For John and Sheila Ware

Rosie HARRIS

Love Against All Odds

WILLIAM HEINEMANN: LONDON

Published by William Heinemann 2007

2 4 6 8 10 9 7 5 3 1

First published in Great Britain in 2007 by
William Heinemann
Random House, 20 Vauxhall Bridge Road,
London SW1V 2SA

www.rbooks.co.uk

Addresses for companies within The Random House Group Limited
can be found at: www.randomhouse.co.uk/offices.htm

The Random House Group Limited Reg. No. 954009

A CIP catalogue record for this book
is available from the British Library

ISBN 9780434020386

The Random House Group Limited supports The Forest Stewardship
Council (FSC),the leading international forest certification organisation. All our
titles that are printed on Greenpeace approved FSC certified paper carry the
FSC logo.Our paper procurement policy can be found at:
www.rbooks.co.uk/environment

Mixed Sources
Product group from well-managed
forests and other controlled sources
www.fsc.org Cert no. TT-COC-2139
© 1996 Forest Stewardship Council
FSC

Typeset in Palatino by Palimpsest Book Production Limited
Grangemouth, Stirlingshire
Printed and bound in the UK by
CPI Mackays, Chatham ME5 8TD

Love Against All Odds

Acknowledgements

Once again my thanks to everyone at Random House for their continued support and above all to my editor Georgina Hawtrey-Woore for all her cooperation; she's a real star!

A big thank you to Caroline Sheldon of The Caroline Sheldon Literary Agency who always has good advice at her fingertips.

Chapter One

Gaynor Sanderson hesitated as she reached the warehouse, then, after removing her school hat with its distinctive badge, and lowering her school bag from her shoulder, she left them both on the floor inside the sliding steel door of the workshop.

Shaking her long brown hair free from its regulation hair band so that it framed her oval face, she walked quietly through the corrugated iron building towards the long wooden bench where a young man in dark blue overalls was working. He had his back to her, and she moved so quietly that he was unaware of her presence as she crept up behind him until she startled him by clapping her hands over his eyes.

'Guess who?' she whispered, kissing his cheek.

Barri Hughes jumped, dropped the chisel he was holding, and swore.

'Damno di, Gaynor, you shouldn't come creeping in like that!' he gasped as he turned round. 'One of these days we'll get caught and then it will be the sack for me!'

Despite his remonstration, Barri Hughes was smiling broadly. Seventeen, strikingly good-looking with well-spaced deep blue eyes under thick dark eyebrows, and close-cropped thick dark hair, he had an air of easy good humour. Confidently, he pulled her into his arms and kissed her soundly on the mouth.

'Should you be doing that?' she teased breathlessly, when he released her a couple of minutes later.

'Probably not.' He grinned as he started to take her back into his arms again.

'That will do, Barri Hughes, you can wait until I see you later on tonight if you want another kiss,' she told him archly, quickly twisting away out of his reach, but smiling invitingly, her hazel eyes full of promise.

'Except that you won't be seeing him tonight or ever again if I have my way!' an angry voice declared.

They both looked round guiltily as a barrel-shaped man wearing a khaki coat-style overall strode purposefully towards them. His manner was menacing, and his face dark with anger. 'I've told both of you countless times that this sort of behaviour has got to stop. Since neither of you takes the slightest notice of what I say, this time I will be making sure that it does end, and end for good,' he threatened.

'Please, Dad, don't start telling Barri off,' Gaynor pleaded. 'It was all my fault!' She giggled and slipped her hand through her father's arm. 'I crept up on him and gave him a fright and he was cross with me so we were just making up.'

'I know exactly what happened because I was watching you both from my office window, and damn silly behaviour it was and all,' Ieuan Sanderson told them with asperity. 'If that chisel Barri was using had slipped, he'd have had a nasty gash on his hand and he might even have lost a finger.'

'I'm sorry,' Gaynor said penitently. 'That's why I was kissing him to make up for startling him like that.'

'It's still no excuse,' her father rasped. 'He didn't have to kiss you back.'

'Look, Mr Sanderson—'

'If you are going to say that she was leading you on, Barri Hughes, then don't bother. She has only just turned fourteen and she's still at school, and because of that she doesn't know any better,' Ieuan Sanderson declared pompously. 'You are older than her, and you've been working for almost three years, so you should be able to behave properly.'

'Dad! I'm only still at school because I'm training to be a teacher, otherwise I'd be out working like Ellie and the rest of my friends,' Gaynor protested sulkily.

'That will do, cariad! I'll deal with you later,' Ieuan Sanderson told his daughter firmly. 'As for you,' he said sternly, turning back to Barri, 'get on with your work. I shall be having a word with your father about your behaviour.'

Barri's mouth tightened into a narrow line, but he said nothing. He thought that Mr

Sanderson was being very unfair. He couldn't understand why he was so determined to prevent him and Gaynor from seeing each other. They'd practically grown up together and he'd always thought that their families were close friends. He'd never do anything to hurt Gaynor, but he knew it was a waste of time trying to reason with her father when he was laying down the law.

He could tell from the way she tossed her head and glared at her father that Gaynor was also annoyed by his interference. Like Barri, though, she remained silent knowing how futile it was to argue with her father. All he could do was give her a reassuring wink before she walked away, and hope that she wouldn't get it in the neck when her father got home, although he rather thought she would.

Ieuan Sanderson knew that both Gaynor and Barri thought he was hard on them. Even his wife Florence was not above reproaching him for being so protective about their young daughter and didn't seem convinced when he insisted that it was because she was their only child, and very precious to him, which was why he wanted only the very best for her.

Seeing her kissing and carrying on with Barri Hughes went against the grain. He knew Barri was regarded as an upstanding young man, but in his opinion Barri's attendance at chapel was not nearly as regular as it should be. His father,

Simon Hughes, was conscientious like himself. Both of them were deacons, both sang in the choir, and both officiated in the general running of things.

Ieuan and Simon had known each other for almost fifty years, ever since they were youngsters. When they left school, they'd started work together as apprentices at Ferndale Forge, the steel works in their home town. They'd both married and settled down only a few doors apart. It had caused a slight rift in their friendship, though, when he'd been made undermanager and Simon merely a foreman, because it gave him authority over his friend.

It had been the natural order of things that when Barri left school at fourteen he also came to work at Ferndale Forge. Now, almost three years later, he had nearly completed his apprenticeship. He was a bright, good-looking boyo and, in Ieuan's estimation, he should be out enjoying life with lads of his own age, not mooching around with a girl as young as Gaynor.

Living as they did within a stone's throw of each other in Lake Street didn't help matters because it was easy enough for them to spot each other the moment they went out of the door. What was more, they knew each other's movements so well that it was a simple matter for Barri and Gaynor to arrange to meet up when they were coming in, or going out.

At one time it had seemed mere friendship

between the pair of them, but lately Ieuan was convinced that things were becoming far too serious. He didn't want his girl's head filled with fancy notions about getting married. He wanted her to have some experience of the world before she settled down, and when she did he felt that she deserved someone better than Barri Hughes.

He was only too aware that he had never stretched his own wings, never ventured out of Ferndale either to look for work, or for a home when he and Florence had married, and there had often been times when he wished that he had.

It was a nice enough place with its pretty views out over the valley, its chapels and an assortment of shops in the compact little high street, but it had none of the worldliness of Cardiff, Newport, Swansea, or even Pontypridd.

The majority of the men who lived in Ferndale worked at one of the nearby pits. He'd avoided going underground himself, and so had Simon Hughes, but you could hardly call their jobs in a small steel works much of an improvement on mining. Mostly it was hot and dirty with its sweltering furnaces, the cacophony of noise, and the harsh smells that assailed the back of your throat. Handling molten ore and shaping metal was almost as dangerous as being underground in one of the pits.

6

Ieuan didn't want his girl marrying a steel worker, or a miner, or any other blue-collared worker if it came to that. He wanted something better for her. He'd like her to have a husband who worked in an office, wore a smart suit and a shirt with a white collar; a man who had clean hands and clean fingernails. A chap who used his brain not his brawn, and who came home at night looking as spruce as he'd been when he'd left home that morning.

He was pretty sure that Florence felt the same, only she was afraid to voice her thoughts aloud in case it upset him knowing that he had never achieved such an ambition himself.

Florence was part of the trouble; she was far too passive and lenient. Sometimes she seemed to be almost afraid to have any opinion and she rarely put her foot down where Gaynor was concerned. She'd always been a doting mother, but, he thought irritably, there was a limit to how much tolerance she ought to show.

Another problem was that Florence was very friendly with Ceri Hughes, Barri's mother, and she wouldn't want to say anything that might upset her. Yes, he sighed, Florence was a bit of a mouse. Perhaps that was his fault in a way, he reflected. He liked to rule the roost, and he expected her to do as he told her. He had no patience with time-wasting backchat or arguments. Someone had to be boss and in their house, and that was him, every time.

Whenever Ieuan reprimanded Gaynor, and

she argued with him, Florence made sure she kept in the background. She usually disappeared into the kitchen on the pretence of making them all a nice cup of tea. What she should have been doing was staying right there beside him, backing him up. He was fed up of being handed a cup of tea and being advised 'to sleep on it because everything would look better in the morning'. He was also irritated with hearing her consoling Gaynor and telling her to be a good girl for her dad. What she ought to be doing was pointing out the pitfalls of getting involved with Barri Hughes when she was still only a schoolgirl.

In some ways Gaynor took after her father. She liked to have her own way, and she made sure that she always did where her mother was concerned. When it came to dealing with him, however, then she knew that he expected to be obeyed.

As a young child she'd been malleable enough; his little angel. It was only in the last couple of years that she'd started digging her heels in, answering him back and showing her mettle by being awkward.

He wondered if perhaps Barri was egging her on, giving her ideas about independence, and filling her head with thoughts of their having a future together.

He'd have to lay his cards on the table with Simon Hughes. He'd asked him enough times to stop Barri chasing around after Gaynor and yet he'd done sod all about it so there was only one answer. Barri had to go. The sooner he left Ferndale the better.

He'd suggest to Simon and Ceri that their boy went to sea or moved somewhere really far away. Knowing them both as he did, however, then probably Cardiff would seem like the end of the world to them even though they could go down and visit him from time to time.

There would be tears and recriminations from Gaynor, but once Barri had left Ferndale she'd soon settle down and spend more time with some of the girlfriends whom she'd been ignoring lately. As a result, instead of being so obstreperous through spending far too much time with Barri, she'd be his sweet little girl once again.

There was no time like the present, he resolved as he made his way back to his office, a partitioned-off corner of the main shed. He'd sack Barri right away, but he'd have a word with Barri's father first and tell him what he was proposing, and his reason for doing it. He felt he owed Simon Hughes that much.

He wasn't sure how Simon would take it; in fact, it might mean the end of a lifelong friendship, but he was quite certain that it would be saving his Gaynor from getting involved in something that they'd all come to regret later on.

Gaynor would be aghast that he could do

such a thing, and that was another reason why he would need Simon's cooperation in the matter; why it had to be a joint decision.

Even though his mind was made up, Ieuan Sanderson was still reluctant to do it, knowing the upset that it was bound to cause to all concerned. Ferndale was such a close community that when people heard what had happened the discord might even affect the rest of the work force if they decided to take sides.

Perhaps it would be better, he reasoned, if Barri could be persuaded to leave of his own accord. People would understand that, and Simon and Ceri might even be proud of the fact that their son had decided to spread his wings because he wanted to try and better himself. Maybe he didn't have to involve Simon at all.

Ieuan searched in the drawer of his desk for the cigarettes he kept there. As a rule he didn't smoke while he was working, but there was always the odd occasion when things became so difficult that he needed a cigarette to calm himself down. This was certainly one of those days, he thought grimly as he lit up, took a long draw on it, and then slowly exhaled.

Ten minutes later, his mind was made up. It was no good shilly-shallying any longer. This was one occasion when he certainly didn't need to sleep on it! It was something that had to be done, not only for his own peace of mind, but for Gaynor's future, and the longer he put it off the harder it would be to do.

In all fairness it would be best if he had a word with Barri right away and let him know exactly where he stood. He'd offer him the alternative of leaving Ferndale Forge of his own free will, or of being sacked.

There was no time like the present, Ieuan decided as he stubbed out his cigarette, came out of his office, and called out to Barri that he wanted a word with him.

He tried to disregard the jaunty way Barri responded to his summons. There was no doubt that he had no idea what was coming, Ieuan thought, and for a moment he felt uneasy about how Barri might react.

Barri listened to him in silence, a look of disbelief on his face as he heard the terms: he was to hand in his notice right away and clear off to Cardiff or Newport or one of the other big towns, and have nothing further to do with Gaynor, or he would be sacked.

'I'm trying to make things as easy as I can for you and your family. We don't want tongues wagging or any embarrassment, now do we? This way is the best for all concerned. Go tonight, understand? You can tell your folks any tale you want, I'll back you up on whatever you say.'

'And what about Gaynor? What do I tell her?'

'That's the whole point, boyo, you don't tell her anything.'

'You mean I just vanish, without a word! No explanation, no forwarding address?'

11

Ieuan breathed a sigh of relief. 'That's it; that's exactly what I mean!' he agreed.

Barri's handsome face darkened. 'I can't do that, it would break her heart!' he protested. 'She thinks the world of me; we're planning a future together.'

'You may think so and she may believe that, but I won't entertain the idea for one minute.' Ieuan's eyes narrowed. 'Before you say that you'll run away together let me remind you that she's only a child and she's still at school. If you try any nonsense of that sort I'll have the law on you.'

'Duw anwyl!' Barri shook his head and ran his hands through his hair. 'I can't believe I'm hearing this,' he exclaimed. 'What are you trying to do? She'll be devastated, mun!'

'Nonsense! She'll be upset, I grant you that, but in a month or so she will have forgotten all about it.'

'Have you thought what she will think about me ditching her like that without a word of explanation?'

'I'll be there to counsel her so don't let that worry you,' Ieuan told him stiffly. 'Go home, pack your bags, tell your parents that you want to see a bit more of the world before you settle down, and leave Ferndale tonight. I'm not asking you, Barri, I'm telling you, and what's more I'm prepared to give you twenty pounds out of my own pocket to make it possible for you to do as I ask.'

Chapter Two

Gaynor Sanderson flung open the living-room door, her pretty face puckered with suppressed tears. 'What have you been saying to Barri,' she demanded, looking accusingly at her father who was sitting by the fire in his favourite armchair and who didn't even look up when she came bursting into the room.

'What are you on about, cariad?' He frowned, lowering the evening paper he'd been reading.

'You know quite well what I'm talking about,' she stormed, slamming the door shut. 'You've said something to Barri to stop him from meeting me this evening, haven't you!'

'I haven't seen or spoken to Barri Hughes this evening,' he said mildly.

'You saw him before he finished work, though. You said something to him then, I know you did.'

'In that case, why are you asking me about it?'

'Did you tell him he was to stop seeing me?' she demanded, her voice rising hysterically.

When her father didn't even trouble to reply Gaynor looked across the room at her mother who was sitting at the table industriously darning a sock and trying to ignore what was going on.

'Mam, have you any idea what Dad said to Barri?' she demanded. 'Come on, tell me if you know what is going on.'

Florence carefully removed the wooden mushroom she'd placed inside the sock to hold it in place as she worked, and put it down on the table beside the pile of darning still waiting to be done. Then she examined the neat darn in the sock she was holding before she replied. When she did, she spoke directly to her husband, not to Gaynor.

'Ieuan, I think you should explain to Gaynor exactly what has happened. The poor girl won't rest until you do.'

Ieuan Sanderson carefully folded his newspaper in half and laid it aside, then he regarded Gaynor resignedly. 'Very well, I'll give you the facts, girl, and once I've done so I don't want to hear any more about it. From now on I don't want Barri Hughes's name ever to be mentioned again in this house by either of you. Now, do you both understand?'

'Heavens above, why ever not?' Florence Sanderson gasped in surprise.

Even as she uttered the words she clamped her hand over her mouth, and looked apologetically at her husband.

Ignoring her outburst, he continued to address his remarks directly to Gaynor.

'I've warned Barri Hughes a great many times that he is showing you far too much attention. You have not yet left school and I don't

14

want him filling your head with a load of old nonsense about getting married and having a future together. What is more, I certainly don't want any sort of hanky-panky going on between the two of you which could result in you landing up in trouble.'

'Hanky-panky! I don't know what you mean,' Gaynor muttered, her face going bright red with embarrassment.

'I rather think you do,' her father told her grimly. 'If the reason you don't understand is because you don't know right from wrong, then there is all the more need for you to stop seeing him.'

'Barri cares too much about me to do anything he shouldn't,' Gaynor defended tearfully.

'If he cares as much about you as all that then he would have listened to what I told him months ago, and left you alone. Instead he's completely ignored my warning,' her father reminded her.

'You couldn't expect him to stop seeing me altogether, especially since you've never even mentioned to me that you didn't want us seeing each other,' Gaynor argued.

'If I had done, would you have taken any notice?'

Gaynor shrugged. 'Probably not, but I could have told you that you had nothing to worry about because we never do anything we shouldn't.'

'That's as maybe; the action I've taken, my girl, is what any good father would take. Now,' he unfolded his paper again, 'can we drop the subject?'

'You still haven't told me what it was you said to him that stopped him from meeting me tonight. You haven't sacked Barri, have you?' Her voice rose in consternation. 'You wouldn't do something like that, would you, Dad?'

'No, Gaynor, I haven't sacked Barri; he decided to leave of his own accord.'

'I don't believe you! He wouldn't do that because he loved his job,' she exclaimed in wide-eyed disbelief.

'Are you calling me a liar, girl?' Ieuan rumbled, his voice deep with suppressed anger.

'No, of course not, Dad,' Gaynor said quickly. 'I think, though, that you must have mis-understood what he said to you because Barri wouldn't dream of doing a thing like that, espe-cially without telling me first.'

'Which only goes to show how little he cares about you,' he told her dismissively. 'Barri's left, and you can take my word for it that you won't be seeing him around any more because he's not only leaving his job, he's also going to leave Ferndale as well.'

'No! No, I don't believe that for one minute. He can't have done! He's taking me to Darren Park on Sunday.'

'He might have told you he would, but it won't be happening,' her father stated

16

pompously. 'He's cleared off, girl; gone for good. He's going down to Cardiff, spreading his wings. He says he wants a bit of life, see. You'll forget all about him if you have any sense.'

'I don't believe a word of it,' Gaynor said in a shocked voice. White-faced she turned back to her mother. 'It's not true, is it, Mam?'

'If that's what your dad says then it must be right. Barri is three years older than you, cariad, so, like your dad says, he's probably decided that he wants to see something of life. It's the way with lads of his age,' she ended lamely.

'Not Barri!' Gaynor insisted. 'He wouldn't do a thing like that, not without talking it over with me first. We've always told each other everything. He wouldn't keep something like that a secret.'

'He probably knew you'd go off the deep end if he tried to explain things to you, that's why he said nothing,' her father declared. He shook his newspaper noisily. 'Now, can we have a bit of quiet so that I can read my paper!'

'Yes, leave your dad in peace, cariad,' her mother said in a cajoling voice. 'We'll go into the kitchen and we'll have a nice cup of tea and then talk things over,' she added, pushing her pile of darning to one side.

'No, I'm sorry, Mam. I haven't time for drinking tea. I'm going round to ask Mrs Hughes if she knows what is going on, and to find out if Barri really has left Ferndale as Dad says. If he has gone to Cardiff then she might have his address.'

'No!' Ieuan slammed his fist down on the arm of his chair. 'I won't have you going round there with your heart on your sleeve, you silly child. Where's your pride? He's walked out on you, so accept that and face up to it. Hold your head high, cariad, don't go chasing after him like a moonstruck rabbit. Now either go in the kitchen with your mother, or get upstairs to your room. That's my final word on the matter. Do you understand!'

'But, Dad—'

'Be quiet! I've had enough backchat from you for one night, so up to your room with you.'

'No, I'm going into the kitchen to talk to Mam,' Gaynor told him defiantly.

'I'm beginning to think you are hard of hearing! I said you were to go to your room and that is exactly what I meant!' Ieuan Sanderson rustled his newspaper ominously.

'Do as your dad says, Gaynor,' her mother told her gently. 'Run along now and I'll make a pot of tea and bring you up a cup.'

'You'll do nothing of the sort, Florence. You stay right here and get on with your darning,' Ieuan thundered. 'I said Gaynor was to go straight up to her room and that is what she is going to do. Furthermore, she can stay there until she has calmed down and got a civil tongue in her head once again.'

Gaynor knew it was useless arguing with her

father when he used that tone of voice. Tossing back her hair, she did as she was told. Once in her room she flung herself down on her bed, pummelling the pillow as she tried to work out whether or not he was telling her the truth.

She had known Barri ever since she could remember. Along with dozens of other kids of assorted ages they'd played together both out in the street and in the local park.

She knew her best friend Ellie was jealous of the way Barri singled her out as they grew older and they became special friends. When he started work Ellie had warned her that he would want to go his own way and go out with his workmates so she would have to make do with seeing less of him. It hadn't happened, though. Barri remained as close as ever.

Barri's mam and dad had always made her welcome and treated her as if she was one of their own. Until Barri had started work her mam and dad had been the same with him. After school they would go into each other's houses and be given a jam butty, or a welsh cake spread with butter, to keep them going until their main meal. Then they'd be told to run along and play outside until their dads came home from work.

One of her nicest memories was going on a Sunday school outing when she'd been quite small, about seven years old. It had been a gloriously hot sunny day in August and the huge charabanc had been packed with mothers and children. They'd all taken picnics and bottles of pop to enjoy when they got there and along with most of the other children they both had a brightly painted tin bucket and a little wooden spade.

They'd gone to Barry Island for the day and she remembered that when they arrived she had been told to sit with her mam and a group of smaller children, while the bigger ones went off together to do more exciting things. The boys rolled up their trouser bottoms and the girls tucked their skirts into their knickers and they walked barefoot down the sand and splashed and paddled in the sea.

Barri had offered to take her and to look after her, but the idea was poo-poohed and she'd been left to play with her bucket and spade along with the rest of the younger ones. She'd been so upset about it that when no one was looking she had sneaked off. She'd meant to go and find Barri, but the beach was so packed with people that in next to no time she was lost.

There'd been a hue and cry once it was discovered that she was missing, and though they looked for her everywhere, no one could find her. Eventually Barri had found her hiding behind a beach hut and had taken her back to the rest of the group.

Her mam was all for spanking her but Barri had stood up for her and said he would look after her for the rest of the trip. And he had, she recalled with a smile. He'd even taken her down to the water's edge and let her paddle in the sparkling water before the tide finally turned. She'd wanted to run after it, but he had held her hand and said that once the sea ebbed away like that it went for miles and miles and she would be completely lost and no one would ever find her again.

Instead, he'd taken her by the hand and they had walked back up the wet, dappled sand to where her mam was waiting and he had made her turn around and look at the trail of footprints they'd left behind them.

'Look, yours and mine, side by side,' he'd told her. 'For the rest of time that's how we'll always be, always in step with each other and walking side by side.'

When they played with other children and they divided up into two teams Barri always insisted she was with him, even though she was often the youngest and smallest. And even if it meant that his side lost the game because she had difficulty in keeping up with the bigger children he had never seemed to mind.

When a crowd of them played hopscotch, or marbles, or tops, depending on what time of the year it was, he always made sure no one ever bullied her. If she was accidentally pushed over and grazed her hand, or her knee, then he was always there to dry her tears and comfort her.

After they grew too old for such childish games

they would sit on one of the low walls, hold hands, and exchange ideas about everything under the sun. Some of the boys would hand round cigarettes, but they always hid them if they saw a grown-up approaching. Barri would never let her try smoking a cigarette; he said it wasn't for girls, not nice ones like her, anyway. When the others tittered or jeered, he scowled at them and threatened to 'knock their blocks off if they didn't shut up', and because he was bigger than most of them they stopped doing it.

They had not only faced their small world together, but had also made wonderful plans about what they would do in the future when they were grown-up. They were both so happy in their home surroundings that they had no desire to move away. They didn't want the noise of a big city like Newport or Cardiff, nor did they want to be out in the remote countryside with nothing but baaing sheep for company. They wanted to stay in Ferndale for ever.

'We'll go on holiday every year of our lives, mind,' Barri had assured her. 'We'll go to places like America and Australia and we'll take a trip to Holland where all the tulips come from, and to France where they eat frogs' legs for dinner. We can even go to Germany now that the Pied Piper has got rid of all the horrible old rats.'

'I don't want to go to Eskimo Land because it will be too cold and I don't want to go to Africa because it is so hot there that people don't wear any clothes,' she'd told him.

He'd agreed with her about that and assured her that they would never go anywhere she didn't want them to go and also that he would never go anywhere without her.

Yet now he had, or so it seemed. She couldn't believe that he would betray the trust that had built up between them all the time they were growing up. That was why she couldn't for one moment accept what her dad had told her about Barri deciding on the spur of the moment to clear off; to leave Ferndale without a word to her about what he was doing or where he was going.

There was only one way to find out, and that was to go to Barri's home and ask his mam what was going on, but if her dad found her doing that she wasn't too sure how he would react in his present mood.

Chapter Three

Gaynor marked off another day on her calendar; it was something she had been doing every night, ever since her dad had told her that Barri had left Ferndale. It had gone on for over a month now and she'd told herself that if there was no word from him by the end of July then she was going to accept what had happened and put Barri right out of her mind.

Perhaps her dad was right after all and Barri was fickle, and wanted to spread his wings and see something of life outside of Ferndale.

But even if he did want to do something like that, he could have told her about it, not simply leave her high and dry. He hadn't even sent her a postcard, she thought bitterly.

She wasn't the only one who felt let down. Although her dad had told her she wasn't to go and ask Barri's mam or dad what had happened, she'd bumped into Mrs Hughes one morning when they'd been waiting for the postman. Both of them were hoping that there would be some news from Barri, so it was only natural that they should ask each other if they'd had a letter from him yet.

'Clearing off like that without any warning. I didn't know a thing about it until I found a note pinned on his pillow that said "Gone to Cardiff",' Ceri Hughes said indignantly. 'That was it! Not a word of explanation. What on earth happened? Tell me, Gaynor, did the two of you have a falling out of some sort?'

'No, it was nothing to do with me,' Gaynor assured her. 'He stood me up. We'd agreed to meet at seven o'clock, but when I got to Darren Park there wasn't sight nor sound of him. I hung around there for almost an hour and then ...' She sniffed back a sob.

'Go on, cariad. What happened after that?'

'I went home again,' Gaynor said lamely.

'You never thought to come and ask us where he was?' Ceri Hughes said in surprise.

'Well, no. I didn't want it to look as if I was chasing after him.'

'Is that a fact?' Mrs Hughes looked doubtful. 'Are you sure, Gaynor, or was it because your dad has been telling you that my Barri was too old for you, and because he wanted you to concentrate on your studies and this business of becoming a teacher?'

Gaynor's eyes widened. 'Whatever makes you say that?'

Mrs Hughes said nothing for a moment, then she spoke very slowly, weighing up her words carefully, as if afraid that she might be saying something she shouldn't. 'It was what Barri's dad said when I showed him the note.'

25

Gaynor looked at her expectantly. 'Go on, what did he say?'

Again Mrs Hughes hesitated. 'My Simon said that he didn't think your dad approved of the two of you seeing so much of each other. Is that true, Gaynor?'

It was Gaynor's turn to dither. 'I'm not too sure,' she said diffidently, a flood of colour staining her cheeks.

Ceri Hughes regarded her shrewdly. 'Is that the truth, cariad? You are a bit young to be going steady. After all, Barri is quite a bit older than you; a man, in fact, while you are still a schoolgirl.'

'You grown-ups are all the same,' Gaynor told her bitterly. 'Like I told my dad, we always behaved ourselves.'

'So that's what's at the bottom of this kerfuffle. Your dad has been poking his oar in and putting my boyo in his place, has he! Just because your dad's one of the managers at Ferndale Forge he thinks he rules the roost there. It's a wonder he didn't sack my Simon at the same time.'

Before Gaynor could answer Ceri Hughes turned on her heel and walked back into her own house and slammed the door shut behind her.

Although they'd passed each other in the high street several times since then, they hadn't spoken.

When Gaynor mentioned the matter to her

26

mam, Florence had avoided the question and pretended she didn't know what Gaynor was talking about, but in the end she'd admitted that Ceri Hughes didn't speak to her either.

'She seems to blame us for Barri clearing off like he did without a word to any of us. Rubbish, mind you, cariad. We had nothing to do with it. I told her how upset you were, devastated, in fact, but it made no difference.'

'Can't you find out from Dad exactly what happened?' Gaynor pressed.

Her mother shook her head. 'Best let alone,' she said firmly. 'You know your dad, once he says a matter is closed then that's it. Over and done with, so to speak. No point in raking things up again.'

'I need to know why he went, Mam,' Gaynor protested.

'The best thing you can do, cariad, is get on with your life,' her mother told her firmly. 'Forget the past; we all have disappointments in our lives. I know how you must be feeling, but what's done is done. Forget about Barri and later on, when you are a bit older, find yourself a new boyfriend.'

'What's the point of doing that? Dad would send them packing the moment he thought they were getting too keen on me,' Gaynor told her sulkily.

But, as time went by, Gaynor knew that her mam was right. She had to forget about Barri and start living again. According to gossip, although she hadn't heard from him, his mother had and was telling people that he'd found a good job down in Cardiff.

Her best friend, Ellie, was sympathetic, but because Gaynor had pushed her to one side and devoted all her time to Barri when he'd been around she, too, had made a new life for herself.

Unlike Gaynor, Ellie had left school the minute she was fourteen and had started work in the office at one of the local mines. Now she was going out with one of the junior clerks and so she was the one who didn't have much time to spend with her girlfriends.

'I tell you what, Gaynor.' Ellie's round face shone with enthusiasm. 'There's a new chap just come to work in Davey's office and Davey has been asked to take him out on Sunday and show him around. You could come along as well and make up a foursome if you like,' she suggested, when for the umpteenth time Gaynor asked her to go out somewhere.

Gaynor hesitated. After the rows she'd had with her father about Barri Hughes she didn't think he would be very happy about her going out with this chap Ellie was talking about. If he was already working then he was bound to be as old as Barri, if not older.

'He's only eighteen,' Ellie went on as if reading her mind. 'He's come over from Germany to study the way we do things in the coal mines over here. Davey has the job of

28

looking after him. They've promised that when this fellow goes home again they'll send Davey over there to the place where he works so that he can see the differences for himself.'

'I'm not sure,' Gaynor said hesitantly. 'I think I had better ask my dad first.'

'I understand, but it would be nice if you did come. Davey will probably be gabbing away to this chap so I'll be left out in the cold if I'm there on my own.'

'I'll try. What's this fellow's name?'

'Claus. Konrad Claus. I've only met him once, but he seemed ever so nice. His hair is so fair that it's almost white and he has the brightest blue eyes you've ever seen.' She giggled. 'He clicked his heels and kissed my hand when Davey introduced us.'

'Is that what they do where he comes from?'

'It must be! He talks a bit queer, too; it's almost as if he is giving orders.'

'What's his job in the office?'

'I'm not too sure; I think Davey said that Konrad was studying to be a surveyor. He seems to know an awful lot about how coal is formed under the ground and all that sort of thing.'

When Gaynor mentioned all this to her mam and dad as they ate their evening meal that night, she was very surprised at how impressed her father seemed to be. To her amazement he appeared to quite like the idea that she would be meeting the young German.

'He sounds very intelligent,' he said enthusiastically. 'That's the sort of person who could be of help to you if you are going to be a teacher; the kind of chap I would like to see you take up with one day.'

'Ellie has asked me if I'll go with them on Sunday when Davey shows Konrad Claus around Ferndale,' she said cautiously.

'A very good idea! Why not bring all three of them back here afterwards and we can show Konrad some Welsh hospitality. Your mother will bake some Welsh cakes and make some bara brith. He'd enjoy that with a cup of tea.'

Gaynor hesitated. She felt angry that he could welcome this unknown foreigner into their home when he didn't want Barri there. She was on the point of saying so when she caught her mother's warning glance, and instead of voicing her opinion she merely nodded and agreed to do just that.

Ellie was also very surprised by Mr Sanderson's attitude, but as they both agreed, you never could tell how grown-ups were going to react, especially fathers.

By the time it came to Sunday Gaynor was beginning to wish she had never mentioned Konrad Claus because her dad had never stopped talking about him. He seemed to know an awful lot about the Germans and kept telling her how smart and efficient they were and how she could learn a lot from knowing a chap of that sort.

Gaynor knew that her mother was nervous

in case they didn't like him, or, worse still, he didn't like the food she offered him.

'I believe the things they eat are quite different to what we have,' she kept saying worriedly. 'Supposing he doesn't like Welsh cakes or bara brith?'

'Of course he will like them, everybody does, especially when you make them,' Gaynor told her. 'Anyway, if he doesn't, then what does it matter? He can always go home and have a meal afterwards if he's still hungry. I'm far more worried about what I shall say to him. It'll be all right while we are out and Davey is telling him about Ferndale and so on, but afterwards, when they come here, he'll expect me to talk to him, won't he?'

'I doubt if you will be able to get a word in edgeways.' Her mother smiled. 'It seems to me that your dad will be monopolising him and asking him a thousand and one questions, poor boyo.'

It turned out that Mrs Sanderson was closer to the truth than she could imagine. Her husband completely dominated things on Sunday afternoon when Gaynor arrived back home after an enjoyable outing with Ellie, Davey and the young German guest.

Gaynor was well aware that her father read the *South Wales Echo* every evening, but until he began talking to Konrad she had no idea that he had amassed so much general knowledge.

The others listened in silence as the two of them discussed everything that was going on in the outside world, from the sinking of the *Titanic* just over a year earlier to the fact that the Norwegian explorer Amundsen had managed to reach the South Pole ahead of the British explorer Scott.

Gaynor waited with bated breath when Konrad started talking about the discovery in Peru of the lost city of the Incas because she was quite sure her dad would know nothing about that. To her surprise he seemed to know a great deal about it.

When Konrad mentioned the British Suffragette movement, however, Ieuan frowned and shook his head and raised a finger to his lips. 'We'd better not discuss that topic in front of the ladies,' he warned. Konrad coloured up, bowed, and quickly apologised for his insensitivity. From then on they talked about the sort of work Konrad hoped to do, and the exams he would have to take in order to become a surveyor in his own country.

'Of course, it will all depend on what happens in the rest of the world in the near future,' Konrad said with a shrug of his shoulders. 'When I return to the Fatherland I will probably have to do service in the German Army.'

Once again, sensing Konrad's patriotic enthusiasm and not wanting to cause any conflict between them, Ieuan changed the topic and began discussing the new car that had been invented by Henry Ford of America. 'It's called the T-Ford and he claims that it is going to be cheap enough for even the ordinary working man to be able to afford one. I hope that comes true!'

Konrad agreed with him, but he appeared to be even more fascinated by the future of flying, insisting that one day it would also be possible for anyone to fly anywhere in the world.

'It has been a great privilege to sit at your table and discuss so many things,' Konrad told him as he took his leave. 'I am very surprised, Mr Sanderson, that you work in making steel. I would think with all your knowledge you should be in parliament.'

His parting tribute brought a smug smile to Ieuan's face. 'A very intelligent young man, even if he is a German,' he pronounced when the door closed behind Konrad, Ellie and Davey.

Gaynor merely smiled and said nothing. She could see what her dad meant, though; Barri would never have been able to match her dad in a discussion like that. Probably the most they had ever said to each other was to comment on a rugby score, which horse had won the Derby, or some Union matter that affected them both.

Over the next week, although she still missed Barri, Gaynor found herself thinking about Konrad quite a lot. When Ellie asked her if she wanted to make up a foursome again the following weekend, she agreed.

'Davey has suggested going to a dance in Pontypridd on Saturday night.'

Gaynor looked doubtful. 'I'd love to come, but I'm not sure that my dad would let me go,' she said uneasily.

'Can you find out and let me know tomorrow? If you can't come, I'll have to ask someone else, otherwise Konrad will have no one to dance with, will he?'

Much to Gaynor's surprise her dad offered no objection at all; her mother was more difficult, though. She protested that Gaynor was too young for outings of that sort and pointed out that she didn't have the right sort of dress.

'Then you'd better make her one. You can run her up a frock, can't you?' Ieuan Sanderson said impatiently.

'Of course I can if you don't mind her going out with this Konrad,' Florence murmured.

'Mind? Why should I mind?' Ieuan asked tetchily.

'I thought you might feel he is too old for her. He is eighteen you know; older than Barri.'

'Don't be ridiculous, woman!' Ieuan told her dismissively. 'There's no comparison between them. He's not a factory worker, now is he, but a highly intelligent young man and that's what counts. Being older than Gaynor is all to the good; it means he's more responsible.'

The next few days were some of the most exciting Gaynor had ever known. When she told Ellie that her dad had not only said that she could go, but also that her mam was going to make her a new dress, Ellie was quick to tell

34

her what it ought to be like. She even came home with her to make sure that Gaynor's mother understood how important it was to have the right sort of dress.

From then on, when she wasn't studying, Gaynor found that going out with Konrad became the most exciting and important thing in her life.

There seemed to be only one thing about Konrad that didn't find favour with her father and that was the fact that he showed no interest in attending chapel. He was always polite when the subject was raised, and occasionally accompanied them on special occasions, but it was quite obvious to Ieuan that Konrad's religious conviction, especially when it came to attending chapel, was sadly lacking.

As the weeks went by, Gaynor found herself agreeing with her father that an educated man with ambition was a far more exciting companion than a mere steel worker. Konrad was not only clever but he was good-looking and charming. He was also passionate, and she soon discovered that his behaviour when the two of them were on their own was very different from the staid, serious Konrad who discussed politics and world affairs with her father.

Sometimes Gaynor was almost frightened by the extent of Konrad's passion. Although Barri had assured her he loved her deeply he was careful never to overstep the mark. He had never asked her to do more than exchange kisses or indulge in warm, tender cuddles.

Konrad wanted a lot more from their relationship than that. Little by little he took her deeper into the realms of lovemaking, doing it so subtly that she found herself encouraging him, she was so eager for more revelations.

When she did appear to be slightly reticent, usually because she was fearful of what the consequences could be, Konrad solemnly promised that he wouldn't let any harm come to her. He constantly told her that if she loved him as much as she said she did, then she would trust him implicitly; and when she assured him that she did he became extremely passionate.

Her lovemaking with Konrad temporarily obliterated the memories of what she had felt for Barri. They had only been children, she told herself philosophically. What she was experiencing with Konrad was something quite different; ecstasy beyond description.

Her father never questioned what was going on between them. He liked Konrad so much that when Florence voiced concern, and said she thought that Konrad and Gaynor were seeing far too much of each other, and that it could result in heartache, he dismissed her fears contemptuously.

'What's wrong with you?' he demanded. 'After all we're doing to help our daughter to become a teacher and better herself, do you want her to end up marrying a bloke who works down a pit? Think yourself lucky that she is moving on, and that she has found herself a chap who is going places.'

'Yes, he'll be going back to Germany when he's finished his year here,' Florence told him with spirit. 'A couple of months back amongst his own folks again and he'll forget all about our little Gaynor.'

'Rubbish! He's in love with her, besotted by her. You can see it in his eyes, and in the way he's so protective of her.'

'He's domineering and she's changed since she's been going out with him.'

'She's growing up! She's stretching herself intellectually to keep up with him. She's beginning to realise that there is a world outside the narrow confines of Ferndale.'

Florence Sanderson knew better than to argue with her husband, so from then on she kept her opinion to herself, but it pained her to see the way Konrad was exercising so much power over Gaynor. No matter how hard she tried to accept the situation and say nothing she saw trouble ahead.

The trouble when it did come was not at all the sort of thing she had anticipated. There had been rumours of war in the air for many months, but, on a bright June day in 1914, Konrad appeared on their doorstep while they were still having breakfast.

'I have been recalled to the Fatherland,' he told them bluntly. 'I have to return immediately.'

He clicked his heels and bowed politely. 'I would like to thank you all for your hospitality. It has been most enjoyable and given me a valuable insight into the people of this country.' He paused and walked over to Gaynor and lifted her hand to his lips. 'You have been a wonderful friend, I will never forget you . . .'

'What do you mean, never forget me?' She stared at him, bewildered. 'You'll write to me, you'll come back again . . .'

His face was an icy mask. 'No, fräulein, our friendship is over. Now, I return to the Fatherland because my country needs me. Soon, in fact very soon indeed, our two countries will be at war with each other so it is unlikely that we will ever meet again.'

Chapter Four

There was a stunned silence after the door slammed shut behind Konrad Claus. Gaynor found herself shivering even though it was a hot summer day. It was like a nightmare, she thought; it couldn't be happening. Konrad couldn't be walking away and out of her life for ever, simply because there was some sort of trouble in his homeland. What had it to do with him?

As if aware of her unspoken thoughts, Ieuan slammed a fist down on the table. 'It's the assassination; it's that archduke being killed in Sarajevo last week. There's going to be trouble,' he went on, his voice heavy with concern. 'Things have been building up for months and now there will be a terrible reaction. There's war in the air. You mark my words, both of you.'

'What has war got to do with Konrad? He's training to be a surveyor . . .'

'Training to be a spy, more likely,' Florence interrupted, her voice trembling. 'That's what he was, I can see it all now, he was sent over here to spy on us all.'

'Stop your stupid ranting, woman,' Ieuan

39

ordered contemptuously. 'What do you know of such things? Talk sense; how could a young lad like that be a spy?'

Florence fiddled nervously with the lace collar of her blue cotton dress. 'What else was he doing here? He was always asking ques-tions, trying to find out about all the places around here and how we did things and so on.'

'He was intelligent and eager to broaden his outlook,' Ieuan rasped. 'What did you expect him to do while he was over here, walk around with his eyes shut?'

'He certainly didn't do that,' Florence agreed vehemently. 'He even asked me where our water supply came from! Now why would he want to know a thing like that? And why did he ask Ellie's dad if he would take him down the pit to the coal face and show him how they dug for the coal?'

'Konrad was training to be a surveyor so of course he wanted to see how things were done. He would be expected to know details like that when he got back home,' Ieuan exclaimed irritably.

'Shut up, both of you!' Gaynor wailed. 'Stop talking about him like that. I don't care whether he was a spy or not, he was my boyfriend and I want him back.'

Pushing back her chair she headed towards the door, tears streaming down her face.

'Where do you think you are going? Come back here at once,' Ieuan ordered.

'I'm going round to Ellie's house to see if she knows what this is all about.'

'Why would she be likely to know any more than we do?' Her father frowned.

'Davey may have said something to her; Konrad might have told him more than he has told us.'

'Well, they did work together so you could be right,' her father admitted. 'Dry your eyes first and be careful what you say though, cariad. Don't let yourself down by making a song and dance about what's happened. You don't want her, or anyone else in Ferndale, to know that you've been let down.'

'She has, though,' Florence moaned. 'The truth is she's been jilted again. My poor girl made a laughing stock and left high and dry. What are people going to say? This is the second time a chap has run out on her. That Barri Hughes cleared off without a word to any of us, not even his own mother.'

Gaynor didn't stop to hear any more of her mother's diatribe. Trying hard to hold back her tears she headed towards Beech Street.

Ellie was shocked by the news. 'It's the first I've heard about it,' she admitted, her dark eyes wide with dismay. 'Davey hasn't mentioned anything about Konrad leaving and I'm sure he would be the first to know. I'll ask him when I see him tonight. He's doing overtime, so he won't be home for another hour.'

'Shall I come back later then?' Gaynor asked.

41

'If you like.' Ellie sounded rather uncertain. 'It might be better if I came and told you after I've seen him.'

'We could go and meet Davey together,' Gaynor suggested hopefully.

Ellie shook her head. 'No, the state you are in, it would be better for you to wait at home,' she said kindly. 'You don't want the whole of Ferndale to see you in tears, now do you?'

'You think the same as my mam; that Konrad's gone and won't be coming back, don't you?' Gaynor said dejectedly.

Ellie's round face was full of compassion as she put her arms around her friend. 'I'm not sure. He was . . . there was something military about him . . . the way he walked, the set of his shoulders. It was as if he'd been in a training camp.'

'We know he had,' Gaynor reminded her. 'He said all the young men in Germany had to take part in drilling and training even before they left school. He wasn't in a special squad or anything.'

'Well, no, I suppose you're right about that,' Ellie agreed.

'Please, Ellie, let's both go and meet Davey,' Gaynor begged. 'The sooner I hear direct from him the reason why Konrad has gone home the better.'

As the two girls walked up towards Blaen Pit they talked non-stop about Konrad. The only thing Gaynor didn't mention was that her mam thought he was a spy.

She still couldn't believe that her mam had actually said that, or that she even thought he might be one. Spies were the enemy and even though Konrad was a German, it didn't mean that he was one. She couldn't bear to think of such a thing. She was sure there was some personal reason to do with his family as to why he had found it necessary to scurry off back to Germany, and that once it was resolved then he would come back again, to Ferndale and to her.

Davey knew no more than they did; in fact, he didn't know as much.

'I have no idea,' he said in a puzzled voice. 'He was at work first thing this morning, and then he was called into the manager's office and when he came back to his desk he gathered together his notebooks and his belongings and tidied up. He didn't say a word and I was too busy to ask him what was happening. I knew he couldn't have been given the sack because he wasn't really employed by Blaen Pit; it was some sort of arrangement with his company in Germany, so I thought that perhaps he was being moved to another department.'

He listened to what Konrad had told Gaynor, shaking his head from time to time.

'He'll be back,' Davey told her confidently. 'He wouldn't walk out on you like that, I thought you'd be getting wed before us,' he added with a hearty laugh. 'Me and Ellie said you'd be off back to Germany when Konrad finished his stint over here.'

43

Gaynor smiled wanly. 'When was he due to finish working with you?' she asked.

Davey pursed his lips. 'Not until Christmas, as far as I know. I'm not too sure, but I can probably check on it for you tomorrow, if you really want to know.'

Gaynor nodded eagerly, her dark eyes glittering with unshed tears. 'Yes, please, Davey, I would like to know,' she admitted.

In spite of all Davey's assurances that Konrad would be back again before she knew it, Gaynor wasn't at all confident that he would be. When he had come to their house that morning he had seemed so different from the young man she had fallen in love with. He'd been cold and detached and so patriotic with his talk of the Fatherland and service to his country. It was almost as if he had already left them and was planning his new life back in Germany. Suddenly he seemed to be a stranger.

His mention of war between their two countries had frightened her. She didn't know much about war or politics except what she had learned in history lessons at school, but there was something ominous in his predictions.

If Konrad was a spy, she reasoned, then of course she would never see him again. Was he, though? She kept remembering all the countless questions he'd asked, especially the serious ones directed at her father. He had been so knowledgeable about the geography of Wales and the way the British government worked and matters of that sort that now, looking back, she realised there could well have been a purpose to all his probing questions.

Did that mean that their relationship had just been a passing whim on his part, or had it been something special as he had claimed it was? It was something she wasn't sure about and she knew it was going to keep her awake at nights until she heard from him.

She went over everything they'd talked about, all the confidences they had exchanged, and it hit her like a hammer that he had told her hardly anything about himself whereas she had told him everything there was to tell about her life and family.

She didn't even know where he lived in Germany and that was something Davey said he couldn't help her with because he didn't know either.

'Those details are kept in the pit manager's office and I don't have any way of looking at them,' he explained.

'Don't you know any of the men or girls who work in there? Wouldn't they tell you?'

Davey shook his head. 'I'm afraid I can't help you. You'll have to wait until Konrad returns.'

As the weeks went by and there was no word from him, both Gaynor's parents gradually lost patience with her downcast looks and lacklustre attitude to life. They kept pointing out that it was a good thing he had gone, as the chance of there being a war was becoming more and more probable, so she had best forget about him.

4 August 1914 was a date that Gaynor would never forget. She hid her trembling lip and her tears until she reached the seclusion of her bedroom, where she flung herself down on her bed and let her tears flow, her whole body shaking.

The official announcement of war put paid to all Gaynor's hopes and dreams. She accepted that Konrad would never come back now; she could never hope to see him again. She still didn't think that he had been a spy; simply a deluded conscientious fool who put his country before their love and friendship.

For weeks she was submerged in her unhappiness. Listening to her father talking about the progress of the war, about the British troops landing in France and then, weeks later, the same troops retreating from Mons after heavy casualties, was all gibberish to her. In October, when she heard that the Germans had dropped bombs on Paris, she even wished that she could have been there because it would have brought to an end the dire misery that engulfed her life.

By Christmas she was in such a state of despair that she didn't think that she could face 1915 knowing what she would have to face in the New Year. Her parents had no idea of her condition and she couldn't bring herself to tell them that she was expecting a baby; Konrad's child. What on earth would they say?

She didn't tell Ellie either. Secrets were hard

to keep in Ferndale and she had already had to endure whispers and pitying glances when the news got out that Konrad Claus had left her in the lurch. Her mother's contention that he was a German spy was also voiced by a good many other people.

She didn't know much about having a baby, except for what she had gleaned in the problem pages of the women's magazines Ellie sometimes lent her. As far as she could work out, her baby was going to arrive sometime in the early spring of 1915.

When she began to develop an enlarged stomach over Christmas, and her mother told her she was eating too much and getting fat, Gaynor didn't argue with her. As long as her mam thought she was putting on weight and had no idea that she was expecting a baby, she could forget about it herself.

In January, when none of her clothes fitted her properly, Florence became worried in case there was something terribly wrong with her. When she insisted that Gaynor ought to see a doctor she was shocked beyond belief when Gaynor told her she was pregnant.

'I don't know what your dad is going to say,' she fretted. 'It's such a disgrace! You're not even married! You can't keep it, you know that, don't you? It will have to go.'

'Stop talking about it as if it was a stray kitten, Mam!' Gaynor said crossly. 'It's a baby, my baby and it will be your grandchild.'

'Yes, and the father is a German spy! What do you think people are going to say when they find out? None of us will be able to hold our heads up. We must talk it over and plan what we can do to stop the gossip. Does anyone else know?'

'No, I haven't told anyone,' Gaynor muttered sulkily.

'Not even Ellie? Because if you've told her, she will have told that Davey and he'll have told everyone at work. What's more, Ellie will have told her own mam and, before you know it, the gossip will be all round Ferndale like a rash.'

Gaynor clapped her hands over her ears to shut out her mother's tirade. 'You're not listening, Mam,' she insisted when Florence finally stopped ranting. 'I haven't breathed a word to anyone, not even to Ellie.'

'Well, you don't need to tell people now, do you? They can see for themselves. One look at you and they'll know exactly what's wrong,' her mother said tartly.

'You didn't notice, so why should anyone else?' Gaynor protested.

'Huh! I know people and how they gossip! One whiff of scandal and it's like a forest fire. One spark sets it off and before you know what is happening, it's running wild.'

'If you don't say anything, then I certainly won't,' Gaynor assured her.

'There will be no need to do so, you silly girl.

In about a couple of months' time, if not sooner, you'll have a little bundle in your arms and you won't be able to hide that.'

'That's it then,' Gaynor retorted, her hazel eyes narrowing. 'We can stop talking about it because people will be able to see for themselves soon enough.'

'Not in Ferndale, they won't! Don't think for one minute that me and your dad are going to stand by and see you walk down the high street with a little bastard in your arms, my girl.'

Gaynor stared at her mother in alarm. Normally she was so quiet and complacent, but now her mouth was a thin hard line and there was such a look of fury on her usually placid face that Gaynor was taken aback.

'So what are you going to do?' she challenged with an air of bravado, 'look the other way?'

'Call it that if you like,' her mother told her furiously. 'What I am going to do is make sure you go away somewhere as soon as possible. Once you've had the baby we'll arrange to have it adopted. People know you are training to be a teacher so I'll say you've gone on a special course down in Cardiff, or something like that.'

'And who is going to believe that sort of trumped up tale?' Gaynor laughed scornfully. 'Dad certainly won't.'

'We'll have to tell him the truth, of course. Whether other people believe what we tell them or not is of no consequence whatsoever. If you've not breathed a word to anyone, no one

49

can prove otherwise. When you come back in a month or two's time no one will ever dream of what has happened, as long as you never let on.'

'You mean as long as I don't bring the baby back with me!'

'Of course that's what I mean!' Florence's face softened and her voice became pleading. 'It's all for the best, Gaynor, what do you want with a baby at your age! Bringing it up would be a lifetime's commitment. If you have it adopted you can make a clean start. Forget all about it and about that German spy.'

'And if I don't do what you ask? If I don't have it adopted, but decide to keep it and bring it up?'

'You'll do so without any help from us,' her mother hissed. 'As it is, I dread to think what your dad is going to say when I break the news to him, so telling him that you want to keep it is quite out of the question. He's a good, God-fearing man and—'

'Good? God-fearing? You make me laugh, Mam! If that's the case, then I don't think he will want me to give away my baby to complete strangers, now will he?'

Florence's mouth tightened again. 'You know as well as I do, Gaynor, that he is a man who is proud of his standing in the community. He has earned the respect of people, especially at chapel, and when they find out that you are expecting a baby it will undermine all that.'

In that Florence was right. She waited until they had all finished eating their evening meal before she broke the news to her husband. Ieuan listened in silence then vented his displeasure in no uncertain terms. Gaynor was left in no doubt that she had sinned to such an immense degree that he could never forgive her.

His dark eyes glinted angrily as he stated, 'I hold you, and not Konrad, responsible for the dilemma, and I blame your mother for not counselling you to make sure that such a thing couldn't happen,' he railed. 'When I took you to task about your behaviour with Barri Hughes you assured me that you knew right from wrong. In which case you must knowingly have let Konrad Claus take advantage of you.'

Gaynor defended herself angrily, reminding him of the encouragement he had given her to better herself by favouring an educated white-collar worker, but this only made matters worse. He even went as far as to reprimand her for being no better than she should be.

'First it was that Barri Hughes and then the moment I manage to get rid of him you take up with this German fellow and this is the result,' he stormed. 'I find it hard to believe that after all the sacrifices we have made so that you can stay on at school and pass all the tests and exams to become a teacher, and the moral example we have set you, that you could sin in this fashion. You have let us down, Gaynor, and you most certainly have let yourself

51

down. There is only one way out of this and that is to do as your mother has already told you; you must go away somewhere and as soon as this child is born arrange to have it adopted.'

'And if I won't give up my baby?' she asked quietly.

Her heart was pounding as she waited for his answer, although she could tell from the look on his face what it would be. Nevertheless, she felt she had to make one last stand.

She could put aside her feelings for Konrad because she was convinced that he would never be coming back, but the baby was as much a part of her as it was of him. No matter what happened, she couldn't bring herself to abandon it, not even to please her parents.

Chapter Five

The atmosphere in the Sandersons' house during the first few weeks of 1915 became unbearable. Ieuan Sanderson refused to speak to his daughter, and even went so far as to turn away from her whenever possible, as if he couldn't bear the sight of her.

Florence Sanderson tried to breach the gap between the two of them, but her doleful expression didn't help matters. Her main concern was that the news that Gaynor was expecting a baby would get out and then there would be so much gossip that she would be ashamed to walk down the high street.

Once it reached the ears of the people who attended chapel, it would cause such a scandal that neither she nor her husband would ever be able to hold their heads up again.

Florence went on about this so often that Gaynor dreaded being on her own with her mother. She spent more and more time up in her bedroom viewing herself in the mirror. People must know that she was pregnant she thought worriedly.

When Miss Lloyd, the headmistress, took her to one side and questioned her, Gaynor decided

53

that she must act before her parents took matters into their own hands and forced her into doing something she didn't want to do.

Nothing had gone right for her since Barri had been sent away, she thought sadly. She was pretty certain the rumours were right and that he had gone to Cardiff. In the days when they had exchanged confidences he had once said that he had been there for the day and he thought it was the most magnificent, exciting place in the world.

Would finding him solve her problem or only make it worse, she wondered? She realised that what she had felt for Konrad had been infatuation and that she still loved Barri and always would, but what would he think when he realised that she was pregnant? Would he stand by her simply because until he'd left Ferndale they had meant so much to each other? Was it a chance she dared to take?

After several more sleepless nights she made up her mind. Time was running out so she would go to Cardiff and try to find Barri, but if she didn't then she'd manage on her own somehow. Whatever happened she was determined to keep her baby even though her parents were united against her doing so.

If only she'd left school at fourteen, like Ellie had done, then she'd have some money, but she only had the pocket money she'd saved up over the years.

Counting out her hoard didn't take very long

and was very disappointing. Ever since the day when she had first been given a penny a week pocket money she had always been made to save half of it. The same at birthdays and Christmas when, in addition to her present, she was always given a bright silver sixpenny bit that had to go straight into her money box.

All those years of saving amounted to only just over ten pounds. She wasn't sure how far that would go when she had to pay for somewhere to sleep as well as her food. The train fare to Cardiff would also make a big dent in it. She had to do something, because she couldn't stay in Ferndale, she thought unhappily.

If she didn't manage to locate Barri then she'd have to find some sort of charitable institution that would take her in and help her. They were always collecting for fallen women and the homeless at chapel, and if they did that in a small place like Ferndale, then they must do even more in big cities like Cardiff.

If she was able to get a job, then things mightn't be too bad, but in her condition, and with her lack of experience, she wasn't too sure she would be able to do so. She'd worry about all this when she reached Cardiff. For the moment, the important thing was to plan how she was going to get away without her mother becoming suspicious.

Probably the best thing would be to wait until Sunday and then say that she didn't feel well enough to go with her parents to chapel. Every day her mother commented about what she looked like and worried that someone would guess her secret, so they'd probably be quite relieved and not make a fuss about it, she thought wryly. She'd pack a suitcase, and while they were out of the house she would make her escape, she decided.

Cardiff was different from anything Gaynor had ever experienced in her whole life. By the time the train from the Valleys arrived at Cardiff Central it was packed with soldiers and seamen who had joined it along the way, and they were all carrying kitbags and wartime paraphernalia.

She felt so frightened for a moment she wished she'd never undertaken such a madcap plan. She wondered if she turned round and caught the next train back to Ferndale whether she could manage to sneak home again, tear up the note she had left for her parents, and forget she had ever planned to leave.

Common sense told her that it was quite impossible to do that. For a start they would arrive home from chapel long before she could get back to Lake Street. They would have read her note, know what her intention had been, and because it was defying them by going against their wishes, there would be repercussions. And she vowed she would never willingly give up her baby.

She'd made her choice and now that she was

in Cardiff on her own the best thing she could do was take a deep breath and get on with it.

Even though it was Sunday, as she left the station the streets nearby seemed to be crowded and she had no idea which way to go. She felt faint; it was a long time since she'd had breakfast and she longed for a cup of tea, but she had no idea where to go to get one.

She stood on the edge of the pavement looking around uncertainly. In one direction there seemed to be lots of shops, but because it was Sunday, they were all closed, some with their windows shuttered. Even so she decided to walk that way.

It meant crossing the road and she felt quite nervous because she'd never seen so much traffic and it was coming from all directions. Most frightening of all were the trams. Gaynor had never seen anything like them. They seemed to glide along on metal rails and long metal poles extended from the roofs of them up into the sky where they were attached to some sort of wire.

As she tried to cross the road one of these monsters bore down on her, scaring the life out of her. Desperately she tried to run and get out of its path, but as she did so the heel of her shoe became trapped in one of the shiny metal rails that crossed the road at that point like some terrible trap.

The last thing Gaynor heard was the wild clanging of a bell, and the screech of metal against metal as the huge monster shuddered to a stop, but not before it had clipped her, knocking her down and sending her suitcase flying.

She lay on the ground unable to move and was aware that there were people all around her, talking to her, questioning her, touching her, feeling her arms and legs as if to make sure she was still in one piece. She tried to speak but words wouldn't come. Her mouth was so dry and her tongue seemed to be choking her.

When strong arms lifted her out of the path of the traffic, she made no resistance. She let them prop her against a lamp-post, her suitcase at her side. Tentatively, she tried moving her arms and legs, her feet and hands, and was relieved to find they were intact and working. Yet she was in pain, terrible griping pain, and her clothes were wet through as though she had been lying in a puddle.

Bewildered, she looked down at her soiled clothes and shuddered. The road and pavement were dry and she felt ashamed to admit that she had lost control and wet herself.

She sat very still as people continued to ask her if she was all right, or if she was hurt in any way.

'I'm all right, thank you. Please leave me for a moment to get my breath back.'

As she kept repeating this, those who had gathered out of curiosity began to wander away. In the end only two people remained; a large middle-aged woman and a small, thin man with a sad face and a drooping moustache.

'You'd better get up from there or your baby's going to be born on the pavement,' the woman told her abruptly. 'Come on, take my arm and I'll walk you home. Where do you live? Down the docks?'

Gaynor shook her head. 'I don't live anywhere; I've only just got off the train.'

'Running away from home are you?' the woman said bluntly. 'Well, you can't hang around here, not in your state. The best thing you can do is go along to the Institution and see if they will take you in.'

Gaynor looked at her, bewildered. 'I've no idea were that is,' she whispered.

'Get up and I'll take you there,' the woman told her briskly, holding her hand out.

Pain grabbed at Gaynor as she took the woman's hand and let herself be pulled to her feet. Groaning, she clung on to the lamp-post as she felt her knees buckling.

The woman looked at the man who was still standing there, staring at them with a vacant look on his face.

'You'd better help,' she ordered. 'You carry her suitcase, and I'll support her. It's not far to go, just to the top of Bute Street. Come on, there's no time to mess around.'

'You are very kind, but I don't think I can walk anywhere,' Gaynor gasped helplessly.

'You've no choice, girl. Now come on, start

59

helping yourself. Put your arm through mine and lean on me. Ten minutes and you'll be safe and sound. They'll take good care of you there. It's a hostel for girls like you. And they'll get the baby adopted afterwards.'

'No . . . no . . . I don't want to give my baby away,' Gaynor protested, letting go of the woman's arm.

'Well, that's as maybe,' the woman scoffed. 'You know your own business best, but if your family wanted it, then you wouldn't be running away and you wouldn't have ended up here in Cardiff without any idea of where you are going to spend the night. Come on, it's the best place for you and you can sort out what you do with the baby after you've had it.'

As another wave of pain swept through her, Gaynor knew she had no choice. Obediently, she slipped her hand back inside the woman's arm and leaned heavily on her as they made their way across the Hayes and headed towards Bute Street.

When they stopped in front of a grim, grey-stone building, Gaynor shuddered. More than ever she wanted to turn and run, but she felt so ill that she put up no resistance as the woman went up to the front door of the building and banged on it with the heavy iron knocker.

The man who was still following them tapped her on the shoulder and then dumped her case on the pavement, touched his cap and hurried away before she could even thank him.

The door was opened by a skinny young girl with short red hair, who was wearing a green overall; she stared at them blankly.

'This young girl was knocked over by a tram and it seems to have started off her labour, her waters have broken,' the woman pronounced. 'She's got nowhere to go, so this seems to be the best place for her.'

The young girl stared from one to the other of them for a minute as if she didn't understand, then, as Gaynor doubled over in pain, she said, 'I'd better fetch Matron.'

Matron was a tall, thin woman dressed in a smart dark blue uniform. 'What's her name?' she demanded, ignoring Gaynor and addressing the woman who had helped her there.

'Don't ask me, I only gave her a hand to get here after she was knocked down.'

Matron frowned. 'Well, girl, what is your name and where are you from?'

Gaynor shook her head. She didn't want to tell her anything. She tried to back away but her legs felt too weak to carry her. When the woman who had befriended her disengaged her arm, she had to cling on to the door post to stop herself from falling.

What happened after that wasn't clear to Gaynor. The woman hurried off and she had no alternative but to struggle inside the grim building under the eagle eye of the woman in the dark blue uniform who picked up her suitcase.

In a daze, she let herself be led down a gloomy corridor and into a small room which seemed to be completely bare apart from a narrow iron bedstead and a bucket in one corner.

The matron took down a dark grey cotton garment that was hanging on the back of the door and handed it to Gaynor.

'No nonsense, now. Take off your clothes, put this on, and sit on the bed until someone comes to attend to you,' she ordered crisply.

'There's been a mistake,' Gaynor protested. 'I don't want to be here.'

'You've not much choice, have you?' the woman snapped. 'As I understand it, you have nowhere else to go.'

'I . . . I'll find somewhere.'

'You are in labour and if you won't tell me your home address I can hardly let you out on the street. Now, for the last time, where is your home?'

Gaynor shook her head stubbornly. 'I'm from the Valleys . . .'

'Exactly as I thought! You're one of those silly little Welsh trollops who get themselves into trouble and then come down here to Cardiff with the idea that because it's a big city and no one will know who you are, then you can bury your shame here. We get your type all the time. While you are here you will do as you are told and as soon as your baby is born we'll arrange for it to be adopted and then you can be on your way.'

'No, no, you don't understand; I don't want to give away my baby I want to keep it.'

The woman gave her a pitying look, then turned on her heel and walked out, shutting the door behind her. Gaynor rushed after her, protesting hysterically as she heard the grating sound of a key turning in the lock.

Alone in the cell-like room, she sank down on the bed and held her head in her hands. What had she done! What sort of a mess was she in now? She ached all over and the fierce stabbing pains low down in her back were like something she'd never experienced before. The woman who had brought her here had told her she was in labour, but she had no idea what to do or how long it was going to last.

As the pains grew worse she looked around, wondering if there was a bell or something she could use to summon help. Her throat was so dry that she couldn't call out. She needed a drink of water. She wanted someone to hold her, to comfort her. As another contraction gripped her body, she wished there was someone there to explain what was happening to her.

Terrified, she banged on the door with her fists, but still no one came. She lay down on the bed, exhausted, as wave after wave of pain swept through her. She was sure she was going to die, all alone in the cold bare little room.

In between the spasms she seemed to drift off, not to sleep but into some sort of oblivion, only to be brought back to reality again as another contraction took possession of her.

When she could stand no more and was quite sure the end was coming and that she really was going to die, the door suddenly opened. It wasn't Matron, but a stout young woman; she wore a nurse's starched white apron over a dark green dress which had the sleeves rolled up to the elbows. For a moment she stood there, saying nothing, listening to Gaynor's moans and studying her agonised writhing.

'Why aren't you undressed and wearing a gown?' the newcomer demanded. 'Come on, off with your things and get into this,' she added, picking up the grey gown, which was still lying on the bed.

'I don't think I can, I'm in too much pain,' Gaynor moaned as she struggled to sit up.

'Grin and bear it and get on with it, I haven't all night,' the nurse said sharply.

'What do you mean? I don't know what I'm supposed to do,' Gaynor gasped.

'Get your clothes off, put on this gown, and next time the pain comes, push as hard as you can.'

'Push? What do you mean?'

'Just do as you're told,' the nurse told her impatiently. 'Take a deep breath and bear down.'

Although she felt physically exhausted, Gaynor did her best to obey. An hour later, as a new day dawned, wracked with pain and sure she was going to pass out at any moment,

Gaynor felt a sudden release from the tremen-dous pressure that had been holding her body in its grip for so long. It was followed by a faint wailing sound.

'You've got a girl. Skinny as a rabbit, but she'll live. Come on, sit up and feed her.'

Gaynor struggled to do so and found herself being hauled roughly up the bed and then the baby, wrapped in a piece of coarse grey towelling, was put into her arms.

'Get on with it then! You know what to do, don't you?'

'No, not really,' Gaynor admitted, looking down at the bundle in her arms. 'Can you show me?'

The nurse hesitated, and then touched by the pleading in Gaynor's eyes she shrugged. 'Here,' she moved the baby into a different position in Gaynor's arms. 'Hold her like that and stick your nipple into her mouth and she'll do the rest.'

Left alone with her baby daughter, Gaynor enthusiastically studied the tiny round face and the delicate little hands and feet. Suddenly all the pain and distress leading up to the baby's birth was forgotten. The baby had the same fair hair and blue eyes as Konrad, but this was her little daughter.

As the tiny body stirred against her, Gaynor felt a protective tenderness well up inside her. She might be penniless and alone in a strange city but no one was going to take this little miracle away from her.

Chapter Six

Gaynor found that the time she was allowed to spend with her baby was limited to half an hour every four hours each day while she fed her and changed her nappy. In between, the baby was whisked away to another room and she was expected to concentrate on scrubbing and cleaning, or helping in the laundry room. She also had to work in the kitchen preparing food for the other inmates of the hostel, or for the down-and-outs who called there once a day for hot soup and a crust of bread.

Often she heard babies crying, and whether it was because they were hungry, or because they needed changing, she was never sure but the sound tore at her heart strings.

As she went about her tasks, she schemed and planned as to how she would get away, but it seemed to be impossible. For a start, her own clothes had been removed and she wouldn't get them back until she was released. Since she was forced to wear the grim, grey serge dress which was the uniform for all the inmates, she would be recognised the minute she walked out into the street, especially if she had a baby in her arms.

Over the days she came to know several of the other new mums. Some of them were almost due to leave and resignedly accepted that their babies were being adopted.

When she protested, and even wept with frustration after having been told that this would happen to her baby, too, they were surprised by her attitude rather than sympathetic.

'You don't want to be lumbered with a young baby,' the other women told her when they found out how young she was. 'Think yourself lucky that it will be found a home. You'd never be able to bring it up when you have no husband or family to help out.'

Gaynor steadfastly refused to accept their advice. She declared fiercely that no matter what anyone said she intended to keep her baby.

'They won't let you do that, you know. All the babies born here have to be given up for adoption,' they told her. 'You must have known that was part of the deal when they took you in,' Saratina, a plump olive-skinned girl, who was about the same age as Gaynor, pointed out.

'They never mentioned it to me,' Gaynor protested. 'I was brought in here because I had an accident; I was knocked over by a tram and a woman who stopped to help brought me here. I had no idea what was happening.'

'Well, you know now, cariad.' Agnes, one of the older women, guffawed. 'You've had your kid and they'll keep it. They've probably already told some couple that they have a new baby girl for them and fixed the date when she'll be handed over.'

'When do you think that will be?'

Agnes shrugged. 'How old is she, about eight days, isn't it?'

Gaynor nodded. 'That's right.'

'Well, then, another couple of days and she'll be going. They usually do the handover on the kid's tenth day and then they keep you here for another four days to make sure that there is no chance of you finding out where the baby's gone.'

The colour drained from Gaynor's face. 'That's terrible!' she exclaimed.

'It's what happens. Your baby went yesterday, didn't it, Saratina? That means only another three days and then you'll be out of here yourself.'

Gaynor faced them all defiantly. 'No one else is going to have my baby, I don't care what any of you says,' she declared, struggling to keep her voice steady.

The women exchanged looks of amusement as they pushed back their chairs and went to get on with their day's chores. Only Saratina remained behind. Clutching hold of Gaynor's arm, she said in a low voice, 'Do you really want to keep your baby?'

'Of course I do!' Gaynor's voice rose shrilly.

'Shush!' Saratina held a finger to her lips. 'I

have an idea. We'll talk about it later, when we can be on our own.'

The thought that someone was at last taking her seriously, and was prepared to help her, increased Gaynor's determination that she would do anything to stop them taking her baby from her. She hadn't even got a name for it but now, in a rush of gratitude towards Saratina, she decided to call the baby Sara.

Saratina's scheme was daring and left Gaynor breathless with admiration. She still found it hard to comprehend and begged her to go over it again.

'Listen carefully then,' Saratina told her. 'Your baby is due to be adopted tomorrow, the same day as I'm due for release. Your baby won't be taken back to the nursery after her early morning feed, but put in a special despatch room. There's a fancy cradle in there with frills round it and a pretty crocheted coverlet to make the baby look more appealing,' she explained.

'It's my day for discharge, but before they let me go at nine o'clock I have to scrub the front steps so that they are spotlessly clean for when the people who are going to adopt arrive. To do that I take a box out there containing the scrubbing brushes, pumice stone and all the rest of the stuff. What I will do is put your baby in that box, go outside with it, then take the baby and hide her. Half an hour later, when I leave the hostel, I'll collect the baby from where I've hidden her and take her home with me.'

'It's terribly risky,' Gaynor protested.

'It will work,' Saratina said confidently.

'Here,' she pulled a scrap of crumpled paper out of the pocket of her dress and passed it to Gaynor. 'I've written my address down. When you leave here in four days' time, you come there and then you can have your baby back. It's as simple as that.'

Gaynor looked uncertain. 'Where will you put little Sara until you are free? That's what I'm calling her,' she added shyly. 'I've named her after you. A shorter form of your name.'

Saratina looked at her in wide-eyed surprise and giggled.

'So where exactly will you hide her?' Gaynor persisted.

'There's an entry running down the side of this place and there's a broken wall halfway down and the bricks have all fallen into a heap. I'll put her in amongst them and no one will spot her.'

Gaynor looked doubtful. 'What happens if she cries? Someone might hear her.'

Saratina shook her head. 'I doubt if they'd take any notice. If a passer-by does hear a baby bawling, they'll think it is coming from this building.'

'What if a dog finds her?'

'No chance. I'll wrap her in a blanket and cover her over with newspapers and an old sack. Nothing will find her. She'll only be there for about an hour.'

It sounded feasible but Gaynor was still unconvinced.

'What's wrong now, what are you looking so worried about?' Saratina asked impatiently.

'Suppose you don't want to give her back to me when I get out and come to your house to collect her?' Gaynor blurted out.

'Not give her back to you?' Saratina's dark eyebrows shot up. 'If I wanted a baby, I would have had mine at home and kept it, wouldn't I? I only came here to have it because it was the easiest way of getting rid of it afterwards. By the time you get out, Gaynor Sanderson, I'll be fed up with looking after your kid and only too pleased to hand her back to you.'

'So why are you so willing to help me and to take the risk of saving my baby like this?'

Saratina shrugged. 'I don't know, really. Except that you seem to be so keen on keeping her.'

'Oh I am; I must stop her from being adopted,' Gaynor assured her.

'And I'll help you. I've told you my plan, but you've got to promise me on your baby's life that you'll say nothing to my mam about where we met, or that I have just had a baby. She thinks I've got a job where I have to live in and that's why I haven't been home for the last six months. Swear now!'

'I won't say a word, I promise I won't,' Gaynor assured her. 'There's just one thing, though; won't your mam think it odd that you arrive home with my baby and I'm not there with you?'

'She would if I didn't tell her a good story,' Saratina agreed.

'So what are you going to tell her?'

Saratina was silent for a moment, screwing up her eyes in concentration. 'I shall say you were a friend I worked with – you were in service like me. You had a bad time having the baby and they want you to stay in hospital for a bit longer so I've said I'll look after your baby until you come home.'

'Will she believe that?'

'Why not? There's no reason why she shouldn't,' Saratina said defensively.

'You said you haven't been to see your mam for months and then you turn up with a very young baby ... won't she be suspicious?' Gaynor said in a puzzled voice. 'She might think it is yours!'

Saratina laughed. 'I'm Spanish, haven't you noticed the colour my skin is, and my black hair? Your baby's hair is so fair that it is almost white and her eyes are bright blue. No matter how hard I tried I couldn't end up with a baby that looked like that. All my brothers and sisters have jet black hair, dark eyes and olive skin, the same as my mam and dad.'

'You said your mam didn't want any more babies in your house and that was why you never told her you were having one,' Gaynor argued.

72

'We don't, but this one will only be there for a couple of weeks. You'll be out of here in a few days' time and then once you're on your feet . . .'

'That's not quite the truth, though,' Gaynor reminded her. 'I have nowhere to go, no one to turn to. I daren't go back to my parents . . .'

'We'll worry about that after you come out,' Saratina told her cheerfully. 'Now, make sure you can read that address and remember, not a word to anyone here about what we are doing and when you get to my place, don't you ever breathe a word to anyone in my family about me having had a baby. Understand? I didn't want my baby because we've always had a houseful of them. My mam has one almost every year, there're half a dozen younger than me. It takes my mam all her time to feed us and care for us now that my dad has died. She certainly doesn't want another added to their number, certainly not one of mine . . .'

'You mean because the father won't marry you,' Gaynor murmured sympathetically.

'No, because I wouldn't marry him. It was all a mistake. I'll tell you the whole story some-time, when we've got more time to talk. For the moment, all you need to know is that my mam must never know that I've had a baby.'

Gaynor looked puzzled. 'I still don't understand how you managed not to tell her.'

'I told you, I left home nearly six months ago. She thought I was in service and living in. I wasn't, of course. I had a job for a while and

73

then after that I lived rough. That's how I ended up in here. Like you, I collapsed in the street and some do-gooder bundled me into this place. Now, you've got to promise me you'll say nothing to my mam. Swear now!'

'I promise!' Gaynor agreed. 'I won't say a word!' She concentrated on the smudged writing on the scrap of paper and read aloud: 'Vario, Sophia Street.'

'That's right, now remember it and don't tell anyone else,' Saratina warned as she snatched back the scrap of paper. 'I'm going to destroy this. I don't want anyone here knowing where I live,' she warned.

'And I certainly won't tell them,' Gaynor promised again.

'Good! When you leave here come to Sophia Street and ask for the Varios' house. Everyone knows us so it won't be difficult for you to find.' Saratina smiled.

'I . . . I don't know where Sophia Street is, though,' Gaynor said anxiously.

'Off Bute Street, of course!' Saratina told her impatiently.

'Where's that, though? Bute Street, I mean?'

Saratina looked at her in astonishment. 'You must know where it is; this place is in Bute Street. Simply follow this road down towards the docks and Sophia Street is one of the roads off on your right. You can't miss it.'

'Fine! I'm sure I'll find it,' Gaynor agreed with more confidence than she felt.

'If your baby is being taken for adoption tomorrow, Monday, then you will be told you can leave on Friday, so I'll expect to see you on Friday morning.' Saratina smiled. 'Now, don't breathe a word to anyone. Oh, and don't say goodbye to me when I leave, it might make someone suspicious when they find your baby is missing.'

Gaynor nodded as though in agreement, but her heart was thundering and her mind was churning with all that was happening. She trusted Saratina and she was sure that if she did manage to get her baby out of the building, then she would look after it until she was able to be there. She was worried, though, in case she wouldn't be able to find Sophia Street. Saratina had made it all sound so easy, but she had no idea where to go.

Next morning, Gaynor tried to keep her mind on cleaning the office and corridors, which was her allocated job that day, but she was listening to every sound and watching everyone else's movements.

She saw Saratina walk past with her big box of cleaning materials and could hardly stop herself from rushing to see if her baby was in it. She watched her bring the box back about twenty minutes later and then waited a nail-biting hour until she heard some of the others calling out goodbye and good wishes as Saratina made her departure.

Gaynor wondered what would happen next.

She wasn't left in ignorance for very long. About half an hour after Saratina had left, the commotion began when Matron sent one of the other women to make sure that Gaynor's baby was ready for the adoption procedure.

The moment she came scurrying back to report that the baby was missing a general hue and cry ensued.

The mystery deepened when no one seemed to have seen the baby since its six o'clock feed that morning. No one had visited the hostel, and the only person who had left it had been Saratina when she was discharged. Several people could affirm that she had only had a small brown paper bag with her brush and comb in it, so there was nothing to implicate her.

The couple who were waiting to adopt the baby were closeted in Matron's office for almost half an hour. Eventually, when there was still no news of the missing baby, they left after being assured that they would be contacted again as soon as there was some news.

No one told Gaynor that her baby was missing and she knew she dare not ask any questions. Her anxiety deepened when she heard rumours that Matron was talking about informing the police.

After a heated discussion, and a meeting with some of the other officials, there were rumours that it had eventually been decided that it might be better to do nothing, simply offer the couple another baby.

As they had never seen the one they were to adopt, they could be told that the baby had been found shortly after they had left, and that would be the end of the matter, someone explained. Matron said that although no one seemed to have any idea where the missing baby could be, she was quite sure that it would turn up in time. It wasn't as though it could walk out on its own accord.

Gaynor felt outraged by such callousness. If her baby really had been missing, then it seemed no one was in the least bit worried about it. One of the women even suggested that perhaps it had been taken away by the Alsatian dog from the butcher's nearby.

'Fortunately the baby's birth hasn't yet been registered,' Matron was overheard to comment. 'As usual, we delayed doing that until the baby was adopted, so all we have to do is claim that it has died. No one is likely to ask to see the body. We often have stillborn births, or babies who expire from natural causes within a few days of birth, so it will be accepted without question.'

Gaynor couldn't believe that she could dismiss the matter so casually or that no one suspected Saratina. All she had to worry about now was whether Saratina had found the baby safe and sound and was looking after it.

She was desperate to find out for herself. A few more days, and then she would be able to hold little Sara in her arms, she thought jubilantly.

The time went so slowly that Gaynor wanted to scream, but she forced herself to remain calm and tried to stay indifferent to the hullabaloo that was going on all around her.

The night before she was released, Gaynor was unable to settle. All the things she had ever seen or done in the whole of her life paraded through her mind in a steady stream. The harder she tried to sleep the more wide awake she felt.

There were so many problems ahead that she became frightened. She had no home, no money, and because she had never worked, she had no references. She couldn't even tell people where she'd once lived in case they made contact with someone and then everyone in Ferndale would know where she was. They might even find out she'd had a baby and that would distress her parents, because it would be considered such a disgrace.

If only her mam and dad had been more reasonable; if only they'd let her have her baby and live at home and bring it up, then she wouldn't be in the mess she was in today, she thought resentfully.

For one wild moment she thought of going back to Ferndale, with Sara in her arms, to see what would happen. After all, Sara was their grandchild; surely they wouldn't turn her away?

Even as the thought went through her mind she knew what the result would be. Of course they'd disown her; they would probably slam the door in her face. Her father would be so incensed that he might even denounce her as a sinner in front of the entire congregation in chapel.

Her pillow became soaked with tears as she thought about what a terrible disgrace that would be, and how it would upset her mother. As dawn approached, and the sky outside began to lighten, she resolved that this was the last time she would cry about what had happened. The past was over and done with; there was no going back, no time for regrets or recriminations.

It was a fresh day dawning and she was about to start out on a new life. From now on her only concern would be Sara; everything she did would revolve around her.

Eager to get started, she began to dress. As she slipped the rough grey serge dress over her head she stopped. She wouldn't be wearing this any more; she would be able to wear her own clothes. She wondered if they would still fit her; if they didn't, then what would she do?

Saratina would know what to do, she thought confidently. Once she was with Saratina and baby Sara everything in the world would come right.

She had no idea where Sophia Street was, but Saratina had said that the hostel was at the top of Bute Street and that all she had to do was to walk towards the docks until she came to a turning on the right called Sophia Street and then she'd easily find the Varios' house.

Excitement at the thought of being reunited with her baby overcame her anxiety. It would be so wonderful to hold her in her arms again and to be able to cuddle her for as long as she wished, knowing that no one was going to take her away again.

Chapter Seven

Once she managed to find Sophia Street, Gaynor had no trouble at all finding the Varios' house. The front door and window frames were painted in a vivid yellow so that it looked like a bright sunflower peering out from the dingy grey, brown and black of the other houses in the long row.

As she drew nearer she smiled to herself when she saw that not only were there bright red curtains at the front-room window, but when she looked up, she saw that the ones in the front bedroom were a vivid blue.

She knocked on the door and even before it was opened by a diminutive little girl with huge dark eyes and shoulder-length dark hair, she could hear music mingling with the sound of voices coming from inside.

Close on the girl's heels was a boy in a ragged jumper, dragging a battered teddy bear by its ear, and a slightly younger boy who was sucking his thumb and clinging on to the back of the girl's dress.

They stood in the doorway staring at Gaynor, but not saying a word. From somewhere deep inside the house she heard Saratina's voice asking who it was. When none of the children answered, she called out, 'Saratina, it's me, Gaynor. Can I come in?'

Suddenly Saratina was there in the hallway, pushing the children to one side and hugging Gaynor as if they hadn't seen each other for months.

'Come in. You found us all right? How are you, come on in. The kettle's boiling.'

She paused and hugged Gaynor again then shooed the gaping children back inside the house as she pulled Gaynor into the narrow hallway.

Above the sound of the music, Gaynor could hear a baby crying and suddenly she found that her cheeks were wet with tears of thankfulness, so relieved was she to know that little Sara was safe and sound.

Saratina fussed over her, taking her into the living room, shooing all the children away, before rushing to fetch baby Sara who was wrapped in a multi-coloured crocheted shawl. When she had made sure that Gaynor was settled into an armchair Saratina brought her a bottle to feed the baby with while she went to make them both a cup of tea.

While Sara was taking her bottle, Gaynor looked around the living room in astonishment. There were so many different colours in the room that it made her feel giddy. Two of the walls were a bright orange, the other two a vibrant yellow and the door was bright green. The carpet was a vivid motley of reds, yellows, blues and greens and there was a rug in front of the fireplace that had brilliant red poppies on a pale lilac background.

The brown armchairs had yellow and red cushions piled on them and the fawn sofa had pale green and yellow cushions and a gaily striped blanket thrown carelessly over the back.

On the high mantelpiece, which had a dark red velvet valance trimmed with pink satin bobbles hanging from the edge of it, there was a row of multi-coloured glass vases. On the window sill a bright pink jug was filled with enormous paper flowers in vivid shades of purple and orange. Gaynor had never in her life seen anything quite so colourful or lively, so completely different from the dull orderliness of her own home back in Ferndale.

Not only was the room as bright as a fairground but there was also music coming from another part of the house. Gaynor wasn't sure if it was someone playing a guitar or music from a gramophone, but it was loud and lively.

Gaynor cuddled Sara closer, pulling back the multicoloured shawl and studying the baby's little arms and legs, marvelling at how they were beginning to fill out and how much she seemed to have grown in less than a week.

A feeling of pride surged through her. 'You're going to grow up into a beautiful little girl and make your mam proud of you,' she assured her daughter as she rested her lips on the child's brow in a fervent kiss.

'She's going to be like her mama then,' a man's voice said softly.

Gaynor looked up, startled. A tall, dark haired, dark eyed man had come into the room so quietly that she hadn't noticed.

He stood smiling down at her, holding a guitar in one of his hands.

'Who ... who are you?' she gasped. 'You frightened the life out of me.'

'Pedro. Pedro Vario. I'm Saratina's brother.' He smiled widely, flashing strong, even teeth that gleamed whitely against his olive skin. 'You mean she hasn't told you about me?'

'No, Saratina hasn't mentioned you ... I don't know why.'

He laughed again. 'I do! She sees me so little that when I'm not ashore she forgets all about me.' He sighed. 'Also, she blames me for her misfortune because I introduced her to the scoundrel who betrayed us both.'

Gaynor felt uncomfortable, remembering that Saratina had told her that no one in her family knew about her baby and making her promise not to mention it under any circumstances, yet her brother seemed to know all about it.

Seeing her confusion, Pedro gave a low laugh. 'Saratina has told you not to mention a word about what happened to her, has she? I am glad she has decided to take my advice over that. I was the one who suggested that she should leave home before our mam got a hint of what was in the offing, so make sure you say nothing.'

'I won't. I promised Saratina I wouldn't breathe a word.'

'Good. It has been hard for her, mind you, but it would be even harder on mam if she ever found out. Our mother is very religious and has always brought us up quite strictly. One moment of weakness on Saratina's part, that was all it took . . .'

'And it was a friend of yours?' Gaynor murmured.

'Hardly a friend,' Pedro told her grimly. 'A fellow sailor and Saratina was young and vulnerable and fell for his charms. In one brief weekend he swept her off her feet and seduced her. As soon as she was aware of the results she was devastated. As it is she has compromised her soul; she will carry the guilty secret with her to the grave.'

'Now it's all over she can put it all behind her,' Gaynor told him confidently.

Pedro shook his head, his dark eyes blazing with anger. 'How can she ever do that? You are obviously not a Catholic or you would know that she will never again be able to take communion because she can never confess about what has happened.'

'No, I'm not a Catholic but I don't see that what happened needs to have such a long-lasting effect.'

'He was not a Catholic and if she was to confess her sin she would probably be excommunicated. If she doesn't confess, then she is

85

barred from taking Holy Communion. Either way, my poor sister is damned and my mother would be devastated.'

'I thought that whatever you told the priest in the confessional was supposed to be secret,' Gaynor argued in a surprised voice.

Pedro shrugged. 'Our priest would know, so Saratina would never feel comfortable in his presence. Whenever he came to the house to see Mama, or they met him in the street, her guilt would flare up anew and sooner or later it would spill over and Mama would find out about it. As it is, she has only delayed her punishment; she will never be cleansed and she will remain in limbo for ever!'

Gaynor shook her head in bewilderment; she didn't know what to say. It was all beyond her. At chapel there were dire warnings of the perils attached to sinning, such as fire and brimstone in the life ever after, but from what Pedro had just told her there were even worse things to be endured in their faith.

Pedro scowled and crossed himself. 'May God forgive the scoundrel who seduced my sister; I never will. True, it is all in the past and now she is ready to start afresh, but if Mama ever heard that Saratina had given birth in the workhouse the disgrace would kill her.' He frowned. 'Could you not have done the same? Had your baby adopted and started afresh?'

Gaynor didn't know what to say; she turned her head to avoid Pedro's penetrating, dark stare. She wondered what his reaction would be if he ever heard the truth about the father of her baby and learned that he had been a German; one of the enemy he and his fellow sailors were now facing.

She busied herself wrapping the shawl back around her daughter's tiny body. She kept her head lowered so that he couldn't see the tears that had come into her eyes at the words 'shame' and 'workhouse'. She wished he would go away. It was no wonder Saratina hadn't told her about him, she thought angrily, if he questioned and upbraided her in this fashion.

She was aware that Pedro was waiting for her to say something, so, taking a deep breath, she squared her shoulders and looked up at him.

'I feel no shame,' she told him furiously. 'The shame lies with my parents; they are the ones who should feel shame because, like your family, they seemed to think that having a baby out of wedlock was a disgrace. All they achieved by turning me out was to punish an innocent child even before she was born. I intend to put the humiliation of having to go into the workhouse out of my mind. She is the most beautiful baby ever and I shall spend the rest of my life making sure she is cherished and—'

She broke off as she saw he was scowling. 'So how will you do that when you have no home and no job? You don't even know if my sister can provide you with a bed.'

'Saratina is my friend; a very good friend. In

her heart she probably envies me because I still have my baby and because of that she will do whatever she can to help me.'

Pedro's manner suddenly altered. 'You're right, Saratina will,' he agreed. 'My sister's a saint.'

Gaynor looked at him puzzled. 'You've changed your tune!' she said sceptically.

Pedro shrugged. 'I speak as I find. I spend most of my life at sea out of touch with my family and when I return and find so much has happened in my absence ...' He stopped speaking as Saratina came into the room.

'Oh, you two have already met.' She smiled. 'Now, I want you both to be good friends ... understand? You are my two favourite people. Gaynor's had it rough, so treat her gently and no sermonising, OK? Pedro sails again in two days' time, Gaynor, so you won't have to put up with him for too long. With the war becoming more intense every day it will probably be a long time before he has shore leave again.'

Gaynor nodded understandingly, but as her eyes met Pedro's, she felt a frisson of alarm that he would be going back to sea so soon, even if he had been rather judgemental. Since war had been declared it had become a very hazardous occupation and she felt apprehensive about the dangers he would have to encounter.

You must be mad, she chided herself; you've only known him for ten minutes and he's already made it plain that he thinks you've behaved disgracefully.

She gave a mental shrug; she had plenty of problems of her own to worry about, her own future was also extremely hazardous at the moment and, as Saratina said, Pedro would be leaving in a couple of days so what did it matter what he thought. Saratina had said she could stay there for the present and that was all that mattered.

In a few days, after she'd adjusted to her new surroundings, she'd find a job so that she could plan her future. With any luck she would be able to find a place of her own before Pedro came back from his next trip. In the meantime, she'd accept his sermons with a smile, for Saratina's sake, even though she was quite sure she could never be friends with him.

She found it hard to understand how someone as broadminded and understanding as Saratina could have a brother who was so judgemental.

Men, she decided, were the cause of so many problems. They demanded purity and innocence in their own loved ones, yet they were invariably the cause of other women's downfall.

When it happened, they blamed everyone but themselves. They were hypocrites. Pedro was one of the worst she'd ever encountered.

Gaynor's first meeting with Saratina's mother, Maria Vario, was equally disturbing for her. Saratina had warned her that her mother knew nothing at all about her pregnancy and had emphasised how important it was that she never heard about it. Pedro had said much the same thing, and so Gaynor was on tenterhooks in case she said something she shouldn't.

Mrs Vario was an older version of Saratina. She was short with flashing dark eyes, dark hair drawn back into a fat bun at the back of her head, and a round, olive-skinned face. As a result of years of child-bearing she appeared very stout and motherly.

She greeted Gaynor with a beaming smile, telling her what a lovely baby Sara was and sympathising greatly over the fact that Sara's father had died as a result of the war.

'These terrible battles! They are killing off all the beautiful young men. I dread the thought of my Pedro having to go back to sea again, but that is his life. He joined the Merchant Navy just before war was declared and he is no coward, so it is impossible for him not to return to his ship. I pray every night that God and the Blessed Virgin will watch over him and keep him safe.'

Gaynor nodded in agreement but, before she could speak, Maria Vario had started reminiscing about how her own husband had died at sea leaving her with a young family to bring up and how difficult life could be.

'I missed my Saratina so much; she is such a good girl, she helps me so much with the babies,' she went on. 'I know she thought that going into service and living away from home was a good idea because it was one less mouth to feed, and she could send her wages home, but the money she sent now and again was very little and in no way made up for the loss I felt. These rich people, they have so much yet pay such small wages to the people they employ to look after their domestic needs. Now she will live at home again and find work nearby. It is one of the advantages of war that they need women for the factories and they pay them well. She says you will be doing the same.'

'Yes, I will have to work to support myself and little Sara,' Gaynor murmured.

'So terrible to have no family to help you at a time like this,' Maria said sadly. 'I have agreed with Saratina that you can stay here with us so that we can help you.'

'That is extremely kind of you,' Gaynor murmured. 'I am very grateful.'

She felt overcome by the offer. She wished she'd had more time to talk to Saratina and to find out exactly what she'd told her mother and what they had agreed between them.

'Yes, you need not worry, I will care for your baby while you work.' Maria smiled. 'She will be looked after like one of my own.'

'How many brothers and sisters does Saratina have?'

'I have six children. Pedro is the eldest, and then Saratina and the little ones are Miguel, José, Margarita and Sanje. Until now he has been thought of as the baby of the family, even though he will be starting school later this year. I thought I was going to be lonely not having a baby in the house to care for, but now' – she smiled warmly – 'I will have your little Sara. My children already adore her.'

'Are you sure it is not going to be too much trouble?' Gaynor asked hesitantly.

'Trouble! That is a word I do not like. She is a blessing, not trouble. The good Lord sent you to us and we will do his bidding. She is already one of the family and soon I hope you will feel that you are as well.'

For the first few days, Gaynor found the noisy chatter, the friendly squabbling, and all the laughter and banter, was almost too much for her after the strictly disciplined, silent routine of the workhouse.

At night she and baby Sara shared a room with Saratina and Margarita and Gaynor was so worried that Sara might waken and disturb them that she hardly slept a wink.

Gaynor looked so red-eyed and washed out that before Pedro left two days later he told his mother that he thought Gaynor and Sara should move into his room.

'I know Miguel was looking forward to being in there and not having to share with José and Sanje, but I have spoken to him about it and we have reached an agreement.'

Gaynor found it was wonderful to have a room all to herself, even though it was the smallest room in the house. It was over the scullery and at a different level from the other bedrooms. As she went down the three steps from the landing she really felt that she was in a place of her own. She also felt confident that even if Sara did wake and cry it was unlikely that she would disturb the others.

At night, before she drifted off to sleep, she thought about Barri and her intention to find him, but she had no idea how to start doing so. For some unaccountable reason she felt she didn't want to tell Saratina about him.

Gaynor soon began to think very seriously about finding work. She had been at the Varios' almost a week, which was plenty of time to get used to her surroundings and to fit in with the family, and, although Maria hadn't mentioned money, she knew it must be an added burden having to feed her and provide for little Sara.

Saratina had already found herself work at Curran's, the factory on the banks of the Taff where they were making armaments. It was long hours and hard work, but when Gaynor expressed a willingness to join her, Saratina looked pleased and promised to find out if they were still taking women on.

Gaynor found factory life even harder to tolerate than being in the workhouse. Countless times she wished she was back in Ferndale, which seemed like an oasis of tranquillity compared to where she was now.

She felt stressed by all the noise, the dust,

the fumes and the coarse language of the other women. Most of them were married women whose husbands had been called up and were now in the army, and many of them were revelling in their new-found freedom. They had money in their pockets each week and no one at home ordering them around. A few of them had very young children whom they'd had to put into someone else's care while they worked, but the majority had children who were old enough to look after themselves and, in many cases, able to help to look after their younger brothers or sisters.

Saratina sensed Gaynor's unease about working there. 'We don't have to stay here, you know; you can try something else if you want to. I've heard that the electric tram company are taking women on because so many of the men have been called up.'

'What sort of work would that be? Surely I wouldn't be expected to drive one!' Gaynor shuddered as she thought about the huge green monsters that charged up and down along the glittering tramlines in the centre of the main roads, and she remembered her accident.

'No.' Saratina laughed. 'We'd be conductresses. We'd wear a uniform and take the fares and ping the bell to tell the driver when to stop and start.'

'We? You mean you'll come as well?'

'Of course! I'm fed up of working here, I fancy a change.'

'Would they be regular hours or would we have to do shift work like we do here?'

Saratina shrugged. 'I don't know. Anyway, what does it matter? My mam will look after Sara no matter what sort of hours you're working.'

Gaynor nodded. 'Do they pay as well as they do here in a factory?'

'I don't know the answer to that either, but we could go along to their office and find out all about the job and check if they have any vacancies.'

Chapter Eight

Florence Sanderson was filled with a sense of unease. She had barely exchanged half a dozen words with her husband in as many days. Although neither of them would openly admit it they were both extremely worried about the same thing; what might have happened to Gaynor.

It was now almost two months since the Sunday she had left home without a word to either of them, and there had been no news from her at all. Most of her friends had either gone off to war or, in the case of the girls, were doing some sort of war work so there was no one left who might know where she had gone.

Added to which, there was a general air of depression in Ferndale as bad news from the Front seemed to arrive daily. Already there had been news of quite a number of casualties and this had brought sorrow not only to their immediate families but also to their friends and neighbours as well.

As an explanation for Gaynor's absence, Florence had told people that she had gone away to do war work. She wasn't sure if they believed her, but because she had always been rather reserved no one questioned her about this; indeed, no one even asked where Gaynor had gone or how she was getting on.

As a family they were already under a cloud of suspicion when her fears that Konrad had been a German spy became widespread. Ieuan had even found that some of the people at chapel even stopped talking about the war when he was around.

The one exception had been Ellie. She had hounded both of them from the day Gaynor had left home, wanting to know if she had gone to Cardiff to look for Barri Hughes as she had vowed to do and, if so, where was she living, because she wanted to go and see her. Ellie claimed that she, too, was fed up with life in Ferndale and felt there would be plenty of openings in Cardiff for girls to do more worthwhile work than she was doing now.

'Give me Gaynor's address so that I can write and see what she thinks of the idea,' Ellie pleaded. 'She might be able to tell me where I can stay while I look for work, and where there're jobs going. Either way, it would be nice for us to be together again as I've missed her since she left.'

Ellie had seemed very much put out, Florence reflected, when she'd said she couldn't do so because Gaynor was on the point of moving and she didn't have her new address.

'Well, give me her old address and I'll ask them where she's gone,' she persisted.

When Florence refused to do even that, Ellie had approached Mr Sanderson with the same request, but he hadn't bothered to be so polite. He'd sent her on her way telling her that if she hadn't encouraged his daughter in her wicked ways then Gaynor would still be at home and would never have become pregnant in the first place. He'd refused to believe Ellie when she'd exclaimed in a shocked voice that she had known nothing about this and that she'd never understood why Gaynor had left Ferndale in such a hurry without even saying goodbye.

'Don't mention that girl's name to me ever again,' he told his wife, angrily.

'Not mention Ellie? Why ever not?'

'Not her . . . your daughter's name.'

Her face flushed. 'She's your daughter just as much as mine!'

'She's no daughter of mine or she would never have behaved as she has done,' Ieuan declared in a domineering voice, his face red and angry. 'She's wanton and wicked and if she ever returns to Ferndale she is not to put a foot over our threshold and you're not to have anything to do with her. Do you understand?'

Florence didn't answer. She knew that when her husband was on what she termed his 'high horse' there was no possibility of reasoning with him. She knew he was disappointed in Gaynor, but in her eyes he was partly to blame for what had happened. He was the one who had encouraged her friendship with Konrad Claus.

98

She also realised that when Konrad had suddenly decided to return to Germany Ieuan had been almost as shocked and upset as Gaynor.

Florence had other concerns. Night after night she lay awake until the early hours of the morning worrying about Gaynor and the reason she had left home. She was quite sure it had not been because she was upset about Konrad Claus going back to Germany, or her own foolhardy behaviour, but because she was so determined to keep the child she was expecting.

She wished she did have Gaynor's address so that she could see her again and find out how she was. Not that she would dare to go to Cardiff herself, she thought with a shudder, but she was sure she would be able to persuade Ellie to do so on her behalf.

Gaynor would have had the baby by now, and she wondered how she was coping. As an only child, she had led such a sheltered life. She would have no idea what to do with a baby or how to look after it. With no one to care for her, no home, and no one to support her, she must be in dire trouble.

Ever since Gaynor had gone she prayed as she'd never prayed in her life before; not just when she went to chapel on Sunday, but every hour of the day and long into the night. She missed her daughter daily and regretted the fact that they had driven her away.

Her own concern over Gaynor and what might be happening to her took precedence over the horrors of the war that were reported daily in the newspapers.

There were even times when she thought that those mothers who lost their sons in battle were better off than she was; at least they knew what had happened to their beloved ones.

She still had her memories, of course, Florence thought with a sigh. She'd been so happy when she had learned that the baby she'd longed for was a little girl. Ieuan, unfortunately, had been disappointed, but she supposed that was only natural because like most men he had wanted his first born to be a son.

'Next time it will be a boy,' she'd told him apologetically. But there hadn't been a next time; for some inexplicable reason there had been no more children.

Florence had loved every moment of Gaynor's childhood. She'd dressed her in dainty little dresses and pretty bonnets so that she always looked enchanting. She'd been worried when it was time for her to go to school, but she'd hidden her feelings, knowing that Ieuan would have no patience with her if he saw her in tears over it.

Gaynor had loved being with all the other children and in due course Ieuan had taken great pride in her ability to learn. It had been his decision that instead of leaving school she should stay on and study to become a teacher.

Florence sighed; he'd been a good father in many ways, even though he had appeared to be a hard man because he kept his true feelings hidden and found it hard to express any affection. She sometimes felt, though, that he'd been far too dogmatic and critical about Gaynor's achievements and overly strict with her, especially in public.

He was always intent on being seen as an upstanding member of society and a pillar of the chapel; so much so that he always expected Gaynor to behave in an adult way. She'd tried to accept that, but when he had begun laying down the law about who Gaynor could play with and who she couldn't, what she could wear and what she couldn't, and even controlling what books and magazines she read, then she had felt it was her duty to speak out.

Ieuan refused to discuss the matter; but instead, he made it abundantly clear that he felt his authority was being undermined.

Whenever that was the case his reaction was silence. Again, she didn't mind for herself, but the hurt look on Gaynor's little face when she tried to tell her dad something and he ignored her completely, or else stood up and pushed her to one side and then walked out of the room, was more than she could stand.

The biggest rows had been over Gaynor's friendship with Barri Hughes. It was something Florence had never been able to comprehend because, not only did Ieuan and Barri's father work together, but the entire Hughes family were also members of the chapel they attended. In fact, the two families couldn't have been closer and Barri was such a nice boy and so trustworthy and he cared deeply about Gaynor.

She'd had visions of Barri and Gaynor marrying when they were old enough to do so and eventually making her and Ieuan proud grandparents. Sending him away had upset her almost as much as it had Gaynor. She would never understand why Ieuan had thought that Barri wasn't good enough for her.

Even worse, in her eyes, was his encouragement of the young German.

She'd suspected that Konrad was taking liberties with Gaynor and now she wished she'd asked her outright if that was true.

She knew that Ieuan put the blame on her for Gaynor getting into trouble and then running away from home. He claimed it was because Gaynor was so ashamed of herself that she couldn't face them and refused to listen when she told him that she was sure that it was because Gaynor didn't want to have the baby adopted.

Ieuan Sanderson felt that life had handed him a raw deal. All his life he had wanted a son. He'd pictured him, a big strapping lad with a mind that was razor-sharp. A clever lad who didn't earn his living by working in a factory and toiling with his hands, or down in a coal mine, but by using his brains. He'd dreamed that he'd be a professional man; a lawyer, a doctor, or a teacher. He'd go off to work each morning dressed in a dark suit, gleaming white shirt, smart Ulster, shiny bowler and carrying a leather briefcase full of important documents relating to his livelihood.

It hadn't happened, of course. Florence had failed him. She'd only produced one child and that had been a daughter instead of the son he'd longed for.

As the years passed, and he watched Gaynor grow from a placid baby into a lively young schoolgirl, and he realised that there never would be a son, he had adapted his ambition. If he couldn't have a white-collared son, then an educated son-in-law would be the next best thing.

He had tolerated Gaynor's friendship with Barri Hughes as being inevitable when they were growing up because they only lived a few doors away from each other and the families were close.

He and Simon Hughes might both have started out working in the same factory, but he'd proved his own superiority; he'd got promotion and now, in his fifties, he was Simon's boss; another factor which made Barri an unsuitable match for Gaynor.

Barri was a good-looking young boyo, polite and hard working, but he was only a factory worker and not the sort of chap he wanted as a husband for Gaynor, especially when it became obvious how intelligent she was and when her headmistress suggested that she should train to become a teacher. The minute he saw that they were getting too close for his peace of mind he'd put his foot down and when Simon Hughes continued to ignore the problem there had been nothing else for it but to tell young Barri that he must go away.

Florence had been filled with misgivings, of course. She was sensitive about Gaynor's feelings, but he was more concerned about his daughter's future than with her broken heart, since he knew that would soon mend. And it had, he'd been right about that, he thought triumphantly.

Konrad Claus had not only been studious, but also had good career prospects. Ieuan had welcomed him into his home, encouraged Gaynor to take an interest in him, and had been pleased when their friendship flourished.

It had been a real blow when the young German suddenly announced he had been recalled to the Fatherland. Whether the rumours that he was a spy had any foundation or not, Ieuan didn't know and now, since he'd vanished completely from the scene, it no longer seemed very important.

Gaynor packing her bags and leaving Ferndale without a word so soon afterwards had been another blow. Holding his head high and ignoring the rumours that flew around following her departure hadn't been easy, especially in chapel.

Again he blamed Florence. It should never have happened; she should have made sure that Gaynor didn't get into that sort of trouble. She'd always been too lenient and soft with the girl; she should most certainly have stopped her leaving.

With hindsight he wished they'd handled matters differently. Gaynor most definitely couldn't be allowed to keep the baby she was expecting. Florence was right about that, but she had obviously not done a very good job of explaining this to her.

To make matters worse, Florence didn't even know where she'd gone! Although they both suspected that she'd gone off to Cardiff, they found it impossible to discuss the matter with each other.

If Florence had made sure she had an address, or at least a promise from Gaynor that she would send one as soon as she was settled, then he could have gone to Cardiff and made sure she was all right and told her that she could come back home again as soon as she'd had the child adopted. He would have been prepared to forgive and forget.

As it was, since they didn't have that information, he had hardened his heart and now intended to banish her from his thoughts altogether.

He'd always been a law-abiding upright man with high expectations of himself, his family and the future. He'd tried so hard to make sure that Gaynor had the same ideals. Now, he felt that he had failed completely; he was even too old to fight for his country.

If he'd had the son he'd dreamed about, then his boyo would now be representing him as a soldier. He'd be looking smart in his uniform and doing his bit to conquer the enemy.

A daughter was no good when it came to these sorts of things although, if she was still living at home, then at least she could have done some kind of war work, even if it was only helping to raise funds or knitting socks and gloves for the boyos who had been sent to the Front.

Chapter Nine

Working for the Cardiff tramways was so different from working at an ammunitions factory that at first both Saratina and Gaynor were intrigued by the novelty of their new environment, especially Gaynor, who had never been on one. At first, remembering her accident, she was very nervous, but once she was inside the tram her confidence returned.

Although the trams clanged and rattled like enormous tin cans as they made their way along the tramlines, inside they were mostly of wood. Downstairs, Gaynor was surprised to find that narrow bench seats ran the full length on either side. Upstairs, though, the seats were in pairs with a narrow aisle between them. The backs on each pair of seats could be pushed back and forth so that passengers could always face the way they were going, because the tramcar itself could be driven from either end.

Their uniforms were in a navy serge material and consisted of an ankle-length skirt, a tight-fitting jacket, and a broad-brimmed hat which they agreed looked quite smart.

'The uniform would be even nicer if it was

the same as the livery on the fleet of trams,' Saratina sighed.

What they weren't quite so happy about was the heavy equipment they had to wear strapped across their chest. There was a large leather money pouch and a shiny metal holder containing different coloured tickets and a punch. Each time they took a fare they had to select the right ticket – single, return or child – then punch a hole in one side of it and hand it over to the passenger.

Also pinned to their chest was a round enamel disc that bore the same number as the one on their documents and pay packet.

'These cross-over straps feel so uncomfortable,' Gaynor protested as they started their second day's training. 'They're so cumbersome when you reach up to tug the leather cord to tell the driver when to stop and when to start again.'

'They certainly are,' Saratina agreed. 'Especially for me, because I have to stand on my toes to reach the bell pull.'

'All that stretching may help you to grow,' Gaynor laughed.

They spent the rest of their training practising how to balance as the tram swung round corners. They were also instructed on how to reverse the backs of the slatted wooden seats when they reached the terminus so that passengers would be facing the right way when the tram was driven back into the heart of the city.

'The passengers can always do it themselves

if we forget,' Saratina pointed out. 'Anyway, some of them like having their backs to where they are going, or if they're with a group of friends they like being able to sit facing them so that they can talk.'

'That's not the point. The seats should always be facing in the right direction,' their instructor told them. 'The driver will sometimes check to make sure you've done it when he walks through to the driving position at the other end of the tram, remember.'

They were also checked out on their ability to run up and down the twisting staircase to the upper deck. Then they were handed a list of rules and regulations about not allowing passengers to stand strap-hanging while the tram was in motion, and how to deal with unruly passengers or passengers who refused to pay their fare.

'Will we get many of those?' Gaynor asked anxiously.

'There's usually some late on Fridays and Saturdays when the men have been boozing, but don't worry, we try not to have girls doing the late shifts.'

'So what is the biggest problem?' Saratina asked.

'Your biggest problem is watching out for fare dodgers; usually women who try to avoid paying for their kids.'

'How do they manage that?'

'They often claim that the child is under five

years old and therefore can travel free; or else they send them to sit further along the tram and pretend they're not theirs. When you go to get the money off the kiddie, the child says that his mam has already paid. This sometimes works if they have several kids and the mother pays for a couple of them.'

'The other fare dodgers are the strap-hangers who stay near the door and when you ask them for their money hop off, even when the tram is moving quite fast. There's nothing you can do about them, of course, except make sure that no one is permitted to stand on the platform if there are any seats available, or if there is standing room inside.'

Despite all the rules they both agreed that the work seemed quite manageable. They went over everything time and again when they got home at night to make sure they knew what to do, yet both of them admitted that they felt nervous on their first day as conductresses.

'It wouldn't be so bad if we were together,' Gaynor sighed as they hurried down Bute Street towards the terminus at the Pier Head.

'We won't be on our own, though, not on the first day,' Saratina reminded her. 'There will be an experienced conductor on board as well. He will be there to keep an eye on what we do and he'll put us right if we go wrong.'

The weeks that followed were a revelation to both girls. For the first few days their main concern was the terrible ache they felt in their legs from running up and down the stairs to collect fares from those brave enough to ride on the open top deck no matter what sort of weather it was.

In a very short time they learned to intercept the passengers who were going upstairs as they boarded. This was possible when things were not too busy. Early in the morning, though, again around lunchtime, and in the evenings between five o'clock and half past six, people jostled with each other to get on, and clambered up the stairs before they could issue them with tickets. Then they had no choice but to go upstairs as soon as they had collected the fares from those travelling inside the tram.

'I've begun waiting till they start to come downstairs again and nabbing them before they can get off,' Saratina confessed.

'What happens if an inspector gets on and goes straight upstairs and finds that there are passengers who have no tickets?'

'One did the other day and I told him that I hadn't had time to go up.'

'Did he believe you?'

Saratina shrugged. 'I suppose so, he didn't say anything more.'

'I think I'll give that a try,' Gaynor said thoughtfully, as she stirred her cup of tea. 'I hate those stairs, I'm scared stiff of falling. When the tram is going fast you get shaken to bits, and if it goes round a corner, then you get

111

thrown hard against the handrail. My side is a mass of bruises.'

'I dread it when there's a wind blowing. Or if it's raining. You can get soaked through in next to no time and your hands are so cold you find it difficult to punch the tickets.'

'You always catch the wind and rain when you are standing on the platform,' Gaynor agreed. 'I feel sorry for the drivers who have to stand there even when it is blowing directly into their face. I always try to get inside, but if the tram is full, and there are a lot of strap-hanging passengers, you can't.'

Their other problem was the driver who was their partner for the shift. They were rarely with the same one for more than two or three days and every driver seemed to have his own methods and quirky ways. Some even had silly little rules about how the bell pull should be used. The general rule was one pull for stop and two for go ahead, but one of the older men insisted on three pulls for go ahead, just to make sure he had not misheard. Often he didn't hear the single bell signal because of all the other noises and went sailing past the scheduled stop thinking that no one wanted to get off.

'Deaf as a post, the silly old dodderer,' Saratina declared angrily after spending a day partnering him. 'He'd be better off at home tending to his allotment.'

'He's probably one of the retired drivers who've been recalled because all the younger chaps have either been called up or have volunteered,' Gaynor sighed.

Despite their complaints, they appreciated that the money they were paid was almost as good as they would earn in Curran's munitions factory and, having tried that sort of work, they knew they much preferred to be working as conductresses.

Shift work, though, presented problems. The Vario house was always so full of children that they found it difficult to sleep during the day. Baby Sara's crying was not the only distraction when the other children were at home.

Even so, Gaynor liked shift work when it meant that she was at home during the day and could help to look after Sara, or even take her out in the big high pram that Mrs Vario had used for all her other children. It was clean though battered through years of constant use, but as far as Gaynor was concerned she couldn't have been prouder if it had been gleaming and gold plated.

She liked nothing better than to take Sara out for a walk in it along the Glamorgan Canal embankment, or on a sunny day to Grangetown Gardens. If she didn't have time to go that far, she would stroll around Loudon Square, pausing to sit under one of the trees and watch the delight on Sara's little face as she looked up into the greenery swaying above the pram.

It was at times like this, when she could sit quietly and reflect back on all the many changes that had happened in her life, that Gaynor thought about Barri. She still wondered if he had come to Cardiff after he had left Ferndale so suddenly and, if so, whether he was still here. She wished she could have met up with him again, but Cardiff was such a big city that it seemed highly improbable they would ever do so.

Her own life had taken so many twists and turns since then and she wondered if his had done the same. Had he forgotten about her, found a new love, she wondered? Perhaps by now he was married and might even have a child himself.

In all probability he had joined the army as soon as war was declared. It was more than likely that he was fighting far away in the trenches in France, she thought philosophically. And then she prayed that he was being kept safe.

The only thing Gaynor felt really sad about was that she didn't have more time to enjoy her baby's company. Sara was growing so fast. In next to no time, or so it seemed, she was sitting up in the big pram and looking around. She'd already cut her first tooth and was being weaned, and very soon she would be crawling. Every time she came home from work, Mrs Vario seemed to have some new accomplishment to relate to her.

She knew she should be feeling happy that Sara was in such good hands and was so well-looked after, but she kept feeling that she was missing out on so many important milestones in her baby's life.

There were times when she felt like a lodger in the Varios' home and that Sara was Maria's child, not hers, and it worried her. As little Sara began to take more and more notice of her surroundings, and happily held out her arms to Maria, rather than to her, it made Gaynor feel almost like an interloper. But she knew she had little choice but to accept the arrangement.

By the time Pedro came home again on shore leave at the end of August 1917, Gaynor was not only accustomed to the Varios' constantly noisy lifestyle but also often joined in their singing and laughter.

Pedro's arrival signalled a time for partying even though they were all finding it was harder and harder to buy the sort of food they liked. Pedro, however, because he was in the Merchant Navy, managed to bring things that had been in short supply for ages. These included bottles of wine and the pungent rum that Mrs Vario regarded as a medicine as well as being her favourite tipple.

Although she had very little taste for any of these, Gaynor enjoyed the atmosphere as they partied and feasted and she found herself growing more and more interested in Pedro. Their relationship had undergone a subtle change; he no longer seemed to be so critical and she found herself not only enjoying his company but actually looking forward to him being with them.

She noticed that he took quite an interest in Sara and if Maria asked him, he would often rock Sara's pram if she was fretful or dangle a little toy in front of her to distract her when she was tearful. Gaynor was relieved to find that far from the baby causing an uncomfortable rift between them she actually seemed to draw them closer together.

Whenever her shifts permitted, Gaynor liked to take Sara out in her pram to one of the nearby parks or for a walk; Pedro often accompanied her and would help her with the pram when they were crossing a road.

Pedro was also eager to spend as much time as he possibly could out enjoying himself and several times they went dancing with Saratina. Then, on one occasion, they went on their own and Gaynor knew she would never forget that evening.

Strolling home under a dark velvet sky studded with twinkling stars and with a full moon shining down on them after they'd spent the evening dancing was so magical that it was like being in an enchanted world.

When they paused, and Pedro took her into his arms and began kissing her it built up a longing inside her that was unquenchable. She'd responded so ardently that Pedro crushed her closer, his own passion mounting.

As they clung to each other in the moonlight

their need for each other was so great that words were unnecessary.

The rest of Pedro's leave passed in a mist of desire and fulfilment; they had eyes only for each other and they were oblivious to the teasing remarks from Saratina or the questioning looks from Maria about the two of them spending so much time together.

When Gaynor had to go to work, Pedro often went with her, riding on her tram from the depot at the Pier Head and back again. She snatched every moment she could to talk to him, and felt frustrated when passengers boarded and she had to break off to collect their fares.

He teased her about the severity of her uniform; its ankle-length, navy serge skirt and prim button-to-the-neck jacket with its shiny metal buttons and her full-brimmed felt hat which almost hid her face. Laughingly, he told her that it was an image he'd carry in his mind till they met again.

On his last day of shore leave Pedro spent his final precious hour riding with her on the open platform of her tram, his kitbag safely tucked away underneath the stairs. Surreptitiously they held hands, communicating their feelings for each other through the pressure of their entwined fingers

On their third trip from the city centre to the Pier Head they both knew that this had to be the last one. Pedro's leave was over and he had to go or he would miss his boat and then they would think that he'd jumped ship and deserted.

As the tram juddered to a stop at the Pier Head he stood on the edge of the platform, his kitbag over his shoulder, and, after a tender farewell kiss, jumped down on to the roadway. As he strode away without a backward glance, his final words rang in her ears and put a song in her heart.

Those precious words, 'Promise you'll wait for me, Gaynor. The next time I come ashore we'll get married', echoed in her head for a long time afterwards.

As she blinked back her tears and watched him disappearing into the distance, her tremendous relief and love for Pedro dissolved all the guilt she had been feeling for submitting so readily to his passionate lovemaking.

Chapter Ten

Gaynor found the time when she was on the trams so busy, and the time she spent at home with baby Sara so demanding, that when she did get to bed she immediately fell into a dreamless sleep from sheer exhaustion.

Even so, she felt that her life was a bed of roses compared to some of her colleagues. Those who had men folk at the Front lived in constant dread of hearing that they had been killed or injured. When they did get news from their loved ones and learned of the terrible discomfort they were enduring in the trenches, some became despondent, while others were angry and bitter.

Although the newspapers were full of accounts of what was happening on the Somme and at Ypres the personal details hinted at in individual letters were always far worse than anything that was reported officially.

News of what was happening at sea was equally harrowing and Gaynor was concerned about Pedro's safety. She mentioned it to some of the people she worked with, but most of them merely shrugged it away. She couldn't say anything about it when she was at home because she didn't want to distress Maria or upset Saratina. She suspected that they were just as worried as she was, but they put a brave face on it all because of the younger children.

Life with the Varios was busy and noisy. Maria had her hands full coping with all the children. Food was not only in short supply but very expensive, and because there were so many of them to feed Maria struggled to make every penny she received from Saratina and Gaynor each week go as far as it possibly could.

Gaynor also had her own personal problems. She couldn't understand why, when she was leading such an active life, running up and down stairs on the tram for eight hours at a time, and then helping Maria out at home and tending to baby Sara, she could still be managing to put on weight. By rights, she reasoned, she should be losing weight, not gaining it.

She reasoned that it must be the filling stews and stodgy puddings that Maria dished up. They were always so tasty, and she was always so hungry, that even though she fully intended to eat less she always ended up clearing her plate.

Saratina laughed at her. 'I bet there are countless people who wished they had your problem,' she commented drily. 'Half the people in Cardiff are going hungry and you're complaining because you are putting on weight.'

120

Gaynor smiled. 'Yes, I know you are right,' she admitted. 'I'm probably being greedy and eating more than I should.'

'Rubbish, my mam treats us both the same, whatever she puts on your plate is the same as what she puts on mine.'

Gaynor didn't argue, but she did try not to eat so much, a ruse that was quickly spotted by Maria Vario.

'What's going on?' she demanded. 'Are you sick or do you no longer like my cooking?'

When Gaynor assured her that neither was the case and that apart from feeling tired she had never felt better, Maria told her to eat up what was on her plate and not to be so wasteful.

'I hope you are not going to set a bad example to the little ones when it comes to the special feast I hope to provide over Christmas,' she told Gaynor. 'I have scrimped and saved so many foodstuffs over the past months so that there will be a plum pudding and special cake and the children can celebrate the festive season in the traditional manner as it is only right they should do.'

'That will be wonderful,' Gaynor agreed enthusiastically. 'Sara will be old enough this year to really enjoy it.'

Even as she spoke, Gaynor felt wistful about the lovely Christmases she had known as a child and wished her own parents could be there to share the magic with Sara. For a wild moment she was tempted to write to them, to see if they would like to meet Sara. Then she hardened her heart as she remembered the way they had reacted when they knew she was expecting a baby, and how insistent they had been that she must have it adopted.

She had managed to make a life for herself and Sara so she didn't need their help or approval. Maria had filled their place in Sara's life.

Ever since she had left home she had managed to put most of her memories of the people she had known in Ferndale out of her mind; all except Barri. She found herself constantly thinking about him.

Would she even recognise him, she wondered? He might have already ridden on her tram and she might have punched out a ticket and handed it over to him, and not known who he was.

Somehow, she didn't think that was very likely. They had known each other so well that she was sure they'd both recognise each other immediately, even though they were quite different people now to the boy and girl who had exchanged confidences and built so many dreams for the future together.

She still couldn't help being curious about what had happened to him. Was he a soldier, or had he gone to sea? Had he ever gone back to Ferndale, perhaps to look for her only to hear the gossip about her and Konrad and find that she had gone and no one knew where?

Whenever these thoughts came to her she found herself wondering what would have happened if her father hadn't sent Barri away. Would they have made a life together, and would at least some of their dreams have come true?

Although Sara with her fair hair and blue eyes couldn't possibly be Barri's child, there were times when Gaynor wished that she was. Despite her affair with Konrad, Barri still had a very important place in her heart.

Even now, when she knew Pedro intended to marry her next time he came home on leave, she couldn't completely forget Barri.

Determined to live for the moment, Gaynor threw herself wholeheartedly into enjoying Christmas 1917 with Maria, Saratina and the rest of the Vario children. She had no idea what Maria had managed to acquire to put into the Christmas pudding which she mixed up in the biggest basin she could find, but it smelled wonderful. They all took a turn at stirring it and were told to make a wish, but warned that they mustn't say what it was or else it wouldn't come true.

Little Sara loved every moment of it. It took them all their time to keep her under control as she toddled around the house trying to play with the paper chains and other decorations that the Vario children had made and which festooned the living room, adding to the medley of colours already there.

The children were tired on Christmas Eve but far too excited to settle. They had all draped a sock over the end of their bed in anticipation of a visit from Father Christmas. Maria, Saratina and Gaynor had been collecting little surprise items for ages. Now they divided these between the socks and added a shiny new penny, a screw of raisins and a small apple to each one. It was almost midnight, however, before they could distribute them and go to bed themselves.

Even though both Saratina and Gaynor had to work some of the time on Christmas day, the entire family enjoyed the occasion to the full – although Maria kept saying how much she wished Pedro could be with them.

Gaynor's only regret was that she was still putting on weight and although she said nothing to the others she secretly resolved that once 1918 started she was determined to eat less, whether she was hungry or not, because even her uniform felt tight and uncomfortable.

Keeping to her resolution was not going to be easy because it was her nineteenth birthday at the very start of January and the Vario family loved to put on a feast to celebrate such occasions.

Maria made jellies and pink blancmange, which the younger children loved, as well as a special cake, and Saratina had iced it. Maria had even saved some of her homemade mincemeat from Christmas so that there could be mince pies as well.

124

Because Gaynor's shift didn't finish until six, the children were allowed to stay up late so that they could all celebrate her birthday together when she came home.

After they'd eaten, Saratina organised a sing-song, starting with 'Happy Birthday to Gaynor' and the excited little crowd were singing it at the very tops of their voices when there was a loud knock on the front door, making them all stop abruptly.

'Perhaps one of the neighbours has come round to complain because we are all making so much noise,' Saratina laughed as she went to answer it.

They were all laughing and shouting and crowding into the hall behind Saratina as she opened the door and then suddenly they all went quiet as they saw that it was a uniformed telegraph boy standing there holding out a small, bright orange envelope.

The colour drained from Saratina's face as she took it. Hesitantly, she turned round and passed it over the heads of the smaller children to her mother.

Maria took the little envelope and stood there holding it for a long moment, clenching her lips tightly together before lifting the flap and drawing out the flimsy piece of paper from inside.

She stared at it blankly as if unable to make any sense of what was written on it.

'Mam, shall I read it to you?' Saratina asked in a whisper.

Maria nodded and handed it to her.

Saratina's lips formed the words but no sound came from them and her face became ravaged with grief as she looked at her mother.

'Is there any answer, missus?' the telegraph boy demanded impatiently.

Maria and Saratina both shook their heads.

The boy nodded, but still lingered on the doorstep until Gaynor hurriedly stepped forward and pressed a couple of pennies into his outstretched hand.

Grinning broadly, he touched his cap in a salute of thanks and rode off on his bike whistling cheerfully.

As Gaynor closed the door, Maria silently held out the telegram to her so that she could read its contents.

Gaynor's eyes misted as she read the words: 'Regret to inform you that your son, Pedro Vario, together with the rest of the crew of the *SS Resolution*, has been reported missing presumed drowned when this ship was torpedoed in the Bay of Biscay.'

The younger children, sensing that something terrible had happened, obediently scuttled upstairs to bed when Saratina asked them to do so.

In silence she and Gaynor cleared away the debris of the party celebrations and washed up the dishes. Then, while Gaynor went up to tuck all the children in, Saratina made a pot of tea which they took through into the living room.

Maria was sitting hunched up in an armchair, rocking herself backwards and forwards as tears streamed unchecked down her cheeks.

'Pedro, my first born,' she moaned. 'A watery grave the same as his father. How can God keep doing this to me when I try so hard to serve him well?'

Saratina held her mother close, trying to comfort her, but nothing she said could calm Maria or console her in her grief.

Her sobbing continued unabated for hours. Eventually, between them, Saratina and Gaynor persuaded her to go to bed. Gaynor warmed up some milk and poured a generous portion of rum into it in the hope that it would help Mrs Vario to sleep.

She was so completely exhausted that the hot toddy had the desired effect, and within half an hour Maria was fast asleep. Gaynor and Saratina were equally worn out so they made themselves a nightcap and went to bed.

Gaynor found she couldn't get off to sleep. She tossed and turned and wished she hadn't made herself a hot drink because she felt so bloated and uncomfortable. It was as if the whole of her insides were in turmoil. Suddenly she sat bolt upright in bed, gripped by anxiety, fear making her almost choke. She knew now what was wrong with her, why she was putting on weight, and even what was causing the strange churning movement inside her. There was no doubt in her mind at all: she was pregnant.

Rapidly she counted and recounted the time since Pedro had been on leave. She went over it again to be sure. Ever since Pedro had gone back to sea she had been so preoccupied with coping with her new job and caring for Sara that she had never given a moment's thought to the possibility that she might be pregnant again. There was no question about it at all; it was over four months ago. She was pregnant; her discomfort was from the movement of the baby she was carrying.

She was too stunned to cry or even to think clearly. In some ways it was like a rerun of what had happened when Konrad had told her he was going back to Germany. She was once again pregnant and alone in the world. This time, though, she already had a young daughter who would have only just turned three when the new baby – Pedro's baby – was born. How on earth was she going to manage? And how could she not have realised sooner?

She lay awake all night trying to figure out if she ought to tell Maria or whether it would be better to say nothing to either her or Saratina until she absolutely had to.

They were both so full of their own grief that they probably wouldn't want to hear about it at the moment. She was quite sure that Pedro had never told them that they were to be married the next time he came on leave. She had never mentioned it to them, preferring to keep her wonderful secret to herself. Now she would have to tell them, but would they even believe her?

On the other hand, Mrs Vario might be overjoyed to know that at least there would be a child in a few months' time to be a lasting reminder of her lost son, even if it was conceived out of wedlock.

Why had this terrible disaster happened? What was there about her that seemed to bring trouble to the men who loved her? First it had been Barri banished from his home almost as if he were a criminal without even having a chance to tell her what was happening. Then Konrad, displaying such coldness and sense of duty to what he termed the Fatherland that he had walked out on her, unaware that she was expecting his child. Now, just when she thought she had found love and happiness and a chance of a future, Pedro was lost at sea and once again she was faced with having to fend for herself and their coming child as best she could.

Why did so much tragedy come her way? Her father would probably say that she was being punished for her sins.

Could she rely on Saratina to support her yet again if she decided to keep the child?

Sliding further down into the bed and pulling the covers up over her head she tried to obliterate all her troublesome thoughts. She was so desperately tired that she couldn't think clearly. Perhaps the answer would come to her as she slept. There was nothing she could do at this time of night. It wouldn't be fair to waken Saratina and burden her when she was grieving for her brother.

Things would look different in the morning; everything could be resolved if they all pulled together. Between them they'd manage to work something out, she told herself optimistically.

Chapter Eleven

Gaynor's hopes of seeking Saratina's advice on the best way to break the news to Maria were dashed the next morning. Saratina wakened her and, the moment she opened her eyes, asked her if she could help see to the children because her mother was too ill to do so.

'She's in such a state of collapse that I think I will have to get the doctor in,' Saratina explained. 'I've never seen her like this, not even when Dad died. She's aged ten years overnight and she isn't responding to anything I say,' she added worriedly.

'Give me five minutes and I'll be dressed,' Gaynor told her, throwing back the covers and scrabbling for the clothes she'd taken off the night before. 'What shift are you on?' she called as Saratina left the room.

'I'm staying home today; I can't leave Mama, not the state she's in.'

'But . . .'

'Let's leave it for the moment. Help me get the young ones off to school and then we'll try and make some sort of plan.'

'Saratina, listen to me. You'll lose your job if you don't turn in,' Gaynor said worriedly.

'Ssh!' Saratina nodded towards José who was listening to their exchange, 'We'll talk about it later. Let's give them some breakfast and get them dressed ready for school.'

The next half an hour was a mad scramble to make sure the children weren't late. As well as ensuring they had something to eat they had to pack up lunch boxes for each of them. Before they were ready to leave the house there was a panic to find lost gloves and scarves and to help them into their coats before sending them on their way with warnings about keeping together and taking care when they were crossing the road.

By this time Sara was awake and calling out for attention, so Gaynor dressed her and prepared her breakfast while Saratina made a fresh pot of tea and took a cup of it and some toast upstairs to her mother.

As they finally sat down to their own breakfast, it felt as though the two of them had already done a day's work.

Fortunately, Gaynor was not due to report to the depot until midday, so she had plenty of time to help Saratina make the beds and tidy up the house.

'Are you still going to call the doctor?' she asked at mid-morning as they stopped for a cup of cocoa before Gaynor left for work.

'I'm not sure,' Saratina said worriedly. 'She's sleeping so soundly at the moment that she might be over the worst of it when she wakes up again. I think I'll wait and see how she is because I don't want to spend money on a doctor if it isn't necessary.'

'No, of course not,' Gaynor agreed, 'especially if you are going to be off work for a few days yourself because they are bound to stop your money.'

'That reminds me, can you let them know at the depot that I won't be in today? You'd better say I'm not well. That'll do for now. After you get home this evening we'll have to sit down and decide what we are going to do from now on.'

The inspector was extremely angry when Gaynor told him that Saratina wasn't coming in to work, despite her excellent attendance record.

'You girls are all the same with your trumped-up excuses,' he ranted. 'You're always taking time off and messing up the rota. You seem to forget that there's a war on and we all have to pull our weight and do our bit. Where would we be if the boyos who are in the trenches over in France decided they wanted to take a day off whenever they weren't feeling a hundred per cent fit?'

He was so angry that Gaynor didn't dare try to explain what had happened. She didn't think he would have very much sympathy if she did. Rumour had it that he had already lost both of his sons on the battlefield as well as one of his brothers.

It did make her realise, however, that even though it wasn't the ideal time to tell Saratina that she was expecting another baby, she would have to because, more than likely, she wouldn't be able to go on working on the trams herself for very much longer. It would probably be better if she was the one to stay at home and cook and clean for the family and Saratina held on to her job. The thought of what she would say to Saratina and how they were going to manage worried Gaynor all day.

Telling Maria and Saratina that she was pregnant was one of the hardest things Gaynor had ever had to do. They both looked at her in stunned silence. She also had the feeling that neither of them believed her when she said that she and Pedro had been planning to get married when he next came home on leave.

'Why did he never say a word about this to me?' Maria exclaimed, a look of bewilderment on her face.

'He only asked me as he was leaving,' Gaynor explained weakly. 'He spent the last couple of hours before he rejoined his ship riding on the tram with me. The very last thing he said as we reached the Pier Head and he finally had to leave, was to ask me to marry him the next time he came home.'

'He couldn't have known that you were expecting his baby . . . not then,' Maria protested.

'He didn't. He was asking me to marry him because we were in love.'

'Neither of you told us that you were in love with each other,' Saratina pointed out defensively. 'I'm sure he would have told me even if he wanted to keep it quiet so as not to upset Mama.'

'Well, no, it was something private between me and Pedro,' Gaynor explained, her colour rising.

'Why on earth would he want to marry you and to take on the burden of a three-year-old?' Maria protested.

'Pedro was very fond of little Sara,' Gaynor reminded her.

'That's as maybe. We're all fond of Sara, but it doesn't mean we want to spend the rest of our lives bringing her up.'

Gaynor felt crestfallen. She had hoped that Maria would have been pleased to hear about their plans to marry, and she had hoped that Maria would welcome the baby when it was born, but now she wasn't so sure. She seemed so morbidly scornful about the idea of Pedro wanting to marry her.

As Gaynor turned to Saratina, hoping for a word of support, she was shocked by the look of hostility in her friend's dark eyes.

'I trusted you, Gaynor,' she said bitterly. 'I never for one moment thought that you would try to steal my brother from us. My mother needed him to help support her; his money has been essential for our welfare since my dad was drowned.'

135

'I wasn't going to steal him away,' Gaynor retorted in a shocked voice. 'But you surely didn't expect him to stay single the rest of his life,' she added defensively.

'I certainly didn't expect him to go behind my back and plan to get married without telling me,' Maria declared. She fished her handkerchief out of her sleeve and mopped at her face. 'This is such disturbing news and, coming on top of that terrible telegram yesterday, it's giving me palpitations.' She pressed a hand to her prominent chest and gasped for breath. 'Saratina, can you fetch me some Sal volatile? Quickly, before I pass out.'

Saratina rushed into the kitchen and reached up to the top shelf of the pantry for the little dark green bottle containing the precious medicine. Very carefully, she measured out five drops into a small glass and then diluted it with a little water and carried it back into the living room.

Gaynor sat unmoving, wondering if she had done the right thing after all. She waited until Saratina had held the glass to her mother's lips and Mrs Vario had managed to swallow the contents. She watched with growing alarm as, still gasping for breath, Maria lay back in her chair and closed her eyes.

Saratina remained at her mother's side until she was sure that she had recovered from her panic attack. When her mother eventually opened her eyes and pulled herself up straight in her chair, Saratina asked Gaynor to go and make a pot of tea.

'I know just how terrible my mam must be feeling, Gaynor, because the shock of your news has left me shaking as well,' she said accusingly.

Gaynor was glad to escape to the kitchen. While she waited for the kettle to boil she thought back over the last few minutes and wondered if Saratina and her mother had both been so upset by the thought of Pedro getting married that they had barely listened to the other piece of news she had told them. Surely that would be of even greater concern than the news that she and Pedro had planned to get married.

As she poured out cups of tea for the three of them, she wondered whether she should repeat that part of her news, or whether it would be better to say nothing for the moment, and leave it for a few days.

As soon as she had taken a sip of her tea, however, Maria broached the subject herself.

'So you're pregnant, or so you say,' she commented acidly, looking Gaynor up and down critically.

'Yes!' Gaynor pushed her hair back behind her ears and waited for the onslaught she was quite sure would follow. The silence was intimidating and she looked anxiously from Saratina to Maria and back again, aware that they were being as censorious as her parents had been when she'd told them that she was expecting Sara.

'How do we know that you are telling the truth?' Saratina demanded.

Gaynor smiled timidly. 'That's the reason why I've been putting on weight,' she told her.

'It's taken you long enough to realise it, hasn't it? Strange that it was only when the telegram arrived that you suddenly announced you are expecting his baby,' she added caustically.

'We've no way of knowing that it is his,' Maria intervened sharply. 'You might just be looking for a father for your baby after having had a fling with someone. You might only be saying that it's my Pedro's child because you know that he can't deny it.'

'That's a terrible thing to say,' Gaynor declared in a shocked voice.

'Well, this is not the first time that you've got yourself into trouble, now is it?' Mrs Vario snapped accusingly. 'You've already had one baby and no father to help you bring it up. It seems to me, Gaynor, that what you've done once you are quite happy to do again. I can't think what my Saratina is doing associating with someone like you. She has been brought up to know right from wrong, and I'm not at all happy for her to be friends with a girl of your sort.'

'Girl of my sort!' Gaynor was so incensed that she was on the verge of blurting out what had happened to Saratina and how the two of them had come to meet in the first place.

As she started to speak, Saratina shot her a

138

warning look and Gaynor bit her lip. There was nothing to be gained from revealing Saratina's guilty secret. Far better to keep quiet and ensure that Saratina was on her side, she decided. In the future she was going to need every bit of help she could get and if she had to resort to blackmail in order to obtain it from Saratina, then that was what she would do.

As they stared into each other's eyes Gaynor was aware of the fear flickering behind Saratina's dark gaze and felt confident that from now on she could rely on her to help as much as possible.

At first Maria refused to believe that Pedro had said that he and Gaynor would be married when he next came home on leave.

When Gaynor assured her that it was true, and reminded her that she was pregnant with Pedro's baby, Maria pondered in silence. Then her face hardened. 'We've only your word for that,' she repeated as she stared at Gaynor. 'Why should we believe you?'

'I've been putting on weight,' Gaynor reminded her. 'Look,' she patted her rounded tummy. 'That's Pedro's baby! Give me your hand, you can feel it moving.'

'Rubbish!' The scorn in Maria's voice was as cutting as a knife. 'It's probably wind or sheer gluttony.'

Gaynor shook her head and smiled wryly. 'Believe me, I wish it was simply one of those reasons.'

139

Maria's eyes narrowed. 'Why don't you get rid of it, then? You're not a Catholic, and you've most certainly not got any morals, so what is there to stop you?'

Gaynor shook her head. 'I couldn't do a thing like that. I wasn't able to even consider it when I was expecting Sara any more than I could agree to allowing her to be adopted. I won't get rid of this baby or let it be adopted either.'

'You expect me to help you raise this one as well, do you?' Maria said scathingly.

'I was hoping you would help me, the same as you did with Sara,' Gaynor said quietly. 'After all, Maria, this one will be your grand-child.'

'You'll never be able to prove that my Pedro is the father. Like I've already said, you know it's safe to claim he is because he is never going to come back, so he can't deny it. That baby in your belly could be any man's child; someone you've taken up with and you've been meeting after finishing your late-night shifts.'

Gaynor shrank back as if she had been hit. 'That's a terrible thing to say, and you know full well that it is not true. I've never been out with anyone except Pedro since the day I came to live here. Saratina will tell you the same,' she insisted as she saw the look of disbelief on Maria's face. Turning, she pleaded, 'Tell her, Saratina. You know that I am telling the truth.'

Saratina stared at her coldly, shaking her head and shrugging her shoulders while holding her

140

hands wide. 'Don't involve me in your argument; I don't know what you get up to. I didn't even know that you were carrying on with my brother . . . that's if you were. Mama's right, it could have been with any man for all we know.'

Gaynor stared at her, unable to believe her ears. Once again the temptation to break her promise and denounce Saratina was overwhelming, and began building up inside her till she thought she was going to explode from the drumming inside her head.

Then it was dissipated as Saratina said quietly, 'We all make mistakes from time to time, Mama, so don't take on so. Gaynor probably *is* telling the truth about her and Pedro. In a few months' time, when she has had the baby, we should know for certain if she's telling the truth or not by it's colouring.'

'And if she isn't telling us the truth?'

Saratina gave another of her expressive shrugs. 'We'll deal with that when it happens. Like I said, if it is Pedro's, we'll know the moment it is born,' she added confidently.

Chapter Twelve

Gaynor's second baby, another little girl, was born early in June 1918 and she named her Rachael. The birth was as unlike Sara's as it was possible to be. This time it took place in her own bed in the Varios' house with Maria and Saratina at her side and Peggy Miller, the local midwife, also in attendance.

When Sara was brought in to meet her new sister she was overawed by the tiny scrap that her mother was holding in her arms. She stroked the baby's cheek very gently, and when Saratina explained that they must go downstairs and leave the new baby and her mummy to sleep, Sara gently kissed baby Rachael on the cheek. 'I'll come back and see her again after I've had my tea,' she promised gravely, her blue eyes shining enthusiastically.

Over the next few weeks, although Saratina seemed to accept the newcomer, it became apparent that Maria was unable to. All the old resentment that she had displayed when Gaynor had first told her that she was expecting Pedro's baby seemed to flare up anew. She had obviously been hoping for a boy to replace Pedro and the sight of the new baby seemed to irritate her because it was a girl.

As the weeks passed, the situation seemed to get worse rather than better. Whenever Gaynor tried to talk to Saratina about it she merely shrugged and told Gaynor she hadn't noticed anything different about the way her mother treated the new baby.

'You're imagining it. You're probably suffering from depression. Lots of new mums do, so I'm told.'

Gaynor tried hard to believe her and was careful to keep Rachael out of Maria's way as much as possible, but the hostility was there. She sensed it by the way Maria looked at the baby and by the frown on her face whenever the baby cried. She never offered to nurse Rachael or to do anything at all for her.

More and more Gaynor wished she could move away. Maria still appeared to be as fond as ever of Sara. She seemed amused by her prattle, and this only made the way she ignored the new baby all the more noticeable.

Gaynor felt increasingly uncomfortable about it all. Perhaps if she could get away for a few days, then Maria might come to her senses and realise how very much a part of her family they had become. Gaynor reasoned that perhaps she would miss them so much that when they came back home again she'd be so pleased to see them that she would make a fuss of Rachael as well as of Sara.

Gaynor gave it a great deal of thought and decided that, since she had no money or friends whom she could go and stay with, then there was only one place she could go, and that was back home to Ferndale. The only problem was that after all this time she was still not too sure she dared risk doing so.

It was such a long time since she'd left and all that time there had been no word exchanged between herself and her parents. She'd had no contact at all with either Ellie or anyone else she had known when she was growing up. It was her own fault, she kept telling herself, because she had never let any of them know where she was.

Again, the longing to be reunited with Barri was overwhelming. Perhaps he was living back in Ferndale again, and if she paid her parents a visit she would meet up with him.

The more she thought about it, the more homesick she felt. In the end she resolved that she would go back. If Saratina would lend her the money for her train fare she'd risk the outcome and pay them a visit.

At first Saratina wasn't too keen. 'How are you ever going to pay me back when you're not working?' she said reluctantly.

'I'll ask my mam and dad to give it to me and I'll repay whatever you lend me the moment I get back,' she promised.

'You'll have to wait until next payday, then, because I'm skint at the moment.'

It was two weeks before Saratina could scrape together enough money for Gaynor's train fare. 'How long are you going to be away?' she asked as she handed it over.

'I don't know. They mightn't want me to stay at all,' Gaynor said hesitantly.

'Bit of a waste, then, to be spending all that much money on the off chance, isn't it?'

'I know that,' Gaynor agreed, 'but I have this tremendous longing to see them again. Things aren't right here, not since Rachael was born. If I could get them to agree to me going back there to live I think your mam would be glad to see the back of me and my children, don't you think?'

Saratina shrugged hopelessly. 'Heaven alone knows. Mama's certainly been in a very strange mood ever since we heard the news about Pedro.'

'I'd hoped that the baby would take his place in her heart,' Gaynor said wistfully.

'It might have done if it had been a boy.'

Gaynor drew in her breath sharply as she heard the condemnation in Saratina's voice. Knowing that she couldn't afford to fall out with Saratina, she bit back the hasty retort that sprang to her lips.

'I think the best thing would be for Mama to think that we've gone for a day out together, then if you decide to come back she won't need to know that you were trying to get away from her,' Saratina stated.

Gaynor looked shocked. 'Is that necessary? I appreciate what a good friend you've been, Saratina, and I'm sure it's only because of the way you've stood up for me that your mam hasn't thrown me out before now, but do we have to deceive her like that?'

'It might be safer to do it that way. If Mama knew the truth she might say that she didn't want you to come back here and then where would you be if your own folks didn't want you either? Let's face it; they've never once been in touch with you since the day you left home, now have they?'

'Only because they don't know where I am,' Gaynor retorted defensively.

Saratina shrugged. 'Well, it's up to you. I'll cover for you if you want me to. I'm going out for the day on Sunday with Sandy, but I'll tell Mama it's with you.'

'Sandy?' Gaynor frowned. 'You don't mean Sandy Peterson, the ginger-haired inspector, surely?'

'Yes. What's wrong with him?'

'Well . . . well, nothing, I suppose . . . except that he's old enough to be your father.'

'Hardly, he's only thirty-five!'

'I thought he was married. And what would your mam say?'

'He was . . . once. His wife died last year.

And anyway, Mama doesn't need to find out. Anything else you need to know?'

'I'm sorry, Saratina. I'm not criticising. I was a bit surprised, that's all.'

Saratina shrugged again. 'You haven't said if you want me to say you're coming out with me on Sunday or not.'

'Yes, I think it probably would be a good idea ... just in case.' She smiled.

They made their plans carefully before they mentioned anything to Maria.

'Bit unfair, leaving me to look after the other children all on my own,' her mother complained. 'Why can't you take them along with you as well?'

'Oh come on, Mama,' Saratina protested, 'we're taking both the little ones. The others wouldn't want to come with us anyway, they'd far rather be out swinging from the lamp-posts or playing hopscotch. You won't see much of them.'

'Except when they're hungry,' her mother grumbled.

Gaynor felt on tenterhooks in the few days leading up to the Sunday they were planning their deception. Although she said nothing to Sara about where they were going, she was worried about what might happen if, later on, Sara told Maria that they hadn't been out with Saratina after all.

If her own parents were agreeable to her going home to Ferndale, then it wouldn't matter if Maria did find out, she kept telling herself. The trouble was that she wasn't at all sure that it was all going to work out as she hoped.

On Sunday morning she was up early, had fed and dressed Rachael, and was washed and ready herself, before Sara was awake.

At first Sara was very excited by the news that as soon as they'd had their breakfast they were going out for the day. Then her happy laughter turned to tears when she realised that Mama Maria was not going with them as well. She clung on to her, begging her to come as well.

'Mama Maria is going to make a special meal for when we all come home again,' Gaynor told Sara.

There were even more tears from an over-excited Sara when, an hour later, they parted company from Saratina on the platform at Cardiff General.

'I want Saratina to come on the train with us,' Sara stormed. 'You said we were all going out together,' she sobbed.

No matter how hard they tried to reason with her they were unable to make her understand that she was going with her mam and baby sister and that, although Saratina wasn't going on the train with them, she would be there waiting at the station to meet them when they got back.

'You could always call the whole thing off

and come back home, I suppose, seeing as you haven't told your folks you are paying them a visit,' Saratina suggested.

'Yes, I could do that, but what would I tell your mam?'

'I'm sure my mam would understand if you told her that Sara was playing up and far too upset for you to go ahead with our plans for the day and that I've gone off on my own.'

'No.' Gaynor shook her head. 'I'm not giving in to Sara and letting her spoil all our plans like that. She'll be all right once we are on the train. She's never been on a train before so she'll love it.'

Saratina raised her eyebrows. 'I wouldn't count on it. She seems to have a right fit of the miseries and no mistake. I only hope she behaves herself when you reach Ferndale or they certainly won't invite you to stay on,' she muttered as she bundled them all on to the train and slammed the carriage door.

Once she was on her own with her daughters, Gaynor found a biscuit for Sara, and as the train pulled out of Cardiff station she gave Rachael a bottle. Her own nerves were jangling and she dared not think about how she was going to handle things when they reached their journey's end. With any luck, she consoled herself, Rachael would have finished her bottle and would be fast asleep long before then and so she would be able to give Sara all her attention. Perhaps if she told her a story about where

149

they were going and who they were going to see it would take the child's mind off her disappointment because neither Maria nor Saratina were coming with them.

To her surprise, before she had even finished her biscuit Sara curled up beside her and was asleep. When she roused her as the train approached Ferndale, Gaynor was relieved to find that all the child's disappointments seemed to have been forgotten. Sara was wide-eyed and curious, full of questions about where they were and who they were going to see.

Gaynor found it strange to be back in Ferndale. As they walked along the high street and made their way to Lake Street all the old memories came rushing back. The high street didn't seem to have changed at all. The same shops were still there, but all of them were closed and shuttered because it was Sunday.

Her heart was pounding as she walked down Lake Street. She wondered what her parents would say when they opened the front door and found her there on the doorstep, a toddler at her side and a sleeping baby in her arms.

She was shaking like a leaf as she rapped on the front door, then took a step back, forcing a smile on to her face in readiness to greet her mother.

Her smile slowly faded when the door opened and it was her father, and not her mother, who was standing there.

His face froze as he recognised her. They

stood for what seemed to be an eternity, staring at each other like complete strangers. Apart from being a little more grey, he seemed to be no different at all from when she had last seen him. Grim-faced, portly, dressed in his best suit, he was obviously about to go to chapel.

'Hello, Dad,' she said nervously. 'I ... I thought it was time I paid you a visit.'

'Then you thought wrongly,' he said curtly. 'You are not welcome, so go.' As he spoke, he stepped back into the hallway and started to close the door.

'Dad!' Words failed her. She had not expected a rapturous welcome, but she hadn't expected him to behave so coldly and to turn her away.

Before the door closed completely she stretched out her hand and tried to push it open again. 'Is Mam there? I came to see her. She'll want to see her grandchildren.'

Her father didn't answer, but the door jarred painfully against her outstretched hand as he endeavoured to close it and she drew back with a yelp before he slammed it shut.

For a moment she stood there on the pavement, unable to believe what had happened. Sara started to snivel, but Gaynor was too upset herself to say or do anything other than take the child's hand and pull her away.

As she did so she heard the door open again and she turned round quickly, hoping that her dad had had a change of heart and was going to invite her in after all.

Instead, she saw her mother coming towards her, waving her hand and calling to her to stop. Gaynor thought she looked thin and unhappy and noticed that she was wearing her best dress, and that in her haste she'd not even stopped to remove the pinafore she had on over it.

Before they could reach each other, her father had come rushing out of the door, shouting angrily. As he intervened, grabbing Florence by the arm and dragging her back inside the house, Gaynor saw the colour drain from her mother's face and for a moment she thought her mother was going to faint.

As she took a step towards them her mother screamed out, 'Go away, Gaynor, go away, while you're safe. Don't try to defy him or it will be worse for both of us.'

'Take her advice, cariad, you can only do your mam harm if you come back here.'

Gaynor turned to see that Mrs Hughes had come out of her own house a couple of doors down and was standing there listening to what was going on.

'Your dad's like a madman these days,' she went on. 'Never been the same since the day he sent my Barri packing like he did. Broke my Simon's heart . . . and mine!'

Gaynor shook her head in bewilderment. She tried to gather her thoughts together, but it felt as if a great gale had blown through her head leaving it numb and empty.

'Barri!' Her voice croaked as she uttered his name. 'Do you know where he is?'

Mrs Hughes shook her head sadly. 'Never a word from him since the day your dad drove him out of Ferndale.'

'And Ellie? Do you ever see her these days?'

'She went off to work in a munitions factory after Davey, that chap who worked in the same office as she did, and whom she was going out with, was killed at the Front. She didn't like the factory so she went to help out on the land somewhere in Somerset. The last I heard she'd married some farmer or the other. She's never been back to visit and her mother has stopped talking about her.'

'Do you think Barri did go to Cardiff?' Gaynor persisted.

'He did.' Mrs Hughes sighed. 'We had a post-card from him, but when I wrote to him it came back marked "gone away". By now he's prob-ably fighting for his country. Or he could be lying dead, rotting in some old trench over there in France,' she added bitterly.

Gaynor bit her lip; she had no words of comfort, and she grieved over Barri's disap-pearance every bit as much as his mother did. 'And how is my mam? She looks so old and frail and I didn't get a chance to speak to her.'

'We're all looking old, cariad. This war has taken its toll on every one of us, what with the worry about all our young boyos being caught up in it and so many of them losing their lives, poor dabs. The ones who should be out there fighting, old sods like your dad, are safe at home,' she added angrily, as she turned and made to go back indoors.

'I'm sorry, Mrs Hughes, about Barri; well, about everything.'

'I'm not blaming you, cariad; it's not your fault the way things turned out. By the look of things you have your hands full and problems of your own these day.' She smiled. 'I'd ask you in, but my Simon never speaks to your dad these days so he wouldn't like it. Anyway, it would only be stirring up old hurts now, wouldn't it?' she added apologetically.

'I understand!' Tears of self-pity filled Gaynor's eyes as the door shut behind Mrs Hughes. Her arms ached from carrying Rachael and she thought how comforting it would have been to be sipping a cup of tea, and having a friendly chat.

Rubbing away her tears with the back of her hand, she moved the baby into a more comfortable position in her arms. Then, taking hold of Sara's hand once more, she began to walk towards the high street and the railway station.

As she sat on the deserted platform waiting for the train to take them back to Cardiff she wallowed in her own misery. The future seemed to be so bleak that she wondered if it was even worth going on. She'd heard stories about people who had ended their life by throwing themselves in front of an oncoming train and she wondered if perhaps that was what she ought to do.

No one seemed to care about her or want her. Maria had made it plain that she was no longer welcome in her house. Saratina had done all she could, but since Sandy had come into her life even Saratina had less and less time for her.

She'd really thought that by now her own parents would be ready to forgive and forget, but her dad was as vitriolic as ever. He'd even seemed to have caused an irreparable rift between her and Barri's family.

One moment of courage and then it would all be over. No more worries, no more being rejected by the people she loved, simply oblivion; dark velvet blackness.

She gave herself a mental shake. What was she thinking about! What about Sara and Rachael, she chided herself. What would happen to them if she wasn't around to care for them, and love them? Unless, of course, she took the two of them along with her?

She was conscious of the noise of the approaching train; she could see the huge plume of swirling white smoke as the iron monster came charging down the rails thundering towards the platform where she was standing. It was now or never, she told herself. Jump, go on girl, jump!

She looked down at her two babies and her deep love for them overwhelmed her. She couldn't do it! It would be wrong to sacrifice their little lives simply because her own father's heartlessness had left her feeling so miserable and depressed.

Chapter Thirteen

As the feeling of animosity between herself and Maria Vario began to increase, Gaynor knew that it was important for all of them that she should move out of the Varios' home as soon as she possibly could.

Although they hadn't openly asked her to leave, Saratina had dropped a great many hints that since she was the only one who was working and bringing home any money it was becoming difficult for her mother to make ends meet these days.

On more than one occasion she had said, 'If only we had a spare room, then mam could take in a lodger and their rent would make a terrific difference.'

Whether she was intended to take it that way or not, Gaynor immediately assumed that what Saratina was implying was that if only she would move out she would share her mother's room and then they could rent out the room they used and that would help solve everything for them. As it was she was not paying any rent and not contributing any money for her keep. Maria even bought the necessary baby formula for Rachael, which she constantly reminded Gaynor about, adding to her feelings of guilt.

If her parents had been willing for her to go back to Ferndale, as she had hoped, then there would have been no problem, but since her father had turned her away, there was nowhere else she could go except to the workhouse. She shuddered at the thought because she knew if that happened she would be separated from her children, and she simply couldn't bear that.

Trying to find some other solution seemed impossible. Everybody in Sophia Street seemed to be friends of the Varios, so she could hardly discuss the matter with them or even ask their advice. In the end, she plucked up courage and one evening when she and Saratina were both in the kitchen washing up after the family's evening meal she faced her with the problem.

'You are right, it would make a difference if you moved out and we could let the room we are using,' Saratina agreed as she lifted a plate out of the bowl of soapy water and passed it to Gaynor to dry.

'I know, but I have nowhere to go. Have you any ideas?'

'I have, actually.' Saratina swirled the soapy water round in the bowl thoughtfully. 'I've been wondering whether to mention it to you, but I didn't want to upset you.'

'Go on, what is it?'

'Why don't you rent a house?'

'Me, rent a house!' Gaynor interrupted,

laughing derisively. 'How do you think I could do that when I haven't a bean to my name? In fact, I still owe you the money I borrowed for my train fare to Ferndale and I can't even find a way to pay that back.'

'Yes, well, listen to my idea,' Saratina stated as she plunged another pile of plates into the washing-up water. 'If you rent a house, then you can let out most of the rooms and the money you get for those will not only pay the rent, but will keep you and your children in food and clothes.'

'As an idea it's great,' Gaynor agreed, 'but who is going to let me take on a house when they find out I haven't even got a job? The letting agents would not only want references but also rent in advance.'

'I've thought of all that and I think it might be possible if I asked Sandy to vouch for you. If he said you were a responsible sort of person and that you had once worked for the Tramways and so on, they'd probably agree to let you have the tenancy of a house. In fact, I'm sure they would.'

Saratina expanded on her idea as they finished doing the dishes. 'Think about it,' she told Gaynor as she emptied the dirty water out of the enamel bowl and wrung out the dish-cloth and put it to dry. 'If you want to go ahead, then we'll have a look around and see if we can find the right sort of place for you and I'll ask Sandy if he'll give you a reference.'

Gaynor thought about nothing else for the next few days. It was early September and the weather still mild enough for the children to enjoy being taken out so she began systematically exploring all the roads in the Bute Street area right down to the Pier Head to see what houses were empty and available to rent.

Most of the ones she looked at were either so dirty or in such a terrible state of disrepair that she shuddered at the thought of trying to live in them. They had been neglected all through the war because not only was money needed for other things, but the paint and materials needed to do them up were in short supply.

She was on the point of giving up when she found a small terraced house in Eleanor Place that seemed fairly suitable. Although it was in the heart of Tiger Bay and rather shabby it looked fairly clean and there were no smashed windows or broken doors. A further advantage was that it appeared to be partly furnished so that meant she would be able to move in straight away if she could persuade the landlord to let her rent it.

She was feeling quite excited when she told Saratina all about it and asked her to come and have a look at it. Saratina was quite impressed and agreed that it did seem suitable.

'All I have to do now, then, is to try and persuade the landlord to let me rent it.'

Saratina looked thoughtful. 'I think you might do a lot better if you let Sandy go and ask about it. Sandy was saying that there are a couple of conductresses who are looking for somewhere to live. If he explained all this to the landlord, or the agent representing him, then he'd be more likely to convince them that they should let you have the place.'

'That would be wonderful,' Gaynor agreed, 'but why is he going out of his way to do so much for me?'

'Probably because I've asked him to do what he can to help, of course.' Saratina smiled. 'Also, he is very anxious to find somewhere for these new conductresses to live and this sounds like the ideal solution all round.'

They didn't tell Maria till the arrangement was complete. When they did she said very little, but Gaynor thought she seemed less tense in the days that followed. She even offered to look after Sara and Rachael so that Gaynor could go on her own to clean the house in Eleanor Place and get it ready for herself and the lodgers who would be moving in at the same time.

Sandy Peterson was as good as his word. Not only did he negotiate the rental terms for the house in Eleanor Place on Gaynor's behalf, but he also arranged the rent which the conductresses were going to pay Gaynor, and, with the full agreement of all concerned, he deducted it from their wages each week.

'I'll pay the rent direct to the letting agent for you,' he told Gaynor. 'That way, not only will you have no worries, but there will be no chance of you getting into arrears. You'll have no rent to pay out yourself each week, either, so the money you charge your lodgers for providing them with meals and doing their laundry will be all yours to live on,' he pointed out.

Gaynor was very grateful. Even so, she found it was not as plain sailing as she'd expected it to be. She was not used to budgeting because Maria had seen to all that when she had been living with the Varios. She found it quite a responsibility to spin out the money and to provide them all with nourishing meals as well as squeeze a shilling or two out of what they paid her for her own needs and those of the children.

As she sat with paper and pencil trying to work out the best ways to allocate her meagre income she kept telling herself that she would soon get used to doing it. At least she had her own place, she reminded herself. What was more, there was no unpleasant atmosphere or uncomfortable feeling that they didn't want her there.

The three young women Sandy had found were ideal lodgers. The eldest, Susan, had said she wanted a room to herself so she had taken the small back bedroom. The other two, Betty and Iris, were in their early twenties and had been friends all their lives so they were sharing the middle bedroom. The largest of the bedrooms, which was at the front of the house, she'd kept for herself and her own children.

They were usually on different shifts so they were seldom all at home at the same time. When they were, they seemed to get on well and enjoy each other's company immensely.

Susan was married and her husband was away at sea. She was the quiet one and liked nothing better than to sit nursing Rachael or telling stories to Sara.

Betty and Iris were younger and full of life. They came from a small village near Tonypandy and enjoyed their free time to the full. They kept Gaynor amused, as well as envious, with their wild clothes and the crazy hats they wore when they weren't in uniform.

Their exploits when they went dancing had her and Susan doubled over with laughter. Both Betty and Iris had boyfriends but they were in the army. Although when they went out they were never short of men friends, much to Gaynor's relief they never brought any chaps back to the house.

She had hardly settled into her new home when, in November 1918, peace was declared; the war had ended. The excitement of all the celebrations and street parties to mark 11 November was tempered for Gaynor by the knowledge that once the men came home again, they would want their jobs back. There would be no need for the Tramways to employ women any more.

'I don't know what I am going to do when that happens,' she confided in Saratina. 'I've become so friendly with the girls who are lodging here and they are so fond of Sara and Rachael, that we are like one big family,' she sighed.

'Surely, you don't mean you'd rather we were still at war.' Saratina scowled.

'No, of course I don't. It's simply that I don't like the idea of losing my lodgers. Life without them is going to be very quiet and uneventful. What's more, I don't know if I will be able to afford to stay on in Eleanor Place.'

'You could always find a job,' Saratina suggested.

'How can I do that? It will be at least another year before Sara is old enough to go to school and Rachael is still only a baby.'

'Then find some new lodgers,' Saratina laughed. 'There are always people looking for somewhere to live.'

'Not women, though. There will be hardly any women going out to work at all now the war's over. Once the men are demobbed they'll all be claiming their jobs back.'

'Then you'll have to take in men, won't you?'

'I know, but I am not too keen on doing that,' Gaynor protested. 'It wouldn't be the same as living in a house where there're only girls around the place!'

'Well, worry about it when it happens,' Saratina said impatiently. 'Sandy says it will be months before the jobs are all sorted out. The Tramways don't mind employing women because they pay them less than the men.'

Saratina was quite right, Christmas came and there was still no talk about any of Gaynor's lodgers losing their jobs. Life at Eleanor Place remained as happy and companionable as ever. Gaynor cooked meals to fit in with her lodgers' varying shifts and in return, when they weren't working, they helped to keep Sara and Rachael amused.

It was almost three months into 1919 before the blow fell. By then the men who had been soldiers were being demobbed at a tremendous rate. Those who had jobs to come back to were demanding to be reinstated and there was upheaval and confusion everywhere.

One by one the women who had been employed by the Tramways were told that their services were no longer required. Susan was the first of Gaynor's three lodgers to leave. She had only taken the job because her husband had been called up, and she was happy to give up work the moment he was demobbed.

Betty and Iris were also eager to return home to Tonypandy the moment they heard that their boyfriends were about to be demobbed.

Without their money coming in each week Gaynor was left almost destitute. In order to buy food for herself and the children she had to spend the few shillings she had squirrelled away while her lodgers had been paying her for their keep.

Although she was as frugal as she could

possibly be, and bought only the absolute necessities, such as bread and milk, she knew that what little money she had would only keep her in food and coal for about three weeks at the most. She was at her wits' end to know what she was going to do after that.

To make matters even worse, towards the end of the second week she received a letter from the letting agency to say that unless her rent arrears were paid immediately they would have no alternative but to ask her to vacate the house.

She was so upset that she went straight round to Sophia Street to confide in Saratina and ask her advice.

'You'll have to do as I suggested and find some more lodgers, even if it has to be men.'

'I suppose you're right,' Gaynor admitted.

'You should have done it right away, and then you wouldn't be in this mess,' Saratina pointed out sharply.

'Do you think Sandy Peterson could recommend some who would be reliable?' Gaynor asked contritely. 'If he could do that and continue with the same arrangements as before, it would be a tremendous help.'

Saratina gave her a withering look. 'You mean you haven't heard that Sandy Peterson has vanished?'

Gaynor looked at her in dismay. 'When did this happen? You mean he's walked out of his job without a word to you?'

'I've just told you; he's vanished and the police are looking for him.'

Gaynor looked bemused. 'Oh, Saratina, how terrible; you must be so upset, you were so close. What do they want him for? What's he done?'

'He's been fiddling the takings. Kept most of it for himself instead of handing it over.'

The colour drained from Gaynor's face as she pulled the letter she'd received that morning out of her pocket and passed it over to Saratina for her to read.

They both stared at each other, wide-eyed with horror. 'Dammo di! This means that he hasn't been handing over the rent on your place, either,' Saratina declared in a shocked voice.

Gaynor snatched the letter back and read it through again. 'I thought they were asking for the last three weeks since I've lost my lodgers,' Gaynor groaned, 'but look, it's for the last three months! How am I ever going to repay that much when I have nothing at all coming in?'

'Oh, Gaynor, I am so sorry!' Saratina put an arm around her shoulders and hugged her. 'He's done the dirty on both of us. The best thing you can do is to go and see the letting agent and explain the situation and ask him if he will give you time to pay it. I don't hold out very much hope, mind,' she added worriedly.

'Perhaps it would be better if I leave it for the moment and try and find some new lodgers first. If I can go along with some of the money, he will be more likely to listen when I ask whether I can pay back what is owing over the next few weeks,' Gaynor said hopefully.

'Few weeks! Don't talk daft, cariad. It's going to take you months, probably a year, to pay back all that's owing. I don't think they will be prepared to wait that length of time for their money. They're going to insist that you move out right away.'

Chapter Fourteen

Gaynor wished that Saratina was able to go with her to see the letting agent because she had never felt so nervous in her life. She'd thought about asking Maria to look after Sara and Rachael for a couple of hours but then, at the last minute, she'd changed her mind. Perhaps the agent would take pity on her and perhaps be more lenient when he saw that she had a young family and she explained to him that letting rooms was the only way she could provide for them.

The office address on the letter she had received was in the Hayes and since she couldn't take the pram on a tram it meant a long walk. Sara was complaining that her legs were aching before they were halfway along Bute Street. When she started to cry, Gaynor sat her on the pram, warning her that she would have to sit still or she would squash baby Rachael.

By the time she reached the office she was feeling not only apprehensive but also footsore and breathless. It was the last straw when the smartly dressed girl on the reception desk asked her if she had an appointment and she said she hadn't.

'In that case, I am afraid you will have to make one and come back another day,' she stated authoritatively when Gaynor shook her head.

'I've come about this letter I received from you and it says you needed to see me as soon as possible, otherwise you intend to evict me . . .'

'Arrears is it?' the girl interrupted in a sneering tone. 'Well, wait here a minute, and I'll see if there is anyone in the office who can deal with it.'

She disappeared through a door behind her and Gaynor could hear her going up to the offices above. There was a long wait and still the girl didn't come back. Sara was already becoming fractious, and although Rachael had been asleep when they arrived she was now waking up. Gaynor felt at her wits' end because she knew that any minute now Rachael would be demanding a feed.

Having come so far, and rehearsed what she was going to say, Gaynor was reluctant to leave without dealing with the matter, so she banged on the desk and called out for attention.

The girl looked extremely annoyed as she came back to her desk. 'If you'd made an appointment, then you wouldn't have had to wait,' she pointed out. 'As it is, Mr Loch who signed that letter you've brought in isn't here at the moment.'

'Surely there is someone else who can deal with it!' Gaynor said crossly.

'Only Mr Hughes, and he doesn't usually deal with clients and certainly not when it is a matter of people being in arrears,' she added loftily.

'Well, perhaps he can come down off his high horse for once,' Gaynor snapped. 'You can go and find out and tell him that he had better come and talk to me, because I have no intention of leaving here until I've seen someone.'

With a haughty sniff the receptionist minced past Gaynor and strutted towards a door at the far side of the room. She gave a light tap on the door and, without waiting for a reply, opened it and walked in.

Quickly Gaynor turned the pram around, grabbed hold of Sara's hand, and followed her.

As she wheeled the pram through the door the girl swung round with a shrill little scream. 'I'm sorry, Mr Hughes, I know you've said that you don't want to deal with any of the clients, but this woman was so persistent. I told her to wait . . .'

Gaynor stared past the girl to where a man, dressed in a dark blue suit, was sitting at a desk entering figures in a ledger. There was something vaguely familiar about the shape of the dark head, the slant of the broad shoulders. Then she drew her breath in sharply as he looked up. It couldn't be, she told herself, and yet, he reminded her so much of Barri that she felt disorientated.

'Gaynor . . . Gaynor Sanderson? It is, isn't it?'

As he spoke, the man was on his feet and moving towards her. She stared back at him, a look of incredulity on her face as she whispered his name aloud.

His face was so badly contorted, with puckered skin and ugly red scars, almost obliterating one side of it, that she stared at him aghast. This cruelly disfigured man couldn't be the handsome Barri she'd known and loved, she told herself.

The dark eyes and the deep voice were both as she remembered them, though, and stirred up so many memories that her mind was in a whirl.

She sensed the receptionist was staring from one to the other of them, openly curious, and she felt an overwhelming relief when, with a brief glance in the girl's direction, he said, 'You can leave us, I'll handle this matter. Close the door behind you, please.'

The moment they were alone he came around to her side of the desk and stretched out his hands and held Gaynor's. 'It really is me,' he said wryly. 'I'm sorry about the way I look. It happened while I was in the army. A grenade was tossed into the trench I was in and it went off full in my face,' he explained.

'Oh, Barri, what a terrible thing to happen; you could have been killed.' Gaynor gently released one of her hands from his grip and tenderly stroked the crumpled discoloured skin of his cheek. 'Does it hurt very much?'

172

He gave her a lop-sided smile. 'Not now. It certainly did at first. It looks unsightly, though, that's why I stay in the background and never see any of the clients if I can help it. Some of them are quite frightened by the way I look.'

'They wouldn't be if they knew you.' Gaynor smiled fondly. 'I recognised your voice, but—'

'You couldn't believe the face belonged to me,' he added a trifle bitterly.

'Oh, Barri! I didn't mean it like that at all; it was just that I was taken by surprise. It's so long since I last saw you, and I wasn't even sure when you left Ferndale whether or nor you had come to Cardiff. No one seemed to have any idea about where you'd gone, not even your mother or Ellie. When I first arrived here I was confident that I would be able to find you, but so much happened . . .' She shrugged hopelessly, not finishing what she was saying.

Barri looked across at Rachael in the pram and Sara, who was clutching its handle tightly, peering at him with a puzzled look on her little face. 'You've been kept busy in other ways,' he observed sardonically.

'This is Sara, and the baby is Rachael,' Gaynor told him with a tremulous smile. 'Come and say hello to Barri,' she urged, pulling Sara forward.

Sara pulled back and gave him a coy little smile, then hid her face in Gaynor's skirt.

'So you're married,' Barri commented.

Gaynor shook her head. 'No!'

'But you have been? What happened . . . was he another casualty of the war?'

Gaynor shook her head. 'No! It's a very long story,' she said.

'You mean you'd rather tell me all about it some other time,' Barri said, looking in Sara's direction.

Gaynor nodded quickly. She was relieved that he was being so tactful.

'So why are you here? Did I hear the receptionist say something about arrears?'

Hot colour flooded Gaynor's face. 'I'm afraid so. I had an arrangement for my rent to be paid by a man called Sandy Peterson. I now discover that he has vanished and that many other people have also been cheated as well as me.'

Barri listened intently to Gaynor's account of how she had come to be so much in arrears. While she was speaking, he drew a writing pad towards him, and from time to time made notes.

'I don't think you have any chance at all of ever recovering this money from Sandy Peterson,' he told her bluntly when she finished speaking.

'Oh dear!' Her face fell. 'Will I still have to repay it to you?' she asked worriedly.

'I'm afraid so, but I am sure we can devise some sort of system whereby the repayment can be spread over a period of time that will make it easy for you to do so,' he told her quickly.

174

Gaynor bit her lip as she studied him covertly. Wondering what he would think when he realised that she had no income whatsoever and that she had never been married.

Barri looked so smart and respectable in his neat dark blue suit, white shirt and light blue tie, and from the size of his office it was obvious that he held a position of responsibility and she felt a sense of relief that he was the one dealing with her problem.

She was suddenly conscious of how shabby she was in her black cotton skirt and plain white blouse, which was frayed at the cuffs. Even the pram that Rachael was sleeping in was old and battered because it had been used for all the Vario children. Sara's dress was too small for her and she had outgrown her little canvas shoes so that she'd resorted to cutting a hole in the tops to make room for her toes.

'I will need some more time to go through your records,' Barri told her as he tapped the papers in front of him with his fountain pen. 'You'll have to give me a day or so to arrange things.'

'If I've got to come back again,' Gaynor frowned, 'can I be sure that it is you I see next time?'

'Of course! I'll make sure that I am the one who deals with this matter,' he promised. 'I will have to consult several other people about what is to be done, which is why you will have to come back again,' he explained.

'Thank you, Barri.' As she began to man-
oeuvre the pram towards the door he stood up
to help her. 'Look,' he said hesitantly, as he
limped across the room, 'perhaps it would make
things easier if I came to see you. It must be
quite a long walk from Eleanor Place for this
young lady,' he added, ruffling Sara's dark hair.

'Yes, that would be very helpful,' Gaynor
agreed, 'but with your bad leg, wouldn't you
find it difficult to come all that way?'

'It looks far worse than it is.' He grinned.
'These days I hardly notice it.'

'In that case then, when would you be able
to come?'

'Well, we both have a lot to talk over because
there is so much catching up to be done, as well
as the matter of the arrears, so perhaps we
should make it one evening, after these two are
tucked up in bed and asleep,' he suggested.

Gaynor stared at him for a long moment, a
thousand and one questions bouncing around
in her head, before she nodded in agreement.
Then, out of curiosity, she asked bluntly, 'Won't
your wife mind if you come to see me in the
evening?'

Barri shook his head. 'I haven't got a wife,'
he told her gravely.

Her relief was so great at knowing that he
had never married, and had no ties, that she
burst out laughing; she quickly recovered
herself, however, when she saw the look of
confusion on his face.

They stared at each other for a moment in silence, almost as if afraid to voice out loud what they were thinking.

Gaynor no longer noticed his scars and puckered skin; he was once again the handsome boyo she had been so close to when she was growing up.

As she walked home down the length of Bute Street with a tired and bored Sara balanced on the pram and a whimpering little Rachael struggling to sit up and constantly being pushed back down again by Sara, her mind was so full of images of the past that the children's squabbling barely registered with her.

She felt overjoyed at finding Barri again after all this time. She tried not to keep thinking about the fact that he wasn't married and neither was she, but she found that it was impossible not to do so.

She still loved him as much as she had ever done, but she had no way of telling what his feelings were for her. He had changed from an exuberant youth full of schemes for the future into a sombre man. She wondered if that was because of his war experiences, and his bitterness about the way his life had been changed because of her father's actions all those years ago.

Next time they met she would tell him every detail about her past and she hoped he would confide in her about everything that had happened to him since he'd left Ferndale. After that, it was a case of letting fate take its course, she told herself optimistically.

Barri Hughes took an early lunch. He needed to get out of the office, and away from the curious stares of the receptionist. He wanted to be on his own so that he could go over every-thing that had happened that morning.

He'd been shocked to see how shabby and weary Gaynor had looked. True, it had been six years since he'd last seen her. Yet to have seen her changed so much, from a carefree schoolgirl with shiny dark hair and sparkling hazel eyes into a careworn mother of two small children, with her hair pulled back into a straggle under her faded straw cloche hat, had saddened him.

She had obviously been equally shocked by his appearance. All the bitterness that he had felt when he first saw the result of his facial injuries flared up anew. When he was growing up he'd never worried about how he looked, but now the way people stared, or shivered and quickly looked away again, often cut him to the quick.

He knew he'd been regarded as good-looking by some of the girls at school, but he had thought very little about it because he wasn't interested in them. Gaynor had been his friend, his soul mate, and together they'd planned and dreamed about the sort of life they would have together in the future.

When Ieuan Sanderson had sacked him,

giving him no chance to even explain to Gaynor what was happening, he had been determined to forget her, but he never had. She'd been constantly in his thoughts from the moment he had left Ferndale. She'd been his talisman all through the dreadful months that had stretched into years when he had been in the trenches.

Lying in a hospital bed after he'd been injured, his only thought was of getting back to Ferndale and seeing her again. Then, when he'd taken that first look at his face after they had removed the bandages, his heart had sunk. Right away he knew he could never face Gaynor while he looked as he did.

Much later still, when he knew that his broken leg had not healed properly and that as well as his facial disfigurement he would always walk with a limp, it set a permanent seal on him ever trying to contact her.

He hadn't even returned to Ferndale. He knew his mother must have been heartbroken when he had left and it didn't seem fair to make her go through the even worse ordeal of seeing him in such a sorry state. Far better for her to retain her memories of the good-looking son she'd always been so proud of, not a man whose face was little better than that of a gargoyle.

He wondered if Gaynor was still in touch with her family, or even with his. He should have warned her not to say that she had seen him. His family assumed he'd died in battle and he wanted it to remain that way.

Somehow, from the look of her clothes and shabby appearance, and the fact that she was living in one of the most squalid areas in Cardiff, he didn't think that she could be in touch with her family. Her mother, if not her father, would have done something to help her, especially now that she had two children to bring up as well as herself to look after.

Remembering the children, one a mere baby, and the fact that she said she wasn't married, and never had been, puzzled him, but he didn't want to venture into speculation.

There was so much he didn't know about her that he couldn't wait to see her again, and he wondered just how forthcoming she would be when next they met.

In the meantime, he thought worriedly, there were the rent arrears to be sorted out. These went back over three months, which meant there would be a pretty high figure outstanding. How on earth was she going to manage to pay it off?

Chapter Fifteen

Gaynor spent the next few days in a state of expectation as she waited for Barri to call. She kept thinking about how she could pay off the money and told everyone she knew that she had rooms to let. The woman in the corner shop had agreed that she could put a card in the window. She also said that she'd tell her old man to make it known that she was looking for lodgers when he went for his evening pint down at the pub.

Telling herself that she was really doing it in readiness for her new lodgers, Gaynor cleaned the house from top to bottom. Since the weather was still mild, she took the children out for a walk every afternoon so that they were so tired that Sara was ready for bed by half past six each evening, just in case Barri turned up.

It was three days before he came, and when he did, it was shortly after five o'clock, much earlier than she had anticipated. She was still struggling to feed Rachael and at the same time persuade Sara to sit at the table and eat her tea.

As she opened the door to him she realised how dishevelled she must look with a print wrap-over pinny covering her blouse and skirt to safeguard them from Sara's sticky fingers and to protect them when she spoon-fed Rachel.

As she took Barry into the untidy living room she was conscious of how shabby it was and wondered what on earth he must think of her and their home. After the way she had worked so hard to make things look nice she wanted to cry with frustration.

Before she could do more than greet him rather awkwardly and ask him if she could take his hat and coat before he sat down, Sara had scrambled down from the table and walked towards him.

'You're the man with the funny face,' she stated, staring up at him, wide-eyed.

'Sara! That's very rude!' Gaynor gasped. 'I'm so sorry, Barri,' she said apologetically.

'Not at all; she's only stating what she can see.' He smiled back at Sara. 'You're quite right, I have got a funny face,' he said solemnly. 'You have a very pretty face, though,' he added. 'In fact, you look exactly like your mam did when she was your age.'

'You knew my mam when she was four years old?' Sara asked, her big blue eyes widening in surprise.

'Oh yes, we went to school together.'

'I'm going to school soon. In one year's time I will be five, and then I will be able to go to school, won't I, Mam?' she turned to Gaynor for confirmation.

'Yes, but only if you eat up all your tea.' Gaynor smiled.

'Can Barri have some as well?'

'I've already had my tea,' he told her. 'I ate it all up so that I could come to see you.'

'Oh!' Sara stared at him in surprise, and then she gave him a beaming smile and climbed back on her chair and began to finish eating the food on her plate.

'My, you do have a wonderful way with children,' Gaynor observed drily.

The exchange broke down any remaining barriers between them all. Barri nursed Rachael and, with Sara's help, gave her a bottle. Then he carried them both upstairs to bed, leaving Gaynor to clear up in the living room before following them up to tuck the children in.

'I bet you didn't expect to have to do that,' Gaynor laughed as they came back downstairs and made themselves comfortable and Gaynor poured out a cup of tea for them both.

'I enjoyed it. They're lovely children. It's hard that you have to bring them up on your own. I'm sure you must be worn out by the time you get them to bed.'

'The three lodgers I had, the tram conductresses I told you about, were very good, and they helped me a lot with them,' Gaynor confided. 'I'm already missing them.'

'So does that mean that at the moment you have no lodgers at all?' Barry frowned.

Gaynor shook her head. Bit by bit she recounted all that had happened to her since they had last seen each other. He listened in silence, but she was aware of the conflicting emotions that registered on his face and in his eyes.

'You've had a tough time of it,' he murmured when she'd finished. He stretched out a hand and took one of hers in his, studying it thoughtfully.

'I expect you've also had a pretty rough time over the past five years,' she commented drily. 'Are you going to tell me what happened after you left Ferndale?'

'Only if you make a fresh pot of tea,' he teased.

Barri's story was equally disturbing for Gaynor. He'd come to Cardiff, found some lodgings in Cathays, and ended up working in an ironmonger's shop.

'They treated me as a dogsbody,' he said bitterly. 'I was the delivery boy, floor sweeper and general gofer. I spent most of the day picking things up and putting them away after everyone else. I hated it. As soon as war was declared I volunteered for the army.'

'And you were sent to France?'

'I was. I went over there the moment I'd finished my basic training,' Barri agreed grimly.

He helped himself to sugar and stirred it into his tea, moving his head from side to side as if he was troubled by the memories he was reviving by talking about it.

'It was tough. It was wet and muddy in the trenches. We were short of food and it was bitterly cold. The winter over there in France is more severe than it is here, and our uniforms weren't designed to keep out that sort of cold. The Germans were not only much better equipped and better trained than us, but they were more used to that sort of weather. We didn't stand a chance.'

He paused and, reaching out for the teapot, refilled his cup. In silence, Gaynor added some milk to it and pushed the sugar bowl towards him.

'It was the day before my twentieth birthday when this happened,' he went on, running a hand down his face. 'One minute we were scraping mud off our boots, and the next, there was a whooshing noise, followed by a deafening explosion. I found myself flung backwards; something was stinging and burning my face as though I had fallen into a fire. I could hear someone screaming, and all I wanted them to do was to shut up.'

Barri paused and ran his hand through his hair. 'It must have been me screaming, because I learned later that no one else had been seriously hurt; not on that occasion, anyway. All the boyos who were in that trench with me died, eventually – every single one of them – but that was much later on, when they were fighting in another battle, some time after I'd left the unit.'

'So what happened to you after you were injured?' Gaynor asked, her voice full of concern.

'I was treated by some of the medics, patched up, and sent to a hospital tent behind the lines. The place was packed; there weren't sufficient drugs to go around, nor enough doctors to tend to our wounds. There were too few nurses to look after us. Those who were only walking wounded did what they could to help the rest of us. My head and face were so bandaged that I couldn't see what was going on, and my leg was broken, so I couldn't do anything to help myself, let alone help anyone else. I just lay there, day after day, wishing that when I went to sleep I wouldn't wake up again.'

'So how long was it before they brought you home?'

His face tightened and she could see it was difficult for him to talk about it.

'Days, weeks, I lost count of time. I tried to work it out afterwards, and I think it must have been about two weeks before they brought me back to Britain, to an army hospital. It was a temporary place, a specially erected collection of Nissan huts somewhere in the country at the back of beyond. They put my leg in a splint and, later on, they put a plaster cast on it, but it was too late; it had already shrunk.'

'Which is why you have a limp,' she said sympathetically.

He nodded. 'Yes, and my face was a complete mess. It had been neglected so long that the skin had withered and become so distorted that they said they couldn't do anything to improve it. Well, you can see that for yourself,' he added bitterly.

'They managed to save your sight, though. It could have been much worse. Think how terrible it would have been if you had been left blind.'

He shrugged. 'At least I wouldn't be reminded of my disfigurement every time I comb my hair, or pass by a shop window and see my reflection in the glass. I wouldn't have to steel myself day in and day out to meet the shock and revulsion in other people's eyes when they meet me. Fortunately, I can hide away in my office, so I don't have to meet many people while I'm working.'

'Except when they barge in on you without asking permission,' Gaynor said contritely.

Barri smiled. 'Quite a firebrand, aren't you? Whatever happened to the sweet little girl I knew in Ferndale?'

'She would probably have screamed in horror and fainted, or else run away, when she saw what had happened to you.'

'Would she? Is that how you felt, Gaynor, when you first saw this?' he asked harshly, running his forefinger down the deep scar that stretched from the corner of one eye right the way down his cheek to his chin.

Gaynor shook her head. 'I hardly noticed it; I only saw the boyo I'd once been in love with and who had vanished without a word, leaving me heartbroken.'

187

'I didn't vanish, I was banished! Your father gave me no choice. He issued an ultimatum and I was too young and far too scared to defy him.'

'I know, I know. I worked that out, eventually, but it was not until quite a long time afterwards.'

'And that is when you became involved with the German bloke, this Konrad Claus who is Sara's father?'

Gaynor bit her lip. 'I was young, I was missing you, and Ellie and Davey were so close that I felt lonely.'

Barri shook his head. 'You allowed him far more liberties than you did me,' he commented with a smile.

'Yes,' she admitted ruefully, 'I'm afraid I did and I paid the price for it. In the end, once Konrad went back to Germany and my mam and dad found out that I was pregnant, I lost both of them and my comfortable home, didn't I?'

'One way and another, because of your dad, Ferndale also lost both of us,' Barri observed sadly.

'Sara was born at almost the same time as you were injured,' Gaynor murmured reflectively.

'Sara.' Barri smiled. 'She called me the man with the funny face. That was almost a compliment.'

'Small children speak as they find. They are

188

instinctive in their reaction, there's no pretence. Often when they are outspoken like that it is embarrassing because many people take offence, or think the child is being rude.'

Barri didn't answer for a moment, then he smiled. 'I didn't; I thought it was a compliment; well, an acceptance, at any rate. Children are less critical and so much more accepting than adults. Rachael is too little to notice, but at least she wasn't scared when I leaned over her pram, or when I nursed her,' he added with a wry smile.

'Why should she be?'

'And you? Did you really mean that you're not scared, or threatened by my ugly disfigurement?'

'I've already told you; I see only the boyo I knew when I lived in Ferndale.' Rising from her chair, Gaynor moved closer and, taking his face between her two hands, studied it carefully. 'The same as it ever was,' she whispered as she gently kissed the scars on his puckered cheek.

Barri looked at her, his gaze intense, but then he stiffened and drew back.

'We must talk,' he said firmly. 'I came here to put forward one or two suggestions to try and help you clear the outstanding arrears of rent on this place; that is, if you still want me to do so?'

'Of course; I quite understand.' Gaynor sat bolt upright in her chair, feeling as if she had been slapped. 'You want this to be a strictly business meeting,' she added, hoping that Barri didn't think she was only being nice to him because she needed his help.

'Right then, shall we get started?' He moved their cups and the rest of the tea things further back on the table to clear a space and then spread out some papers.

Gaynor tried to listen to what he was saying, but her mind was in turmoil. Seeing Barri again brought back all the feelings for him which she had kept submerged for so many years, so she found it wasn't easy to concentrate on all the advice he was giving her.

'Is that all quite clear, now?' he asked as he stopped talking and began to collect up the papers he'd spread out and to stack them together in a neat pile. 'If I leave these with you, then after you've looked through them, you can get in touch with me again if there is anything you don't understand.'

'Yes, very well, I'll do that,' Gaynor promised. Uppermost in her thoughts was not the rows of figures that Barri had compiled, but the fact that any minute now he was going to leave. Desperately she wondered what she could say to make him stay longer.

'It's a big undertaking, I do realise that,' Barri commented as he began to put on his overcoat. 'If I am going to stop the owner asking us to send in the bailiffs, however, I have to be able to convince him that I have a commitment from you that you will be reducing the outstanding arrears by an agreed sum each week. I will, however, ensure that your first payment doesn't have to be made until the end of next week, to give you time to find some new lodgers. Have you managed to find any new ones?'

She shrugged. 'Not really,' she admitted. 'I've put the word out, but no one has turned up yet.'

'I'm sure they will,' he told her confidently. 'If I hear of anyone I think might be suitable then I'll send them along to see you,' he promised.

'Thank you, Barri.'

'You know, you might find it a lot easier if you considered having another family share the house with you rather than take in two or three lodgers.'

She looked at him, startled. 'A family!' She almost choked on the words.

'It would be a lot less work for you; you wouldn't have to cook or clean for them, the wife would do all that. You might even find that the husband would help with any small maintenance jobs you needed doing around the place.'

'They wouldn't be paying me as much as I'd get if I was looking after lodgers though.' She frowned and shook her head emphatically. 'It wouldn't work; I need every penny I can get; don't forget I have two children to feed . . . and myself.'

Barri hesitated, fingering his scar nervously. He wanted to tell her that he would like to help her with her money problems, but he wasn't sure how she would take his offer because he sensed how independent she was. Having found Gaynor again he didn't want to lose her, certainly not by saying or doing anything that would cause a rift between them.

Gaynor took his reticence to imply that he didn't want to be too involved with her plans for the future.

As she showed him out she wondered if they would ever be as close as they'd once been, but she was determined to at least try and maintain contact, even if it was only as a friend.

Chapter Sixteen

The first of Gaynor's prospective lodgers, a middle-aged man, arrived the next day. He had been recommended by the woman from the corner shop. He was a widower and was working in the shipyards at East Moors.

His name was Bevan Powell and he seemed so quiet and ordinary that Gaynor took to him at once. He claimed he neither drank nor gambled and only smoked a pipe.

They agreed amicably on the rent for the small single room at the back of the house. He asked if Gaynor could provide him with breakfast and an evening meal and they agreed that he would find his midday snack himself.

It was a good start, but she was still worried about how she was going to find the fifteen shillings at the end of the week to pay her rent and something off the outstanding arrears as she'd agreed with Barri.

Two days later, Thomas Pritchard, a thin, gaunt young man with a muffler round his neck and who told her that he had not long been demobbed, came looking for lodgings for himself and his mate, Dylan Jenkins. When she explained that it was a double room, but assured him that there were two single beds in there, he shrugged his thin shoulders and said that would suit them fine.

Thomas and Dylan also wanted her to provide them with an evening meal, but said that neither of them had time to eat breakfast before they left in the morning. They were both navvies working down at the docks and they said they always had a hearty fry-up mid-morning in one of the dockside cafés which kept them going for the rest of the day.

They all asked her if she would do their washing and mending, which meant that she was kept busy from the moment she opened her eyes and gave Rachael her early morning bottle, till she flopped into bed after she'd washed up and tidied around after the evening meal. However, it did enable her to keep to the arrangement she'd made with Barri about repaying the arrears she owed.

The only problem was that she had to hand over the money before Barri's office closed on a Friday night which meant taking it all the way up to the Hayes the minute her lodgers arrived home with their pay each Friday.

'Would it make it any easier if I called round on a Friday night to collect this?' Barri asked when, the third Friday in succession, she turned up at the office as they were on the point of locking the door. 'I'm sure it must be difficult for you when you have to bring both the children and walk all the way from Eleanor Place.'

Her face lit up with relief, and then she frowned. 'It's very good of you to offer, but that would mean you'd be late getting home yourself on a Friday evening.'

'That wouldn't matter. I'm in no hurry; there's no one waiting for me. I usually stop and buy some fish and chips and then sit and eat them on my own.'

'In that case, then if you come yourself to collect the money, why not stay and eat with us? You can always buy fish and chips another night,' she added with a smile.

He looked pleased at being asked, but still hesitated. 'I'm sure you've got better things to do with your time than to spend it cooking a meal for me,' he protested.

'I have to cook anyway for my lodgers, so I'm only asking you to join us,' she pointed out.

She wanted him to come so much that it hurt. Ever since they had met up again a few weeks earlier she'd not been able to put him out of her thoughts. She wondered if he wanted to see her as much as she longed to talk to him again.

As she worked around the house she'd gone over every detail of what he had told her about his time in the army. It often made her feel guilty about what had happened to him because things might have been so very different if her father hadn't insisted on him leaving Ferndale Forges when he did.

Sometimes she let herself daydream about

what life could have been like for them both. By now he would have been a foreman and she might have been a teacher, and they might even have been making plans to get married.

Or they might have already married and have two little girls like Sara and Rachael, only Barri would be their father. Their home would be a nicely furnished little house with friends and family all living nearby. Next year, when Sara started school, she would have been going to the same one that her mother and Barri had attended, instead of one where there were dozens of barefoot fatherless children of all nationalities.

The thought of Barri sitting down to a meal with her, one she had cooked, filled her with so much pleasure that she could hardly wait for his answer.

Regretfully they wouldn't be alone; there would be three other men sitting round the table and Sara and Rachael would be in bed upstairs, hopefully asleep.

She was already wondering about what she should cook. With a sense of dismay she realised that she knew nothing about what he liked to eat. Perhaps there were things he hated. They'd sometimes shared sandwiches when they'd been at school and she tried to remember which ones had been his favourites and which he'd handed over to her.

Anyway, she reminded herself, it didn't really matter, because she had to keep to a strict budget so he'd have to have whatever she could find that was a bargain when she went shopping.

Unless, she mused, she cheated and made something special and then cut back on what she fed her lodgers for the rest of the week. All's fair in love and war, she told herself and for her part it was certainly love.

Barri had been in her thoughts constantly since they'd met up again and now her love for him was deep and solid; stronger than ever; a love that she knew would remain constant for the rest of her life and, more than anything, she wanted to share it with him.

She gave herself a mental shake; you're getting ahead of yourself, cariad, she told herself, he hasn't even accepted your invitation yet!

'I must say that sounds like a tempting arrangement, if you're sure it won't be putting you out.' He smiled.

She was so relieved, so happy, that she couldn't speak.

'It's not worth going home, all the way to Cathays, so if I come straight from work, then I'll be there about half past six. Will that be all right?' he asked anxiously.

'That will be fine. I'll do my very best to have the girls in bed before you arrive.'

'Don't worry, I'd be happy to help with them.' He smiled. 'Sara might like me to tell her a story.'

Barri's words danced in Gaynor's head like sunbeams as she pushed the cumbersome pram with both girls in it all the way back to Eleanor Place.

Her feeling of euphoria carried her through the whole of the next week. By six o'clock on the following Friday the house had been cleaned, the shabby furniture polished, and the table spread with a clean white tablecloth in readiness. A savoury-smelling cawl was bubbling away and ready to be dished out.

As soon as she had the children fed and undressed ready for bed, she changed into her best white blouse and a navy blue skirt, covering them with a blue and white apron to protect them while she finished off the cooking. She told Sara that Barri was coming and that if she was very good, and was in bed when he arrived, then he would tell her a bedtime story.

Sara was impatiently waiting for Barri's arrival and the moment she heard his knock on the door she was halfway down the stairs, calling out to him to come and tell her a story. He barely had time to remove his hat and coat and say more than a breathless 'hello' to Gaynor before Sara was clutching hold of his hand and dragging him back upstairs.

Gaynor had told her three lodgers that she had invited a friend to join them for their evening meal, but she didn't explain anything more about him or the real reason for his visit.

Barri was still upstairs telling a bedtime story

to Sara when Gaynor was ready to dish up. Bevan, Thomas and Dylan were already seated when he came down.

As Gaynor made the introductions she was quick to notice the mixed looks on the faces of her lodgers as they saw Barri's face for the first time.

To save embarrassment she attempted to explain to them all why he was so disfigured and told them some of the details of how he had been injured during the war.

The two younger men exchanged looks and from then on dominated the conversation with tales about their own war exploits. The two of them had been in the same regiment, but since they had never gone overseas, their experiences, and the conditions they'd lived in, all sounded pretty mild to Gaynor compared to what she knew Barri had endured.

Bevan also listened in silence. Then as he laid his knife and fork down on his empty plate he managed to change the subject by saying how much he had enjoyed his meal.

This sparked off another diatribe from Thomas and Dylan as they listed their favourite foods and when and where they'd eaten the best meals of their life.

As Gaynor dished up the stewed apples and custard she'd made for pudding she wondered what Barri was making of all this. Perhaps inviting him to join them had not been such a good idea after all, she thought uneasily.

The moment Bevan finished eating he stood up, thanked her for the meal, and said he would be spending the rest of the evening in his room.

'Won't you wait and have a cup of tea with us first,' Gaynor asked.

'No thank you, cariad, that was a fine meal as always; I've had all I want.'

'We won't bother with any tea drinking either, we're off down to the pub for a couple of beers,' Dylan announced as he and Thomas scraped back their chairs.

'That's right!' Thomas gave Gaynor a knowing wink, 'we'll be off out and leave you and your boyo the chance to have some time together on your own.'

Gaynor felt the colour flooding her face and couldn't bring herself to look at Barri. She hoped he didn't think she had planned this in advance, even though she wanted to be alone with him more than anything in the world.

To hide her confusion she began to clear the table and when he tried to help she said sharply, 'I don't expect my guests to help, make yourself comfortable in the armchair while I see to all this and then I'll make us both a cup of tea, that's if you don't want to clear off to the pub as well?'

The moment the words were out of her mouth she could have bitten off her tongue. What on earth had made her say something like that, she wondered? Grabbing hold of the pile of plates and pudding dishes that she'd stacked up while she was talking, she carried them out into the kitchen, her eyes misted with tears of frustration.

Barri left Eleanor Place shortly after nine o'clock. As he walked along Adelaide Street and turned into James Street, heading for the tram stop near Clarence Road Bridge, he felt very uneasy about Gaynor's three lodgers.

The older man, Bevan Powell, seemed to be quiet and respectable, but he didn't like the attitude of the two younger men one little bit. He certainly didn't like the idea of Gaynor having to deal with them, especially when Bevan Powell was up in his bedroom or out of the house.

He'd half intended to hang on until they returned from the pub, just to make sure that they weren't drunk, or started behaving obstreperously. He'd hesitated, because he wasn't sure what Gaynor would think of the idea. He didn't want to outstay his welcome, especially if this was to become a regular weekly event. Nonetheless he was concerned about Gaynor.

As he boarded the tram and it clanged its way along Corporation Road, he was tempted to go back again and make sure that she was all right. Then he reminded himself that she was no longer the naïve little girl he had known in Ferndale, but a twenty-year-old woman with two children, so she should be able to take care of herself.

Even though she was living in Tiger Bay, Eleanor Place was one of the better parts; in fact only the Glamorganshire Canal divided it from Grangetown, he consoled himself.

His other concern was that, judging from the furnishings in the house, she must be having a desperately hard time to make ends meet. He calculated that after paying the rent and arrears, and providing meals for three grown men, as well as herself and two children, she would have barely anything left over.

He spent the rest of his journey back to the centre of the city trying to work out how he could help her without appearing to be doing so. He kept wishing that he had given her a false set of figures and then he could have paid off some of her arrears out of his own pocket. It was too late to do that now and he was pretty sure she would be indignant if he offered to do so.

The only solution he managed to reach was that perhaps she would let him take along little presents for the two girls each time he went there. Sweets, fruit, the occasional book or toy would surely be permissible.

He'd like to take them more substantial gifts, like clothes or new shoes, but he felt it was too soon to do that.

Perhaps later on, in a couple of months or so, when he was more certain about how Gaynor regarded him these days, it might be acceptable for him to start doing something of the sort, he mused. He wanted to be sure that she really did feel the same about him as she'd done when they were growing up.

As he sat on the tram and studied his profile in the darkened glass of the adjacent window he felt an overwhelming bitterness that he was now so disfigured. How could any woman want him with a face like that?

Gaynor had shown so much understanding but had it been from the heart, or had she merely been trying to be kind and to make him feel less sorry for himself? He kept remembering the way she had taken his face between her hands and let her fingers trace the deep scar that ran right down his face. She hadn't shuddered or drawn back but, fool that he was, he had pushed her away.

Tonight, it had merely been a warm smile when he'd left. He'd wanted to take her in his arms, hold her close, and tell her how much he loved her. He wanted her to know that he longed to be able to take care of her, and her two little girls.

If only she'd let him help her as he longed to do, then he'd make sure they wanted for nothing. He would enjoy it because he was sure that it would bring him the happiness that had been missing from his life ever since he'd had to leave Ferndale.

Chapter Seventeen

It was Friday again, the first Friday in May 1920, and Gaynor was looking forward to Barri's weekly meeting. So, too, was Sara, who not only enjoyed having him read a story to her before she went to sleep but also eagerly anticipated the new treat he always brought with him.

'I wonder what it will be this time?' she asked her mother as she helped her to put out the cutlery for the evening meal. 'Last week it was a new book for me and a cuddly bunny for Rachael, and the week before that it was a big Easter egg each and they were in a mug that had our name on it.'

'Yes, well, that was a special present because it was Easter,' Gaynor reminded her. 'You shouldn't expect a present every time Barri comes, you know.'

'Why not? He always brings us one.'

'Yes, I know he does, and it is very kind of him, but you still mustn't expect him to do so. He doesn't have to, and I don't want you feeling disappointed if he arrives without one.'

'I know that!' Sara told her scornfully. 'It's because he likes me and Rachael. Perhaps when he gets to like you a bit more he'll bring you a present,' she added thoughtfully.

Gaynor tried not to laugh. Barri had left her in no doubt that he liked her a great deal, but she suspected that, like herself, he was so happy with the situation at the moment, that he didn't want to spoil everything by rushing things.

There were times when she wished that he would say something about his feelings. If everything was out in the open then she'd be able to scotch the winks and innuendoes that she had to tolerate all the time from Thomas and Dylan.

Each week, the minute they'd all finished their meal, the two of them enacted the same ritual about going to the pub for a drink. They never failed to joke that they were only doing it so that she and Barri could be alone, although they all knew quite well that it was their normal practice to go for a drink on Friday night because it was payday and they had money in their pockets.

She knew their comments irritated Barri and she found it increasingly embarrassing, yet she didn't know how to stop them from making them. It was not the only time that Thomas, especially, rubbed her up the wrong way. She often wondered if she should ask either Bevan or Barri to have a word with them about their snide, suggestive remarks.

She kept putting off doing so because she didn't want to involve Bevan if she could help it. Since he was living under the same roof as Thomas and Dylan she was worried in case it caused an unpleasant atmosphere. She was reluctant to involve Barri because she was sure it would bring taunts and even more embarrassing implications from Thomas about their relationship.

She was also well aware that although Dylan was the quiet one of the pair, he supported Thomas in everything he said or did. She often caught them exchanging looks before Thomas said something that she found far too personal or even impertinent.

Since losing one of them would automatically mean both of them packing their bags and going, she kept quiet because she couldn't afford to lose their money. She talked to them as little as possible so as to give them no opportunity to become too friendly with her. Even though they paid her regularly, it was still difficult to make ends meet – not only because of the rent, but also because of the additional heavy drain on her resources to pay off the arrears she owed.

At first she had hoped that Sandy Peterson would be caught and would be made to make good the money he had stolen, and so her debt would vanish. But as the weeks became months and there was no news about him at all, she realised it wasn't going to happen. Saratina, who was still very bitter about being jilted by him, told her she was a fool to ever think he might be caught.

'Even if he was,' she pointed out, 'the Tramways would have first cut, so you wouldn't stand a chance! There were half a dozen conductresses who also lost money because of him,' she reminded Gaynor. 'He was supposed to be putting some of their wages into a savings club, but instead he kept it for himself.'

Gaynor tried to talk to Saratina about Thomas, but she didn't take it very seriously.

'Tell him to shut up or you'll boot him out,' she advised.

'I can't afford to do that,' Gaynor pointed out, 'I need his money each week to pay off the rent arrears.'

'He doesn't need to know that. He's got a cushy billet here, what with his meals and his washing and mending all done for him so he won't want to have to go looking for somewhere else. He knows it wouldn't be half as good, so call his bluff. Make him toe the line, it's your house; he's only a lodger.'

Gaynor knew that Saratina was right, and she wished she had the courage to do as her friend told her, but she felt far too nervous to confront Thomas.

As it was, things came to a head without any intervention on her part. When it did, though, much as she had feared, she lost not one lodger, but two.

Gaynor knew that on at least two occasions Thomas had seen money passing between

207

herself and Barri, and the look on his face had been a mixture of curiosity and sneering.

What exactly he thought was taking place she wasn't sure, but knowing Thomas and his frequent unpleasant insinuations, she was determined to find some other way of handing over the money each week to Barri.

'In future, I'll put it in an envelope and put it into your coat pocket as I hang it up when you arrive,' she told him, and explained her reason.

Barry frowned. 'You're making it look all the more suspicious if he sees you doing that,' he argued.

'That's the whole point; he won't see me do it. I'll have the money in an envelope in my apron pocket, and as I hang your coat on the peg in the hall, I'll slip it into the inside pocket.'

'Very well, if that's what you want to do,' he agreed. 'I'd sooner tell Thomas outright that it's no business of his and at the same time tell him to stop making all these suggestive jokes he seems to enjoy so much. He's a nasty, slimy little bloke, and I think it would be a good idea if you got rid of him.' He held up a hand as she was about to interrupt him. 'I know you can't do without the rent he pays you, but I am sure you will be able to find someone else, a married couple, perhaps, if Dylan goes as well.'

Although she tried to be very discreet about putting the money in Barri's pocket she felt alarmed a couple of weeks later when he claimed it wasn't there. She immediately suspected that Thomas might have discovered what she was doing and was playing a joke on them by removing it.

Barri was not amused when Gaynor put this forward as a possibility.

'I definitely put the envelope in your coat pocket,' she told him. 'If I couldn't pay it, then I would have told you so. I haven't missed a single payment since you arranged it.'

'I know, and that's why I'm so annoyed,' he told her. 'I am well aware how difficult it must be for you to find it every week and that's why I am so angry about him playing such a silly prank.'

'That's if he has taken it.'

'Well, where else has it gone? Both the children are in bed and they couldn't reach up to take anything out of my pocket. Bevan is hardly likely to do a thing like that! Anyway, he was already sitting at the table when I arrived and I saw him go straight upstairs to his room after we finished our meal, like he always does.'

It was almost eleven o'clock before Thomas and Dylan arrived home. They were both singing and Dylan stumbled against the wall as they jostled each other through the front door.

'Duw anwyl! I've never seen them like this before,' Gaynor exclaimed in astonishment.

'Be careful what you say to them,' Barri warned. 'They're both fighting drunk. Heaven knows how much they've had.'

As the two men lurched into the kitchen demanding a cup of tea and something to eat, Thomas was suddenly violently sick all over the floor.

The smell was horrendous and both Gaynor and Barri recoiled. Hastily he pushed her back into the passageway and closed the door on what was happening in the kitchen.

The general noise and pandemonium brought Bevan out of his room. He stood at the top of the stairs calling down to know what was happening. Simultaneously, the two girls woke up and Sara began calling out for Gaynor.

'You go on upstairs and try and calm her down,' Barri told her. 'I'll try and deal with these two. Bevan, I could do with some help down here,' he called up the stairs and waited for the older man to come down.

The two men looked at each other with raised eyebrows as the noise of retching, followed by violent groans, came repeatedly from the kitchen.

'Come on now, lads,' Bevan said calmly as he pushed open the door. 'You're scaring the life out of those two small girls with all your noise and the stench in here is overpowering. What about one of you boyos clearing this mess up?'

'Why don't you bugger off back upstairs, old man, and mind your own bloody business,' Thomas exclaimed between a spate of violent hiccups.

Bevan ignored him. 'Dylan, you'd better open that back door and let this boyo out into the yard before he spews up again,' he ordered firmly.

Dylan staggered to stand up so that he could do as he'd been asked, but his legs were so unsteady that he had to catch hold of one of the shelves to steady himself, and as he did so, he swept a whole pile of dishes on to the floor.

Thomas rocked with laughter then tried to clamp his hand over his mouth before being violently sick again.

'Dammo di! This is a terrible state of affairs, mun,' Bevan muttered, running his hand over his chin and frowning at Barri.

'I certainly agree! I can't leave Gaynor and those two children in the house with these two hooligans, that's quite certain,' Barri said worriedly.

'Don't worry about that, mun, I'll be here! I'll look out for her and see she comes to no harm,' Bevan promised.

'Yes, I know you will, Bevan, but I'm still not sure that you'd be able to deal with them on your own; not while they are in this drunken state. What would happen if both of them turned rough at the same time?'

'That's true, I suppose,' Bevan agreed reluctantly. 'I'm not as fit as I used to be,' he admitted. 'Age taking its toll, I suppose,' he added with a wry smile.

It was the early hours of the morning before

Thomas and Dylan quietened down and Bevan and Barri between them had managed to restore order to the kitchen and clean the place up to the best of their ability.

They had refused to let Gaynor help and wanted her to go on up to bed and try to get some sleep, but she had insisted on staying in the living room. When she finally saw the state of the kitchen and all the smashed dishes, she was in tears.

Thomas and Dylan had both taken themselves off upstairs to sleep off their hangovers, so Gaynor made a pot of tea and insisted that Bevan stayed and drank a cup with them.

'What I don't understand,' he said, looking puzzled, 'is where those two boyos got the money from to get as sozzled as they did. Both of them told me they'd lost heavily on the horses today and after they'd handed over what they owed to a chap at work they said they'd have barely enough left for their lodgings.'

Gaynor and Barri exchanged glances and when Gaynor gave him an almost imperceptible nod Barri said, 'Well, I think we may know where they got some extra money from.'

Bevan listened in silence as Barri told him about the money that was missing from his coat pocket.

'You see, the reason Barri comes here on a Friday is to collect my rent money to save me having to walk all the way up to the Hayes with it so late at night,' Gaynor explained. 'We

212

were at school together, that is why he is being so helpful,' she added quickly, in case Bevan wondered about such an arrangement.

'Did either of those two boyos know about all this?' Bevan asked, looking worried.

'I think so.' Gaynor nodded thoughtfully. 'I'm pretty sure that a couple of weeks ago Thomas saw me passing money over to Barri. At the time he pretended not to take any notice, but I think he worked out what was happening and why Barri was coming round here every Friday night.'

'And you say that some money went missing from your coat pocket tonight, Barri?'

Barri nodded. 'Gaynor always takes my coat from me when I arrive, and she's started slipping an envelope containing the money into the inside pocket as she hangs it up.'

'Then it looks very much as if that is what's happened,' Bevan agreed. 'One of them took the money. So what are you going to do about it?'

'Chuck both of them out as soon as they sober up in the morning,' Barri said emphatically.

'Perhaps we should see if they can explain first,' Gaynor said hesitantly. 'Otherwise I'll be losing both my lodgers before I have a chance to get any new ones.'

'Better that than have those two reprobates living under your roof,' Bevan growled. 'Don't worry, cariad, I'll put the word around down at the shipyard and I'm pretty sure you'll have a couple of new lodgers in next to no time.' He stood up. 'Thank you for the tea. Now, I'm off to my bed.'

'Thank you for all your help tonight, Bevan,' Barri told him, holding out his hand to the older man and shaking it heartily, 'it was greatly appreciated.'

Gaynor and Barri sat without speaking until they heard the click of the lock as Bevan closed his bedroom door.

'Do you really think we should tell Thomas and Dylan to go?' Gaynor asked worriedly as she poured out another cup of tea for herself and Barri.

'I most certainly do! In fact, I'm not leaving here until I see them packed and out of the house.'

Her face clouded as she ran a hand through her hair. 'What about the rent and the arrears? I'm going to have to owe it for this week and if I don't find any new lodgers right away, then I won't be able to pay next week either.'

'I've already told you that I'll take care of that, so don't worry about it,' Barri said firmly. He took one of her hands and held it between both of his own. 'Your safety and that of the two girls is more important than owing a couple of weeks' rent,' he told her very emphatically.

'It's all very well for you to say that,' she argued, 'but I've been in trouble once over getting into arrears, and I don't want the worry of that all over again.'

'I've already said I will take care of it! There won't be any problem, I promise you. Now, why don't you go on up to bed and try and get some sleep.'

She looked at him uncertainly. 'What are you going to do? The trams will have stopped running a long time ago so you won't be able to get home.'

'I've no intention of going home and leaving you here on your own while those two scoundrels are still in your house. I'll make myself comfortable in the armchair, probably doze off for an hour or two, and then as soon as it's daylight I'll get those two young devils up and send them packing. The best thing you can do is to stay upstairs in your bedroom with the girls and try and ignore any noise or commotion going on down here.'

Chapter Eighteen

Although Barri had been so confident that Gaynor would have no difficulty in finding new occupants for her big middle room, it was still empty three weeks later. Several men had asked about it, but either they couldn't afford to pay the sort of rent she was asking or they didn't like the idea of having to share with someone.

Barri told her not to worry, and that he was quite prepared to pay both her rent and the arrears till she found some new lodgers, but Gaynor wasn't happy about this.

'I'll give it another few days and then perhaps I'd better try reducing the rent. Perhaps we can come to some arrangement where I don't have to pay you quite so much each week off the arrears?' she suggested. 'I know it will mean that it will take me a lot longer to pay them off,' she added with a forced smile, 'but the mess I'm in now, and all the money I already owe you, I won't be free of debt for years to come anyway.'

Barri drew in his breath sharply. He wasn't sure if this was the right moment to speak out and offer Gaynor a permanent solution to her problem.

Although he'd thought of nothing else since she had come back into his life, he still hadn't resolved exactly what to say to her. If he expressed himself badly, he would ruin everything, he thought morosely.

He wanted to be sure that she understood that there were no strings attached to his offer. Yet, it was equally important that he didn't make it sound so much a business set up that she wouldn't know what his true feelings were.

For him, meeting up with Gaynor again was like a dream come true, but was it the same for her? Even though she always seemed pleased to see him when he came to Eleanor Place on a Friday night, he wasn't sure why. Was it purely politeness because they'd been friends for most of their lives, or was it relief because she didn't have to trek all the way up to the Hayes, pushing that huge pram with both of the girls in it?

He admired the way she had struggled to be independent but he could see that it was becoming more than she could manage, even if she didn't realise this herself.

Each time he saw her she seemed to be thinner and her frown more pronounced. Sometimes, he sensed that she was so tired that it took her all her time to be patient with Sara when the child insisted that it was too early for bed because it still wasn't dark, or made some other trivial excuse in an attempt to stay up.

Although Sara was nothing at all like her

mother in looks and colouring, her cute antics and facial expressions reminded Barri so much of Gaynor when she'd been younger.

She had Gaynor's turn of phrase, the same cheeky audacity, and her ability to raise a smile even when she was being scolded all brought back memories of their days together in Ferndale.

Perhaps, he reflected, that was why he was so fond of Sara, although he was becoming equally attached to little Rachael. Three years younger, she was a much more placid child than Sara. She had dark hair and eyes like Gaynor, but her round face and chubby little arms and legs had a delicate olive glow, obviously inherited from her Spanish father.

He thought he'd had a hard life but Gaynor seemed to have fared far worse than he had. She'd certainly been unlucky in her love life and he wondered if her heart had been broken too many times for her to risk letting herself ever fall in love again. If only it was possible to turn the clock back and provide her with all the happiness he had promised her when they had been young.

As Gaynor dished out their meal that Friday evening, and he started eating the fish pie that was more potato than fish, he asked himself for the hundredth time should he chance it, was this the right time to offer Gaynor a way out of her predicament?

He waited until the meal was over, the table

cleared, and Bevan, as usual, had gone off upstairs to his room. Avoiding her eyes as she passed him a cup of tea, he said as calmly as he could, 'There is a way to solve your problem, you know.'

'Go on, what's that?' she looked at him expectantly.

He stirred his tea vigorously, still avoiding her eyes. 'You could give up this place ...'

'Oh yes? And do what?' she asked quizzically. 'Are you going to suggest that I should camp out in a shop doorway, or live on a barge on the Glamorgan Canal?'

He gave a tight smile. 'No, I was thinking that you could move into my place.'

'Really!' Gaynor took a sip of her tea, trying to calm her excitement; willing herself to be cautious. 'That sounds fine, but where will you live?' she demanded as she carefully replaced her cup on the saucer, hoping that Barri wouldn't notice how much her hand was shaking.

'I wasn't planning on moving out. It's a four-bedroomed house, so it is much bigger than this place, which means you could have your own rooms,' he went on quickly. 'You wouldn't have to see me at all if you didn't want to.'

She looked at him with raised eyebrows.

'I mean it,' he went on hurriedly, stumbling over the words in his eagerness. 'I go out first thing in the morning and I don't usually get home again until seven o'clock at night, especially on a Friday, and ...'

He stopped. He could see she was laughing. He breathed more easily. At least she wasn't annoyed by his suggestion, he thought with relief.

'Not a very flattering way of asking me to move in with you, is it, Barri?' she teased. 'Whatever happened to that romantic boyo I knew in Ferndale?'

'He lost his charm along with his looks by the sound of it,' he remarked with some exasperation. He drained his cup and put his cup and saucer back on the table. 'I'm afraid I've put it rather badly, haven't I!' He laughed awkwardly. 'I was trying to make it clear to you that it could be a strictly business arrangement – if that was what you wanted.'

'Why, is that the way you would like it to be?' Gaynor asked softly, her eyes unwavering as they met his.

He shrugged self-consciously, running a finger down the scar of his puckered cheek. 'I can't really hope for anything more than that, now can I?' he said grimly. 'What woman would want a man who looked like I do? I've got a face like a gargoyle or some grotesque character on a Toby jug.'

'Don't forget about your limp; you've forgotten to mention that,' Gaynor chuckled softly.

Barri's face hardened. 'No, I haven't forgotten about that! I'm hardly likely to do so. Peg leg Pete, that's me all right; all I need is a parrot on my shoulder and I could get a job in a circus,' he snapped.

Suddenly Gaynor's teasing and laughter turned to tears; her arms were around his neck and her lips on his. 'You stupid fool, how silly you are,' she said fiercely. 'I've wanted to hear you say you still care for me and returned the feelings I have for you from the moment I walked into your office. I told you then and I'm telling you again now, I'm not in the least bit concerned about the scar on your face. To me you are still the handsome boyo I was head over heels in love with when I was growing up. No one has ever truly replaced you in my heart and they never will . . .'

'No one will ever stand a chance of doing so from this moment on, cariad,' he told her triumphantly as his arms tightened around her and his mouth claimed hers.

'And will you promise that if I move in with you then you won't hide away in the attic, or wherever it was you were planning to take refuge?'

'Of course I will. It's not usual for a husband to do that, is it?' he asked with affected seriousness.

'Husband?' her eyes widened. She pulled away and stared at him intently, as if trying to convince herself that he wasn't joking.

'After what you've said about the way you feel about me, surely you don't think I'd let you move into my house unless you did agree to marry me,' he said with mock severity.

As she nestled back into his arms he said

tenderly, 'Do you remember all the things we planned when we were growing up? We made up our minds while we were still at school that we were going to be married and have a home of our own.'

'Yes, and we even planned the sort of house we would live in.' She sighed. 'I really can't believe that after all this time it is going to come true. Do you know, I don't even know where you live, Barri!'

'Then the very first thing we must do is go there so that you can see if you and the girls like it and think you will be happy living there. It's in Roath, not very far from the park, and there's a school only a couple of streets away, so it will be ideal when Sara starts school in September.'

'I wonder what Sara is going to make of all this?' she mused. 'What are we going to tell her – about us, I mean.'

'She seems to like me well enough,' he said confidently. 'She still calls me the man with the funny face, so she might even like the idea that I am going to be her dad.'

Gaynor nodded. 'She talks of nothing else especially on a Friday; she can't wait for you to come and tell her a bedtime story.'

'We'll also have to explain to Bevan and give him time to make other arrangements.'

'Unless we invite Bevan to come and live with us.'

'You don't want to do that, do you?' Barri frowned.

'No, of course I don't,' Gaynor agreed. 'But I wouldn't like to leave Bevan homeless, not after the way he's always been so kind and helpful.'

'It shouldn't be too difficult for him to get fixed up. If he can't, well, there is a very small box room, so I suppose he could have that as a temporary measure.'

When they told Bevan of their plans he said he was very pleased for them, but that he'd rather not go with them.

'It would be too much of a journey from Roath to East Moors for me each day, boyo,' he explained to Barri. 'Give me a week or two to sort myself out if you can, and I'm sure I'll be settled in somewhere else by then.'

'There's no rush,' Barri assured him, 'so make sure you find something suitable. It's going to take me a couple of weeks or so to make the arrangements for me and Gaynor to be married. It'll be in a register office, by the way, so I was wondering if you'd like to come along and be a witness?'

Bevan smiled broadly. 'I'd be honoured, boyo!' He held out his hand and shook Barri's firmly. 'I'd like nothing better. She's a lovely lady, is Gaynor, and you're a lucky fella, mun!'

Gaynor and Barri were married on a lovely summer day at the beginning of July 1920. The war was over and though a flu epidemic was still raging throughout Europe, and there had even been deaths from it in Cardiff, Gaynor and Barri considered the future was bright and they were both full of optimism.

Bevan Powell, looking spruce in the navy blue suit he'd hired for the occasion, along with Rhys Downes who was Barri's boss at the letting agency, acted as the two witnesses.

Gaynor wore a cream voile dress under a light blue linen coat and a flower-trimmed blue straw cloche hat. Sara, wearing a pretty light blue muslin dress trimmed with cream lace, and Rachael, in a pale pink muslin dress trimmed with blue smocking, stood beside her holding hands and looking adorable.

Afterwards they all enjoyed a leisurely meal at a restaurant in St Mary Street. Sara chattered away like a little magpie, keeping them all entertained, but little Rachael was so worn out with all the excitement that she fell asleep on Gaynor's lap long before they'd all finished eating.

After saying goodbye to Bevan and Rhys Downes and inviting them both to come and visit them some time in the future, Gaynor, Barri and the two girls went back to Barri's house, their new home.

As they alighted from the tram, Barri carrying the sleeping Rachael and Gaynor holding Sara's hand, Gaynor felt as if she was in a trance. The husband she had always dreamed of having, two lovely little girls and a comfortably furnished home erased all the problems of the past.

Her only regret was that neither of them had invited any of their own family, or indeed even told them about their marriage. She had been tempted to do so, but after she and Barri had discussed it at great length, and she had told him about what had happened when she had gone to Ferndale with the two children, he had decided that it was better if they didn't.

In his case, he explained, it would probably cause his mother more distress. As far as she was concerned he had vanished and he felt it was best for things to remain that way rather than for her to see him so disfigured.

In her heart, Gaynor didn't think this was true. She was sure that his mother would be overjoyed to know that he was alive and well. Whether he was disfigured or not he was still her son, but she remained silent, not wishing to argue with him since he felt so adamant about it.

From now on he wanted them to forget the past completely, to start a new life. They had their own family, Sara and Rachael, and so he felt that they ought to put the ghosts of the past out of their minds completely.

The minute they walked through the front door Sara dashed upstairs to the bedroom she was to share with Rachael. Barri had promised them both a new doll each and she was eager to see what hers was like. He had said that it would be sitting on their bed waiting for them when they returned home after the ceremony as long as they'd behaved themselves. Her shout of delight when she found it could be heard right through the house.

'Look, Mam, look!' Her excited cry brought a smile to both Barri's and Gaynor's faces. 'Look, Mam,' she yelled again as she burst into the living room. 'My new doll's got a dress exactly the same as mine . . . and it looks like me. Its got fair hair and blue eyes!'

'Was there one for Rachael as well?' her mother asked as the child she was still holding stirred, opened her eyes, and then reached out a hand to take the new doll.

Sara quickly pulled it back out of her reach. 'I don't know; shall I go and look?'

'You'd better, since you don't seem to want her to play with yours,' Gaynor pointed out.

Sara hesitated for a moment; then, her face serious, she carefully sat her new doll down on a chair and ran back into the hallway. 'Don't let Rachael touch it while I'm gone, will you?' she called as she scampered up the stairs.

Sara returned in a matter of minutes with an identical-sized doll, except that this one had dark hair and eyes and was wearing a pink dress with blue smocking and a blue sash tied round the middle.

'It looks like Rachael and it's dressed the same as her,' she announced with satisfaction.

'Well, now, isn't that lucky; it means that you will always be able to tell them apart and there will be no squabbling over them.' Gaynor smiled.

Sara nodded seriously then climbed up on Barri's lap and planted a big wet thank-you kiss on his cheek. 'I'm not going to call you funny face any more,' she announced solemnly, 'I'm going to call you Daddy.'

Chapter Nineteen

Gaynor checked the date on the calendar; in three weeks' time it would be 1 March 1929 and Sara's fourteenth birthday. She'd been just five years old when they'd moved to Bangor Street, and she and Barri had been married for almost nine years.

Barri had lost his job at the letting agency quite soon after their wedding when the agency had been forced to close because of financial problems and for several months they'd despaired of him ever getting another one. To make ends meet, she'd had to go out charring while he stayed home and looked after Sara and Rachael. It hadn't been too bad because by then Sara had started school and Rachael had been a very placid toddler.

Although Barri didn't seem to mind looking after the two children he'd been very depressed because he was convinced that no one would ever want to employ him because of his facial disfigurement and the fact that he walked with a limp.

Then their luck had changed. He found a new job in the housing department of the City Hall and in so many ways it was a hundred times better than his last one. A couple of years ago he had been promoted to the position of assistant manager and there was every possibility that he'd be made manager before it was time for him to retire.

He'd grown to love Cardiff and he was so proud to be working in its finest building and playing such an important part in the way the City Corporation housed its citizens.

Generally speaking, Gaynor decided they'd been happy, fulfilling years, and her love for Barri, and his for her, had never waned; if anything, their love had deepened. He had been a strong dependable father to both Sara and Rachael as well as to his own daughter, Keris, who was now seven. Gaynor's eyes misted as she recalled the joy and fulfilment her birth had brought them both.

Like all families there had been the usual ups and downs. The girls had contracted the usual childhood illnesses and there had been one or two minor accidents resulting in cuts and bruises, but life had been so busy that the time had flown.

There had been a great many changes in Cardiff since the war had ended. It seemed a lifetime ago since she and Saratina Vario had been conductresses while the men had been away fighting. Now, even the trams they had worked on together were being replaced by motor buses.

In 1926 the General Strike had caused a

massive disruption for about six days. Miners from the Rhondda had come to Cardiff in droves carrying placards demanding more money and better conditions in an attempt to draw attention to the hardships they were suffering.

As they marched through the centre of the city she couldn't help wondering if any of them were from Ferndale and perhaps had been at school with either herself or Barri.

Two years ago she had taken all three girls along to watch King George V perform the opening ceremony at the National Museum of Wales. Afterwards, accompanied by Barri, they had gone round it and seen all the incredible wonders on display.

The sensation this year was the first talking pictures which were being shown at the Queen's Cinema in Queen Street, and although Sara didn't yet know about it, that was to be her birthday treat. As a special outing they were taking all three girls along to see *The Jazz Singer*, a full-length talking film starring Al Jolson. Gaynor knew Sara and Rachael would love it, but she was a bit worried that it might be a little too grown-up for Keris.

There would also be a birthday party at home for Sara and her friends. Rachael and Keris had been busy planning all sorts of surprises to make it really special. In fact, they were looking forward to it almost as much as Sara was, and she had said that both of them could invite one of their friends along as well.

Sara was quite grown-up for fourteen. She was tall and well developed and with her lovely thick blonde hair that was so long and silky and her big clear blue eyes she was a real heart-breaker. When she'd been little she had been a real chatterbox, but these days she was rather haughty and reserved; almost cold sometimes. She had such a cool, calculating stare when you asked her a question, or told her to do something, that Gaynor frequently found that it was quite intimidating.

She was very bright at school and quick to learn. There had been times when they'd thought it might be a good idea for her to train to be a teacher, but Sara had turned down their suggestion.

'I wouldn't have the patience to be bothered with young children. I want to work in a really posh office; perhaps in the accounts department at the City Hall.'

She had been so insistent about this that in the end Gaynor had persuaded Barri to find out if there were any openings. Eventually he had arranged for her to start work as a junior in the treasurer's department as soon as she left school.

When he had told Sara she had given a smug, self-satisfied smile as she thanked him. She would be starting there after the holidays and as a birthday present she'd asked for new clothes that would look right for work.

'I want to choose them myself,' she told her

231

mother. 'Perhaps we could have a trip to James Howell's department store, just the two of us. They have some very smart skirts and dresses displayed in the window that are exactly the sort of thing I want.'

'At very smart prices, if I know anything about it,' Gaynor protested. 'What's wrong with the Bon Marche or one of the smaller shops in one of the Arcades?'

'You'll be asking me to pick up a bargain off one of the stalls on the Hayes open market next,' Sara argued. 'The new clothes will be my birthday present, remember?'

'I know that,' Gaynor agreed, 'all I'm saying is that Howell's is the most expensive shop in Cardiff and I think we should have a look round first.'

'Perhaps I should have asked Dad, not you,' Sara told her icily. 'I'm sure he won't want me turning up at the City Hall looking like a poor relation.'

Barri laughed when Gaynor related their conversation to him later that evening when they were alone. 'I suppose we'd better humour her. All the juniors are very stylish so she's probably scared to death of looking out of place on her first day,'

'Not her! She's brimming with confidence! In fact, I sometimes think she's too big for her boots these days,' Gaynor retorted exasperatedly.

It wasn't the first time that Sara had used the

divide and conquer technique to get her own way. Ever since she'd been quite young, if one parent turned down her request then she found a reason to ask the other, not even admitting that she had already made the request and been turned down.

There was a cold analytical side to her which worried Gaynor. Frequently she detected the shrewd tenacity that her own father had admired so much in Konrad Claus and it sent uneasy shivers through her.

As far as possible she avoided mentioning either Konrad Claus or Pedro Vario who had been Rachael's father. She wasn't even sure that either girl knew about them. They had both been so young when she and Barri had married that she had never thought it advisable to go into any details about their different parentage because it was all so very complicated.

Now that Sara was older, though, it was obvious that she was aware that Barri was not her or Rachael's real father, if only because their colouring and Keris's were so completely different.

Several years ago, after Saratina had been to see them, she had asked why Rachael looked so like her.

At the time, because she'd had no ready answer, Gaynor had ducked the question and changed the subject. She knew that Sara had been far from satisfied and often caught her closely studying both Rachael and Keris as if checking out the differences between herself and them.

Sara knew, of course, that Barri was Keris's dad because she had been seven years old when Keris was born and had helped look after her when she had been a baby. She'd enjoyed rocking her cradle, and she had insisted that Rachael, who had only been four years old, should sing the baby to sleep.

'Why don't you do it,' Rachael would protest.

'Because I can't sing, silly, and you can.'

That was true, Gaynor thought with an inward smile. Sara had a voice like a corncrake while even from the time she was about two years old Rachael had been possessed of a sweetly pretty voice. She was always singing nursery rhymes and simple songs to her dolls when the other two were not there.

Sara's talent lay in organising her two sisters, bossing them around and making sure they did as they were told. She was meticulously neat and tidiness was an obsession with her. She always insisted on putting things away in their right place.

There had been so many rows because Rachael was the exact opposite and no matter how Sara tried to organise the bedroom they shared the result was always ruined due to Rachael's untidiness.

In the end, in order to maintain peace in the home, Gaynor had suggested that perhaps it would be better if Sara moved into the small bedroom that had been Keris's nursery ever since she was born and let Keris be the one to share with Rachael.

Looking very smug, Sara promised to think about it. Barri hadn't approved. He had thought it was better for Sara and Rachael to continue to share so that Rachael could learn how to be tidy.

'Sara will soon drill her into doing it,' he said. 'Anyway, have you asked Keris what she feels about it? She always has had a room to herself and she might prefer to be on her own.'

Sara overheard their exchange and told him calmly that she had definitely decided that she wanted to have a room to herself and that it was time he stopped favouring Keris simply because she was his daughter.

Taken aback, Barri assured her he wasn't showing Keris any preference. 'I'm your dad as well as Keris's,' he reminded her.

'I know you look after us and you let us live in your house, but you are not really my dad . . . or Rachael's,' she said coldly.

'I don't think you know what you are saying,' Barri told her calmly. Inwardly he felt both hurt and shocked by Sara's words.

'Oh, yes I do,' she retorted, standing soldier straight and holding his gaze defiantly. 'We were already born when you met Mam. I was five and Rachel was two years old when you and mam got married and we moved here.'

Before Barri could think of a suitable answer

she added triumphantly, 'You've only got to look at us to see we are not your children; we're not a bit like you.'

After that, Barri had persuaded Gaynor that the time had come to have a quiet talk with Sara and explain who her dad was and what had happened to him.

It had taken Gaynor quite a long time to do so, because she had put it off for as long as she could. When she finally did explain to Sara that her dad had come from Germany and that he'd had to go back there when the war had broken out, Sara had stared at her in silence. For several weeks afterwards she was in a mood and refused to talk to either Gaynor or Barri.

Rachael had been about seven years old when Gaynor heard Sara telling her that she wasn't her real sister and that was why they didn't look a bit alike. Gaynor had wasted no time in taking Rachael aside and explaining to her about Pedro.

'He was Saratina's brother,' she said gently, 'that's why you look so very much like her.'

'Did he sing?' Rachael asked softly.

'Yes, he had a beautiful voice and he played a guitar.' Gaynor smiled.

The next Christmas they bought Rachael a little guitar and she was never happier than when she was strumming away on it and singing little songs, usually ones she'd made up herself.

After that the questions and the teasing had

stopped, but occasionally Gaynor sensed that there was an icy barrier between Sara and the rest of the family. There were times when she seemed to be studying them intently, as if she was analysing the differences between them. If one of them spoke to her she either ignored them completely or was snappy and irritable.

By comparison, Keris was a little angel. She was warm, lovable and amenable. Gaynor sometimes had to agree with the two older girls that Barri spoiled her or showed her favouritism, but she understood and never voiced it aloud.

He was so proud of her, and never stopped commenting on the likeness there was between Gaynor and Keris, and how Gaynor had looked and behaved when she'd been that age. It was easy to see that without a shadow of doubt Keris was the culmination of all his dreams.

In so many ways Gaynor felt the same way, but she did her best to avoid letting it show. She tried to treat all three girls exactly the same and to ensure that they knew she loved them all the same as each other. When they had been younger it had been fairly simple. They didn't seem to mind that their dresses were handed down from one to the other, or to grumble if their hairstyles were similar.

Lately, though, the pattern seemed to have changed. Sara was determined to choose her own clothes and her style was not in the least suitable for either Rachel or Keris.

When Gaynor mentioned this to Barri he smiled understandingly. 'She'll soon be earning her own money so I think you will have to let her develop her own taste. I don't think you need worry that she will go to extremes. She is very prim and proper and doesn't seem to think much of the latest flapper styles.'

'Not for work, perhaps, especially when she knows we are paying for them, but if we don't exercise some control over her you never know what she will buy.'

Worrying about how Sara dressed, or even how she spent her money, proved to be the least of their problems.

Sara had only been working at the City Hall for about three months when trouble flared. They thought she had settled in because she seemed to enjoy her work. Furthermore, she had already enrolled at night school and was studying hard so that she could take an examination that would give her the necessary qualifications for possible promotion.

It was Barri, not Sara, who told Gaynor about the problem. It had reached his ears that some of the other juniors had been teasing Sara about the way her dad looked and limped as he walked. At first she had apparently tried to ignore them, or defended him. Finally, in order to stop their taunts, she'd told everybody that he wasn't her real father anyway.

Her outburst had raised prying questions from his colleagues and he had been forced to admit that what she said was quite true. He pointed out that he had brought her up since she'd been five years old and had always regarded her exactly the same as if she was his own child.

'I think another quiet talk with Sara is on the cards so that we can try and sort this out,' he told Gaynor.

They were both hurt and astonished when she declared that she didn't want to go on working at the City Hall and, what was more, she intended to go to Germany and look for her real father.

They both tried to reason with her but Sara refused to listen to either of them or to let the matter drop. In a hard, determined voice she said that if Gaynor wouldn't help her to trace him then she would run away and find him herself.

'You're talking utter nonsense,' Gaynor told her. 'Germany is a vast country and I've no idea where he lives. What is more, he doesn't even know you exist. He didn't know I was expecting a baby when he went home.'

Far from making Sara abandon the idea, this information only seemed to spur her on. A few weeks into 1930 Gaynor found a note pinned on to her pillow which read in block letters:

GONE TO FIND MY DAD.
DON'T COME LOOKING FOR ME.

Chapter Twenty

Gaynor was beside herself with worry about Sara's absence. She kept saying over and over again what a foolish girl Sara was and listing all the dangers she might encounter.

'How can she possibly think she can get to Germany when she has no money? She'll be back home again in a day or two,' Barri assured her.

As the days passed and she didn't return and there was no news about her he became as uneasy as Gaynor was but in a different way. He was much more concerned about the political state of Germany and that Sara might be mistaken for a spy, and this only added to Gaynor's distress.

'She'll never manage to get there because she hasn't the money for her fare. She's taken her post office savings book, but there're only a couple of pounds in it. Since she started work she's spent her wages on clothes instead of saving them.'

'Perhaps she'll stow away on a boat, that's what I would do,' Rachael told them.

'Stop talking so silly,' Gaynor scolded, but she had to admit that it was a possibility she hadn't thought about.

The moment she and Barri were on their own that night Gaynor's first question was, 'Do you think we should go to the police and tell them that Sara is missing?'

'I've already done that, cariad,' Barri reminded her. 'I reported it a couple of days after she left home.'

'Did they take it seriously?'

Barri frowned. 'Of course they did! Why wouldn't they?'

'Oh, I don't know. What did you tell them exactly?'

Barri looked uncomfortable. 'The truth of course! I had to tell them that I wasn't her natural father and that as far as I knew he was living in Germany and that his name was Konrad Claus.'

'So what will that do? It's in another country.'

'Well, I suppose they'll contact the police over there. They must have ways and means of tracing criminals . . .'

'Sara's not a criminal,' Gaynor interrupted, angrily.

'No, I know that. I meant that they must be able to exchange information when they are trying to trace someone who has run away from their own country.'

'Perhaps you ought to tell them that she might have gone by boat, smuggled herself on board as a stowaway like Rachael said.'

'That's only Rachael being dramatic; you know how she tends to build things up and elaborate.'

241

'Yes, but she usually only does it when it means she can be the centre of attention.'

'It's still a possibility, though. It's about the only way she'd get there. It would be easier to do that than to try and get on a train. Even if she did get as far as the coast by train, she'd still have to go on a boat in order to cross the Channel to get to Germany. It would be much easier to go straight there on a cargo boat from here.'

Barri shook his head in bewilderment. 'I don't know what to think,' he admitted. 'How could she manage to do that without being spotted, that's what I don't understand?'

'Someone might have helped her,' Gaynor suggested.

'Who on earth would do that?'

'One of the crew? Sara's a very pretty girl, you know Barri, it wouldn't be difficult for her to get friendly with one of the sailors and ask him to smuggle her aboard.'

'It would be more than his job was worth; he'd be sacked on the spot.'

'That would only happen if he was found out. If he was a bit of a daredevil, he wouldn't think twice about the risk involved.'

Although they left no stone unturned a month later, when there was still no news of Sara, Gaynor reluctantly tried to resign herself to the situation.

'All we can hope is that when she manages to find Konrad Claus she gets in touch with us and lets us know she is all right,' Barri commented.

'Or comes home again because she fails to find him,' Gaynor said bitterly.

'Somehow I don't think she'll do that,' Barri said quietly. 'Sara would hate having to admit defeat because her venture was a waste of time. You know that she has always found it impossible to say "sorry" even when she is in the wrong.'

'I don't want her to say sorry; I just want her back safe and sound,' she said tearfully.

'I know, I know.' Barry patted her shoulder consolingly. 'I do understand how you feel, but for the sake of the other two we've got to try and carry on as normal.'

'If that's what you think is best,' Gaynor agreed tearfully, 'but I'll never give up hoping,' she added determinedly.

Without Sara in the house life seemed to be much quieter and calmer. The door to the small room that had been Sara's was kept tight shut. Once a week Gaynor went in there and tidied around. Each time she did so she checked every drawer and shelf in the vague hope that there might be some clue that would reveal that, unknown to them, she had been in touch with her father before she left home and it might give them some idea where she was.

Without Sara there to keep them in order both Rachael and Keris seemed to become more difficult to control. Rachael in particular was resentful when Gaynor started imposing restrictions on where she would let them go on their own.

'Just because Sara's skedaddled I don't see why we're been stopped from having fun,' Rachael argued when Gaynor not only insisted that they were to come straight home from school every night, but also stopped them from going to the park to play unless she was there to keep an eye on them.

Gaynor refused to change her mind; even when Rachael appealed to Barri.

'All my friends are laughing at me because I'm not allowed to go to the park with them unless Mam comes as well,' she protested, her huge dark eyes full of tears.

Barri understood Gaynor's reason for being so protective and backed her up. 'I'm sorry, Rachael, but neither you nor Keris are to go anywhere on your own,' he said firmly.

When Rachael came home and told them that she had been selected to take part in the end-of-term concert at school Gaynor still insisted that she could only stay late for rehearsals if either she or Barri came to meet her afterwards.

Rachael sulked, pouted and wheedled in an attempt to stop them doing this. 'You'll make me look so daft in front of all the others if you do that,' she protested, but they both told her that was the rule and she must keep to it.

Rachael stopped arguing when she realised that they were both adamant, but a couple of

244

weeks later they received a letter from her teacher, Miss Davis, requesting them to call and see her as she was having problems with Rachael.

'She has become extremely disruptive in class, and her school work has gone rapidly downhill,' Miss Davis told them. 'She always used to be near the top of the class in the weekly tests but these days she is usually bottom.'

'Perhaps it's because she's spending too much time rehearsing for this school concert,' Barri said mildly.

Miss Davis refused to even consider this was a possibility. 'Her work was already in decline and causing problems long before we started rehearsing,' she said stiffly.

'Then why didn't you let us know about it before now?' Gaynor questioned.

'I was hoping it was a temporary lapse of concentration; it does sometimes happen with girls of her age,' Miss Davis pointed out. 'In Rachael's case it has now gone on far too long. She is a lovely girl and I am concerned about her because as things stand at the moment her inattentiveness could ruin her chances of getting a worthwhile job when she leaves school. In fact, I would be reluctant to provide her with a reference under the circumstances.'

'We'll have a talk to her and try to find out why she has lost interest in her school work,' Barri promised as they shook hands and prepared to leave.

'She will never be quite as clever as her older sister, of course,' Miss Davis remarked as they reached the door. 'Sara was a very bright pupil! I understand she is working at the City Hall, so how is she getting on?'

Gaynor and Barri exchanged looks, and then Barri said quietly, 'You mean you haven't heard?'

Miss Davis frowned. 'No! What is it that I should have heard about Sara?'

'Sara ran away over a month ago,' Gaynor told her in a flat, tight voice. 'We are not sure where she is at the moment but we think she may be in Germany. She left a note to say she had gone to look for her father.'

'Oh dear! Well, this might be the problem that is affecting Rachael's work,' Miss Davis said thoughtfully. 'I'm sure she must be missing her sister.'

Again Gaynor and Barri looked at each other uncertainly. 'We are not too sure,' Barri admitted. 'Sara was certainly a strong influence on both Rachael and Keris, but they seemed to have accepted that she has gone away. As far as we can tell, neither of them is worried about it.'

Although Gaynor and Barri took Rachael to task about her lack of interest in her school work it didn't seem to worry her very much. She merely shrugged and explained dreamily that it was because she had been spending all her time learning and practising the solo she was going to sing in the school concert.

'Well, nice though it might be to be playing such an important part in the concert, you mustn't let it interfere with your school work,' Barri warned her. 'You do understand that, don't you?'

Rachael gave Barri one of her warm, wide smiles and assured him that she did and promised to try harder. She said it in such a light-hearted way, though, that neither he nor Gaynor held out much hope that she would do so.

Another big problem was that the summer holidays were imminent and Gaynor wondered how on earth she was going to manage to watch both Rachael and Keris every minute of the day once they broke up from school.

In the past she'd always been quite happy to let them go to Roath Park on their own as long as they promised to stay together. Sara, of course, had been there last year, Gaynor reflected, and she had never let the other two out of her sight. This year it was something she would have to do herself.

Planning what they would do every day for a whole month was a daunting task, Gaynor soon discovered. If the weather was warm and sunny then they wanted to be out of doors. Both of them resented the fact that they weren't allowed to go and play with their own particular friends.

'You can always invite them to join us in Roath Park,' Gaynor pointed out.

Keris quite liked this idea and asked if they

could take a picnic and then she'd ask her friends to bring one as well, but Rachael was quite scornful about the idea.

'My friends won't want to play with Keris and her lot,' she protested, tossing her thick dark hair in disdain. What's more they will want to do something more exciting than sit around on the grass and have a picnic.'

'Well, it needn't only be a picnic, you can play games afterwards,' Gaynor pointed out.

'With you sitting there watching us all the time and telling us not to make so much noise,' Rachael protested in a resentful voice.

Gaynor looked at her in despair. She didn't know this new Rachael. She was still the same dark-haired, dark-eyed beautiful child she had always been, but the warmth had gone out of her. In the past she had been smiling and lovable, but these days she was as prickly as a hedgehog.

'I tell you what,' Gaynor compromised in an attempt to smooth things over, 'what about us taking a picnic, but afterwards you and your friends do whatever you want to do?'

'Well, it won't be playing stupid childish games with Keris and her bunch,' Rachael told her. 'My friends prefer to sit and talk about things.'

'That's all right, you can sit and talk or you can play games; whichever you prefer to do.'

'If we sit and talk, then you will be able to listen in to all our secrets!' Rachael exclaimed in annoyance.

Gaynor shook her head and tried to hide her smile. What sort of secrets could they possibly have that they wouldn't want her to overhear, she wondered.

'No, I won't listen to what you are talking about,' she promised. 'All I ask is that you stay somewhere nearby so that I can keep an eye on you. If Keris doesn't want me to supervise her games then that's all right as well. I'll bring my sewing or read a book. Now, can we all agree on that?'

Keris was quite happy to go along with this arrangement and, rather reluctantly, Rachael accepted as well.

Barri offered to take the girls off her hands at the weekends, but Gaynor longed for his company so much that she usually went with them.

Twice during the holidays they went to Barry Island because Keris loved playing on the sand, building sandcastles and paddling in the sea. Rachael seemed bored by such outings and simply sat on the sand chewing one of her fingernails and looking fed up.

It was one of the hottest Augusts on record and day after day Gaynor found herself packing up picnics and trundling off to Roath Park. She could hardly wait for September when the two girls returned to school and once again she would be able to have some time on her own.

Her daily routine of housework, which had sometimes seemed so mundane, now had a positive appeal. She'd spent so little time at home lately that the place was beginning to look neglected, she reflected.

Barri smiled when she told him this. 'Relax, enjoy yourself, make the most of each day; you never know what's around the corner.'

Barri's comment repeated itself over and over in Gaynor's mind when one week into the new term Miss Davis sent a boy round to the house with a note asking why Rachael hadn't come to school.

Shrugging on her coat Gaynor accompanied the boy back to school so that she could confront Miss Davis and find out what she was on about.

'I wouldn't normally go to such lengths simply because a pupil was away for one day,' Miss Davis pointed out quite sharply.

'Of course, I do understand, it was very considerate of you,' Gaynor murmured contritely.

'After all the problems we had with Rachael last term I had a suspicion that it wasn't merely a cold, or something trivial like that. In fact, I wondered if you even knew she wasn't here,' Miss Davis explained.

'No I didn't know,' Gaynor agreed. 'She set off for school with Keris this morning the same as usual and now you are saying she hasn't been here all day.'

'That's right.'

'I wish you'd let me know earlier – first thing this morning, when she didn't answer the register.'

Miss Davis stiffened. 'As I've already said, it is not my practice to send a message round to the parent's house simply because a child hasn't turned up. I was making an exception in Rachael's case, but only because—'

'I know, and I'm grateful for what you have done,' Gaynor interrupted. 'I wasn't criticising you, Miss Davis. I spoke without thinking because I am so worried.'

'I'm sure you are,' Miss Davis agreed. 'I didn't want to ask Keris, where Rachael was, not after the problems you've had with your elder daughter.'

Gaynor stared at her in dismay. 'You mean you think that Rachael might have run away the same as Sara did?' she asked in mounting alarm.

Miss Davis shrugged. 'I wouldn't go as far as to say that, but if she isn't here, and she isn't at home with you, then where is she?'

Chapter Twenty-One

Gaynor walked away from the school in a daze. She was tempted to go straight to the City Hall and see what Barri had to say about Rachael's disappearance. Then, realising that it was unlikely that he would know any more than she did, she decided that there was no point in worrying him.

In all probability, she told herself, Rachael would come home at teatime and she'd have some logical explanation about where she'd been. Either that or she'd pretend she hadn't played truant at all which would mean that she'd have caused a storm in a teacup and worried Barri over nothing.

Her head felt so woolly and she longed for a cup of tea. She also felt the need to talk about what had happened with someone who wasn't too involved, in the hope that perhaps they could see more clearly than she could why Rachael was behaving so oddly.

Poor Rachael. Sara going off to try and find her father would remind Rachael that her own father was dead so she couldn't go looking for him even if she wanted to do so.

Suddenly she thought of Saratina. She didn't

see very much of her these days, but they were still good friends and Saratina had always helped her when she was in trouble. She hurried towards the nearest bus stop, hoping that she would find her at home now that she was only working part-time.

They'd been through so much together that Saratina would understand her concern and she knew Rachael well enough to be able to put herself in the girl's shoes and perhaps explain what might be troubling her.

As she walked down Sophia Street she smiled to herself as she caught sight of the Varios' brightly painted house. It stood out from the rest of the street as it had always done and it lifted her heart to see the motley of bright hues.

She really should visit Maria Vario more often, she told herself. Maria was getting old, and so stout, and she had such swollen legs that she rarely went out. And relations between them had thawed somewhat over the years. Saratina was the only one still living at home and was her mother's mainstay.

Saratina hadn't been as lucky as her, Gaynor thought reflectively. Sandy Peterson had not only broken her heart, but he seemed to have put her off men for life. He'd been a right scoundrel, Gaynor reflected, but in some ways she was glad he had cheated on her because otherwise she might never have met up with Barri again.

When Saratina came to the door in answer

to her knock her eyes widened with surprise and she smiled broadly. 'My word, this is a surprise, it must be the day when the Hughes family decide to visit the Varios,' she greeted her.

Gaynor looked puzzled. For a moment she wondered what Saratina was talking about.

'Come on in then, cariad, don't stand on ceremony,' Saratina urged, putting a friendly arm around Gaynor's shoulders and pulling her into the living room.

'Mama,' she announced as they went in, 'we have another visitor; here's Gaynor come to see us as well.'

Gaynor smiled and held out her hands in greeting to the old lady then stopped, gasping in surprise. Sitting beside Maria and tucking into a piece of cake, was Rachael.

Gaynor was so taken aback she didn't know whether to laugh with relief, or to shout at Rachael for all the worry she had caused.

'What are you doing here?' she demanded.

Saratina looked from one to the other in bewilderment. 'I thought you knew she was here and you'd come to collect her. Where's Keris? Hasn't she come with you?'

'Keris is at school where this young madam should be,' Gaynor retorted tartly.

Saratina's smile faded. 'You mean you've played truant, Rachael?' she said in surprise.

'She most certainly has,' Gaynor stated before Rachael could recover from the shock of her mother being there or think of a convincing answer.

'We thought you knew she was here, didn't we, Mam?' Saratina repeated in a puzzled voice, looking across at her mother for confirmation.

'That's right,' Maria confirmed. 'We thought you'd sent her because she wanted to know all about her dad. I've been upstairs and I sorted out my box of photos to show her. There're some lovely ones of Pedro when he was a little boy and when he was about her age, as well as one or two taken when he first went to sea.'

'Rachael was asking if we still had Pedro's guitar.' Saratina smiled. 'She says she is going to sing a song in the school concert at Christmas and she was wondering if she could play the guitar as well.'

'She's welcome to borrow it.' Maria smiled. 'We want it back afterwards, mind, because it's one of the few possessions we still have to remind us of him.

'Rachael wouldn't be able to play it,' Gaynor protested. 'She's never had a lesson in her life and the concert is only a couple of months away.'

'I had a toy one when I was a little kid,' Rachael reminded her mother.

'There you are, and she's been doing all right at playing it since she arrived.' Maria laughed. 'She has been born with natural talent, just like Pedro. He never had lessons either. He spotted the guitar in a pawnbroker's shop, picked it

255

up, and started strumming on it and that was that.'

Gaynor nodded politely. Somehow the story didn't ring true and she sensed that Maria was trying hard to win Rachael's affection.

Maria might be Rachael's grandmother, but she had never encouraged her to visit there, not since they had moved to Eleanor Place. Afterwards, when Barri had come back into her life, she had been glad about that; it made things so much simpler.

Saratina had understood; in fact, she had felt the same way. When Rachael had been very small she had made it plain that she thought it was a good idea for them to stay away. Saratina came to see them occasionally, but she constantly pointed out, her mother had cared for enough babies in her life and she didn't want to be lumbered with any more.

There had been times when Gaynor would have welcomed some help; somewhere to leave Rachael for an hour or so when she had to take Sara to the doctor and occasions like that.

Saratina had always said that it wasn't convenient for them to come and stay with her mother and she had never offered to look after them herself. In those days, of course, all her spare time was taken up going out with Sandy Peterson.

Now, Saratina didn't have a man in her life and Gaynor felt uneasy that perhaps she saw things differently. She wondered if, between them, Saratina and her mother might be trying to take Rachael away from her. Mama Maria was probably very lonely, especially when Saratina was at work. All her other children, José, Miguel, Margarita and even Sanje, the youngest, had left home and were living their own lives. They had their own friends and interests and Maria was on her own most of the time.

Trying not to let the concern she was feeling show in her voice, she said as calmly as she could, 'I can see you've had a very nice time here, Rachael, but we must go now or we will be late collecting Keris from school.'

'Keris, Keris, it is always Keris,' Rachael flared. 'I want to stay here with my dad's mam. I can, can't I?' she appealed clutching hold of Maria Vario's hand.

'Of course you can, cariad, you can stay here any time you like. I've not seen enough of you and now you are growing up to be as pretty as my lovely Saratina. You must come and see me more often, I am your grandmother, you know.'

'Can I take my dad's guitar with me?' Rachael begged.

Maria hesitated and frowned. Gaynor could see the struggle going on in the old lady's mind. The guitar meant so much to her, but if it was going to tie Rachael to her side, then she was obviously willing to let the child borrow it.

'I tell you what,' Gaynor said quickly, 'why don't we leave it here for the moment and we can come back for it another day?'

'I need to practise.' Rachael pouted. 'Please let me take it,' she whinged, snuggling up to Maria.

'Why not come back for it at the weekend? It's only a couple of days away. Perhaps you could come and stay for the day?' Saratina suggested, looking questioningly at Gaynor.

'That's all settled then.' Saratina smiled as Gaynor reluctantly gave a nod of agreement. 'You know your way and you're big enough to come on your own, aren't you?' she added.

Rachael's face lit up. 'Oh yes, I can do that,' she said eagerly, then added slyly, 'that's if my mam will let me. She wouldn't let me go out on my own with any of my friends all through the summer holidays. She made me go everywhere with her and Keris; it was no fun at all.'

'Well, I'm sure she will let you come here on your own, as long as she knows where you are. It was naughty of you to play truant and to come on your own today,' Saratina added reprovingly, but her smile as she said it brought a giggle from Rachael.

'Give me a kiss and then run along with your mam, cariad,' Maria told her. 'You come on your own on Saturday and you can sleep here on Saturday night if your mam will let you and go home again on Sunday afternoon.'

Rachael's face lit up. 'Yes please,' she breathed. 'That sounds lovely. Where will I sleep?'

'In the room your dad used to sleep in when

he was a boy, of course,' Saratina told her.

Rachael looked so smug that once again Gaynor felt her own authority had been undermined.

Barri looked surprised but merely shrugged resignedly when she explained all this to him at home. 'You and Saratina have always been such good friends,' he pointed out, 'so why be so suspicious? After all, she is Rachael's aunt.'

'I know that, but in the past Saratina has shown no real interest in her.'

'And you've felt short-changed because of it. Now that she is at last taking an interest in Rachael, you're reacting as if she is trying to steal her way from you.'

'That's what it feels like,' Gaynor sighed. 'Rachael is suddenly so grown-up, far too old and too knowing for her age. She seems to have taken sides with them and joined forces against me.'

'Come on, cariad.' He took her in his arms, stroking her back consolingly. 'She's only going there for one night . . .'

'She'll be spending almost two days with them,' Gaynor interrupted, pulling away from him and dabbing her eyes. 'Two days when she will be allowed to do exactly what she likes; two days when she will strum away on that damn guitar and they'll convince her that she can play it. Two days when she will pirouette around and do her song and dance act and they'll applaud her and turn her head and make her think she is a hundred times better than what she is.'

'Come on now, be fair,' Barry urged. 'She has a pretty voice and she certainly sings well.'

'I know that, but I don't want them filling her head with a whole load of nonsense about how talented she is and that she doesn't need to work hard at school.'

'Come on, come on. You're making a mountain out of a molehill. Let her go; if you try and stop her, then she will resent it. She'll be stroppy and rebellious and we'll all have one hell of a weekend. Let her go and stay with the Varios if she wants to, and we'll do something special with Keris and that will take your mind off Rachael being at Sophia Street.'

Gaynor sighed. 'I know you are right. I suppose I can't control her for very much longer and this is one way of getting used to letting her go.'

'That's the right way to look at it,' he agreed. 'Now, let's plan how the three of us are going to spend the weekend. Remember, you are letting Rachael have a treat so it is only fair that Keris has one as well. The weather is still quite good so if it's reasonably warm and sunny why don't we go to Barry Island for the day? You know how Keris loves going there.'

'Yes, very well, we'll do that,' Gaynor agreed.

'So which day shall we go, or should we wait and see what the weather is like?'

'We'd better go on Saturday because we don't know what time Rachael will come home on Sunday and we don't want her to find us out.'

'Then tell her what time you want her to come back.'

'The trouble is, if she isn't enjoying herself she might want to come home early.'

'You're doing it again!' Barri said exasperatedly.

'Doing what?'

'You are putting Rachael's interest before Keris.'

'Very well, we'll tell her what time she is to come home and we'll wait and see what the weather is like before we decide which day to have out,' she conceded.

'That's better. Now, forget all about it.'

It was bright and sunny on Saturday and so the moment they'd had breakfast they agreed that it was the right day for their trip to Barry Island.

'We can all go as far as the Hayes together and then Rachael will only have to go down Bute Street on her own and we can go along to Wood Street and catch our train.'

Rachael was so excited at the thought of her visit to Maria Vario and Saratina that it wasn't until the last moment when she realised they were all leaving the house together.

'I don't need you to come with me,' she protested sulkily. 'I found my way there before and I can do it again.'

'We're not coming with you,' Gaynor assured her. 'We're simply travelling on the same bus as you are because we're off out for the day. If we come on the bus at the same time as you then your dad will pay so you won't have to spend any of your pocket money on your fare,' she pointed out.

'So where are you all going, then?' Rachael asked, ignoring the bribe.

'We're going to Barry Island,' Gaynor told her. 'It looks like being a lovely sunny day and Keris always likes it there. I'm not sure if it will be warm enough for her to go paddling in the sea, but she always enjoys playing about on the beach and she still likes building sand castles with her dad.'

Rachael looked taken aback and for one moment Gaynor thought she was going to ask if she could come with them instead of going to the Varios'. Then she saw the girl's shoulders go back stubbornly as she tossed her head defiantly. 'I think it's childish doing things like that,' she retorted loftily.

Chapter Twenty-Two

Rachael seemed to spend more and more of her weekends at the Varios'. Gaynor accepted the new order of things, although she was not entirely happy about the division it was causing in their family. She missed Sara and now felt that she was losing Rachael as well and there were times when it saddened her and made her feel that she had failed with them.

With Sara gone and Rachael so frequently with the Varios, Keris was being turned into an only child and this meant that Barri was showing her even more attention.

At one time Gaynor might have talked over her problem with Saratina, but now she had to be very careful about what she said to her, especially if it concerned Rachael in any way.

Saratina had become Rachael's idol. Everything she said or did was based on what Saratina had said or thought. She copied her aunt's hair style, her mannerisms, and asked her advice about everything.

Saratina not only encouraged Rachael to spend a lot of time with her, but she also spent quite a lot of money on her. She bought her clothes, took her to the pictures, and always made sure that she was given the sort of meals she preferred.

Rachael was developing fast, her figure filling out so that she looked far older than her age.

At Christmas, although Gaynor insisted that she must spend Christmas Day at home, Rachael was determined to see in 1931 in the company of the Varios.

'It will be so much more exciting to go there because Saratina is going to take me down to the Pier Head at midnight. We'll be there when they sound all the hooters to let the New Year in,' she said, her dark eyes sparkling.

'Can I come as well?' Keris asked excitedly.

'No, of course you can't, you're not old enough; you're only eight,' Rachael told her almost triumphantly.

''I'll be nine in May and that's quite soon and you're only twelve, anyway,' Keris retorted, her voice trembling because she was so near to tears.

'I'll be thirteen in July, though, and next year I'll be leaving school,' Rachael pointed out.

Gaynor desperately wanted to stop Rachael going to the Varios on New Year's Eve, but Barri pointed out that it would cause bad feeling not only with Rachael but with Saratina as well, since she had already promised Rachael that this was what they would do.

'Let's start the New Year as we intend to go on, a happy family, no more quarrels over things which are not important. If Rachael wants to be with the Varios, then let her go there. Since we've been letting her see more of them she has done much better at school and you have to admit that her performance at the concert was a credit to all of us.'

'She certainly won plenty of applause,' Gaynor admitted.

'And so she jolly well should. She sang like an angel and the way she played that guitar was unbelievable. Miss Davis was absolutely delighted by her performance.'

As 1931 progressed, Rachael was a changed person. A pattern had established itself.

Rachael worked hard at school, was sweet and loving with Keris, and helped Gaynor whenever she was asked to do so. In return she was allowed to go off down to the Varios first thing on Saturday morning and to come back on Sunday evening so that she could be ready for school the next day.

At Easter she asked if she could stay there all over the holiday and reluctantly Barri and Gaynor agreed.

Keris sulked, but they promised her extra outings and treats to make up for her sister not being there but, nonetheless, they could see that she missed Rachael. To try and compensate, Gaynor agreed that she could move into a bedroom of her own and encouraged her to help redecorate Sara's old room; she let her choose new curtains, and helped her to make the room exactly as she wanted it.

Keris couldn't wait for Rachael to see it and was disappointed that she wasn't there to do so.

'Never mind, she will be back next Sunday because you are both back at school again on the following Monday,' Gaynor told her cheerfully in the week following Easter.

As soon as they'd had their midday meal on the following Sunday, Keris started looking out for Rachael. Gaynor suggested a trip to Roath Park, but Keris shook her head.

'Rachael might come back while we're there. I'd sooner wait until she gets home and then perhaps we could both go and she can tell me all about what she did over Easter.'

They waited all afternoon but there was no sign of her and Gaynor was furious. 'She's been with the Varios for over a week, so surely she could have come back on time, if only to be with Keris,' she fumed as she began to prepare tea.

The three of them ate their meal in expectant silence; all of them were listening for the door, for Rachael's return.

'Perhaps we should go and meet her,' Gaynor suggested as she cleared the table. 'Do you and Keris want to do it?' she asked, looking at Barri who was helping carry the dishes through. 'One of us should stay here in case she has already set off for home; we don't want her to find us all out.'

'You and Keris go, if you think it is necessary, and I'll stay here and do the washing-up,' Barri offered.

'I'll say here with my dad,' Keris stated.

Gaynor looked from one to the other of them, perplexed. She knew she was probably making a fuss about nothing, but she still felt one of them ought to go and collect Rachael and make it clear to Saratina that if she was to go down there again then she must come back on time.

'All right, I'll go on my own,' she said crossly, pushing back her chair and stalking out of the room.

As she waited for a bus to arrive she was tempted to turn round and go home again. Then, having come this far, she resolved she might as well go through with it.

As she walked down Sophia Street she compared it with the street they lived in at Roath and suddenly saw it as it really was; a sordid, dirty street in Tiger Bay. It was no fit place for her daughter to visit, she decided. No wonder Barri wasn't keen on going there.

By the time she reached the Varios' front door, all her misgivings about letting Rachael come there every week had gathered into a hard knot and she was quite determined to tell Saratina, and Maria as well if necessary, that it couldn't go on like this.

Normally she would have knocked on the Varios' door and then, knowing it was never locked, pushed it open and walked in. Today, however, she remained on the doorstep, conscious of the litter in the gutter, the fish and chip papers blowing about, the mangy cat sniffing around and the stray dog cocking its leg at every lamp-post.

'Hello, this is a surprise!' Saratina greeted her when she came and opened the door. 'Why didn't you come in? You usually do.'

'That's because I am usually looking forward to seeing you. Tonight I am so angry that I am almost afraid to come inside in case I say something that finishes our friendship for ever.'

'What on earth are you on about?' Saratina asked sharply. 'I think that if any one should be angry it should be us. After all the plans we made for Rachael to enjoy Easter with us, you didn't let her come.'

'Now you're the one who is talking in riddles,' Gaynor frowned. 'What do you mean, she didn't come? She's been here with you for almost a week.'

'She most certainly hasn't! Mama Maria is really upset about it.'

She stopped speaking and the two of them stared at each other in dismay.

'You mean you haven't seen Rachael at all? Not all over Easter?'

Saratina nodded. 'I thought you had decided that she was coming too often. I understood why you might be feeling like that,' she added hastily. 'I'd probably have felt the same.'

'But she did come! She left home first thing on Good Friday as we arranged with you that she would do, so where on earth is she?'

Again they stared at each other, shaking their heads in disbelief that something like this could happen.

'Don't say anything to Mama for the moment,' Saratina whispered. 'She's not too well; her heart isn't strong these days and—'

'Don't worry, I won't say anything to upset her.' Gaynor nodded.

'She'll wonder why you are here, though.'

'Say . . . say Rachael left some of her things behind the last time she was here and I've come to collect them.'

'Go on in and sit with Mama, then. I'll make us all a cup of tea. It will give us both a chance to think and we'll talk about it later, before you leave.'

Rachael was already at home when Gaynor returned to Roath.

'I see you missed each other,' Barri commented. 'I told you she'd be back safe and sound if you waited.'

Rachael looked tired and grubby. Gaynor waited for her to give them an explanation, but it was obvious from the stubborn look on her face that she had no intention of doing so.

Gaynor paused, trying to think what to do for the best. She was not sure whether to interrogate her in front of Barri and Keris or to wait until they were on their own. After a moment's hesitation she decided that prudence was the wisest course otherwise it might develop into a full-scale family row and she wanted to prevent that if she possibly could.

When she said nothing Gaynor could tell from Rachael's attitude that she was both puzzled and relieved.

She probably can't understand why I didn't want to know where she's been or even seem to be interested, Gaynor thought with satisfaction. She waited until Rachael went up to bed then followed her upstairs. 'Well?' she demanded. 'Exactly where have you been since Good Friday? Certainly not staying with the Varios! Saratina was extremely annoyed that you hadn't turned up and didn't even let them know because she had made plans about what you'd be doing. Maria was upset as well. So exactly where have you been all this time?'

'With friends.'

'What friends?'

'You don't know them!' Rachael told her defiantly.

'School friends?'

'No, not really. I met them through my friends at school, though,' she said quickly.

'And you decided to go and stay with them without telling either me or your dad or Saratina? So where do these special friends live?'

'I don't know.' She fidgeted uncomfortably. 'I didn't stay with them at their house exactly,' she explained quickly, 'we went places.'

'I see!' Gaynor took a deep breath and tried to keep calm. 'And what sort of places did you and these new friends visit that it took you a whole week?'

'We went here and there, all over the place, does it matter?' Rachael muttered defiantly.

'It matters very much. Where did you sleep? What did you do for meals? There are a hundred and one things I want to know, so you'd better start talking.'

It took a long time to make Rachael tell the truth about where she'd been and when she finally did, Gaynor was shocked to the core.

'Is this really the truth, Rachael?' she gasped. 'You've spent the entire time with a circus, travelling all over the place with them!'

'I knew that's how you'd be,' Rachael protested. 'You are so old-fashioned, so dull; you never want us to do anything different or adventurous. You think a trip to Roath Park is an exciting outing!'

'You've never even been to a circus,' Gaynor went on, ignoring Rachael's outburst.

'That's where you're wrong! I went with a crowd from school one day.'

Gaynor felt bewildered. 'When on earth did you manage to do that?'

Rachael avoided her mother's hard stare. 'You thought I had a rehearsal.'

'It was ages ago that you stayed late for rehearsals!' Gaynor exclaimed in disbelief. 'You

271

mean you played truant from that as well?'

'Only once. It wasn't exactly playing truant,' she went on quickly. 'I told you I had a rehearsal when I didn't because a crowd of us wanted to go to the circus and we weren't sure that our parents would let us.'

'Go on, tell me how you became involved with them.'

'The circus has been back again since then and one of the boys we'd talk to there suggested that if I wanted to, I could play and sing for them in between the acts when they were putting on a show. And I said yes!'

She stopped, looking frightened, her lip trembling as she waited nervously for her mother's reaction.

Gaynor felt too shocked to know what to say. She needed time to think; time to talk it over with Barri. They certainly couldn't let her get away with it, but the punishment would certainly have to fit the crime.

In fact, she wasn't sure that punishment was the right solution. This was far too serious a matter for that. Making her stay in every evening for a week, stopping her sweets, or any of the other restrictions that she had sometimes imposed when one of the girls had been naughty, was not the right way to deal with this.

They would both have to talk to her very seriously about her behaviour and they'd have to find out a lot more about this circus she claimed she'd been with. They'd certainly have to let Miss Davis know what had happened in case any other pupils were involved.

Gaynor shuddered as she thought of the dangers Rachael could have been in over the past week and dreaded what she might get up to in the future.

Without saying anything else to Rachael, she turned and walked out of the bedroom, closing the door quietly but firmly behind her.

Chapter Twenty-Three

Gaynor and Barri talked late into the night discussing how they should deal with Rachael's escapade.

'We must make her toe the line, otherwise it sets Keris a bad example, and I think we should put our foot down and stop all her privileges,' Gaynor stated firmly.

'Let's sleep on it,' Barri yawned. 'We don't want to do anything rash, now do we,' he prevaricated.

'That's not being rash, it's being sensible,' Gaynor said quietly. 'She is only a child and still at school. We are responsible for her welfare, remember.'

'Yes, I know that, but she is so strong-willed that we have to be diplomatic so that we don't antagonise her and make her so angry that she does something even worse.'

'Antagonise her! What are you on about! She's going to do as she's told in future and I don't intend to let her forget it.'

'Careful, cariad. You are beginning to sound like your dad,' Barri warned. 'Remember how he stopped you, and me, from doing what we wanted with our lives when you were about her age and look at all the trouble that caused.'

'That was quite a different situation altogether. He claims he was trying to protect us from getting into trouble.'

'We didn't like him interfering, though, did we? If he had handled it differently we might both have stayed in Ferndale.'

'No point in thinking about that now,' Gaynor said huffily. 'Things have changed a lot since those days.'

'Parents still act in the same way; they try and dominate their children into doing what they think is best for them and very often they are wrong.'

'Are you saying that it is all right for Rachael to run off with a circus?' Gaynor asked in astonishment.

'Of course I'm not. She's headstrong but at the same time she does know right from wrong. She did come back of her own accord in time for the new term at school and that was probably because she didn't want you to be worried.'

'She didn't think to let Saratina know that she wouldn't be going to their place over Easter, even though she was the one who had made all the fuss about going there.'

'Probably because she was afraid that if she did that then Saratina would come here hot-footed to warn us and you would have been upset all week. As it turned out you weren't worried until late on the Sunday evening . . .'

'Yes, and if things had gone according to Rachael's devious plan then she would have been home before I found out and none of us would have been any the wiser,' Gaynor interrupted.

'We would have done in time. Saratina would have been sure to have asked you next time you met why Rachael didn't go down there for Easter after all,' Barri reasoned.

Gaynor pushed her hair back from her face, yawned deeply, and rubbed her eyes. 'I feel too tired to argue with you, Barri. All I know is that we've got to find a way to deal with this problem and it must be one we can both agree on.'

'We will, cariad, so try to stop worrying about it. Say nothing to Rachael tomorrow morning, let everything carry on as normal. We'll both give it some more thought and we'll have a long talk to her about it tomorrow night.'

It took Gaynor a great deal of will-power not to mention anything to Rachael about her escapade when she came home from school the next evening. She was looking so smug that it made Gaynor all the more determined that she ought to be punished. If Keris ever came to hear about what Rachael had done then she might try and do something similar, unless she knew that Rachael had been severely dealt with and she feared the same fate.

Gaynor and Barri waited until Keris had gone

to bed, but in the intervening time they had managed to talk to each other and had more or less agreed what they were going to say to Rachael.

Gaynor still felt she deserved more than a mere talking to, but as Barri kept reminding her about the way her father had behaved when she was not much older than Rachael she gave way and said she would let him deal with it this time. If there was any further trouble, though, she would take matters into her own hands and that would mean punishing Rachael as she thought fit.

Rachael listened in sulky silence to Barri's lecture on her thoughtlessness, on her being underhand, deceiving them, and letting Saratina and Mrs Vario down.

'So what are you going to do about it?' she asked with an air of bravado that made Gaynor want to slap her.

'First and foremost you will apologise to your mother for all the anxiety you've caused her.'

Rachael shrugged. 'Sorry, Mam, I didn't mean to worry you, but I knew it was no good asking because I knew you wouldn't let me go with them.'

Barri held up a hand to silence her. 'You will also write a letter to Mrs Vario and Saratina and tell hem how sorry you are for not letting them know that you would not be turning up at their house after they'd invited you and made all sorts of plans to give you a good time.'

Rachael scowled but nodded her head in agreement. 'Is that it?' she asked, shifting uncomfortably from one foot to the other.

'No, that is only the beginning. In future you report to your mother and ask her permission before you go anywhere, even if it is only to the park with Keris. Most important of all, you are not to discuss your escapade with Keris. Now, is that all clearly understood?'

Rachael opened her mouth to protest, then thought better of it and simply nodded.

'Right, now go upstairs to bed, after you have carried out the first thing I told you to do.'

Rachael frowned as if not understanding.

'The first thing I told you to do, the most important thing of all in my opinion,' he said heavily, 'and that is apologise to your mother for your thoughtless behaviour.'

'I've already told her that I'm sorry, didn't you hear me?' she muttered rebelliously.

'It was too glib, Rachael. I want your apology to be far more sincere, as if it is coming from the heart. I want you to really mean every word you say.'

'Can I do it when you're not here?' She scowled nervously, darting a look at Gaynor.

'If you wish. I'm going to make your mother a cup of tea so you can tell her while I am out in the kitchen.'

Gaynor knew that saying sorry was always difficult for Rachael but she steeled herself to remain silent until she had done so.

Rachael was shaking with nerves by the time she'd finished and Gaynor couldn't resist taking her into her arms and hugging her.

They were both in tears by the time Barri returned with the tea.

'Off to bed then, Rachael,' he said quietly. 'You can go and see the Varios on Saturday. No, not to stay,' he said quickly as he saw her face light up. 'You'll be going there to apologise to them and to take back the guitar.'

'Do you mean I can never go there again; to stay, I mean?' Rachael asked.

'We'll think about,' he told her. 'A lot depends on how you behave over the next few months.'

'Few months!' Her voice was so shrill, and she sounded so exasperated, that Gaynor caught her breath. She half expected Barri to get really angry, but to her intense relief he merely shrugged. 'It is all up to you,' he said quietly. 'You know what's expected of you so let's see if you can do it.'

Rachael was so anxious to be able to have her privileges restored that for the next few weeks she behaved impeccably. Gaynor was both pleased and relieved and even went as far as to admit to Barri that she thought the way he had dealt with the problem had been the right one.

Saratina had been to see them to find out why Rachael hadn't been down to visit them and Gaynor explained about the punishment that Barri had imposed.

'Ask him if he could have a rethink and be a little bit more lenient,' she begged. 'Mama is not at all well and she keeps asking where Rachael is and why she hasn't been to see us.'

'I'll have a word with him, but I don't think he will relax the rules. He has said to me on the quiet that if she keeps up her good behaviour till the school holidays start in July, then he'll give her more freedom.

'That's not very long away; surely since she's been good ever since Easter he could let her off the next few weeks.'

'I'll have a word with him, but I don't hold out much hope.'

'I'm only asking for you to let her visit Mam, not to stay,' Saratina begged.

'I'll see what I can do,' Gaynor promised.

Saratina came out to Roath three days later. This time she didn't ask if Rachael could come and visit, she demanded that she went back with her right then.

'Mama Maria's so ill that the doctor doesn't think she will pull through,' she said the moment Barri opened the door to her, tears running down her cheeks. 'A neighbour is there with her at the moment, but I must get back. Can Rachael please come with me, Barri?'

'Of course she can,' he told her quickly. 'I'm sorry to hear about your mother. Rachael's having her tea, but I'll call her right away. Would you like Gaynor to come as well?'

Saratina hesitated. 'No, not at the moment.

Perhaps she could come and collect Rachael later on this evening, if that's all right.'

'I'm sure she will agree to do that. Come along in and explain it all to them yourself.'

'No, you do it, I don't want to upset Rachael by saying the wrong thing. I'm sure you can do it better than me.'

'Very well. I'll simply tell Rachael that Maria wants to see her and you can explain the situation on the way. Rachael will be so pleased to see you, and have so much to tell you, that you probably won't get a chance to do so till you are walking down Sophia Street, which might be all for the best,' Barri said thoughtfully.

'Yes, I'll do that; I'll tell her how ill my mother is before we get to the house, then she won't be too shocked when she sees her.'

'Right, and we'll come and collect Rachael at about ten o'clock. We can't let her stay any later than that because she has to get up for school tomorrow morning.'

Things went more or less as Barri had foreseen. Rachael was overjoyed to see Saratina and as they set off for Sophia Street she was chattering away so much that she didn't even notice that Saratina was exceptionally quiet or that she looked upset.

Hearing that her grandmother was so ill was a terrible shock for Rachael. She blamed it on the worry that she had caused them and couldn't stop saying how sorry she was.

'Never mind about that now,' Saratina told

her. 'Remember you mustn't say anything to Mama Maria about your escapade either. All you have to do is to sit quietly by the side of her bed and only talk to her if she speaks to you.'

Rachael was so upset by her grandmother looking so frail that when Gaynor came to collect her later that evening she begged to be allowed to stay there overnight.

'No, it would be better if you went home, Rachael, and came back again after school tomorrow, that's if your mam will let you,' Saratina told her.

'I want to stay here,' Rachael protested. 'It's all my fault that Mama Maria is so ill, isn't it? I'm the one who upset her by not coming here at Easter.'

'No, no, that's got nothing to do with it,' Saratina assured her. 'Mama has not been well for quite a while. Her heart has been playing up for years and now ... well, now it's got worse.'

'Come on, Rachael, Saratina has enough to do as it is without having to look after you,' Gaynor insisted.

'I don't need anyone to look after me, I can help Saratina to nurse Mama Maria,' Rachael pleaded.

'No, Rachael! Please do as your mam has asked.'

Rachael barely spoke on the way home. She sat next to the window on the bus, staring out into the darkness, occasionally sniffing back her unshed tears. When they reached home she went straight up to her bedroom, refusing even a warm drink to help her to sleep.

'She's terribly upset, Barri, I've never seen her like this,' Gaynor said worriedly.

'Sounds like a guilt complex to me. This is a far worse punishment for her than any restrictions we've imposed. Let's hope it teaches her a lesson,' he added morbidly.

Two days later Saratina came to the house to tell them that her mother had died in her sleep.

Rachael was heartbroken. She wept continually and Gaynor had to give Keris a note to explain to Miss Davis the reason why she wouldn't be at school for a few days.

'Rachael says that Mama Maria was her grandmother.' Keris frowned. 'Was she, Mam?'

'Well, yes, I suppose she was,' Gaynor agreed. 'That's probably why she feels so badly about it. You must try and be nice to her and don't say anything to upset her any more.'

'Was she my grandmother as well?' Keris asked.

'No dear!' Gaynor stroked Keris's hair consolingly. 'No, she wasn't you grandmother.'

'Why not?'

'Mrs Vario was Rachael's father's mother,' Gaynor explained.

Keris repeated the words very slowly as if trying to place them in their right order.

'But not mine?' she persisted. 'So who is my

grandmother?' she asked in a puzzled voice.

'My mother and your dad's mother, of course.'

Keris gave an elaborate sigh. 'Does that mean that my dad really isn't Rachael's dad, Mam?' she asked.

'No, he's not, dear. Rachael's dad was Pedro Vario. He died a long time ago.'

'Before you knew my dad?'

Gaynor hesitated. 'No, I knew your dad when I was a little girl at school, but then he went away and we didn't see each other for years and years and—'

'And as soon as you met him again you married each other and after that I was born.'

'Yes, that's right. Now, can we stop talking about it, Keris? You run along to school or you'll be late, and don't forget to give that note to Miss Davis.'

No sooner had the front door closed behind Keris than Rachael came downstairs and began asking her even more questions about why Pedro had been her father but wasn't Keris's.

'He wasn't Sara's dad either, was he?' Rachael asked.

'No, cariad. I explained all this to you a long time ago. Sara's father was called Konrad Claus . . .'

'And that's why Sara ran away to Germany. She wanted to try and find him.'

'Yes,' Gaynor sighed. Was any family as complicated as hers she wondered? All her daughters had different fathers and all her daughters had one thing in common: they were all so strong-willed that she was finding it difficult to handle them.

'Has Sara found her dad?'

'I don't know. She's never let us know,' Gaynor said tightly.

'Perhaps he's dead like my dad,' Rachael sighed. 'Now my grandmother is dead as well. Soon there won't be anyone left alive but me,' she muttered morosely.

'That's silly talk Rachael and you know it,' Gaynor said briskly. 'You have a mother, a father and a sister all living here in the same house as you.'

'Yes but he isn't really my dad, and Keris is only my half-sister. So what relation is Saratina?'

'Saratina is your aunt, because she was your dad's sister,' Gaynor explained.

'My aunt! That's wonderful,' Rachael exclaimed excitedly, 'and she hasn't any children of her own, that's why she thinks I am so special.'

Chapter Twenty-Four

The full meaning of Rachael's cryptic comments didn't become clear until a couple of weeks after Maria Vario's funeral.

Rachael had been down to Sophia Street once or twice to stay overnight with Saratina, but always came back grumbling that Saratina was very busy. 'She's selling everything and she's going to give up the house,' Rachael told them.

'Saratina's planning to move out? Where is she thinking of going?' Gaynor asked in surprise.

Rachael shrugged and changed the subject as if she didn't know the answer or else wasn't interested.

This puzzled Gaynor and several times she tried to find out more from Rachael, but without any success.

When she mentioned it to Barri, he had no idea what Saratina was proposing to do. 'Perhaps she's found herself a boyfriend and is planning on getting married,' he suggested.

'I'm sure she would have said something to me about it long before now if that was the case,' Gaynor told him.

'She hasn't had much time lately, what with

one thing and another,' he pointed out. 'There were weeks when we didn't let Rachael go down there and since then she has been kept pretty busy looking after her mother.'

'That's true, but at one time we told each other everything.'

'A long time ago,' Barri laughed, 'certainly not since we've been married.'

'Oh, I don't know, Saratina's remained a pretty good friend,' Gaynor reminded him with some asperity. 'I'll miss her if she moves away from Cardiff.'

He smiled teasingly. 'Then why don't you go down there and ask her what she's planning to do. You know her well enough to be able to do that without appearing to be merely curious; you've just said what old friends you are.'

Two days later, on impulse, Gaynor took Barri's advice. As she walked down Sophia Street it struck her that this might be the last time she would ever visit the Vario house, if Saratina really was going away.

Saratina was wearing one of her mother's wrap-around aprons over her black cotton dress and had a scarf tied over her dark hair. There were packed boxes all over the place and from the state of the house it looked as though she was giving it a final clean. She didn't seem to be at all surprised to see her.

'I thought you would have come before now so that we could settle up all the details,' she said rather huffily. 'I have had far too much to do to come all the way out to Roath.'

Gaynor frowned. 'What do you mean? What details do we have to settle?'

'About Rachael of course!'

Gaynor looked at her blankly. 'You'll have to explain. I have no idea what you are talking about.'

Saratina stared at her coldly for a long moment. Then she reached for a packet of cigarettes on the mantelpiece, took one out, and offered the packet to Gaynor.

'You know I don't smoke.'

Saratina shrugged as she lit her own cigarette. 'I'll probably need this,' she commented. 'Come on; say what you have to say. I never thought it was going to be easy, but I'm surprised you've left it to the very last minute to start raising objections.'

'Saratina, I have no idea at all what you are talking about. It obviously has something to do with Rachael; what has she been up to this time?'

'She hasn't been up to anything, why do you always have to think the worst of her?' she asked with a humourless smile. 'It was my idea, not hers, but she nearly fell over herself with excitement when I spoke to her about it. You can't stop her now; it would be . . . it would be cruel. She'd be heartbroken.'

'So tell me what I mustn't stop!'

'Her holiday of course.'

'Holiday! What holiday? As soon as she

leaves school she's got to find herself a job.'

Saratina took a long hard draw on her cigarette and let out a thin plume of smoke. 'Has Rachael told you that I am selling up and leaving here?'

'Yes, she has. She didn't say where you were going, though. Barri thought you might be getting married,' Gaynor said with a deprecating laugh.

Saratina's lip curled. 'No thank you! Sandy Peterson was enough for me. No,' she went on more slowly, 'I'm going to Spain, to visit my relatives there. All my brothers and sisters have left home now and have their own lives, so there is nothing to keep me here ... except Rachael. We've grown quite close, you know.'

'I am aware of that! She is my daughter,' Gaynor said pointedly.

'Yes, but she's not your only daughter. The trouble is Rachael is very jealous of Keris. She thinks that both you and Barri favour her all the time and she often feels left out.'

'That's absolute rubbish,' Gaynor defended hotly, her colour rising. 'I've always treated all my girls exactly the same.'

'Oh yes, for the moment I'd forgotten about Sara. Have you ever thought that perhaps Sara left home because she felt the same way as Rachael does?'

Gaynor struggled to fight back the sour taste in her mouth. 'You're talking nonsense!' she defended hotly.

289

'Well, nonsense or not, Rachael feels left out of things and this has been why she seeks me out more and more. She's a lovely girl and we really are very good friends, as well as being aunt and niece!'

'Very well, I accept your relationship is something special and means a lot to you both, but what has this got to do with all this talk about a holiday?'

'I've told you, I'm going to move back to Spain and I'm taking Rachael with me for a holiday. We're leaving next week and she won't be coming home until the very end of August,' she added as she stubbed out her cigarette. 'I'll pay for her passage back to Cardiff and ask the captain to keep an eye on her while she's on his boat.'

'Don't worry too much about it; Saratina is still probably feeling upset after her mother's death,' Barri said sagely when Gaynor told him what was happening.

'That's all very well, but we can't let her interfere in Rachael's life like this. She has no right to take her on holiday without consulting us first,' she said indignantly.

'I'm sure she intended you to know, Rachael simply hasn't told you—'

'I mean before asking,' Gaynor cut in. 'I don't see why we should put up with such interference; I think we should put our foot down and tell Rachael that she can't go with Saratina. This promise of a holiday is probably the reason why she's showing no interest in finding a job or even deciding what sort of work she wants to do.'

Barri nodded. 'Yes, it possibly is, but do you think that it's a good idea to stop it, cariad? If we refuse to let Rachael go then she will be very resentful and heaven alone knows what she will get up to.'

'What do you mean?'

'Look at what happened at Easter when she went off with that circus crowd without a word to any of us. Don't you think it would be much better to let her go to Spain with Saratina? At least we'll know where she is and that she is with someone who will keep an eye on her and not let her do anything foolish.'

'It means she's getting her own way as well as enjoying a fantastic holiday which Keris won't be getting.'

'Well, you wouldn't want Keris to go with them, now would you?' he laughed.

'No, of course I wouldn't, but I bet she would like the chance to do so. She's going to feel very jealous if Rachael gets a treat like this and she doesn't.'

Barry shrugged helplessly. 'Saratina is Rachael's aunt and that's all there is to it.'

'Unless we put our foot down and say that Rachael can't go with her,' Gaynor repeated stubbornly.

'Let's think about it, think very carefully before we decide,' he urged. 'Let's think about the advantages of letting her go as well as the disadvantages.'

'I can't see that there are any advantages,' Gaynor sighed.

'Can't you? Well, I certainly can. It will be like a holiday for you not to have a stroppy thirteen-year-old girl having a battle of wills with you all the time. Whatever you suggest that the three of you do she won't want to do it. If you say you are going somewhere she will want to go some place else.'

'She's always wanted to be different from everyone else; it's usually easy enough to talk her round, though.'

'She'll be bullying Keris and making life hell for both of you. Let her go with Saratina and you and Keris can enjoy each other's company. You'll only have her to please and she is much easier to get on with than Rachael, as well you know.'

Put like that, Gaynor had to admit that it would be quite pleasant not to have to worry about Rachael and her capricious ways. What worried her, though, was that she might be building up trouble for the future. After spending a whole month on holiday in Spain with Saratina, and her countless relations, she would come home even more spoilt and precocious than she was now.

Gaynor tentatively mentioned to Keris what might be happening, anxious to find out her reaction. Far from being upset that Rachael was having a holiday on her own, Keris was delighted that her sister would not be around to dominate what they did or where they went.

'You mean just you and me, Mam, and now and again Dad as well, of course,' she exclaimed, her dark eyes shining. 'We can have days out together, and no arguments. We can go to the sorts of places we like and do all the things we enjoy.'

She was so ecstatic that Gaynor was immediately persuaded that Barri was right and it would be like a holiday for all of them not to have the daily battle of wills.

Rachael turned sulky when she realised that there was no opposition to her going to Spain with Saratina.

'You're glad that I'm going, aren't you?' she said, almost in tears. 'I've always known that you love Keris more than me.'

'We can't win!' Gaynor exclaimed in exasperation. 'You were the one who wanted to go to Spain; we didn't want you to do so when it was first mentioned. Now, when we finally agree because it seems to mean so much to you, you turn round and say that we don't love you. Do you want to go or not?'

'I may as well, since I'm not wanted here,' Rachael told her churlishly.

'You're probably right,' Gaynor laughed. 'Especially when you have all these silly moods and do such silly wildcat things like you did at Easter.'

Rachael's face darkened as she scowled back

at her mother. 'I'll make you sorry you said that,' she hissed. 'I'm going up to pack and I don't need you to help me.'

'Good, because I haven't got the time to do so at the moment,' Gaynor told her calmly.

As she went about her chores, Gaynor felt guilty that she had been so short with Rachael. She was only a child, after all, she told herself. Thirteen was a funny age; neither child nor woman, which was probably why sometimes she was so sweet and loving and at others so prickly that it was impossible to speak to her without upsetting her. She was probably worried because she had no idea what sort of work she wanted to do even though she was almost old enough to leave school.

As she finished the pile of ironing that had mounted up over the last few days Gaynor noticed that there were several items of clothing there that belonged to Rachael and which she'd want to take to Spain with her.

Rather than face her when she was probably still in her bad mood, Gaynor called out to Keris and asked her to take Rachael's clean washing up to her bedroom so that she could pack them in her suitcase.

'Tell her I'm just going to put the tea on the table so hurry up and finish what she's doing and come on downstairs as I'm going to make pancakes because I know they are her favourite and they must be eaten the moment they are cooked.'

Keris was back down in seconds. 'Rachael's not there, Mam.'

'She must be. She said she was going up to pack her suitcase.'

'There's no suitcase there either. Her room's empty and so are all her drawers and her clothes cupboard.'

'Empty, what do you mean? She only needs to take her summer things to go to Spain, so why on earth would she want to take everything else with her?'

As she ran up the stairs to see for herself, her heart was thundering. If Keris was right, and Rachael had taken all her clothes . . . She refused to let herself think any further.

Keris was quite right. Rachael wasn't in the room and her suitcase had gone and, as Keris had said, practically all her clothes as well as her personal belongings were missing.

Gaynor didn't know what to do. She couldn't believe that Rachael had gone without even saying goodbye; not even to Keris. Should she tear after her? With luck she might even manage to catch her before she boarded a bus at the corner of the road. Or should she leave her to get on with things in her own way?

She looked at the clock. Barri would be home in about an hour's time so perhaps she ought to wait and talk it over with him. They could all go down to Sophia Street that evening and find out why she was behaving so badly.

Barri didn't think it was a good idea to chase after her. 'You know where she is and that she's quite safe,' he pointed out, when he got home.

'Well, we don't really, do we? She is supposed to be with Saratina, but she could be anywhere or with anyone. She is so wild.'

'She is also very level headed when it comes to her own welfare and interests. She is hardly likely to walk away from the chance of a holiday in Spain to rough it in a circus caravan again, now is she!'

'So what are you saying we should do?'

'Leave it till she gets in touch with us. You have an address for the Varios in Spain, haven't you?'

Gaynor shook her head. 'All I know is that they come from somewhere near Almeria.'

Barri looked at her in surprise. Then he shrugged philosophically. 'Never mind, if you need to get in touch with Saratina you know where to find Miguel or Margarita, and they'll know where their relations live.'

It was almost a week later before they received a letter from Saratina to say that they were now in Spain and that she and Rachael had decided to make their home there permanently.

'They can't do that,' Gaynor exclaimed aghast. 'I absolutely forbid it!'

'It's a bit late to do anything about it when she's already there,' Barri sighed.

'She must have been planning this before she

left; they both must have been planning it. That's why she took most of her clothes, her winter stuff as well as her summer things.'

'Yes, you're probably right,' Barri agreed frowning. 'Did your sister say anything to you about going to live in Spain?' he asked, turning to Keris.

Keris shook her head. 'She never tells me anything. We aren't even friends these days.'

'Don't say that, you're almost as dramatic as she is,' Gaynor said irritably. 'I'm sorry,' she added guiltily as she saw Keris's eyes fill with tears. 'We're not cross with you, cariad; we are both very worried about Rachael.'

'You mean she's gone now and we'll never see her again, like Sara?' Keris wailed in dismay.

Suddenly she collapsed in tears and ran over to Barri and flung her arms tightly around him. 'You're not going to run away and leave us as well are you?' she sobbed.

Chapter Twenty-Five

Gaynor tried not to let either Keris or Barri
know how much she was missing Sara and
Rachael. If only they would write to her, let her
know that they were safe and happy, she could
have pushed her constant thoughts about them
to the back of her mind. It was the prolonged
silence that troubled her so much.

For the first few days Keris kept constantly
talking about Rachael and wondering what she
and Saratina would be doing. Then she began
speculating about whether Rachael was coming
home again in time for school after the summer
holidays. When she realised that they were all
questions that her mother was unable to
answer, Keris stopped asking about her, much
to Gaynor's relief.

Barri took a week's holiday and they went
to all the places that Keris loved to visit. Once,
when it was raining, they spent the entire day
at the wonderful National Museum of Wales in
Cathays Park. Gaynor let them go on their own;
trailing around looking at things which didn't
really interest her was no fun and it gave her
a chance to catch up with housework, washing
and ironing, so that she would be able to enjoy

their outings to the seaside without a care in the world.

As well as taking a trip to Barry Island, which was always a favourite with Keris, they had outings to Swansea, Porthcawl and Llantwit Major.

Keris enjoyed them all, but she claimed she still preferred Barry Island, so they spent the last day of Barri's holiday there.

Gaynor was worried about how she was going to keep Keris entertained once Barri went back to work, but on the second day, when they took a picnic to Roath Park, Keris met up with some of her school friends and from then on all she wanted to do was to spend the day with them.

Since they were all local children Gaynor accepted that she would probably come to no harm and that it was better for her to be out enjoying herself with them than cooped up in the house.

She knew she couldn't keep her wrapped up in cotton wool for ever. At first she was a little bit worried that some of the boys they played with seemed to be rather boisterous and she hoped there would be no trouble.

At the weekend, Keris wanted to be with Barri. He doted on her and in Gaynor's opinion he spoiled her by always agreeing to do what she wanted to do and going to new places.

'You've been to three new places already this summer,' Gaynor told her when she said they'd never been to Penarth so could they go there for the day.

'It's only half an hour away on the train,' Barri pointed out when he agreed to her request. 'If you don't want to come with us then you can have a day on your own.'

Gaynor didn't want a day on her own. She had plenty of those when Keris was out playing with her friends. When she was at home on her own her mind was full of disturbing thoughts and images of what Sara and Rachael might be doing and worrying about where they were and if they were getting enough to eat.

She knew it was foolish but she couldn't help it. She knew Barri didn't worry about them like she did, which was why she never mentioned her fears to him. Why should he be concerned when they weren't his daughters?

She sometimes thought that he was relieved that they had gone away. He seemed so much easier going nowadays, especially with Keris, and more and more she worried that their younger daughter was being spoiled.

She was quite glad when it was time for Keris to go back to school although in the days leading up to the start of the new term she was also on edge about whether Rachael might in fact return in time for school after all.

If she didn't, then she would need to go and see Miss Davis and explain her absence since she still had another year to do at school before she was old enough to leave.

'Simply tell her that Rachael is living in Spain with her aunt,' Barri advised. 'I wouldn't bother to explain why or say anything else about it.'

'But she's not old enough to leave school yet,' Gaynor protested.

'I imagine they have schools over there, cariad.' He smiled.

'Yes, I suppose they have, but the children and the teachers will all speak Spanish and Rachael doesn't know a word of it.'

'She probably does by now!' he commented drily. 'She's been over there a month and if I know Rachael, she'll pick it up in no time. She isn't a shrinking violet, so she won't want to sit in a corner and say nothing. If she wants to mix and make friends, then she'll have to speak the lingo. If they are staying with Saratina's relations they will all speak Spanish so she'll learn it in no time at all.'

At first Keris grumbled about having to go to school on her own. The promise of a new fountain pen and a propelling pencil for Christmas, providing she didn't miss a single day all term, soon solved this.

By Christmas it seemed to be accepted by all of them that Rachael wasn't coming home. Gaynor still worried about her, but most of the time she kept her concern to herself.

'How can I send Rachael a present or even a card if I don't know where she lives?' Gaynor sighed as she started to make preparations for Christmas.

Barri shook his head. 'Well, you can't, so the best thing to do is to forget about it.'

Gaynor felt that it was bad enough losing complete contact with Sara but she didn't want the same thing to happen with Rachael. Without saying anything to either Barri or Keris she went down to Sophia Street to ask one or two of the neighbours if they had heard from Saratina, but no one had.

It was too late on that occasion for her to go and find Margarita's house, so Gaynor returned home to think matters over. Another day or so wasn't going to make any difference, she told herself.

When she finally did go to the address in Adelaide Street, she found that Margarita was living in a room behind a butcher's shop. It was small, dirty and sordid, and, to her dismay, she found that Margarita had two small children; one a toddler clinging to her skirts and the other a baby only a few weeks old.

Margarita looked scruffy and unkempt, her once beautiful wavy hair was limp and straight with grease and her grubby blouse was stained with food and where the baby had been sick down it. She smelled sour and horrible. She said that she had no idea what had happened to Saratina and she didn't even know that Rachael had gone to Spain with her.

'If she wanted a kid to bring up then she could have had one of mine,' Margarita flared, glaring at Gaynor. 'I never hear from her or from any of the others in the family. I saw José once, he had a kitbag over his shoulder and he was walking along James Street towards the Pier Head. I shouted out to him but he didn't take any notice. I think he must have signed up with the Merchant Navy or something,' she added dolefully.

'Do you think your priest might know where Saratina is?'

Margarita laughed scornfully. 'She didn't go to Mass any more than I do. I haven't seen inside the church for years now.' She smiled tightly. 'And to think that our José and Sanje were both altar boys. Mam used to wash and iron those lace-edged white tops they wore over their black clothes and they both looked like little angels. Underneath it all they were really little devils,' she said with a harsh little laugh.

Gaynor returned home even more depressed. She tried to tell herself that it was much better that Rachael had gone to Spain with Saratina than that she had stayed down in Tiger Bay with her. Not that Saratina would have let herself go like her sister had. Saratina had always been smartly dressed. In fact, she had prided herself on always wearing the latest fashions and had tried to talk her into doing so as well. Gaynor hoped she still did, and that she was now encouraging Rachael to do the same.

As the months passed, Gaynor was well aware that Barri really couldn't understand why, after all this time, she was still so worried and distressed about Sara and Rachael. Whenever she mentioned it he always reminded her that since neither of them had ever bothered to get in touch after they'd left Cardiff it was foolish to keep worrying.

As far as they knew, Sara was still in Germany, but whether or not she had managed to trace her father they had no idea. Much the same applied to Rachael. She was still in Spain, and had obviously made a life for herself, so why get upset because she couldn't send a card or a present for her birthday or at Christmas.

Keris was now almost the same age as Rachael had been when she'd left home with Saratina. She was entirely different to her sisters both in her looks and colouring, as well as in her nature, and much closer to Barri than they had ever been.

Gaynor still felt that Barri spoiled her. He was forever going out of his way to do things that interested her, or pleased her, and she had to admit that she sometimes felt resentful that he showed her so much special attention.

It also worried her the way Keris turned his feelings for her to her own benefit. She didn't wheedle; her approach was far more subtle. She took him into her confidence and asked his advice. It was a form of flattery that seemed to pay dividends every time.

For her twelfth birthday she asked for a bicycle and when they had pointed out that she couldn't even ride she had immediately come up with 'No, but you will teach me, won't you, Dad?' That had clinched it, and he had taken her along to the bicycle shop to choose the one she wanted and then wheeled it all the way home with her balancing on the saddle.

Barri spent the entire weekend helping her to get her balance. On the following Monday night, the moment she came in from school, she took the bike and headed for Roath Park.

Gaynor chased after her to the bottom of the road, calling her to come back, but she took no notice. Gaynor felt sure that she wasn't safe on it because she couldn't ride properly yet. As she watched her wobbling her way on to the main road Gaynor's heart was in her mouth, but she knew it was useless following her; there was nothing she could do about it.

Barri was home before Keris returned and he was highly amused by her daring. 'She's a real tomboy when she wants to be and no mistake,' he chortled proudly.

Gaynor was annoyed, but she said nothing. It seemed pointless to cause a row when she could see even before it started that she would lose out. Barri would support Keris, no matter what she said. He would dismiss her fears for Keris's safety and call her an old fusspot.

In the months that followed, however, it was the crowd Keris associated with that concerned Gaynor most.

The minute she came in from school she was back out again on her bike saying that she was going to meet her friends in Roath Park or wherever they had decided to ride. Only a couple of the girls had their own bikes and Keris wouldn't loan hers to anyone, so most of the time she was riding around with boys not only of her own age but also older.

Although she knew that Barri was right and that they were all from respectable homes, she didn't like Keris spending so much time with them.

'It's good for her, she has no brothers and we don't want her growing up afraid of men, now do we?'

'No, and neither do we want her chasing after boys at her age.'

'What's that supposed to mean? They ride their bikes together, that's all.'

'I don't think it is,' Gaynor protested. 'I went up to Roath Park the other afternoon and she and a couple of other girls were hanging about by the pond with some boys and they had their arms round each other.'

'You mean the girls had their arms round each other?'

'No, I mean the girls had their arms round the boys. They seemed to be larking about and then they started to pair off and that spells trouble.'

'Oh, come on, Gaynor,' Barri protested. 'It's only what we used to do, now isn't it? I used to wait for you, and you used to hang around for me after school so that we could be together.'

'Yes, and look at the trouble it got us into!'

'Not really! We used to talk a lot, all those plans about our future and so on. Day dreaming, exploring each other's dreams. What harm is there in that? We never did anything we shouldn't have done, now did we?'

'No, but then you were old enough to know better. You're three years older than me.'

'Well, from what you've been saying, some of the boys Keris has been going around with are older than her. They probably have as much sense as I had and behave just as honourably as I did.' He grinned.

'Things are different nowadays. We were always very careful not to do wrong.'

'Only because I was scared stiff of your dad!' He chuckled. 'He didn't approve of us seeing so much of each other, did he!' he commented reminiscently.

'No, I'm afraid he didn't like it at all; nor did my mam, if it comes to that.'

'And what happened? It made us all the more determined to go on seeing each other. You, especially,' he teased. 'I can remember how you used to sneak into the workshop at Ferndale Forge on your way home from school after I started work there.'

'Yes,' Gaynor sighed, 'and that was our undoing. That night when my dad caught me kissing you and you made such a song and dance about it, saying I had frightened you. I think if you hadn't done that then he wouldn't have sent you packing.'

'Don't you believe it! He was determined to separate us.'

Gaynor didn't bother to argue with him about it, but she was worried about what was going to happen when the school holidays started in August and Keris wanted to spend all her time out on her bike.

Lately, as she had been trying to explain to Barri, Keris had taken to spending more and more time alone with just one of the boys. He was good-looking and called Idris Williams, but Gaynor didn't know anything about him or his family.

In Cardiff, it wasn't like it had been in Ferndale when she and Barri were growing up and where everyone knew everybody else.

All she knew about Idris was that he was almost a year older than Keris, but when she had mentioned this a few times and asked if he was leaving school in July at the start of the summer holidays, Keris had said that he wouldn't be fourteen by then so he'd have to stay on until Christmas.

That meant he was going to be around all through the summer holidays and even if he did get himself a part-time job, as so many boys of his age did, he would still have far too much time to spend with Keris.

Chapter Twenty-Six

Much to Gaynor's surprise she found that Barri was as worried as she was about how Keris was going to spend her time during the summer holidays.

'This Idris boy might get himself a summer job,' she pointed out, 'so if he does, then he won't have very much spare time to be out with Keris.'

'Mmm! Well, the less time they have together the more they will try to do when they are together now, and you know where that can lead, especially if it is in the evenings. Canoodling is one thing, but if they take it a step further . . .'

'Barri! Keris is only twelve.'

'Yes, well I know that! I've accused you of being a fusspot, but the more I think back to when we were that age, I know how tempting it can be to feel grown-up and to want to experiment, even though I'm not the heavy-handed dad that your father was.'

'No, I agree you're not. You let Keris get away with far too much. In this family it's me that's the ogre, not her dad.'

'You an ogre? I don't think so!' Barri laughed.

'Anyway,' he went on, 'I've thought of a solution; one that will save you and Keris from falling out. I've got some holiday due, so why don't I take that and then the three of us can spend time together and Keris won't want to go out with Idris.'

Gaynor shook her head. 'I think you are wrong about that. If we are going to Barry Island or somewhere like that then she will want him to come along as well and that will only be encouraging him and giving him the idea that we approve of them being such close friends.'

'You might be right, if that's where we were going, but she won't dream of asking if he can come along as well when she hears where we're going.'

'Oh?' Gaynor looked at him questioningly. 'So where are you thinking we should go?'

'Well . . .' he paused and selected a cigarette from a packet of Lucky Strike and lit up. 'I thought that seeing as you are still brooding about what has happened to Sara, we could take Keris over to Germany on a holiday.'

Gaynor's face lit up. 'That's a wonderful idea.' She beamed. Then her face clouded. 'Where in Germany, though? It's a huge country; we have no idea where to start looking.'

'You must have some idea where Konrad Claus came from?'

She shook her head, her eyes filling with tears. 'I remember him once mentioning

Cologne, but I don't think he lived there . . .'

'Cologne, now that sounds promising,' Barri said enthusiastically. 'There's a wonderful cathedral there so we can tell Keris that's why we're going to Cologne.'

Gaynor looked doubtful. 'I don't think she is going to be very thrilled by that idea.'

'Well, we'll tell her something; anyway, that's where we'll go. I'll make the arrangements. We'll probably go by train to Dover then across on a boat and then by train to Cologne.'

Gaynor smiled wistfully. 'It's a great idea, Barri, and I'm grateful for the thought, but won't it be like looking for a needle in a haystack, hoping to find Sara after all this time? We don't even know what she looks like these days.'

'Rubbish. You'd know Sara the minute you set eyes on her.'

'Perhaps; that is if I do manage to set eyes on her.'

'Well, look at it this way,' Barri said in frustration, 'it will get Keris away from Idris, it will give us a different sort of holiday, and it will give you a chance to find Sara.'

Gaynor nodded and tried to look happy about the plan, but in her heart she felt as though she was being torn apart. Their holiday would probably not only open up the wound of being separated from Sara, but renew all her worry and concern. It would be painful to be in the country where she lived and know that she might be walking the same streets, eating in the same cafés, and yet didn't even know she was breathing the same air.

When Barri mentioned the proposed holiday in Cologne to Keris, expecting her to be highly delighted, she frowned and shook her head.

'I don't want to go there.'

'Why ever not? Your mam is hoping we might be able to find Sara.'

'I guessed that,' she retorted huffily. 'Well, I don't want to spend my summer holiday looking for Sara. I would sooner find Rachael, she's the one I miss the most.'

Barri and Gaynor looked at each other in dismay. They were not sure whether to reconsider their plans or to insist that since Barri had already checked out the travel arrangements they should go to Cologne.

'I don't really want to go away anywhere,' Keris went on, ignoring their concerned expressions. 'I would sooner stay here at home and see Idris every day. We've got all sorts of things planned, we're even thinking of going camping.'

'On your own!' Gaynor exclaimed in shocked disbelief.

'If you are missing Rachael all that much, then perhaps we could change our plans and go to Spain,' Barri suggested quickly.

'Spain! Do you really mean it?' Keris's face lit up and her eyes widened in anticipation. 'Oh yes, I'd love to go to Spain, and then we can look for Rachael.'

312

'Well, I don't suppose we'll be able to find her, but I agree, it would be nice,' Gaynor admitted.

Barri looked confused. 'I don't understand you, Keris. You don't want to go to Germany to see if we can find Sara, but you do want to go to Spain to look for Rachael. Why?'

'It's so long ago that Sara left, I don't remember much about her,' Keris pointed out. 'Rachael and I had fun together; I miss her a lot, and I wish she'd come home.'

'You were always squabbling with her, if I remember,' Gaynor reminded her.

Keris shrugged. 'Only friendly tiffs. We got on well really. We shared all our secrets.' She smiled impishly. 'Well, most of our secrets. Anyway, I miss her the most.'

Barri looked at Gaynor and raised his eyebrows. 'Well, are you prepared for us to change our plans and go and look for Rachael instead of Sara?'

'I don't know. I'd already made up my mind about what we were going to do.'

'Please, Mam,' Keris wheedled, sidling up to her and grabbing her hand.

Gaynor tried hard to evaluate what was the best thing to do. If she were to force Keris into going to Germany, she'd probably sulk the whole time and make their life hell. If they abandoned their holiday plans altogether and stayed at home, she'd have to worry of Keris being out with Idris all the time and not knowing where they were or what they were up to. If they went to Spain as Keris wanted them to do, they'd probably have an enjoyable holiday and they might even be able to find Rachael.

'All right; if that's what you want to do, and providing your dad can cancel all the arrangements he's already made for us to go to Germany, then we'll go to Spain.'

'Of course he can, can't you Dad?' Keris declared jubilantly. 'Oh, thanks, Mam, I've always wanted to go there, ever since I knew that Rachael was going there with Saratina. Do you know, Mam, it's three years since Rachael went to Spain.'

'Yes, I know how long it is.' Gaynor smiled sadly. Three years, and every night during that time the last thing on her mind before she went to sleep was wondering how Rachael was, and whether or not Saratina was looking after her properly. It hurt that neither Saratina nor Rachael had ever written to them. Gaynor and Saratina had been such good friends in the old days. It was as if she wanted to cut off all her connections with the past.

It was also almost five years since Sara had left home and gone to Germany and there had never been a word from her either, she reminded herself bitterly.

'Yes, Rachael has probably changed a lot from the schoolgirl we knew,' she agreed.

'I'll recognise her, though,' Keris asserted confidently, 'even if she doesn't know me at first. I've grown so much that she mightn't recognise me,' she explained.

From then on all conversation centred on their forthcoming holiday in Spain and trying to find out all there was to know about Almeria.

They were all a little disconcerted when they did so. Spain seemed to be in turmoil and a man named Franco was causing a lot of problems even though he was living in Morocco.

'That's not in Spain, it's in Africa and separated from Spain by the Straits of Gibraltar,' Keris told them, adding, 'I know because we were told in our geography lesson.'

'Yes, you're quite right, but Franco is planning to return to Spain when the time is right because he wants to become their leader,' Barri told her.

'Does that matter, or stop us from going there?' Gaynor frowned.

'No, I don't suppose it will come to anything,' Barri shrugged. 'We've had upsets here ever since the General Strike but it's been safe enough for people from other countries to come here on visits and for business purposes.'

Keris was much more interested in what was to be seen and enjoyed in Almeria and, more than anything, what sort of clothes they ought to pack.

'I told Miss Davis we were going there to look for Rachael,' she announced, 'and she said that there is a fortified cathedral and there used to be cannons in its towers to defend it against

Turkish people and the North African pirates in the olden days. Oh, and there's a hilltop village called the Alcazaba, and it's all caves there and people still live in them. Bet you didn't know that,' she added cheekily.

'No, but I do know that there's a museum in the centre of Almeria and it's full of all sorts of interesting things.'

'Bet it's not as good as the museum we have here in Cardiff. Idris says . . .'

Quickly Gaynor changed the conversation. She had an uneasy feeling that if they weren't careful Keris would be asking if they could take Idris with them and she was afraid that if she was sufficiently persistent then Barri might give in to her.

Barri must have had the same concern because he swiftly turned the conversation back to Almeria. This time it was about the different kinds of food they would have there.

'Their speciality is fresh sardines in a hot sauce and they also have all sorts of tasty stews with pasta, beans and herbs in them.'

This didn't interest Keris, but Barri continued to distract her by getting out a map and showing her where Almeria was and pointing out some of the nearby attractions like Roquettas de Mar, a fishing village which, he told her, had little white houses grouped all around the harbour.

'How do you know that? You're making it up, aren't you?'

Barri smiled and ruffled her short brown hair. 'You'll have to wait and find out, won't you?' he teased.

'If we don't find Rachael playing her guitar in Almeria then perhaps we should look for her there,' Keris mused.

'Playing her guitar?' Barri frowned uncomprehendingly.

'That's what she was going to do in Spain,' Keris reminded him. 'She said she was going to sing, dance and play the guitar that had once been her dad's. Didn't she tell you?' She looked from one to the other of them enquiringly.

'She'd learned lots of Spanish words before she left,' Keris went on, not waiting for them to reply. 'Saratina taught them to her. She told me some of them. There was *alboreas* – that means a song and dance that gypsies do, but they only do it at weddings. To do it at any other time is unlucky.'

'You seem to know a lot; why have you never told us this before?' Gaynor said sharply.

'She also told me that she was going to do flamenco dancing and learn how to use *palillos*,' Keris went on, ignoring her mother's question.

'*Palillos*, whatever's that?' Barri asked, lifting his eyebrows.

'It's little wooden castanets. You hold them both in one hand and click them together as you dance,' Keris informed him.

'Well, it's a good thing we've decided to go to Spain, seeing you know so much about what goes on there,' Barri told her. 'Neither your mam nor me speak any Spanish so perhaps you'll be able to act as an interpreter for us.'

Keris shook her head. 'Not really! Rachael only taught me a few words, like *balia bien*, which means good dancing and *vamo' ya*.'

'Well, what does that mean?'

Keris grinned impishly. '*Vamo' ya* means let's go.'

Barri smiled. 'Right, Miss Know-it-all, then you'd better start getting your suitcase packed ready, hadn't you, or you might find we leave you behind.'

Almeria was like a dream, the sparkling deep blue sea, the sunlit streets, the misty-topped mountain range rising up behind the city, and the fascinating skyline of the cathedral and the Alcazaba perched on its hilltop was everything they had anticipated.

In the centre of the city was a long avenue with shady squares off it. Sitting outside in one of these squares, enjoying cool drinks or some of the local dishes, Gaynor hoped that she might one day spot Rachael amongst the crowds.

Barri and Keris were so fascinated by all that was going on that they seemed to have forgotten about their reason for being there, but Gaynor hadn't. She never stopped studying the passing people; the wizened older women in their black all-encompassing skirts and black lace shawls, the young barefoot girls and the stylishly dressed younger women. There were so many with shoulder-length, dark wavy hair like Rachael's that many times her heart thudded as she thought she had seen her, then her spirits fell again as she realised it was yet another stranger.

She looked for Saratina, too, but there were so many women of indeterminate age. Some wore their hair cut short, the same as Saratina had worn hers, yet she never saw anyone with her distinctive cheekbones.

Two days before the end of their stay, Keris badgered them to take her up to the hilltop village of Alcazaba.

'Is it safe?' Gaynor said uneasily. 'It's where all the gypsies live up there in those caves, remember. We are foreigners so we could be attacked or robbed.'

'What, all three of us?' Barry joked. 'One look at my face and most of them will be scared stiff in case I put the evil eye on them. They will be more scared of us than we are of them.'

Keris giggled. 'Your face always frightens my friends until they get to know you,' she agreed.

'There you are, then; we'll be quite safe and it's about the only place we haven't visited around here.'

It was hot and sticky and long before they had reached the cluster of houses Gaynor was wishing she'd stayed behind down in one of the shady squares.

As they walked amongst the glittering white

caves, she looked sideways at the primitive dwellings. The interiors seemed to be very gloomy and to have only the barest of furnishings. She shivered; suddenly she had an uncomfortable feeling that someone was watching them.

She was about to reach out and grab hold of Barri's arm for reassurance when a hand lightly touched her shoulder. She swung round in fright, and then gasped when she recognised the young girl at her elbow.

She was dressed in a vivid blue and green skirt and an orange blouse, but the dark wavy hair and dark eyes were so familiar that she almost choked as she gasped, 'Rachael!'

'Mam? What are you doing here?'

Before she could answer Barri had turned round to tell her to hurry up. In seconds he and Keris were back and Keris and Rachael were hugging each other and crying tears of happiness.

'Do you live here?' Gaynor asked in amazement when they had finally calmed down a little.

'Yes, with Saratina and her aunt and uncle,' Rachael told them. 'Come.' She took Keris and Gaynor by the hand and pulled them towards one of the larger caves leaving Barri to follow. 'Saratina will be very surprised to see you all.'

Saratina was less enthusiastic than Rachael, but nonetheless she made them welcome. She invited them into the darkness of their cave and plied them with a long cool drink of orange and lemon juice that was very refreshing.

'You will eat with us and then we must go to work,' Saratina told them as she offered them bowls of *gurullos*, which seemed to be a mixture of stew and pasta.

'Work. What sort of work?' Barri frowned.

'We sing and dance in the circus. Have you not been to see it?'

Keris looked excited. 'No, where is it?'

Saratina and Rachael exchanged glances. 'We will take you.'

'Can you tell us what happens? What do you do?'

'You will see. I sing, dance and play the guitar to keep the patrons entertained in between the acts,' Rachael told her. 'You will be very proud of me; my name is on all the posters because I am one of the stars of the show.'

Gaynor looked questioningly at Saratina.

'What she says is true,' she confirmed. 'Rachael has made quite a name for herself.'

Realisation suddenly dawned on Gaynor's face. 'Do you mean she is Raquela the Spanish Songbird?' she asked in awe. 'I have seen her name on billboards in the market place and at the railway station, but—'

'In her glamorous flamenco dress and her exotic make up and her hair piled up you didn't recognise her as your little Rachael,' Saratina declared with a proud smile.

Chapter Twenty-Seven

Barri had only planned for them to stay in Almeria for a week but Keris was so overjoyed at seeing Rachael again that he suggested that, as he still had another week of his holiday, which he had been planning to spend at home catching up on jobs that needed doing in the house, they should stay on for another few days.

Rachael was also pleased. 'This weekend there will be a very special fair that takes place only once a year,' she told them, her face lighting up with enthusiasm. 'There'll be parades through the main streets of Almeria and our circus will have a very special perform- ance in Plaza Vieja. That's right in the heart of the city,' she explained. 'It will be a magical night, one you will never forget.'

Keris was eager to know what Rachael would be wearing and what sort of dance she would be doing but her sister was tight-lipped and refused to tell her.

'No, you must wait until the night, otherwise you won't be surprised,' she teased. 'I can tell you it will be well worth the wait,' she prom- ised.

When Rachael wasn't working at the circus Keris wanted to be with her. Barri felt that it would be quite safe for her to do so, but Gaynor was on edge.

She didn't like the gypsy quarters, nor, for the most part, did she like the gypsies themselves. They were always very polite to her, but she thought there was a challenge in their sharp glittering eyes as if they resented her being there. She was sure that the only reason she was accepted by them at all was because they knew that she was Rachael's mother.

Their attitude often made her feel uncomfortable. Rachael was so much at home with them all that it was almost as if she was Saratina's daughter and at times Gaynor felt like an interloper.

Keris had no such inhibitions. She laughed and talked to the sharp-eyed, swarthy men and women who lived at Casa de los Puche as though they were all old friends. She let them twine flowers in her hair and laughed along with them when they simply slid straight out again.

She took it in good part when they encouraged her to dance or sing along with her sister, even though they usually shook their gleaming dark heads in disapproval when she finished.

Gaynor watched all this uneasily, afraid that it was making Keris more and more determined to stay in Spain with her sister and that was something she certainly wouldn't allow. She was sure Barri felt the same way although at the moment he showed far less concern than she did when Keris hinted that it was what she would like to do.

Barri was enjoying himself exploring Almeria. He spent a lot of time at the museum and wandering around the wonderful churches, studying their architectural splendour and their history. One of his favourites seemed to be Alcazaba, the old Arab fortress with its three huge walled enclosures.

Often, when they were having their evening meal, he talked about what had gone on in the past. In times of war, he told them, it had held as many as twenty thousand men. Invariably this led to him expressing his concern about the state of things in present-day Spain.

'I thought our General Strike and then the Wall Street crash in America which affected all our trade was bad enough, but here there seems to be an equal amount of unrest. This chap called Franco seems to be at the bottom of it and because of him the country is becoming so divided that there's even talk of civil war.'

He never went any further than that because he could see that Gaynor didn't like talking about war and Keris wasn't in the least bit interested. She was far too excited by what she had seen and done herself that day.

The night of the carnival was spectacular. The day had been so hot that Gaynor felt exhausted but for Keris's sake she rallied and changed into her prettiest summer dress and let Keris choose for herself what she wanted to wear.

Saratina had found them a vantage point to watch everything from and the streets were already packed to bursting point when they reached there.

Keris was impatient for the circus to appear, but there was quite a long time to wait. Several other parades passed before they appeared, but they were all so novel and colourful that she watched entranced.

Then came a huge roll of drums and a fanfare of music to herald the approach of the circus performers.

Rachael, looking breathtakingly lovely in a full-skirted diaphanous white dress that was nipped into the waist with a huge silver sash, and wearing white flowers in her black wavy hair, led the troupe of dancers into the centre of the square. She was strumming on a guitar that was supported by a silver sash crossed over one shoulder. The crowd went wild with applause as she started to sing, in Spanish, a beautiful, haunting song.

The words meant nothing to Gaynor, but the pathos of the song and music touched her heart. Even Barri looked moved by the beauty of it all.

The spell was broken when the rest of the troupe followed her, singing and dancing wildly. Rachael still played her guitar, but now she was accompanied by the complete circus band which comprised of guitars, flutes and drums.

They watched, spellbound, as acrobats performed daring balancing acts right there in the square and clowns tumbled and frolicked and interacted with jugglers and buffoons.

Between each spectacular act the troupe of dancers entranced the onlookers. The performance lasted for almost an hour and then other less spectacular events took over. Vendors began pushing their way amongst the crowd with trays piled high with all sorts of drinks and sweetmeats.

Keris pleaded to stay on until the very end, but since it was almost midnight, and the crowd were becoming increasingly noisy and wild, both Barri and Gaynor felt it was time for them to return to their lodgings.

'Can't we say goodnight to Saratina and tell Rachael how wonderful she looked?' Keris wheedled.

'We will if we can find them. Otherwise we'll go and see Rachael in the morning. Don't forget, tomorrow will be our last day here and then we have to go home.'

Sulkily, Keris accepted their decision and when they couldn't find Rachael she agreed that she was tired and that she'd wait until the next day to see her.

They'd been in bed for about an hour, and Barri was sound asleep, but Gaynor felt so troubled at the thought of going back to Cardiff and leaving Rachael in Almeria that she was unable to sleep.

It was so hot and breathless in the bedroom that she slipped out of bed and went to stand by the open window. Sounds of distant revelry floated up to her on the still, night air. She was about to return to bed when she was aware of a small shadowy figure slipping out of the house, running across the road and heading towards the centre of Almeria.

For a split second she couldn't believe her eyes. Then, her heart pounding, she made her way to the small adjoining bedroom to reassure herself that it hadn't been Keris whom she'd just seen.

The room was in darkness. Cautiously she moved closer to the bed and all her fears were justified. The bed was empty.

She stood there for a moment not sure what to do. Should she waken Barri, or should she slip on some clothes and go in pursuit of Keris herself?

Barri was so sound asleep that she knew it would take her several minutes to rouse him and convince him of what had happened.

Even as the thought was going through her mind she was peeling off her nightdress and pulling on her day clothes. Grabbing a cardigan in case it had turned colder, she crept down the stairs and let herself out of the building as quietly as Keris had done.

She had no idea exactly where Keris had

gone, but she was pretty certain that since she would be trying to find Rachael and Saratina it would have been back to either La Rambla, the long avenue right in the centre of Almeria, or the market area of Plaza Vieja, where Rachael and her troupe had performed.

Her search was fruitless. She didn't speak enough Spanish to be able to ask if anyone knew where she would find them. The crowd was becoming increasingly raucous and she began to fear not only for Keris's safety but also for her own.

Twice she headed off in the wrong direction, lured by the sound of guitar music and someone singing. More and more she wished she had shaken Barri awake and made him come with her.

She was almost on the point of giving up when she spotted Rachael's glittering white dress. It stood out from all the blacks and reds and vivid hues that most people were wearing.

Pushing her way through the dense crowd she finally managed to get close enough to call out to her. 'Rachael! Have you seen Keris? Do you where is she? Is she with you?'

Saratina detached herself from the throng gathered around Rachael and jostled her way through the crowd to Gaynor's side. 'What are you doing here?' she asked in surprise. 'I thought you would have gone home to your beds long before this.'

'We did, but I saw Keris sneaking out and I

tried to follow her. I was sure she was coming back here.'

'No.' Saratina shook her head. 'I think you are mistaken. We've not seen her, not since we were all together at the Plaza Vieja.'

'She must be here somewhere!' Gaynor insisted. 'Can't you ask if anyone has seen her? I've tried, but I can't make anybody understand me.'

'Wait here. Don't move from this spot. I'll see what I can do,' Saratina promised.

Gaynor tried to ignore all the hugs and kisses she received from semi-drunk men and women as they danced and sang all around her. Her thoughts were centred on Keris, worrying in case she had come to some harm.

Rachael and Saratina both failed to find Keris. 'Go on back to your lodgings, Mam,' Rachael urged. 'She most likely got frightened by all the noise the crowd are making and turned tail and went back. She's probably tucked up in bed again by now.'

Gaynor suspected that they could be right. She let them walk with her to the corner of the street where she was staying, but she could see that they were both very tired so she didn't ask them to come any further although she was rather surprised that Rachael didn't insist on coming back with her to make sure that her sister really was safe and sound.

As quietly as possible she crept into the house and back upstairs. Tiptoeing into Keris's bedroom she gasped in dismay. The bed was as empty as when she had left the house; Keris certainly hadn't returned. So where was she, Gaynor thought in alarm?

This time she had no qualms at all about rousing Barri.

'Why on earth didn't you waken me the moment you knew she had left the house and not go chasing all over the place after her on your own?' he exclaimed crossly as he scrambled out of bed. 'Anything could have happened to you.'

'Well it didn't,' she retorted sharply. 'I found Saratina and Rachael and they helped me to look for her but it was hopeless. There's such a dense crowd out there and half of them are drunk and . . .'

'And Keris is out there somewhere mixed up with them,' he exclaimed angrily.

Even as he was talking to her he was pulling on his clothes, running a comb through his tousled hair, and then slipping his feet into his shoes.

'Where are you going?'

'Off out to look for her as I would have been doing ages ago if you'd had the sense to wake me up.'

'We've looked everywhere for her . . .'

'She must be somewhere. Don't make matters worse by saying she's disappeared. You stay here just in case she does come back. And if she does, then for heaven's sake make sure the pair of you stay right here, don't start looking for me! There have been enough wild goose chases for one night.'

It was almost two hours before Barri returned. Dawn was already breaking, the sun rising like a huge crimson banner. He looked weary, his face grey with worry, which only accentuated his disfigurement and made him appear almost saturnine.

He seemed to be too exhausted to speak as he sank down on the side of the bed and shook his head from side to side. 'Not a sign of her anywhere. The crowds have nearly all gone home and most of the streets are empty.'

Gaynor sat down beside him and put her arms around his shoulders, drawing his head down on her breast and silently stroking his hair. She knew how he was feeling but she had no words of comfort or solace to offer. They clung to each other, rocking backwards and forwards.

It was half an hour later when Saratina arrived with the news that they had found Keris. They had spent several hours looking for her after they had told Gaynor to go home, but with no success. When they eventually arrived home they found her there. She was curled up on their bed fast asleep.

'I thought it was best to let her sleep. I told Rachael to get into bed with her so that when she did waken there would be someone there to see she didn't disappear again.'

'Thank you!' Gaynor's voice was husky with

relief. 'You know we are going home today, don't you? As soon as we've booked out of here we'll come and collect her.'

Saratina nodded. 'I'll make sure she stays with us till then. Actually,' she smiled gravely, 'she has mentioned to Rachael that she wants to stay with us permanently, did you know that?'

'She has dropped plenty of hints but that's absolutely out of the question,' Barri told her firmly.

Saratina nodded in agreement. 'I hoped you'd say that.'

'We've lost two daughters, we certainly don't intend losing another,' Gaynor said angrily. 'If I had my way, Rachael would be coming back to Cardiff with us right now.'

'Yes, well, I can't stop you asking her to do so, but I think you will find that is also right out of the question,' Saratina told her curtly.

Chapter Twenty-Eight

As they left Almeria, Gaynor, Barri and Keris barely said a word to each other.

Keris had slept most of the time, cradled in Gaynor's arms, utterly worn out by the events of her last night in Almeria.

Once on the boat, Barri went up on deck to try and clear his mind. He wished now that they had never come to Spain after all; it had been so upsetting, not only for Keris, but for all of them.

It troubled him deeply that Keris wanted to stay on in Almeria. He shuddered as he recalled the sound of her wheedling, pleading voice as she begged to be allowed to stay with Rachael.

He suspected that in Keris's eyes the sort of life that Rachael was living was exciting and glamorous. As far as he was concerned Rachael had sunk as low as she could go.

He blamed himself for letting her go there with Saratina in the first place. The pair of them were now reduced to the company they were keeping. They even dressed and looked like the gypsies they were living amongst.

He accepted that Rachael had a certain amount of talent. She could play the guitar well enough and she had a good singing voice, but he didn't like the way she pirouetted around the streets, dancing like a dervish.

It must be the Vario blood coming out, he reasoned, and he certainly wouldn't want his own daughter behaving in such an abandoned fashion.

He'd never felt so upset in his life when Gaynor had woken him up and told him that Keris was missing and that she'd been out looking for her and couldn't find her.

Thank God Saratina had the decency to bring her back. He was more grateful than she would ever know. He certainly had no intention of telling her that. He had never liked Saratina; she had far too much influence over Gaynor.

Still, he told himself, that was all in the past. Saratina was far away in Spain and Keris would be safe and sound back in Cardiff. Tomorrow, she would be able to pick up the threads of her old life and mix with school friends who didn't have an air of glamour about them to turn her head.

Perhaps in the past he had been a bit too easy on her, but that would change from now on. He didn't want to be a heavy-handed father like Ieuan Sanderson had been, but he intended to lay down certain ground rules and, in future, he'd see that Keris obeyed them.

As she held Keris close, Gaynor felt so relieved that they'd found her safe and sound that she wanted to weep. She knew that Barri had been very worried, possibly even more than she had been. Keris was his daughter and Rachael wasn't, so it was only natural that he put Keris first.

Even so, she reflected, he indulged her far too much. They would have to have a serious talk about it and agree that in future they were a lot firmer.

It had been because they had changed their plans and gone to Spain instead of Germany that all this had happened. It was seeing Rachael looking so glamorous and dancing and singing that had made Keris envious. It was understandable. She was at an impressionable age and things like that meant a great deal. Now if they'd gone to Germany, even if they had found Sara, she wouldn't have been involved in anything like that.

She wondered exactly what Sara was doing these days. She didn't have Rachael's talents, and she'd been so very different; not only in looks, but in her ice-cold, reserved manner. She'd worked so conscientiously at school that they'd even hoped that she might want to become a teacher.

Gaynor smiled at the thought. That was what her dad had wanted her to be. It seemed such a very long time ago now.

Keris slept late on their first morning home and when she woke up she said she was starving.

She pulled a face when Gaynor told her she was too late for breakfast, but stopped grumbling when she was told that there was a full roast dinner waiting for her with her favourite apple pie and custard to follow.

When she made no reference to their holiday and her escapade in Almeria neither did Barri and Gaynor.

'We'll talk to her about it later,' Barry said quietly as he followed Gaynor out into the kitchen with a pile of used plates while she went to fetch their pudding.

'Yes,' she agreed, 'but we must have a talk first. We must both agree on exactly how we are going to handle things.' Gaynor laid a hand on his arm as he started to move away. 'It's important, Barri, we can't let her go on playing one of us off against the other like she's done in the past.'

For a moment he looked uncertain, and then he nodded. 'You're right, cariad. Come on, let's finish our meal in peace.'

'Right, then; you carry in this jug of custard and I'll bring the apple pie,' she told him.

When they went back into the living room the table was empty.

'Where on earth has she disappeared to now?' Barri asked, perplexed. 'We're not going to have a repeat of what happened in Almeria, are we?'

'Don't be silly!' Gaynor laughed.

'Oh, I'm stupid, am I?' he stated in annoyance. 'Then tell me, where is she?'

'Maybe she's gone up to her room to fetch a handkerchief or something,' Gaynor said over her shoulder as she headed for the stairs and called out, 'Keris! The pudding is on the table, come on down before it gets cold.'

When there was no reply she went up the stairs, still calling out to Keris.

Barri was standing at the bottom of the stairs when she came out of Keris's room. 'Gone again, has she?' he demanded.

'Well, she's not in her room.'

Neither of them bothered eating any of the pudding. Gaynor washed up the dishes in silence and stacked them on the draining board while she waited for the kettle to boil. She heard Barri walking along the hall to the front door then, after a pause, the sound of his steps as he returned to the living room.

He was sitting at the table, his head in his hands, when she carried the tray in.

'Come on, let's have this cuppa now that I've made it and then we'll go and look for her.'

'What's the point? We haven't any idea where she's gone, so we may as well wait until she comes home.'

'Then drink this,' Gaynor said as she placed a cup of tea in front of him.

'Perhaps we should have that chat you mentioned,' he said as he stirred two spoonfuls of sugar into his tea. 'After what happened in Spain you'd think she'd mention where she was going, she must know how worried we'd be.'

337

'She probably wasn't thinking,' Gaynor reasoned. 'She'll be back soon.'

She stirred sugar into her own cup and watched in silence as Barri lit a cigarette. Suddenly her face cleared. 'I bet I know where she's gone. She'll have gone to see Idris Jenkins.'

'That's another thing we are going to put a stop to,' Barri interrupted. 'You said she was seeing far too much of him and I should have listened to you.'

Gaynor bit down on her lower lip and made no comment.

'That's only the start,' Barri went on. 'We've got to talk to her about what happened in Spain. She can't be allowed to get away with that either. So far neither of us has said a word to her about it and we should have.'

'We were both too worried at first, and then too relieved when Saratina told us that she was safe and sound,' Gaynor pointed out.

'Yes, well, now we will and we'll start by laying down the rules of the way we want her to behave in future. I expect you to back me up over this,' he added, frowning at her. 'Understand?'

'Of course I will. In the past I've been the one who wanted you to back me up when I've been trying to make her toe the line if you remember.'

As it happened there was no need for either of them to talk to Keris and to lay down the rules as Barri put it.

Keris returned home half an hour later in

floods of tears. She burst into the house and tore up the stairs to her room.

'What the devil is the matter with her now,' Barri exclaimed exasperatedly.

'Keris!' he stood at the bottom of the stairs, shouting her name angrily. 'Keris, come down here this minute and explain your behaviour.'

Startled by the anger in her father's voice Keris appeared at the top of the stairs looking almost frightened.

'You heard what I said. Come on down here this minute.'

'I don't want to,' she protested. 'I don't want to talk to either of you, I hate you both, and I hate everyone.'

'We don't particularly like you,' he retorted. 'Not after the way you behaved in Almeria and certainly not with your behaviour since we came home. Dashing out like that in the middle of a meal without a word to your mother or to me; what do you think this is, a lodging house?'

'Shut up, shut, up shut up!' Keris screamed.

'That's enough! Come down here immediately and explain where you've been.'

'I went to see Idris Jenkins, if you must know. Satisfied?'

'That's where your mam said you might have gone. So why all the tears and blubbering?'

'Because he's dumped me, if you must know!' She edged her way down the stairs and stood looking at him defiantly. 'I suppose you're pleased about that!'

Barri looked nonplussed. 'Why should I be pleased? I've never even met the boy.'

Keris sniffed back her tears. 'Well, it is all your fault.' She scowled.

'It is? How do you make that out?'

'If you hadn't insisted that we all went to Spain on holiday then this wouldn't have happened. If I had been here he wouldn't have gone off with Paulette Fricker. He said he did it because he was lonely! Well, he wouldn't have been lonely if I hadn't gone away on holiday, now would he!'

Gaynor had been listening to their exchange from the living room, determined not to interfere. Now she came out into the hall and held out her arms to Keris.

'Don't cry about Idris Jenkins, he isn't worth it, cariad,' she said softly, stroking Keris's hair back from her forehead and kissing her warmly.

'He was my boyfriend, Mam, and now I've probably lost him,' she wailed.

'You're too young for a boyfriend,' Gaynor told her gently. 'You've a whole lifetime ahead; you'll find someone much better than Idris Jenkins.'

'No, I won't! If you part us now then when I find him again in fifty years' time he'll be old and ugly like Dad,' she sobbed as she pulled out of her mother's arms, pushed past Barri, and headed back upstairs to her room.

'Leave her. Let her be, Barri,' Gaynor said quickly, laying a restraining hand on his arm as he made to go after her. 'Let her cool down.'

'After what she's just said?' he demanded angrily.

'She doesn't mean any of it. She's so upset by what has happened that she doesn't know what she is saying,' Gaynor told him.

Barri shook his head. 'I don't understand you, I really don't and I certainly don't understand her.'

'I do,' she told him softly. 'She's behaving like I did when my father sent you away all those years ago. She feels her heart is broken and that life will never be the same again, just like I did when you left Ferndale.'

'If I ever set eyes on that Idris Jenkins his life will never be the same again,' Barri muttered.

'I don't think he'll be coming anywhere near us. Keris won't want anything more to do with him, you'll see.'

Gaynor was not altogether right. Keris continued to claim that Idris had broken her heart and ruined her life. Alternatively she sobbed and ranted about it for days until Gaynor felt she could stand it no longer and blamed herself that she had once again failed one of her daughters.

Seeing Rachael and realising how happy she was living with Saratina in Almeria had been a bitter pill. She had hoped that when Rachael saw her she would want to come back home, but it had been obvious that it was the last thing Rachael wanted to do. She was revelling in her new lifestyle, enjoying every minute of her singing and dancing routine. She seemed to regard Saratina as a friend and mother all rolled into one. She seemed to do everything Saratina asked of her without any fuss or argument.

It was this more than anything that was so hurtful, Gaynor reflected.

She had failed Sara as well, she thought sadly. Sara had never been in touch, not even after all this time. Probably the best thing she could do was to try and forget both her elder daughters and to stop worrying about them. Instead, she ought to concentrate on Keris. She owed that much to Barri.

She could see how hurt and angry he was about the way Keris seemed to be turning out, but it wasn't too late to turn things around. They could still guide her, and make sure that she didn't resent them and desert them in order to build an independent life like Sara and Rachael had done.

Barri listened to her in silence while she talked this over with him.

'Yes, we must try and make sure she doesn't ruin her life or turn away from us,' he agreed when she'd finished. He held Gaynor close. 'I know how disappointed you must be that Rachael didn't want to come back with us, but you must see now that she is settled and happy and that must be some consolation to you.'

'It is,' she agreed. 'I can't put her completely out of my mind, though, and I don't like the sort of life she is living, but I do realise that I have no need to worry about her any more.'

'And what about Sara?' he asked quietly.

Gaynor shook her head. 'I don't know what to think about her. If only I knew she was as settled and happy as Rachael appears to be, then I suppose I could stop worrying about her as well.'

Chapter Twenty-Nine

As she prepared for their Christmas celebrations, Gaynor felt sad that neither Rachael nor Sara would be with them and she resolved that her New Year Resolution for 1935 was to go to Germany and try and find Sara. She was pretty sure that Barri would be against the idea and that he wouldn't want to come, but she simply had to try and find her in order to set her own mind at rest.

Keris would be thirteen in May, so if she didn't want to come with her either, then she could stay at home with Barri. She was old enough to take care of herself and having to do so under Barri's supervision might make her come to her senses. She might realise how much I do to make her life comfortable, Gaynor told herself.

Ever since they had come back from Spain and she had discovered that Idris Jenkins had found himself another girlfriend, Keris had been unbearable. Sulks, moodiness and downright rudeness were the order of the day.

Barri remonstrated with her all the time, but it had little effect. Gaynor had tried both being strict and being warm and affectionate, but neither approach had brought them any closer together.

She constantly grumbled that her life was ruined, that the only boy she'd ever love had let her down, and that it was all because she had been made to go to Spain.

'You are acting in an extremely stupid manner,' Gaynor explained to her. 'You're only twelve and girls of twelve don't have boyfriends. They have friends who are boys in the same way as they have friends who are girls.'

'Well, I don't have any friends who are girls,' Keris retorted. 'Not any who are special friends like Idris was.'

When Gaynor asked her if she would like to have a party at Christmas, Keris had vetoed the idea saying there was no one she liked well enough to invite.

When Gaynor went to the end-of-term concert she noticed that whereas the other girls in Keris's class had grouped together in bunches of three or four, Keris had remained on her own, looking withdrawn and miserable. Even Miss Davis had commented on it.

'I really can't understand why Keris isn't more popular,' she commented to Gaynor. 'She's such a pretty girl and so good natured and yet she seems to have no social skills whatsoever. Does she have a lot of friends away from school?'

'Not very many. She spends most of her time

with us. We take her to the pictures once a week and I take her to the shops at the weekend. Occasionally her dad takes her to the museum, but for the rest of the time she simply mopes around the house or lies upstairs on her bed reading.'

'She seems to have no interest in anything these days,' Miss Davis agreed. 'Has she said anything to you about what she wants to do when she leaves school? I've tried to get her to talk about it in class but she says she has no idea. Most of the other girls in her form have some idea about where they want to work.'

Gaynor shook her head. 'As you say, nothing seems to interest her these days. She will have to get a job, of course, but there's nothing that she seems keen to do.'

'Well, she's very bright. She could become a shop assistant or even do some kind of clerical job. When we come back to school after the Christmas holidays I'll try and talk to her again and make her realise it really is time she gave it some thought.'

The winter was a cold, wet one; there was snow and ice which made getting around hazardous and everyone seemed to be fed up and miserable.

'We are better off than most,' Barri reminded her. 'I have a good, steady job with a regular pay packet at the end of each week. A great many men are on the dole and their families are struggling to make ends meet.'

346

Their spirits revived with the arrival of spring; with lighter, brighter days and the weather beginning to warm up. Several times Gaynor was on the point of mentioning that she intended to go to Germany, but then held back because she didn't want to have weeks of discussion about it or give Barri the chance to talk her out of it.

When she eventually did mention it to Barry he looked surprised. 'Why go this early in the year; wouldn't it be better to wait until Whitsun?'

'Why do you say that?'

'The weather will be better and the days much longer.'

'Well, that doesn't really matter. Easter isn't until 19 April this year, so that's well into spring and a really good time of the year to go,' she insisted stubbornly. 'If you don't want to come with me, then I'll go on my own.'

'Why not wait until Whitsun,' Barri persisted. 'It's Keris's birthday on 19 May, only a couple of weeks after Whitsunday. We could all go and it could be a nice birthday treat for her.'

Although it meant amending her own plans Gaynor agreed to this. It was better than arguing, she decided, and she didn't mind putting the trip off for a few weeks. The weather would be even better then.

Shortly after Easter there was disturbing news about political matters in Spain and not for the first time Gaynor wished that Rachael would come back to Cardiff. She knew, though, that it was useless trying to persuade her to do so since she was so happy there.

It did make her even more anxious about Sara because Barri was always forecasting that there was going to be trouble in Germany now that Hitler had so much power. She hoped nothing would happen to prevent them going. Even Keris seemed to have brightened up at the thought of the forthcoming trip.

Cologne was different from anything Gaynor had anticipated. The journey had not been without incident. She and Keris had both been very seasick on the boat and Keris had refused to take Barri's advice to go and lie down in a bunk, but had insisted on being taken up on deck.

It had worked for her, Gaynor knew, but it meant that she had been left on her own, her head swimming and her stomach churning each time the boat rolled.

The moment they stepped ashore and were once more on solid ground, however, both of them felt fine, but Gaynor was already thinking about the return journey and wondering how she was going to cope. Perhaps this time she would try and stay up on deck with Keris and Barri, she decided.

Determinedly, she put it to the back of her mind. She was in Germany, it really was the opportunity she had dreamed about; now all she needed was another stroke of luck if she was to find Sara again. She was here somewhere, she was sure about that, and she tried to think of some positive ways of finding her.

Gaynor liked Cologne; she felt at home there because it was so similar in many ways to Cardiff. The river Taff was replaced by the Rhine; the city centre by Cologne Cathedral rather than the beautiful City Hall in Cardiff.

Language was a barrier, just as it had been in Spain, but somehow it didn't seem to matter quite so much. When they had been in Spain, partly because of the heat, and the difference in the appearance of the people who lived in Almeria, Gaynor really had felt as if she was in a foreign country. Here, in Cologne, she didn't feel like that at all.

The weather was kind to them and so they took every opportunity they could to sit at the outdoor cafés in the main strasse. She liked it there; she never tired of watching the passersby, hoping against hope that they might see Sara.

'We probably wouldn't know her if she was one of the waitresses and even brought a meal to our table,' Barri reminded them. 'It's almost five years since she came here, she'll be twenty now, a woman, not a skinny young girl.'

'We could try asking people,' Keris suggested. 'I'm sure most of them would know if there was an English-speaking girl living near them.'

'Needle in a haystack time again, is it?' Barri laughed sardonically. He picked up the Steiner of beer that the waitress brought to the table and took a long drink of it. 'Well, go on then, Keris,' he teased, 'start asking.'

Gaynor was nowhere near so discouraging. She'd come to Germany with a purpose and although she knew it was a long shot she still hoped that it might pay off. Keris was right; someone who spoke English would be noticed and when Sara had first come over to Germany she hadn't spoken a word of German any more than they did.

To encourage Keris to help her, Gaynor made a game of it. She proposed that they should take it in turns to ask people if they knew of any English girl.

Keris entered into it enthusiastically. 'One of us picks the person to be asked and then the other one asks them,' she stated, elaborating on the idea.

Gaynor agreed, but Barri refused to be involved. Sometimes he was amused by their endeavours, at other times rather annoyed. It made no difference. They were both caught up by the idea and had no intention of stopping.

They asked a wide variety of people over the next few days, and received mostly courteous responses. Once or twice they had difficulty in making people understand what it was they wanted to know. Twice they received rude, almost abusive answers, and Gaynor was on the point of giving up when Keris managed to find someone who seemed to have information.

'The teacher girl?' he queried in halting English. 'She gives classes to business people to help them learn how to trade with the English?'

Even when they were told where they could find her, Barri thought it was highly unlikely that it could be Sara. He did concede that this girl might be able to give them more information than they'd managed to get so far.

'At least she will be able to understand English,' he agreed.

The address they had been given was in the commercial area on the outskirts of Cologne. Factories and warehouses seemed to dominate that part of the town and at first they thought their search was going to prove fruitless.

Then, a young man, who looked more like a soldier than a factory worker, said he knew the young woman they were trying to find and offered to take them along to where she worked.

Gaynor was full of misgivings as they followed him up a dingy staircase to a room over a warehouse. When the door opened he carried on a long conversation with the woman seated at a desk inside. Gaynor felt very uncomfortable as they kept looking across to where the three of them were standing and then putting their heads together and talking some more.

Finally they were admitted and told to wait. After scrutinising them once again the severe-looking receptionist disappeared and then returned with a slim, blonde girl who was wearing a dark business dress with white collar and cuffs. 'Yes? Can I help you?' she asked crisply.

'Sara?' Gaynor's voice trembled she felt so anxious.

The girl studied the three of them stonily then her face slowly broke into a smile and all Gaynor's doubts vanished.

There were no hugs or excitement like there had been when they'd been reunited with Rachael. Sara appeared to be far too poised and self-controlled for anything like that.

Quietly but firmly she explained that she was working and must return to her office right away as she had people there waiting for her. 'I have meetings for the rest of the day,' she explained, 'but if you wish, I will meet you later, after I have finished work, and we can talk then.'

Gaynor felt as if they were being dismissed; Keris looked crestfallen but continued to stare admiringly at her ultra smart efficient-looking sister.

Barri nodded his acceptance of the arrangement and took the piece of paper on which Sara had written down the name of the place where they were to meet.

'Come along, Sara is busy,' he said as he shepherded them out of the warehouse building.

None of them made any comment until they had walked back towards the city centre and found a café. Even then they waited until they had been served and Barri had taken a long draught of his beer and Gaynor had sipped at her coffee before they said a word.

'She seems to have a very high-powered job,' Barri commented casually.

Gaynor nodded and took another sip of her coffee. She found it hard to believe Sara's reaction to seeing them after such a long time.

She'd been so distant, so impersonal, almost as if they were all strangers. What had happened to the warm, loving daughter who had been her firstborn? Gaynor wondered sadly. Had there been some tragedy, or traumatic event that had turned her into such an ice maiden?

Even Keris remained silent and on edge. It was as if she was so overawed by their meeting with Sara that it left her unable to make any comment.

It was several hours before they were due to meet Sara and time seemed to drag. Barri suggested to Keris that he should take her to the museum, but she shook her head and said she didn't feel like it.

'A walk around the cathedral, then; we've only looked at it from the outside,' he proposed.

Again she refused. In the end the three of them went for a stroll along the banks of the

Rhine, stopping to listen to some of the street musicians who were entertaining passers-by and watching as people made their way on to the many boats that were offering sightseeing trips.

Keris wanted to go on one of the boat trips but, remembering how ill she had felt as they'd crossed the Channel, Gaynor told her that there wasn't time to do so.

'Perhaps we should go and find out where this restaurant, where Sara said she'd meet us, is,' Gaynor said anxiously. 'We don't want to arrive late and it's in a part of the city that we don't know so we could easily get lost.'

'It will be ages yet before Sara will have finished work,' Barri observed, checking the time on his watch.

'We don't have to stay there! Once we've found it then we might be able to relax and go somewhere and enjoy ourselves.'

Gaynor felt a lot more reassured when they found the proposed meeting place and she discovered that it was in a respectable-looking area even though it was on the outskirts of the city.

Keris wondered if that was near where Sara lived and bombarded them both with questions, none of which they could answer.

'For heaven's sake be quiet and wait until Sara gets here,' Barri said irritably. 'I'm sure your mother will manage to get every detail about her life from her.'

Chapter Thirty

Sara ordered a light meal for them all but only Keris seemed to enjoy it. She listened in awe as Gaynor questioned Sara to try and find out about everything that had happened to her since she'd left Cardiff.

'You took a terrible risk, you know, coming here, a young girl all on her own in a strange foreign city; anything could have happened to you.'

Looking cool and poised Sara dismissed her mother's concern with an impatient wave of her hand.

'Don't start making a fuss. If you'd told me more about my real father then I wouldn't have had to waste so much time tracing him. I did most of that before leaving Cardiff of course.'

'You did?' Gaynor stared at her in astonishment. 'How on earth did you manage to do that?'

'It wasn't all that difficult,' she said in a superior tone. 'You could have done the same if you'd really wanted to find him,' she added, as her brilliant blue eyes met her mother's defiantly.

'I'd have no idea how to go about it,' Gaynor assured her. 'How were you able to do it?'

'I used my brain of course. I worked at the City Hall, I knew how they tracked down people if they needed to, so I used the same methods.'

'So did you manage to trace him?' Barri asked.

'No, not exactly. After he was called up into the army he was killed.'

'Oh my poor dear!' Gaynor stretched out her hand and took one of Sara's. 'Why ever didn't you come back home again?' she asked in astonishment.

'I was living with you in Cardiff when I found that out,' Sara told her curtly as she pulled her hand away from her mother's. 'I've already told you, I knew what I was doing before I left Cardiff. I didn't come over here on a wild goose chase. I came over to find my father's people. Something you never bothered to do.'

Gaynor shook her head in disbelief. 'I can't believe what you are saying. I had no idea what part of Germany Konrad came from, and I certainly knew nothing at all about his family. He never talked about them at all.'

'Who told you that he'd been killed?' Barri interrupted. 'Are you sure you have the right information?'

'Quite sure. I have had it confirmed by the army authorities and his mother has also told me; I'm sure she wouldn't make a mistake about facts like those since he was her only child,' Sara told him coldly.

356

'His mother? You've found his mother?' Gaynor exclaimed in surprise.

'I've been living with her ever since I came to Cologne,' Sara affirmed.

'Well, that's something of a relief. I've had visions of you walking the streets or having to live rough,' Gaynor breathed, her eyes filling with tears.

'You should have written and let your mam know you were safe, Sara,' Barry told her grimly.

Sara shrugged. 'She had you, Rachael and Keris, I didn't think she'd miss me, and Greta Claus needed me, she was all on her own and deep in grief because she'd lost her son.'

'Did she believe you when you told her that Konrad was your father?' Gaynor asked in surprise.

'Of course she did, why shouldn't she?'

Gaynor shrugged. 'I don't know, but she must have had some doubts. A young girl who only speaks English turning up out of the blue with a story like that! I don't suppose for one minute that she even knew I existed and Konrad didn't know that I was expecting you when he suddenly decided that his country needed him.'

'She knew he'd been living near Cardiff and as soon as I told her that was where I came from and that my mother had come from Ferndale and that my father had been called Konrad Claus—'

'She believed you,' Barri finished.

357

'Of course she did! And it was easy enough to prove it,' Sara added complacently.

'Prove it ... how? What do you mean by that?' Gaynor asked, looking puzzled.

'The birthmark at the top of my arm, of course. Konrad had a half moon on his upper arm too and so has Greta Claus.'

'So the outcome of all this is that while your mother has never stopped worrying you have established yourself quite comfortably over here,' Barri commented drily.

'Yes, thank you,' Sara told him coolly. 'I have a very interesting and fulfilling job, teaching English to businessmen so that they can trade with the British without encountering language difficulties. In addition I have the best home life imaginable. Greta Claus can't do enough to make me comfortable; she plays her role of grandmother extremely well.'

'So you have no intention of coming back home to Cardiff with us?' Gaynor asked wistfully.

Sara shook her sleek blonde head emphatically. 'Most certainly not! There is no chance of that at all.'

'I think you should give it more thought, Sara,' Barri told her quietly.

Sara frowned. 'Why? What do you mean?'

'There's a lot of unrest in Germany at the moment. This fellow Hitler—'

'No more!' Sara held up her hand. 'Don't start trying to tell me things I don't want to hear.

Hitler is good for Germany; once he gets the opportunity to do so he will make this a better country than Britain has ever been.'

'Sara! That is utter nonsense! Now listen to me.'

'No, Barri—'

'Barri?' Gaynor intervened sadly. 'He's still your dad . . .'

'He's not. I know he stood in for him while I was growing up and I'm grateful for that, but Konrad Claus was my real dad and his mother is my grandmother and I have no intention of deserting her.'

'Perhaps . . . perhaps she'd like to come back to Cardiff as well,' Gaynor said hesitantly.

Sara's laugh was hard and cold. 'She most certainly wouldn't. Frau Claus is German through and through. She upholds the Fatherland and she has shown me that deep down I'm as great a patriot as my father was.'

'Well, that's that, then,' Barri said stiffly. 'We've come here specially to find you. Keris misses you and your mother is heartbroken because you haven't kept in touch.'

Sara looked from one to the other of them in silence, 'Yet it has taken you all this time to bother to come and find me. What about Rachael? Has she managed to overcome her heartache at me leaving home? Is that why she hasn't come with you?'

'Rachael isn't living with us any more,' Keris pouted. 'She lives in Spain, she's a gypsy now.'

'Gypsy!' The horror in Sara's voice left no doubt about her feelings on the matter.

'No, she's not exactly a gypsy,' Gaynor said quickly. 'She lives in Almeria with Saratina. You remember Saratina?' She smiled hesitantly at Sara.

'Of course I remember Saratina. We lived with her and Mama Maria and her family at one time in an overcrowded house in Tiger Bay, didn't we?'

'That's right, when you were very small. Mama Maria helped to look after you while I was out working.'

'So why is Rachael living with Saratina?'

'Well –' Gaynor hesitated. 'Mama Maria died and Saratina decided to go and live in Almeria in southern Spain and – and Rachael went with her.'

'And now she sings and dances and plays the guitar,' Keris butted in. 'Rachael's ever so pretty and she wears really lovely dresses when she sings in the streets.'

'Rachael a gypsy!' Sara shuddered. 'Well, she'd better not come here! They don't like gypsies in Germany.'

'I don't think this sort of talk is getting us anywhere,' Barri put in hotly. 'Now listen to me, Sara. Things are getting very complicated over here in Germany. It's my opinion that in the very near future there's either going to be a civil war or a war between the British and the Germans. Things are bad in Spain as well;

in fact the whole of Europe is at boiling point. Now, as we suggested earlier, we'd like you to come back home to Cardiff with us. Bring Frau Claus as well, if you can persuade her to come. We'd all feel much happier if we knew you were safe, especially your mother.'

'Is that what you told Rachael? Well, I bet she didn't listen to your bumbling either.'

Barri's twisted mouth tightened grimly. 'I've already lived through one war and believe me, Sara, I recognise the danger signals.'

Sara looked at him contemptuously. 'Just because you fought and got hurt in the Great War you think you can blame the Germans for everything that goes wrong. Well, you can't. I'm here, I like it here, and I have no intention of coming back to Cardiff ever again. That's why I've never written to you and why it has never bothered me that you have never been in touch with me.'

Pushing her plate to one side she stood up. 'It's been very nice seeing you all but I intend to stay here with Frau Claus. She is my grandmother; she loves me and I love her.'

'Very well, Sara. If that's what you want to do then I suppose we'll have to accept your decision,' Gaynor told her quickly. 'There is just one thing, though; while we are over here you must take us to meet Frau Claus.'

'No! Most certainly not. I know what you are trying to do. You want to turn her against me so that she says I have to go home with you.'

'No, I don't want to do anything of the sort!' Gaynor exclaimed sharply. 'I do need to know, though, that you are in safe hands. You are barely twenty, Sara. In the eyes of the law you are still under age; we're still responsible for you.'

'Please, Sara, I'd like to meet your grandmother,' Keris pleaded.

'If I take you to meet her, then will you go back to Cardiff and leave me in peace?' Sara demanded, looking from one to the other of them.

'If that is what you wish,' Gaynor agreed reluctantly. 'We are planning to leave tomorrow, so can we go and meet her now?'

Again Sara hesitated. 'It will be something of a shock for her. I would have liked to have had time to prepare her for your visit,' she demurred.

'Half an hour should be long enough,' Barri said firmly. 'Do you live far from here? If not, then we'll wait here and you can come back for us.'

Sara stared at him frostily, then she beckoned the waitress over and ordered more food and drink for them. 'I'll be back in half an hour,' she stated as she picked up her bag and walked out.

Frau Claus greeted them frigidly. Gaynor had tried to find out something about the woman as they had walked from the café to the apartment block where she lived, but Sara had disclosed very little.

Sara used her door key to let them in, and then led the way along a narrow hallway into a large, very spartan living room. Greta Claus was tall and thin with iron-grey hair pulled back into a tight knot. She wore a plain black dress with only a narrow white collar relieving its severity. Unsmiling, she welcomed them with a restrained handshake, and then a look of horror came into her blue eyes as they rested on the disfigurement on Barri's face.

'You have been a soldier,' she accused. 'One of the enemy who shot my poor Konrad dead and him little more than a boy.'

'I am sure we were both only doing what our country demanded of us,' Barri told her quietly. 'I was very badly injured as you can see.'

'You have been more fortunate than my Konrad; you are still alive,' she stated accusingly.

'Indeed, but for the rest of my life I will carry the scars of what I had to endure both on my face and in here,' he said tapping his head with his forefinger.

Greta Claus stared at him coldly but said nothing. Instead, she waved a hand to indicate to them to sit down.

'You have not come to claim back my granddaughter, I hope?' she asked in stilted English. 'She is a good girl and I need her as company now that I have no son.'

'She is also my daughter,' Gaynor said quietly.

Frau Claus made a deep guttural sound of annoyance. 'You have other daughters. This young one here' – she nodded in Keris's direction – 'and another one as well. Yes? So you have no need of Sara, not like I do.'

'I miss her a great deal,' Gaynor stated, 'but if she wants to stay here with you then I shall not interfere. I only want to be reassured that she is being well-looked after and that she is happy.'

'Happy! Of course she is happy; I give her all the love that I cannot express for my son because your soldiers killed him. I look after her as if she was the most important person in the world because to me she is.'

Gaynor bit down on her lip, trying hard to hold back her tears as she looked searchingly at Sara. She held her breath, hoping Sara would speak up; say something about how much she was missing her family even though she was planning to stay on in Germany, but Sara remained silent.

'I think it is time we left,' Barri said. He stood up and held out his hand to Frau Claus. When she ignored it he moved over to Sara, taking her by the shoulders and bending his head to kiss her but she sidestepped away.

With an imperceptible lift of his shoulders Barri took Keris by the hand and walked towards the door not waiting for Gaynor to say goodbye to Sara and Frau Claus.

364

Chapter Thirty-One

They were all quiet and subdued on their journey back home to Cardiff the next day. They barely mentioned what had happened the previous evening. Even Keris remained quiet and distracted.

In the weeks that followed Gaynor felt devastated by what Greta Claus had said. She knew Barri was deeply hurt and she blamed herself. She should never have insisted on going to Germany to try and find Sara. She should have realised when Sara didn't get in touch with them that it was because she wanted to get right away from all of them.

Although she hadn't been quite so glacial and outspoken as Sara had been about coming home, Rachael had behaved in much the same way, she reflected, and it saddened her that they both felt this way.

With both her elder daughters completely independent there was only Keris left and since they'd come back from Germany she had been so moody that it worried both her and Barri.

She was quiet and listless one minute and only wanted to sit and be cuddled; then suddenly she was so high-spirited and demanding, wanting to go out every night of the week, that they had trouble keeping up with her.

Neither she nor Barri could put their finger on exactly what the cause was. When either of them tried to talk to her about it she either clammed up and refused to say anything or else burst into tears. She insisted that it had nothing to do with the fact that Sara and Rachael had left home, probably for ever. Nor was it because of what had happened last year when Idris Jenkins had dropped her.

Gaynor thought it might be that she was worried about starting work and not having any idea about what she wanted to do. When she broached the subject Keris merely shrugged and said 'I don't much care where I work.'

'Surely there must be something that appeals to you; some sort of job that you would really like to do best,' her mother pressed. 'You don't want to end up working in a factory, now do you?'

Again Keris showed little interest. 'If that's all there is I can do, then I suppose that is where I will have to work isn't it?' she said resignedly.

'Would you like to be a shop assistant? Perhaps you could apply to one of the posh stores in St Mary's Street; somewhere like David Morgan's?'

'Not really. You have to wear a black dress and I'd look frumpy in one of those.'

'Well, what about working in one of the

smaller shops, then, perhaps in one of the arcades?'

Keris shook her head. 'Not really, I don't want to be stuck behind a counter having to smile and talk nicely and deal with awkward customers all day.'

'How about becoming a Nippy in the big Lyons tea shop. I'm sure you would have the chance to meet a lot of interesting people if you were working there.'

'Then I'd have to wear one of those silly caps and a frilly apron! No thank you! I certainly don't want to do anything like that,' she said scornfully.

Nothing that Gaynor suggested seemed to interest Keris in the slightest.

'Stop going on about me going to work, Mam,' she said irritably. 'Miss Davis has already suggested most of those jobs,' she added dismissively.

'What about a job in the City Hall, then? I'm sure your dad would help over that. Shall I ask him to find out if there are any openings at the moment for junior clerks?'

Keris showed a slight flicker of interest. 'That's where Sara went to work when she left school, wasn't it?'

'That's right and she loved it there so I'm sure you would as well.' Gaynor said eagerly.

'Why did she run away to Germany, then, if she liked it there so much?'

For a moment Gaynor thought of saying

nothing, and then she decided that it was much better if they did talk about it. 'You heard what Sara said, she wanted to try and find her real father and she knew he was German.'

'And she found out exactly where he came from in Germany only because she went to work in the City Hall. Why couldn't she have asked you? Or wouldn't you tell her?'

Gaynor sighed. 'I knew he came from Germany but not where and he didn't even know about Sara.'

'And you never wanted to meet his mother and tell her about Sara?' she asked in a bewildered voice. 'If Sara hadn't managed to find out where Frau Claus lived in Germany and gone there to find her, then she would never even have met her grandmother,' she added in an accusing voice.

'Probably not,' Gaynor admitted. 'When Sara was born the war was on and it would have been impossible to get in touch with her then because the Germans were the enemy,' she explained.

'You never told Rachael that Mama Maria was her grandmother though, did you?'

Gaynor bit her lip. 'Mama Maria knew,' she said quietly.

'Rachael didn't, though. No wonder she ran away with Saratina when she found out,' Keris muttered accusingly.

'Look, both Sara and Rachael had a happy home life. Your dad looked after them as though

368

they were his own. I thought they were perfectly happy and that there was no need to make their lives more complicated by telling them about such matters.'

'How was it complicated?' Keris demanded angrily. 'Rachael had met Mama Maria. You lived with her when Rachael was a baby,' Keris argued.

'Yes, but she was far too little to understand anything about relationships of that sort and then we all moved to Roath; before you were even born.'

'You mean when you found my dad?'

'That's right.' Gaynor nodded.

'So what about our other grandmother? You must have had a mother and she would be a grandmother to all of us. And Dad must have had a mother. So I should have two grand-mothers whom I've never even met. Do they both still live in Ferndale where you and Dad were born?'

'It's a long story,' Gaynor said evasively. 'Your dad's mam died a long time ago.'

'And your mam?' Keris persisted.

Gaynor shook her head sadly. 'I have only seen her once since I left home. I went back there when Sara and Rachael were babies, long before you were born, and my dad was so cross with me that he wouldn't let me speak to her.'

Keris looked shocked. 'You've never been to see her since then? You mean she doesn't even know that I exist!'

369

'I'm afraid not. It is such a long time ago I thought it was best to forget all about that part of my life. Your dad feels the same, that is why we never talk about it,' Gaynor said firmly.

Keris gaped at her aghast. 'You mean you've behaved the same way towards your mam as Sara and Rachael have done and yet you are really upset with them because they've made you feel so sad.'

Gaynor started back in dismay. 'It wasn't like that at all,' she protested. 'You don't understand, Keris, my dad wouldn't let me see her. He turned me away when I went to the door.'

It was like that, though, Gaynor thought ashamedly. She should have tried again and it had taken a thirteen-year-old to point it out to her. Now, after all these years, it was probably too late.

To Gaynor's surprise, after her open admission that she no longer had anything to do with her family, or Barri's, Keris's behaviour seemed to undergo a change. She not only seemed to be a lot calmer and more cheerful, but seemed to want to spend more and more time at home with her mother.

Every time they went shopping together, or she showed Keris how to sew, or bake, Gaynor had the satisfaction of knowing that they were sharing similar interests. At last they were doing the sorts of things that mothers and daughters were supposed to do together.

As the bond between them deepened Gaynor

felt a tremendous sense of pleasure in that at least one of her daughters was enjoying her company. Perhaps this time she had got her approach right, even though she appeared to have failed so miserably with her two older girls.

Once Christmas was over Keris began taking more interest in her school work. She still refused to talk about what sort of job she would like to have when she left school.

'It's probably best if we say nothing at all to her about it until she makes up her mind and we see what her final school report is like,' Barri advised. 'I'm quite confident that if she wants to work at the City Hall I will be able to get her a job there.'

Although Gaynor agreed with him that she wouldn't press Keris to make any decision she couldn't help feeling apprehensive. She knew it was silly but she had an uneasy premonition that this was the calm before the storm and that some unforeseen catastrophe was waiting to upset their lives once more.

Barri laughed at her fears and told her not to start talking like that in front of Keris.

At the beginning of June, a few weeks after her own fourteenth birthday, Keris told them that she'd been invited to a birthday party on the following Saturday by Lynda Morgan.

'She's the same age as me and she used to be one of my best friends at school until her parents moved out to Canton,' Keris explained.

'How are you going to get home?' Barri asked.

'Lynda suggested that because it's a Saturday night and we won't have to go to school next day then perhaps I could stay at her place overnight as some of the others are doing?'

'Well, I don't mind, it's up to your mother, of course,' Barri told her.

'I won't be coming home until Sunday afternoon because there's going to be dancing and Lynda says the party will probably go on very late,' she explained excitedly. 'She says we'll all want to have a lie-in the next morning.'

When Gaynor agreed that it would be all right, Keris asked if she could use one of the big suitcases. 'I don't want to go on a bus in my party dress, so I need a big case to make sure that it doesn't get crushed.'

When Gaynor took the suitcase along to Keris's bedroom, Keris gave her a big hug. 'You're the best mother in the world and I'll always love you,' she assured her.

'Hey, steady on, you're going away for one night, not a lifetime,' Gaynor laughed.

When Keris hadn't returned home by eight o'clock on Sunday evening Barri went along to her friend's house to find out why she was so late. When he came back he was looking worried and anxious. 'She wasn't there,' he told Gaynor, 'what's more she never turned up for the party.'

Gaynor felt really alarmed. Immediately she

went up to Keris's bedroom; the party dress that she had been supposed to pack in the big suitcase was still hanging in her cupboard. Not only that but most of her summer dresses were missing, and so, too, were some of her shoes and underwear.

As she stood looking at the depleted cupboard, Keris's words pounded in her head. 'You are the best mother in the world and I'll always love you.'

Had she been saying goodbye, she wondered?

Slowly she went back downstairs and told Barri of her fears.

'Sit down, I'll make a pot of tea,' he told her. 'Try and think if there was anything else she said that might give us some idea of what she was planning to do.'

As they drank their tea, Gaynor told Barri about the long discussion she had had with Keris about grandmothers and how angry she had been because Sara and Rachael had never been told that they had one.

'Well, they both know now,' he pointed out as he poured out a second cup.

'Not about my mother, and she's their grandmother as well,' she sighed.

Barri looked thoughtful. 'Did you tell her that my mother was dead?'

'Yes.' Gaynor nodded. 'I also explained why we had never been to see my mother. I told her it was because the last time I went to Ferndale, when Sara and Rachael were quite small, my father refused to let me speak to her.'

'I think she's been planning this escapade for quite some time,' Barri mused. 'This is why she wasn't interested in talking about a job of any kind. She didn't want to get tied down because she knew she wouldn't be here to do it.'

'What do you mean? Where on earth do you think she has gone? She hasn't much money.' She paused and spread her hands wide as she looked at him in dismay. 'She asked me for her post office savings book last week because she said she wanted to buy a birthday present for this friend.'

'Did you let her have it?'

'Of course I did. You know how we've always encouraged her to be independent, and to budget her money. She knows that if she takes any money out of her savings, and spends it on something, then she has to save up and put it back again out of her pocket money over the next few weeks.'

'So how much money do you think there was in her savings book?'

'I'm not sure, about nine pounds, I think.'

'Mmm! Well, depending on where she decided to go that would probably be enough for her fare.'

They stared at each other, afraid to voice their thoughts aloud. Gaynor was the first to break the silence. 'You don't think she would go looking for one of her sisters do you? She does know where both of them are living now.'

'That's what I am wondering,' Barri agreed. 'Which one do you think is the more likely choice, Sara or Rachael?'

'She's always been closer to Rachael than Sara,' Gaynor said thoughtfully. 'Even when they were small she used to hate the way Sara bossed her around. Since we've met Sara again and seen how cold and calculating she has become I don't think Keris would want to be with her.'

'So it would be to see Rachael again. Do you think she's gone to Spain?'

Gaynor shook her head. 'I don't know what to think,' she admitted. 'I have a feeling that she would have told us if that was what she wanted to do, though. She didn't really like the place where Rachael was living, because she was frightened of the gypsies.'

'She was envious of Rachael's lifestyle, all the dancing and singing, though,' Barri reminded her.

'She can't play a musical instrument and she most certainly can't sing!'

'No, but then neither can Saratina, but she is managing to work behind the scenes organising things so perhaps Keris feels she could do that, or something similar.'

I've got a strange feeling that she wouldn't dare go as far as Spain; not on her own. She's nowhere near as adventurous as the other two were at her age. In fact, I keep wondering if—'

'If she's gone to Ferndale to look for your mother, her missing grandmother,' Barri said before she could voice it aloud herself.

'Exactly!' She looked at him in dismay. 'Oh Barri, what are we going to do about it? We don't even know if my mother is still alive.'

Chapter Thirty-Two

Gaynor and Barri talked late into the night trying to decide which of them should go to Ferndale the next morning and see if that was where Keris had gone.

'I think it is my place to do so,' he kept insisting, but Gaynor wouldn't agree.

'It will mean you will have to take a day off work, Barri,' she pointed out worriedly.

'That's all right, I still have several days due to me,' he reminded her.

'Yes, but later on you might need to take time off and then you won't be able to do so.'

'I know, but it might be better for me to face your father rather than you. The last time you went home he wouldn't let you speak to your mother, remember.'

'Barri, that was almost twenty years ago.' She smiled. 'He'll be an old man by now, he won't have the fire in his belly that he had then.'

'Don't you be so sure. I used to quake in my shoes whenever he took me to task when I worked for him. He didn't have to raise his voice, either!'

'I know what you are saying and I appreciate that you are trying to save me from another family row.' She took his face between her hands and kissed him on the lips. 'I really would rather be the one to go up there,' she assured him.

Barri stroked her hair. 'It might be better still, if we both go together, cariad,' he suggested.

'That still means you taking time off work and we've agreed it doesn't make sense for you to do that.'

'There's no real rush,' he hedged, trying to hide his concern. 'Perhaps we should wait a couple of days, possibly until the weekend, and then there will be no problem about it interfering with work.'

'You mean not look for Keris for a whole week! Supposing she hasn't gone there? What if she has simply run away?'

Barri ran his hands through his hair. 'Look at it this way,' he reasoned, 'if she has gone to Ferndale to find your parents and after making herself known to them she doesn't come back within the next day or two, then at least she is safe and sound. If we go there and she isn't there, then we start worrying ourselves silly about where else she may have gone.'

'I won't be able to rest if I don't know where she is! We're both worried sick as it is, otherwise we wouldn't be sitting here after midnight arguing about it,' Gaynor pointed out.

'Agreed.' He stood up. 'Come on, let's go to bed, cariad. Things will look different in the morning. Who knows, she may be home safe and sound and in time for school by then and we'll be scolding her and asking ourselves why we got so worked up.'

'And if she isn't?'

'We'll make sensible plans. To start with, once I get into work I can phone through to that place where Sara works and speak to her and find out if Keris is there.'

'How can you do that, we haven't got a telephone number for her. We don't even know the name of the company where she teaches English.'

'Don't worry, I can find that out. I know where it is located and they are bound to be on the telephone.'

'What if she isn't there?'

'Sara take a day off!' Barri laughed. 'Come on, cariad, you saw how keen and efficient she was,' he teased.

'You can hardly phone Rachael, though. I shouldn't think they have many telephones in any of the caves in that gypsy village in Almeria. I can't even remember the name of it.'

'No, I don't suppose they do have telephones there, but if I contact the police in Almeria I am sure they will know Rachael and will be able to find out if a very young English girl has suddenly appeared in the area in her company.'

'You think of everything, don't you, Barri,' Gaynor sighed. 'I suppose you are right and I am making a mountain out of a molehill. Women look at these things differently to men and remembering what happened when Sara and Rachael disappeared makes me so terribly anxious.'

'I'm every bit as worried as you are, Gaynor. Keris is my daughter, too, remember, cariad.'

Gaynor bit her lip, sensing the rebuke in Barri's voice.

Long after Barri had fallen asleep, even though she was cradled in the warm comfort of his arms, Gaynor was still wide awake. She spent most of the night worrying about Keris and considering all the possibilities of where she might be.

Repeatedly she went over the discussion she'd had with Keris about grandmothers and more and more she felt convinced that Keris had gone to Ferndale in an attempt to find hers.

She didn't understand why having a grandmother mattered to her so much, unless it was because of some deep-down jealousy because both Sara and Rachael had known theirs whereas she had never even met hers.

Once again I've failed, she reflected. When they'd been younger she had always thought they were a close happy family, but now she was not so sure. It seemed that as they became older both Sara and Rachael had to some degree resented Barri. She realised that he had always favoured Keris, but then she had been the baby of the family and she had tried to explain to the older two that this was only natural.

Keris certainly had been more wilful, more

demanding, and been allowed far more privileges than her two sisters. She didn't blame Barri for this; it was the changing world they were living in.

When the two older girls had been growing up they had never expected to be allowed to go to the pictures every week like Keris did.

Sara and Rachael had been happy playing in the park, but Keris wanted to do more adventurous things. Barri had bought Keris a bicycle, yet neither of the older girls had ever had one.

She was still listing all the advantages that Keris had enjoyed when she fell asleep towards morning. When she wakened Barri had already left for work and for a few seconds she couldn't remember what she had been so worried about the night before.

She struggled out of bed, hoping that Keris was already up and dressed and having her breakfast otherwise she was going to be late for school. It was only when she pushed open her bedroom door that it all came flooding back.

She stared at the empty room in dismay, then tightened her dressing-gown cord and went down to the kitchen only to find that was also deserted.

Barri had eaten his breakfast and gone to work, but there was still tea in the pot. She poured herself out a cup and stood by the sink drinking it and trying to decide what to do for the best.

It was going to be a long day if she did as

he'd asked and waited to see if he could find out if Keris was with either of her sisters. Perhaps she could go to the City Hall at midday and talk to him in his lunch hour. There would still be time for her to go to Ferndale if he had no news.

Keris humped her big suitcase up on to the platform at Cardiff central and then sat down on a seat to think again about what she was doing.

When she'd been plotting and scheming it had all seemed to be such a splendid idea. Now that she had actually packed her case, lied about where she was going, and was at the station, she wasn't sure that it was such a good plan after all.

She could always go back home, of course. She had told her parents that she was staying at her friend's house overnight, though, so they wouldn't be expecting her back till late tomorrow. It meant that she had time to go to Ferndale, find out where her grandparents lived and, if they weren't pleased to see her, or didn't make her welcome, time to come back home and no one would be any the wiser.

That wasn't what she wanted to do, though. When she had heard that Sara had found her grandmother and realised that Rachael had known hers, she'd felt quite jealous.

She had talked to a lot of the girls at school about their grandmothers and they all had lovely stories to tell about how they always made a tremendous fuss of them, knitted them jumpers, sent them presents at Christmas and when it was their birthday, and she'd felt really deprived.

She didn't need a grandmother to do all those sorts of things for her because her mam did them anyway, but it would be nice to know that she had a grandmother, somewhere in the background, if she ever needed her.

She wondered what she looked like. Would she be fat and round with black hair like Mama Maria, or tall and thin and severe-looking like Frau Claus? More likely she would look like an older edition of her mam with brown hair and brown eyes, only her face would be wrinkled or she might have a double chin.

If I got on the train and went to Ferndale I'd be able to find out, she told herself. Unless her mam's dad, who would be her grandfather, refused to let them talk to each other. Her mam had said that the last time she went there he had turned her away and wouldn't even let them speak to each other.

Well, she wouldn't let him do that. She'd stand up to him and insist on talking to her grandmother. She'd tell him she'd come to see them and she wanted to stay and get to know them better, and that was why she'd packed most of her clothes into her suitcase. Perhaps if she explained that her own mam didn't even know she had come then he would see sense.

The announcement that the train she wanted

was coming in to the station decided her. She was going to go to Ferndale, she told herself. Whatever happened she had to find out for herself. If she didn't like them then she'd come straight back. If she decided to stay then she would send her mam a picture postcard to let her know where she was and that she had no need to worry about her as she had about Sara and Rachael.

Barri wasn't at all surprised to see Gaynor waiting for him when he came out of his office at the end of the day. He had half expected her to come to the City Hall at midday to find out if he had any news. He was glad she hadn't because it had taken him quite a while to get in touch with Sara's office and to speak to her and then afterwards to telephone the police in Almeria.

At least he was now pretty certain that Keris was in neither place. He'd asked both Sara and Rachael to promise that they would contact him immediately if she did turn up.

In her pink floral dress under a dark pink duster coat and her white straw hat trimmed with pink flowers, Gaynor looked almost too young to be the mother of three grown-up girls, Barri thought as he hurried towards her.

'Any news?'

He shook his head. 'Well, at least we know she hasn't gone as far as Spain or Germany,' he assured her as he put his arm around her shoulders.

'Which means that she has probably gone to Ferndale . . .'

'And that we don't need to worry,' he said quickly.

'How can you say that,' she flared as she pulled away from him. 'I should have gone there first thing and made sure, not listened to you.'

'If she is there, she is not likely to come to any harm, now is she?' he reasoned.

'I don't know, but I think we should go there right now and find out. I'll certainly be giving her a piece of my mind if she is, worrying us half to death like this'

'Let's wait until morning,' he counselled. 'Let's go and have a nice meal somewhere and plan what we are going to do. I've arranged to take tomorrow off work so we can set off good and early. That will be much better than arriving there when it is almost dark as we'll do if we go now.'

'Supposing she isn't there! We could both be quite wrong and that will mean that she is on her own, heaven knows where, for another night. She could be in all sorts of trouble by then.'

'She's a sensible girl; she'd got enough money to buy food and a place to stay.'

'Stop being so practical,' Gaynor snapped. 'Perhaps you should go round to that Idris Jenkins's house and make sure that she hasn't run off with him.'

'Of course I will if you want me to, but not

until after we've had a meal. I bet you've eaten nothing all day. You can't live on cups of tea alone,' he told her with mock severity.

Although she agreed to them having a meal before they went home, Gaynor refused to consider his suggestion of going to the pictures.

'I thought it would take your mind off things and there are several good ones on at the moment.'

'I don't want to sit in a fusty old cinema in the dark and I certainly couldn't concentrate on the picture, not with all I have on my mind,' she told him crossly.

Barri insisted that she should have a glass of wine with her meal. 'Come on, it will help you to relax,' he told her. 'You were awake half the night and you were still asleep when I left this morning. If we are going to do things my way and go looking for Keris tomorrow, then I want us up early in the morning.'

Gaynor was up long before Barri was awake. She was washed, dressed and almost ready for them to go out. She had made a pot of tea and was about to sit down and drink hers before she took one up to Barri when she heard the rattle of the letterbox.

Putting the cup down so quickly that she splashed the hot tea all over her hand, she dashed to the front door. For a moment she stood there staring down at the picture postcard, quite sure that it must be from Keris yet almost afraid to pick it up in case it wasn't.

386

Chapter Thirty-Three

Keris had never been to a village in the Rhondda Valley before and had no idea what to expect. The long narrow terraces of stone cottages with the mountain in the background reminded her momentarily of the gypsy caves where Rachael lived. These weren't caves, though; they were sturdy stone cottages with slate roofs, gleaming in the hot June sunshine.

She walked down the high street with its neat little shops and thought how different it was from the busy streets and huge stores in the centre of Cardiff. There was hardly any traffic either, no noisy lorries or buses and very few cars.

Quite a few women were out shopping with baskets over their arm, making their purchases and stopping to chat to one another as they moved from one shop to the other.

As she watched them she wondered if one of them was her grandmother. Her mam must be nearly forty, she reasoned, so her grandmother would be one of the older ones. Was she one of the grey-haired old ladies walking with a stick, who had to pause and rest every now and again as they climbed up the steep street because they were breathless?

Her mam's name had been Sanderson so perhaps the sensible thing to do was to ask where the Sandersons lived, she decided, and the best place to do that would be at the post office. She needed a picture postcard to send her mam and dad to let them know she was safe and that they needn't worry about her. She could go in and buy that and a postage stamp and at the same time ask about her grandmother.

"The only person of that name is old Mrs Sanderson who lives in Lake Street. She's on her own; her husband died a couple of years ago.'

'That might be the person I'm looking for,' Keris said slowly. 'Do you know if she has a daughter?'

'Daughter?' The woman wrinkled her brow thoughtfully. 'Now I'm not sure about that. I'm new here, see. Only took over this place about five years ago. Hang on a minute while I serve Mrs Price, and then I'll try and find out for you.'

'I can tell you what you need to know,' Mrs Price said confidently as she moved up to the counter to be served. 'Florrie Sanderson certainly did have a daughter, but she left Ferndale about twenty years ago. I don't think she has ever been back since. Sad, really. Her old mam could do with her help now.'

'You mean because she's a widow?' Keris asked.

'Well, yes, that as well, but it's mainly because she's not in very good health these days. She shouldn't be living on her own. If she has a fall or anything then she could lie there for days and no one would know, not unless the poor soul could manage to get to the door and call out to a passer-by.'

'If it's the lady I think you are talking about, she seems well able to look after herself,' the postmistress intervened.

'At the moment she can manage, but I'm speculating on what could happen,' Mrs Price retorted.

Keris smiled and thanked them both for their help and, picking up her suitcase, said she would go and see if this was the Mrs Sanderson she was looking for.

'She doesn't take in lodgers,' Mrs Price told her. 'She wouldn't be able to look after them, so there's no point you going there to ask if she'd rent out a room. If you are looking for lodgings then—'

'I'm not,' Keris told her crisply. 'Thanks for the information.'

As she went through the door she smiled to herself as she heard the exchange between Mrs Price and the postmistress.

'A right hoity-toity young madam, that one,' Mrs Price commented in a disapproving voice. 'I wonder what her game is? She doesn't come from around here, that's for sure.'

'You're right, Mrs Price, and it's an odd place to come to for a holiday, yet from the size of that suitcase she is obviously thinking of staying for a while,' the postmistress agreed.

There were so few streets in Ferndale that Keris had no difficulty in finding Lake Street, but she wasn't sure which house it was. She thought of starting at one end and working all the way down, but that might arouse suspicion, she thought, as she climbed the steep incline on which they were built.

She was about to turn round and go back to the high street and see if she could find someone else who could tell her when she spotted Mrs Price coming up the steep road behind her.

She smiled. 'Are you following me, or do you live in Lake Street as well?'

'Both, cariad. I've lived here for almost forty years; born here, see. After I married I lived at home with my mam for a couple of years and then me and my Cedric managed to get a house of our own. He worked at one of the pits just outside the village so we were entitled to have one because he was one of their workers.'

'So you probably know which house is Mrs Sanderson's then,' Keris commented.

'Of course I do. Don't you?'

Keris shook her head. 'That's why I am asking you,' she said pointedly.

'Well, I'm not sure that I should tell you. I don't know who you are, see. Never set eyes on you in my life before and there are all sorts of strange people roaming the country. With old Mrs Sanderson being on the frail side and living on her own . . .'

'Oh for goodness' sake,' Keris said impatiently. 'Do I look like someone who would hurt an old lady?'

Mrs Price studied her for a moment with pursed lips. 'Who can say?' she muttered. 'All dressed up like you are you might be planning to steal from her. You might rob her of all her bits and pieces, ornaments and the like, and pack them into that big suitcase, and then make off with them.'

Keris picked up her suitcase and began walking on up the road. She had never felt so angry in her life. Hurt an old lady indeed. All she wanted to do was to find her and explain that she was her granddaughter and tell her how much she loved her.

'Wait, cariad, wait a minute. You've walked right past the house you want.'

Mrs Price stopped about four doors from where Keris had paused. 'I'll knock on the door for you and make sure she's well enough to see strangers.'

'I'm not a stranger,' Keris declared angrily. 'I'm – I'm her granddaughter.'

'Granddaughter!' Mrs Price regarded her suspiciously. 'She's never mentioned you.'

'Probably because she's never met me,' Keris explained. 'She's going to do so now, though,' she declared as she walked up to the door in front of Mrs Price and knocked on it.

It seemed to be ages before the door opened, and then it was only the merest crack and a thin reedy voice asked, 'Who is it, what do you want?'

'Florrie,' Mrs Price pushed Keris to one side. 'Are you all right, cariad? This young girl has been down in the post office asking where you lived. I followed her up here to find out what she was up to and now she says she's your granddaughter.'

'My granddaughter?' Mrs Sanderson sounded bewildered.

'Well, that's what she said,' Mrs Price said triumphantly, 'and she insisted on knocking on your door. Now don't worry, cariad, I won't let her come in or harm you.'

'My mother's name is Gaynor, she was Gaynor Sanderson,' Keris said, standing her ground. 'She left here when she was fourteen, the same age as I am now. She lives in Cardiff and my dad's name is Barri Hughes.'

'Gaynor! Barri!' Mrs Sanderson's voice suddenly sounded stronger and there was a glimmer of recognition in her eyes as she stared at Keris. 'You are like her; like she was as a young girl. She had brown hair. And your face . . .' Her voice trailed off for a moment as she peered short-sightedly at Keris. 'Yes, you are like her, very much like her. And you say your dad's name is Barri?'

'That's right. He and my mam were sweethearts and then he was sent way by –' Keris hesitated. 'He went off to Cardiff just before the war started and then he was in the war and he was badly injured. He and my mam met up

392

again afterwards when they were both living in Cardiff and got married.'

'Barri Hughes. He used to live a couple of doors away. His mam and dad are both dead now,' she sighed. 'Everyone from those days has either died or moved away. It's so lonely without them.'

'You needn't be lonely any longer,' Keris told her. 'I'm here now and I can stay and look after you if you want me to.'

Gaynor picked up the picture postcard from the doormat and turned it over and over in her hands. In the tiny space for correspondence on the back, alongside the address, was scrawled 'I'm all right Mam, so don't worry about me. Love to you and to Dad, Keris.'

She read the few words over and over again, her mind in a whirl. There was no address, nowhere she could write back to or where she could go and find her. She tried to read the postmark but it was too blurred.

As she turned the card over again she felt a rush of relief as she recognised the picture. It was Darren Park! That must mean that Keris was in Ferndale, just as Barri had thought she would be.

Her relief was so great that her knees felt weak. She stumbled into the living room and sank down on the nearest chair. Burying her face in her hands she began sobbing.

When she handed the card to Barri he

recognised that it was Darren Park, even before he read the message, and his reaction was almost the same as hers.

'She's safe and sound, she must be,' he breathed as he took Gaynor in his arms. Holding her tight against his chest he tried to comfort her and control the trembling that was making her shake like a leaf.

'Let's go and find her right now,' she begged, pulling away from him and pushing her hair back from her face and smoothing it into some sort of order.

'Yes, yes, we will, the moment you've calmed down,' he assured her. 'If you turn up in Ferndale in this state you'll frighten Keris and your mother.'

'Is she with my mother, though? We aren't even sure that my mother is alive.'

'Both your mam and dad were alive and well when you took Sara and Rachael to see them, so it's possible that they still are,' he added optimistically.

Gaynor shivered and nodded. 'When my father wouldn't even let her speak to me,' she said bitterly. 'If he's still alive then he won't let Keris speak to her either; not even to explain who she is. Even if she does they mightn't believe her, not even my mother. She has no idea of what's happened to me or that we have met up again; not even that Keris has been born.'

'You don't know any of that for certain. As

I've said before, your father will be quite an old man now; he will have retired and he is sure to have mellowed.'

'No.' Gaynor shook her head emphatically. 'He will never mellow. You don't think I am likely to forget about the way he treated you, do you?' she added scornfully.

'Hush, cariad. That's all in the past,' Barri told her.

'It's all my fault,' Gaynor sobbed. 'I should have kept in touch with her. I should have gone back again, tried to see her; insisted on speaking to her. Keris was right, I could have found some way of getting messages to her if I had tried hard enough. There were plenty of neighbours who would have told her how I was getting on if I had written to them. I'm sure they would have done.'

'It's no good worrying about that now,' Barri said firmly. 'With hindsight we nearly always know we should have done things differently.'

'Poor little Keris, even if she does manage to find them they won't know who she is, so how can she convince them?'

Barry smiled. 'I'm sure they remember what you looked like at that age and she is the spitting image of you.'

'We must go there right away and find out if she's managed to do so,' Gaynor insisted.

'We will, but it's my opinion that she has. You know how persuasive she is when she wants to be. She's probably staying with them;

she wouldn't have sent that card otherwise, now would she?' he reasoned.

'I don't know, I can't think straight,' Gaynor admitted. 'My head's in a complete whirl.'

'Right, well let's have some breakfast and then we'll get ourselves smartened up and we'll be off. We can't go dressed as we are, we look like a pair of scarecrows,' he added with an attempt at making her laugh.

'I don't want to waste time over breakfast,' Gaynor protested. 'I want to go now.'

'Well, I want some breakfast,' he insisted. 'I'm starving and it may be hours before we get another meal. If we have a really good breakfast then we'll be ready to face anything; even your father's wrath, if he is still as fierce as he always used to be.'

'You can't come with me, you have to go to work,' Gaynor reminded him.

'No, I told you last night that I was having the day off. We've got the whole day to sort this matter out so we don't have to rush. Breakfast first and then we'll be off. It's a lovely day, so we'll be able to see Ferndale at its best.'

Gaynor sighed wistfully. 'It's probably changed a great deal after all these years. We'll probably be disappointed.'

Barri shrugged. 'That's true, but if we find Keris and we are reunited with your family, that will be consolation enough.'

Gaynor nodded, and then she reached up and ran her fingers gently down his scarred face. 'You are a good man, Barri Hughes, and I love you very much, I hope you know that?'

'I do and I love you; every bit as much as I did in those days.'

Chapter Thirty-Four

Holding hands, as they had done the last time they had walked along Lake Street together so many years ago, Barri and Gaynor made their way to her old home.

Gaynor took a deep breath as Barri knocked on the door and looked at him with a tremulous smile.

When the door was opened and she saw Keris standing there her feeling of relief was so immense, she could hardly breathe.

'Mam, Dad!' Keris looked from one to the other and then flung herself into her mother's arms, grabbing tightly at the sleeve of Barri's jacket as she did so, as if to ensure that all three of them were in one close embrace.

They both kissed her, kissed each other, and hugged together tightly. There was no need for words, their relief at all being together again was so obvious.

When a thin reedy voice called out, asking who it was at the door, they pulled apart. Wiping away her tears Gaynor whispered, 'Let me go and see her, Keris. You stay here for a minute with your dad.'

'Mam!' Gaynor walked in barely looking

around the familiar living room as she made her way towards the armchair by the fireside and held out her arms to the elderly woman who was struggling unsteadily to her feet.

'Oh, Mam, it's so wonderful to see you again!'

'Gaynor? Oh, my darling girl. After all this time! How I've dreamed of this happening.'

They clung to each other like limpets, their tears mingling.

Her mother felt so frail that Gaynor was afraid of hurting her if she hugged her too tightly. She couldn't believe how much she had aged, how lined her face was or how grey her hair.

As Florence's blue-veined hand, covered with brown liver spots, reached up and stroked her face, Gaynor felt her tears building up anew. Her mother looked so faded and careworn and she felt guilty about the worry she had probably caused her over the years.

She had always thought of her mother as being a fairly tall, upright woman, but twenty years had taken its toll and this frail body nestling against her barely reached to her chest.

Over her mother's shoulder she saw Barri and Keris come into the room and gently disengaged herself from her mother's arms and helped her back into her armchair.

'Barri is here, Mam,' she said gently. 'I'm sure that you remember Barri.'

Mrs Sanderson turned to greet him and there was a beaming smile of welcome on her lined face. 'Barri, so many years have gone by, it's so good to see you again.'

He put an arm around her shoulder and hugged her gently, kissing the top of her grey head.

As she looked up and caught sight of his disfigured face her eyes widened and she peered closer. 'Whatever happened to your poor face?' she asked, her voice laced with concern.

'It happened during the war, when I was in the army. I was badly injured,' he explained briefly.

'Oh you poor boyo; to have had to suffer like that!'

'It doesn't hurt, even though it stops me from being the handsome boyo I once was,' he joked.

Mrs Sanderson nodded sadly. 'Terrible thing, war,' she murmured. 'You and my Gaynor found each other again and now there is this one to bring us all together.' She smiled as she held out a hand to pull Keris closer.

'You both sit down and talk to my grand-mother and I'll go and make us all some tea,' Keris told them.

Florence Sanderson nodded in agreement, almost like an obedient child.

'She's only been here a couple of days but already she has taken charge.' She smiled. 'You've brought her up well, Gaynor. Your little Keris is a lovely girl and a real homemaker. Such a pity that Ieuan isn't alive to meet her.' She sighed.

'He's dead, you know. It was quite sudden. It must be almost two years ago now. The doctor said it was something to do with his heart!'

'I'm sorry, Mam.' Gaynor felt tears prickling her eyes as she reached out and held her mother's hand. She found herself wishing things could have been different between them, but it was too late now.

'You had two other girls, a bit older than Keris, Gaynor; what's happened to them?'

'They're fine ... they ... they've both left home, though,' she added with a sad smile. 'I'll tell you all about them later.'

Gaynor felt reluctant to return to Cardiff and leave Keris in Ferndale, but both she and Barri agreed that it was probably the best thing to do for the moment.

Barri needed to return to work and Mrs Sanderson was far too frail to be left on her own. She was still fiercely independent, though, and strongly refuted Gaynor's concern that she needed looking after.

There seemed to be a tremendous empathy between her and Keris. She seemed to happily accept her granddaughter's presence even though she was obviously aware that it was Keris looking after her and not the other way round.

'Are you sure you don't want to go back to Cardiff with your mam and dad and finish your schooling?' she questioned when Keris insisted on staying.

'You'll be missing all your friends and going to the pictures and everything else that seems to go on down there in Cardiff,' she went on. 'It's deadly dull here in Ferndale; you ask your mam, she'll remember all about that.'

Keris looked questioningly at Gaynor. 'Must I go back with you, Mam? I only have another week left at school and then we'll be breaking up for the summer holidays. When we do I'll be finished with school altogether.'

'Don't you want to be there when you all break up so that you can say goodbye to all your friends?'

'Not really. They've all got jobs to go to and I haven't.'

'And whose fault is that?' Barry said in an exasperated voice. 'We've been on at you for months now to show some interest in what you want to do and to start applying for jobs.'

'There's nothing that interests me,' Keris told him sulkily. 'I don't want to work in a shop or an office. Mam doesn't want me to work in a factory, and I don't want to become a Nippy.'

'So what do you want to do, then, cariad?' Florence Sanderson asked.

'I want to stay here and look after you,' Keris told her with an impish smile.

'You won't find that very interesting,' her grandmother told her. 'I rarely go out anywhere these days. I like to have a nap in the afternoon and I'm in bed by nine o'clock most nights.'

'That's only because you are here on your

own and there is no one for you to do things with,' Keris told her. 'Now, if I am here, you will want to show me around Ferndale and lots of other things. We can walk down to the high street and do the shopping together and I can ask some of your friends to come round in the afternoon for a cup of tea.'

'There're very few of my old friends still alive,' Mrs Sanderson told her sadly.

'Never mind, we can have tea together every afternoon and you can tell me all about when my mum and dad were young. They never talk to me about those days and there are lots of things that I want to know.'

Gaynor and Barri both expected Keris to come home again after a few days complaining that there was nothing to do at her grandmother's house. When she didn't, and the days became weeks, Barri became anxious and insisted that they ought to go back there and see for themselves if she was all right.

'We did promise Keris that we wouldn't keep checking up on her,' Gaynor reminded him.

'Well we haven't. She's been there for over a month now, so I think it is high time we went to see how she is and to make sure that things are working out for both of them.'

'You know how they are.' She laughed. 'Keris has written to us once a week and told you what she's been doing and not to worry about her.'

'Yes, well, that's all very well, but I want to see for myself. I'm not sure how they are managing for money; Keris is another mouth to feed, remember. I thought we could go up on Sunday, but if you don't want to come with me then I'll go on my own.'

'Of course I'll come with you. I'm missing Keris just as much as you are. The house seems dead without her. I'm more worried that she might be making a nuisance of herself and disturbing my mother's routine.'

'There you are, then; if we go to see them, then you can find out if your mother really wants her to stay on or whether she would rather be on her own.'

'I had thought about that because even if my mam wanted Keris to come home Keris wouldn't tell us.'

'That's right!' Barri agreed. 'If your mother has been living on her own ever since your dad died then she might be finding that having a young girl in the house, especially one who is as lively as Keris, is quite upsetting for her.'

Gaynor looked thoughtful. 'There's another thing I've reasoned out. No matter what Keris may say she is bound to be finding it very quiet with only her grandmother for company. This may be quite a good thing because it may make her think about her own future,' Gaynor pointed out.

Barri frowned. 'What do you mean?'

'Well, she simply wouldn't come to any decision about what she wanted to do when she left school would she? She wasn't interested in any of the jobs we mentioned to her. I'm hoping that her stay in Ferndale may have brought her to her senses and now she'll be ready to decide what she wants to do.'

'Do you really think so? She doesn't appear to be fed up with being there. Judging by the postcards she sends each week she sounds cheerful enough.'

'Two lines that are always the same – "everything fine, don't worry about me." I ask you, Barri, does that really sound as if she is enjoying herself? She's fourteen; she should be having fun, not sitting around with an old lady.'

Barri sighed. 'You could be right, I suppose. I don't see how we are going to find out, though. You know Keris; she's as stubborn as a mule and she won't admit that she's made a mistake.'

Gaynor smiled. 'Perhaps not, but I've been thinking that if we leave her there a bit longer she may be only too ready to change her mind and want to have a more exciting life.'

'So what are you proposing?'

'Instead of going there next week let's leave it until the August bank holiday weekend. Last year, if you remember, we took her to Barry Island, her favourite place. When she finds herself stuck in Ferndale over the bank holiday she's going to feel pretty fed up.'

'You just said we would go up there over the bank holiday.'

'Yes, we will, but we won't tell her that. We'll just turn up and you'll see how relieved she'll be to see us. You mark my words. We could even take them both out somewhere.'

Barri looked disappointed. 'If you think that's a good idea. I suppose we should accept what she says on the cards and stop worrying about her.'

'Then in that case leaving our visit for another couple of weeks won't make much difference one way or the other, now will it?' Gaynor stated emphatically.

'No, except that I am missing her and I want to see her.'

'You'll live, you'll enjoy her company all the more the longer you wait,' Gaynor told him, laughingly.

August Bank Holiday Monday was a scorching hot day. As Gaynor pointed out to Barri, it was just the sort of day for an excursion to Barry Island.

'We're not going to Barry Island though, are we,' he said resignedly. 'Perhaps we should have gone up to Ferndale last week, or the week before, and then we could have brought Keris back with us and then we could all have gone there this weekend.'

'We can always go to Barry next weekend, it will be quieter then. That's unless she has made herself some new friends and gone off there this weekend anyway.

'I don't think my mother would agree to her doing that though. She's always been a very cautious person and I imagine she's worse now that she's older.'

The railway station was very busy but the train up to the Valleys was practically empty. Everybody was going to Barry or Swansea, not up to the Rhondda.

Ferndale was like a ghost town as they walked from the station. All the shops were closed and shuttered and there seemed to be no one about. It reminded Gaynor of the time when she had taken Sara and Rachael to visit her parents when they were small.

'They mightn't even be in, you know, because they don't know that we are coming to see them,' Barry said worriedly.

'So where do you think they will be? I can't see my mother going on a trip to the seaside.'

'I know that, but they may have taken a picnic and gone up to Darren Park. That's what we used to do at bank holiday time, now didn't we?'

Gaynor smiled. 'Well, if they're not at home then we know where to go and look for them.'

Keris looked so relieved to see them both when she answered the door that Gaynor felt sure she was right and that Keris was fed up with being there.

'I'm so glad you've come,' she said, relief showing on her face as they entered the house.

'I was wondering how I was going to get some help.'

'Help? What sort of help?' Barri asked in surprise.

'For grandmother. She's feeling the heat and having a lot of difficulty in breathing,' Keris explained. 'She says she's all right but I know she isn't. She's had these attacks before and the doctor gave her some special pills to help her breathe more easily, but she's used them all up.'

'Where is she?' Gaynor asked, looking around the empty living room.

'Upstairs in bed. She's been in bed for a couple of weeks now.'

'Why on earth didn't you write and let us know?' Gaynor exclaimed in alarm.

'I have been writing to you, I've written every week.'

'You always say everything is all right and not to worry,' Gaynor snapped.

Keris shrugged. 'I didn't want to worry you. We are all right, really. The doctor says it is nothing to worry about and that it's only because of her age.'

'I'll decide about that,' Gaynor told her sharply as she headed for the stairs.

'Go quietly, she might be asleep and she's been awake most of the night struggling to get her breath,' Keris warned.

It was apparent to Gaynor the moment she walked into the bedroom that her mother was far from well. She was propped up against a pile of pillows looking frail and her breathing was shallow. Her face was not only drained of colour but there was the faintest blue tinge around her lips.

'You say she has been in bed for several days now?' Gaynor whispered, turning to Keris.

'She hasn't been downstairs for a couple of weeks,' Keris admitted as they returned to the living room.

'Good heavens! So who has been caring for her?'

'I have, of course. The nurse came a couple of times and showed me how to wash her and brought a bedpan . . .'

'And you've been coping with all that on your own!' Barry exclaimed in amazement. 'You should have written and told us. She needs proper care.'

'I like looking after her,' Keris said stubbornly. 'The doctor said I was doing it all right. He calls in quite often to make sure.'

'She should be in hospital, Keris. She needs professional care,' Barri said gently.

'No, she would hate that,' Keris told him, her eyes bright with tears. 'I'm going to look after her, it's what I've promised her and I want to do it.'

'You've done a wonderful job, Keris, but I think it is too much for you to undertake,' Barri told her.

'We came to see if you wanted to come home, cariad,' Gaynor added gently.

'Well, you can see that I don't; that I can't. I'm needed here. I'm looking after her properly. I cook and clean and make sure she is comfortable and—'

'Yes, yes, you've done wonderfully well,' Gaynor agreed, 'but by the look of things she is going to get worse, not better. You may be looking after her perfectly well, but you need someone else here in the house with you in case of an emergency.'

'What sort of an emergency?'

Gaynor and Barri exchanged glances. 'In case she suddenly becomes worse like she has done today, cariad,' Gaynor said softly, putting her arm around Keris and hugging her close.

'With her breathing problems she could have a heart attack,' Barri explained. 'If you are here on your own, then you'd have to leave her while you ran for the doctor.'

Keris shook her head. 'I'd go next door and ask them to go for him.'

'That's all right if they are there, but what about today, for example; are they here or have they gone out for the day?'

'They've gone on a charabanc trip today because it's the bank holiday,' Keris admitted, 'but there's usually someone there.'

'Look, why don't we wait until your grandmother wakes up and then we'll suggest to her that she comes back to Cardiff and stays with us for a while.'

'No!' Keris shook her head. 'I told you I want

410

to look after her. She's my grandmother and now that I've found her I intend to take care of her,' she said determinedly.

'And so you shall,' Barri agreed, 'I promise you that.'

'If we take her back to Cardiff, you will be the one who looks after her until she is better,' Gaynor agreed.

Chapter Thirty-Five

Gaynor decided that it would take far too much organising to bring Mrs Sanderson from Ferndale to Cardiff because she was far too ill to travel by train. It would mean arranging for a taxicab to collect her and Keris as well as all the belongings she was likely to need for an extended visit.

She was so frail and weak that Barri agreed with her that it would be better to leave her in her own place in Ferndale as long as Keris was there attending to her every need.

'I think she will rest better if she is in her own room with all her own things around her,' Gaynor said thoughtfully. 'I can stay if necessary and you can come at the weekends, Barri, or if she gets any worse and needs to have someone with her all the time, day and night, then I'm sure we will be able to find someone.'

'Now don't you worry, Mam, I'll take care of her,' Keris promised.

'You could have your bed in the same room as her if you want to,' Gaynor offered.

'I'm in the little bedroom next to hers so I will hear her if she wakens at all in the night,' Keris assured her.

For the first few weeks Florence Sanderson seemed to rally. She even wanted to come downstairs and sat with them for a few hours each day. Then, as autumn approached and the weather became colder, she took to spending more and more time in bed.

By Christmas, she was unable to manage the stairs at all. They had already decided to spend the Christmas holiday at Ferndale with her so Barri carried her down on Christmas Day so that she could have dinner with them. Afterwards, swathed in shawls and blankets, she sat huddled in an armchair and with her eyes closed as if she felt too weary to keep them open.

When Barri asked, 'Shall I take you back upstairs?' she nodded in agreement and feebly tried to apologise for putting a dampener on their day.

'I'll stay up there with her until she goes to sleep,' Keris whispered to her mother as they'd settled Mrs Sanderson into bed and tucked a hot water bottle wrapped in a piece of blanket down by her feet to keep her warm.

The next morning Mrs Sanderson seemed to be almost too weak to swallow the milky porridge that Keris fed to her from a spoon.

'Is there anything you'd like us to get you or do for you, Mam?' Gaynor asked anxiously. 'We want to make you as comfortable as possible, you know. You have only to say if there is anything you want especially.'

Mrs Sanderson clutched at Gaynor's hand. 'There is something,' she whispered. 'I want to see my other granddaughters. I know I haven't much time left and I am very grateful to dear little Keris for all she has done for me, but I would like to see your other two girls as well, cariad.'

'Of course, I'll see what we can do,' Gaynor promised. 'You do know that Sara lives in Germany and Rachael in Spain, don't you? It may take them several days to get here, that's if they can manage to do so at all.'

Her mother smiled and nodded and squeezed her hand, but whether or not she really understood what was involved Gaynor wasn't sure.

'It won't be easy,' Barri said worriedly. 'I can probably reach Sara by telephone right away, but I won't be able to do that where Rachael is concerned.'

'There must be some way you can get hold of her, Dad,' Keris frowned. 'How did you manage to do it last time you wanted to get in touch with her?'

'Leave it with me, I'll see what I can do,' Barri promised. When he spoke to Sara on the telephone and explained about her grand-mother she agreed to come as soon as possible.

'Sara is on holiday so she is coming right away before her new classes start,' he told them triumphantly.

'And Rachael?'

'I'm not sure.' He shrugged. 'I wasn't able to speak to her, but I have left a message with the chap who helped us make contact with her before so it's just a case of when she gets it.'

Within a few days the entire family were reunited. Gaynor could hardly believe it. She looked round the dining table proudly as she compared Sara's cool blonde beauty with Rachael's dark prettiness and then Keris's blossoming loveliness.

They were all her girls and in her eyes they were all gorgeous, even though they looked so different from each other. She wished they could all stay together, but she realised that was asking too much. They were here now, though, and she intended to make the most of every minute they were all together as a family.

Their presence seemed to bring a new lease of life to Florence Sanderson. Keris was overjoyed when her grandmother began once more to take an interest in what was going on around her.

On the Sunday after New Year's Day, she once again insisted on coming downstairs to join in the family meal.

'I never dreamed that one day you'd all be here with me.' She smiled. I want to make the most of it.'

Keris helped her to put on her best dress, but said that she must have a warm shawl around her shoulders as well. She combed her sparse grey hair and put a generous dab of scent on her best lace-edged handkerchief.

Barri carried her downstairs and helped Keris to make her comfortable in the armchair by the fireside.

Then they all gathered round her, listening to her thin voice as she recounted episodes from her past life.

'I was far too severe with your mam, I was always so afraid that some harm would come to my little Gaynor,' she told them as she clutched hold of Gaynor's arm. 'I shouldn't have let her dad send Barri away when he did but you always obeyed your husband in those days and I thought he was acting for the best. It's too late now to make amends to them, but I can beg my Gaynor not to make the same mistake with you three.'

She sighed as her eyes rested on Sara. 'You're the image of Konrad Claus. I remember the day when he first came to our house. He was such a smart-looking young man, with his fair hair and vivid blue eyes. He had such a precise way with him. He was so different from the local boyos.'

'I never knew your father, of course.' She frowned as her gaze rested on Rachael. 'You must be like him though, because I can see hardly any resemblance to my Gaynor. He must have had lovely dark hair and been very handsome. It must be from him that you get your beautiful singing voice. My Gaynor could never sing, not even when she was at school.'

'He played the guitar too, grandmother,' Rachael told her.

'Such a clever man and you have inherited his talents and I'm pleased to see that you're using them to make a good life for yourself, my dear.'

Her gnarled hand went out to hold Keris's small, slim one. 'And this sweet child, dear Barri's daughter, she has done so much for me. I have her to thank that we've all been brought together at last. She may be only a child, barely left school, but she has such a warm heart, such a lovely gentle girl . . .' She paused to catch her breath.

'I think you should rest now,' Barri said, holding a glass of water to her lips.

Feebly, Florence Sanderson pushed the glass away. 'Gaynor, don't crush her spirit like we crushed yours. Don't make her so rebellious that she runs away from home or you'll live to regret it like I have done all these years. Take care of her . . .' Her voice faltered and seemed to catch in her throat choking her as she struggled for breath.

'Quickly, Keris, fetch her pills,' Barri urged as once again he held the glass to her mouth.

Their efforts were in vain. By the time Keris returned her grandmother was too weak to swallow the pills. Grasping hold of Keris's hand she managed a faint smile before her eyes closed.

Sara and Rachael were stunned by what had happened. Barri tried to console them by gently reminding them that they had been expecting the end to come for several days.

417

'She died happy,' Keris said with a sigh of relief. 'Her dearest wish was to meet you both,' she said looking at her sisters. 'In her last moments she was surrounded by those she loved and who meant so much to her, what could be better?'

Suddenly Gaynor was in floods of tears. 'I should have visited her years ago,' she sobbed. 'She was so right, I was rebellious, and I was also selfish. Her life with my father couldn't have been easy and I should have been there to support her and comfort her.'

Sara and Rachael said they wanted to stay on for a few days so Gaynor and Barri spent several enjoyable hours showing all three of the girls around Ferndale visiting Darren Park and all the other places they'd known when they'd been growing up.

They stayed on for Florence Sanderson's funeral which took place the following week. They laid her to rest beside her husband after a service in the chapel that she'd attended all her life.

'Remember now we are in touch I don't want to lose contact with you again,' Gaynor told Sara and Rachael the next day as they prepared for their journeys home.

'I know you've made satisfying lives for yourselves, and that you are happy where you are living,' Gaynor told them, love and pride shining in her eyes, 'but your dad and me still love you both dearly and we will always be here for you if you ever need any help or feel you want to return home.'

'I will write to you,' Sara promised, laying a hand affectionately on her mother's arm.

'I will as well,' Rachael assured them, giving them both a big hug. 'You must come to Spain again for a holiday. Saratina made me promise to make sure I asked you.'

'That goes for me too,' Sara smiled. 'I mean it,' she affirmed, turning to Barri. 'I know I said some rather nasty things to you when you came to Cologne, but you are the only dad I've ever known and I do care deeply about you and I'm grateful to you for all you did for me when I was growing up.'

As they hugged and kissed goodbye, Sara said sharply, 'What about Keris, what sort of future is she going to have? Perhaps she should come and stay with me in Cologne for a while and see something of the world outside Cardiff.'

'Or with me and Saratina in Almeria and have some fun,' Rachael added quickly.

Keris smiled. 'I'd like to have a holiday with each of you one day, but not until after I've finished my training. Perhaps we could all have a holiday together then.'

'Training! What training are you talking about, Keris?' Barri looked mystified.

'It's something I promised my grandmother I would do,' Keris told them with an impish grin.

'Yes? Well go on; tell us what it is you are planning,' Gaynor pressed impatiently.

'My grandmother said that she wanted me to train to be a teacher because that was what she and granddad had wanted Mam to be and I promised her that I would.

'That is all right, isn't it?' she asked apprehensively as they expressed surprise and she saw the look of amazement on all their faces. 'It really is what I want to do.'